# Celiminal

# Celiminal

PAT IEZZI

authorHOUSE®

*AuthorHouse™*
*1663 Liberty Drive*
*Bloomington, IN 47403*
*www.authorhouse.com*
*Phone: 1 (800) 839-8640*

*This is a work of fiction. All of the characters, names, incidents, organizations, and dialogue in this novel are either the products of the author's imagination or are used fictitiously.*

*Published by AuthorHouse   01/15/2016*

*ISBN: 978-1-5049-6056-4 (sc)*
*ISBN: 978-1-5049-6057-1 (hc)*
*ISBN: 978-1-5049-6055-7 (e)*

*Library of Congress Control Number: 2015918463*

*Print information available on the last page.*

*To my children,*
*Marcus, Maura, and Michael*

"And they believe rightly; for I have sworn upon the Altar of God, eternal hostility against every form of tyranny over the mind of man."
Thomas Jefferson

# Prologue

*Pittsburgh, Pennsylvania*
*Friday, August 31*
*8:45 p.m.*

Owen Roberts shuddered to think about it. Even now, the unsettling events that had occurred years ago disturbed him. The secret experiments and their dire implications had left him with a deep sense of regret and, needless to say, an intense guilt. And now, with nowhere to turn, Owen didn't want forgiveness, but rather to deliver a warning about an impending peril—before it was too late.

After stepping out of the elevator, Owen scanned the empty, half-lit hallway blanketed in alternating ribbons of light and darkness. He again weighed whether a second phone call would suffice rather than a face-to-face meeting with the psychiatrist. Finally, he dismissed the reservation and headed toward the office, hoping to find an answer.

Now and then, a wisp of cool air shot past him from the overhead air-conditioning system, which cooled the anxiety continuing to build within him. In those strips of darkness, he stopped and glanced over his shoulder in fear that someone had managed to track him. Finding no one, he moved on. His weary, measured steps caused the heels of his shoes to squeal at times on the marble floor. A sound swallowed, though, by the ever-present ventilation fan.

He passed several offices marked by last names until he reached the unmarked door and then paused. In the subdued light, a short distance ahead, a bright-red exit sign screamed at him. *That would be too easy*, he thought. It would be a matter of time before they would find him. No. He had no choice. A hundred blank faces flashed through his mind, and he recognized each and every one of them. Their unspoken words egged him on to enter the room.

With a moist palm, Owen grasped the cold doorknob and turned it. The door opened freely to reveal an office illuminated by the soft glow of a desk lamp and the flickering points of city light caught by the floor-to-ceiling bank of windows along the exterior wall.

As he closed the door, a burgundy leather sofa and moss-green, upholstered chairs huddled around an oval coffee table greeted him. To his immediate right, some eight feet away, three side chairs faced a dark cherry desk and credenza. A series of bookcases with what appeared to be medical journals and books extended the length of an interior wall.

While an old grandfather clock marked the minutes, Owen shifted his weight from one side to the other. Time moved slowly but relentlessly, and for him, the gaps in time allowed him to ponder the incidents and encounters of the past few hours. An ominous thought quickly came to the forefront: *Have I covered my tracks sufficiently?*

For the last hour, he had snaked his way through department stores, up one floor and down two, in one door, out another, crossed the street—sometimes twice—always turning, waiting, and looking for the tail that had stalked him the last few days. Despite his valiant efforts to shake the relentless pursuer, he was like an animal caught in a trap: he could maneuver, but not very far.

When the door to the adjoining room swung open, Dr. James Greyson entered, paused for a moment, and then, closing the door and locking it, made his way across the room.

"I stepped out. So I left the side door open," Greyson said as the clock chimed nine o'clock. Oddly, his tone of voice, unlike the warm, pleasant voice on the phone, told a different story—one that telegraphed disguised worry. A slight twitch formed a smile across his face.

The facial lines, once barely noticeable, as Owen remembered him, now were deeply etched across the doctor's thin face. And his dark-brown hair, receding at the temples, was peppered with gray—weathered, undoubtedly, by the demands of his profession. His passion and tenacity were gone from his facial features.

"Thanks for seeing me. The matter called for immediate attention," Owen said as he gripped Greyson's hand and stared into the unwelcoming eyes.

"At this late hour, and on a Friday, no one will bother us. Sometimes I work a little later to catch up on paperwork before the weekend."

"I'm sure you'll understand why I needed to see you. And it couldn't wait. It concerns STAR."

Greyson stared without showing any emotion, but Owen knew it struck a chord—one of displeasure.

"The program ... you and I worked on ... we managed to find a way. It works. And that's why I'm here."

"That's not what I wanted to hear. Impossible. Milsen and I agreed that there was no way," Greyson said dismissively.

"There's no mistake. I really didn't know who else might understand ... you know the consequences."

Greyson had an intimate knowledge of the project. For more than five years, Greyson and Dr. Henry Milsen had worked together on mind alteration—code named DMP, short for Differential Mind Persuasion—for the CIA. They were the dynamic duo, the sparks behind the idea, and Owen wrote the computer program. Their joint research into visual and audio techniques in order to embed messages below the normal limits of the human mind's perception paved the way.

Greyson shook his head and then turned away, staring at the ceiling like a person looking for divine inspiration. When there was none, he retreated to his desk chair. "Consequences. That's an understatement. Something I don't want to know about. For that matter, what do you want from me? I left the CIA years ago. And it's ... it's actually none of my business. It's not my concern."

"But—" Owen interjected.

"The answer is no." Greyson slapped the desktop. "I don't want to be involved. That was years ago, and I washed my hands of the whole mess."

Owen shook his head and said, "It's not the CIA," as he took a seat on the edge of a side chair. "When the director and Milsen were called to answer questions before a congressional subcommittee, DMP was shut down. That was about a year after you left. Like you, the president, CIA, and even the NSA did not want another media investigation. The project was left to die."

Greyson sat back in his executive chair. "Listen. I'm done. I don't want the news media or some terrorist group after me. You can tell Milsen, the CIA, or whoever, that I am not interested."

Owen continued, ignoring his pleas, "After leaving the CIA, Milsen and I accepted positions with a political consulting firm, and so did Bateman. Milsen continued the research. Bateman, like always, wandered off to the more severe psychological techniques, although he did lend a hand now and then."

"Bateman—I should have known."

Owen recalled that Greyson and Bateman were a volatile mix, always in heated arguments. Bateman liked to experiment and subscribed, without question, to the philosophy that the end always justified the means.

"It's not what you think. Milsen and I needed work, and we never thought it would result in anything conclusive. But, by accident," Owen said as he shrugged his shoulders, "we had a breakthrough. That's when he stepped in. He stole the program and claimed all the glory. That was, at first, and—"

Greyson raised his hands to object. "But why … why would you continue? It was bound to come to this, don't you see?" Exasperated by the events, letting out a slow breath, he resigned himself. "I guess it was inevitable." Silence filled the room for a short period before he asked, "Where's the program?" It was more of a command than a question. "Do you have it with you? Where is it?"

Owen could not agree more with Greyson's assessment. Why? He couldn't explain why they had pursued the research. An idea, maybe a challenge, but the results eventually led him to understand the stark consequences and the tempest of fear the program could stoke. Yes, he had had second thoughts, admitting to himself what was at stake. He had even tried to undo what he had done.

"I've got it. And I managed to destroy all the copies and previous versions … that I could find."

"Find? You mean there are others?"

"Well … I'm unsure," Owen paused, "but as an extra precaution, I inserted a self-executing virus on the server where STAR resides. If they try to run it—well, eventually, after a number of attempts, the program will become corrupt."

Greyson shook his head and said despairingly, drawing in a deep breath, "Unsure? That's not good enough. And what happens if they move the program to another server or make a copy of it? Then what? What about Milsen? And where's he in all this?"

"Dead!"

Greyson closed his eyes tightly and rubbed his forehead with his index finger and thumb. Then he looked up and said, "Natural causes?"

"No. The police report said it was an accident. *But ... but it wasn't*. A day before the accident, he and I met with Tony Cervasi, who owns the company that subsidized the research. Things got ugly after Bateman showed him what we had."

"What did you expect?" Greyson retorted.

"No, I realize it. Things simply sort of spiraled out of control."

Greyson leaned forward. "And you think I can help you? Forget it. Go to the authorities."

"Because they—" Owen's assessment was interrupted.

Greyson gave a sideward glance at the door. "Wait a minute … it must be security." He rose to his feet.

But it was too late. The door groaned slightly as it sprung open wide. Owen shot a glance across the room to find a rotund figure with a doughy face and slicked-back black hair had entered. Carl Matalino, the director of security at Cervasi's company, flashed a crooked smile as his eyes swept the room. He pulled a handkerchief from the inside pocket of his black pinstriped suit and wiped his forehead. Another muscular, meaty fellow with dark eyes and a scar running down the side of his face entered behind Matalino.

Owen swallowed hard, thinking Greyson had lured him in, possibly, to put an end to the matter.

Matalino flashed a glance at Greyson and then turned his full attention to Owen. "I guess my sources were right. You'd show up here. Well, I'll give you the answer: that program belongs to us. And we don't take kindly to losing our investment. We know what you did in our mainframe. Hand it over. And then we'll all go home and have a good night's sleep."

"Wait a minute. You can't barge into my office!" Greyson blurted out, with a hand on the telephone. "Who the hell are you?"

"You sit your ass down. And get your damn hand off the phone," Matalino barked. With his beefy finger, he directed his underling to cover the outside door.

Greyson held his ground. "This is a private office …"

For Owen, Greyson's words melted into the background. There was no dealing with Matalino. Owen knew if he handed over the program, it would be his death sentence.

In a lighting fast move, Owen tugged on the electric cord feeding the lamp. Lights out, he grabbed the lamp as it slipped off the desktop and flung it across the room in the direction of Matalino. Wasting no time, he flipped over a chair, and sprang for the outer door.

Finding himself in the hallway, unscathed, he dashed down the hall, summoned by the exit sign. Owen heard, again, in his mind, the victims of their experiment chanting: *Run. Run.*

Within seconds he opened the stairwell door and clamored down the stairs. Grabbing, more than two steps at a time, he nearly fell rounding the corner. Another flight down, and he could hear his pursuer hitting each step.

At the lobby level, he cautiously opened the gray steel door. There, at the exit, he recognized the tail, who had watched his every move, talking on a cell phone. Hearing the thundering footfalls descending the stairs, Owen streaked through the corridor and rounded the corner to face a dead end where a bank of elevators sat open-door. He jumped into a waiting elevator, pressed the button for an upper floor, and then darted out into another waiting car.

"Come on, come on, close," he murmured breathlessly to himself. The doors closed at a glacial pace, but once they did, he pulled the emergency stop button.

Waiting, he could hear one of them say, "He's headed to the tenth floor. Call Matalino and cover the main entrance. And I'll take this elevator. If he wants out, he'll have to pass you at some point."

Moments later, outside the elevator, silence once again returned. Owen hoped luck was with him as he pushed in the emergency button. The doors separated. With care, he slowly peered around the open door. Seeing no one, he emerged. Around the next corner, Owen caught sight of the tail.

As if on cue, Owen's cell phone began to chime. He shook his head in disbelief. Without thinking, he instinctively pulled the phone from his pocket and slid it over the marble floor. Like a loose hockey puck, the phone ricocheted off a wall and slid past Matalino's henchman, who turned his head to follow the ringing cell phone.

In an instant, Owen closed the distance between them, and at full speed, slammed into the tail, causing them both to hit the floor. A trickle of blood oozed from the thug's face. Stunned, but not out, the guy swore and quickly began to regain his senses.

Owen stood, scooped up his cell phone, and sprinted into the lobby, never losing stride as he flew out the main entrance into the night. At an intersection, breathing heavily, he cut between cars in a line of traffic and ran until he reached the alley. Stopping momentarily, he looked back and found a dark figure running in his direction.

Hurriedly punching in a number on his cell phone, he slapped it to his ear as he continued to run, hoping Danielle would answer the phone in time. With each ring, he wondered whether his plan had gone awry. On the seventh ring, his fear heightened. It was only a matter of time before Matalino would question her.

At the end of the alley, he jumped a jersey barrier that funneled cars into a single lane across a bridge to the South Side. Just then, he saw the pedestrian walkway across the bridge was closed, blocking his escape. But he had no time. A car stopped headed in the opposite direction, and two men jumped out to give chase.

With only the headlights from passing cars, Owen angled himself around the concrete obstruction and slowed his pace on a moonless night. As he crossed the bridge, the sound of a tugboat churning up the river virtually drowned out the footsteps closing in on him. Too late, he felt the hard shove from behind. Now he could feel himself free floating, with nothing underneath his feet, his cell dropping from his hand as he grasped at nothingness.

# 1

*New York, New York*
*Friday, August 31*
*9:30 p.m.*

The text message read: Life in danger.

Danielle Madison read it silently to herself, again in an attempt to make a connection between the cryptic words and the reason behind them. Now, with her anxiety ratcheted up a notch, she subconsciously began biting her lip as a roller coaster of emotions, from love to concern, coursed through her. The message left a chilling void within her.

"Mind if I come in?" Karen said as she removed her eyeglasses. But before Danielle answered, her paralegal strode into the office and plopped herself into a high-back chair. Leaning forward, she nodded in the direction of the keyboard in front of two monitors on the desk. "If you checked your e-mails ... you'll find several I sent you from Owen. He never left a number though."

Without acknowledging her, Danielle tapped on her keyboard and pulled up the e-mails. For the last several hours, she had been unavailable, locked in a teleconference meeting with a group of attorneys from the West Coast.

All the messages were marked "urgent," with a short notation: "left no telephone number." The last message was taken more than two hours ago. According to Danielle's cell, the last text message was sent shortly thereafter.

She hadn't heard from him in months, despite leaving phone messages at work for him. And her text messages, like her phone calls, were one-way communications. He never hinted why their relationship came to an abrupt end. She couldn't hide her feelings; she still loved him.

"Did he say anything or when he'd call back?" Danielle asked with growing uneasiness.

"Nope, he hung up … without giving me a chance. Why … something wrong?"

Danielle shook her head, not wanting to discuss the text message, even though she and Karen had discussed Owen's absence on several occasions.

"You and I had this conversation a couple of weeks ago. But I was right … I told you he'd surface."

"I remember," Danielle confessed. Never believing Owen had found someone else, she had to admit his actions left her perplexed. It was as though he didn't want any direct contact, except now and then she'd receive a romantic card in the mail.

Danielle rose from her desk chair and began to stuff the leather attaché case with legal pleadings and a deposition. Snapping the flap on the case shut, her eyes returned to meet Karen's intense gaze. "You know, I need to call him. I'll make it short so that he doesn't get the impression … well, that I'm desperate."

"Good, at least it's a start. You can't play into his hands. How could he just do a disappearing act? I've seen how some of those handsome, single legal associates follow you with their eyes when you walk by."

With a wry smile, Danielle responded, "Not one of them has asked me out." She tugged at the case and dropped it with a thud to the floor.

"It's quite obvious that you've been out of the loop. We've been working fourteen hour days, seven days a week. Nobody's going to ask you out after work. You're here, never home," Karen said, raising her eyebrows questioningly. "And look, you've only got a few more weeks before your last day." Using the chair's arms as a springboard, she said, "Take my advice, I don't want you putting in these hours at your new job. Now … you better get going."

"Yes, ma'am," Danielle said, taking a quick look at her watch. She decided to call Owen later, but her uneasiness hit a few crescendos before they subsided.

"And I wouldn't worry about him … I'm going to be here for the next few hours, so if he calls, I'll tell him to call your cell."

*Yeah, sure.* But a nagging thought crossed Danielle's mind: *What did Owen mean by that text message? Why now?*

Danielle donned her dress jacket, threw the strap of her laptop case over her shoulder, and reached down to clutch the attaché case. She took a deep breath in a vain attempt to calm her anxieties. "Have you noticed Denon's arrogance this political season?"

"Isn't he always? What drives him, I don't know. And nothing stops his egotism at the expense of those he leaves in his wake." Karen responded with a dismissive wave. "Wait a minute; let me help you with that." She removed the black leather strap to the laptop from Danielle's shoulder. "I'll walk you to the front door. I have to lock it anyway." They walked down the corridor past a number of darkened offices. "Oh, one more thing, I know we've been busy, but did you ever take the time to … well, really do some due diligence on your new employer? I mean," Karen probed, "you know, what you're going to be doing there and—"

"You don't have to worry," Danielle said as they reached the outer door. "If I put up with Denon Pierce these last several years, how could there be a bigger problem? And as for Owen, he'll have to face me, but that's his problem, not mine."

With a hesitant nod, Karen handed the laptop to her. "Sure … and my reservations may be just that … reservations," she replied, her voice trailing off.

"Why? Tell me." Danielle raised an eyebrow. This was not the assurance she wanted, and given tonight's message, she didn't need more problems.

"Sorry. We'll talk about it tomorrow."

Danielle smiled faintly, searching Karen's face for some stark foreboding, but her face was expressionless. "See you in the morning." Minutes later, she wearily stepped out of the high-rise into a muggy summer night. As she strode to the corner of Lexington and Fifty-Fourth, she saw couples holding hands and leaning into their dates, with ladies dressed in fashionable shoes and matching bags. Like any Friday night in New York City, the party was just beginning.

Across the street, Danielle hailed a cab in a steady stream of traffic, and with some good fortune, a driver pulled up to the curb a short distance away. With a bead on the blinking tail light, she gritted her teeth, clutched her belongings, and hurried down the sidewalk.

Opening the cab door, she swung the dead weight attaché case into the rear seat and got in, trailed by her purse and laptop. A hand reached out and closed the door behind her. As she turned to gesture a thank you, the figure, with a cane at his side, stepped into the crowd.

Danielle leaned forward and called out her address on the Upper East Side. The driver raised a hand that he understood.

As the cab lurched into traffic, Danielle recalled her day: the fist raised in anger by a defendant outside the courtroom, and his death threat—"I'll see you dead"—reverberated in her mind. And then her earlier encounter with a judge who browbeat her about an evidentiary petition against a state legislator charged with bribery. The judge's unsupported, derisive comments had unnerved her.

*But how would Owen know?*

It was a day she wanted to end. The job entailed too much pressure from all sides. When she entered private practice five years ago with Higgins, Biggs, and Reed, HBR, where she interned during law school, the pay was great and the cases were challenging. That was before the endless days filled with a high octane diet of caffeine, legal briefs, motions, and court appearances. Now at thirty, she understood the adage the city that never sleeps also applied to the private practice of law.

Jolted by the driver's sudden shift to another lane, she was awakened as they swept past crowded sidewalks with couples mingling outside bars and restaurants. Her rationale for resigning her position was quite simple: she wanted a life. And her new position as assistant general legal counsel with a political consulting firm outside Washington, D. C. gave her the opportunity.

But one matter dampened her enthusiasm was Owen. She tried to forget him, though in her heart, she knew that she never would.

Gripping the handle of the attaché case once more, Danielle's thoughts shifted to the task she had to complete by morning. With the November elections in eight weeks, her first priority tonight was to write a trial brief on election irregularities for Denon, who also served as the outside legal counsel to PERC, Political Election Response Corporation, her soon-to-be employer.

Without a turn signal, the driver swerved onto Second Avenue and drove two blocks, coming to a screeching halt in front of her apartment building. After slipping the driver a twenty, she gathered her belongings and stepped out, remembering that she'd stood in the same spot at sunrise, when the apartment building was bathed in sunlight. Trudging up to the entrance, she eyed the apartment lights, which appeared as stars in the dark of night.

As she approached, Jay, the doorman, threw open the door.

"Thanks," she said, angling herself through the doorway. A cool breeze from the air conditioning swept away the close feeling of the night's warm, muggy air.

"Long day, I take it? Looks like you brought your work with you for the Labor Day weekend."

"Politics," she lightly complained. "It's that time of year. Political races, speeches, election irregularities … it's like this every election year. And with my moving, it only adds to my workload."

He shook his head sympathetically. "By the way, when I arrived earlier this evening, I delivered those packages to your apartment. And if you need any help moving, just give me a call."

She nodded and managed a weak smile. The movers she had called the other day had said they would deliver shipping boxes to her.

It seemed like only yesterday when she moved into the apartment complex, welcoming the opportunity to share a luxurious, two-bedroom apartment with her college roommate and good friend, Ann Burk, an advertising executive. They lived in a spacious apartment, well-furnished and stunningly decorated. Now with Ann's upcoming marriage to Greg Myers, another junior associate at HBR, Danielle's move to Washington meant that Ann and Greg didn't need to find another place.

At the secure double doors, which led into the main corridor of the apartment building, she swiped her door key and entered the foyer. Finding an empty car, she took the elevator to the twenty-fifth floor.

Their apartment was situated only two doors down from the elevators. That's when she heard the telephone ringing. Hurriedly, she unlocked the door and dropped her belongings on the floor. As she dashed for the phone, it fell silent at her reach. A fleeting glance at the answering machine told her there was one message.

Pressing the "play" button, she heard: "Danielle, it's Owen." There was a brief pause, and then the message began anew. "The books. You don't have the source code ... access ..." Then a white noise filled the void, with what seemed a howling wind and a sound she couldn't readily identify.

*Yeah, the books.* How could she forget? The New York State Consolidated Laws, the Administrative Code, and the Legal Opinions of the State of New York were sent to her office at HBR. It was his idea of a gift for her passing the bar and accepting a position as a lawyer. A nice gesture, and amusing at the time, but neither the firm nor her office had the room for another library.

Danielle turned up the volume and replayed the message. "I don't have what ... what's that supposed to mean?" As she listened intently, he was out of breath, and the unmistakable sound like a distant fog horn of a boat caught her attention. She shook her head, attempting to assess his phone message. But nothing came to mind.

With that, she returned to the front door. There sat two long, narrow boxes stacked against the wall. Opening the top box, she found the books. She selected a volume, read the cover, and mumbled, *The Early Writings of Thomas Jefferson*? Owen was a nerd, but a loveable one.

Tossing the book aside, she made her way to the kitchen, dragging her laptop and attaché case. Maybe Karen was right. She should forget him and begin looking for someone else.

After making a cup of steaming chai tea in the hope that the caffeine would keep her awake, she turned to page one and began to read the deposition. Three hours later, with heavy eyelids, she got up and stretched, and then seeing the answering machine, she began to sort through images of the past in her mind.

*What was it? There's something I'm missing.* Her mind wandered back months ago when she last saw him. Trying her best, she attempted to resurrect any part of his conversation, but it was murky.

"There's a matter that needs tending to," Owen said.

*Or something on that order,* she thought. But he never said what. And now she had accepted a legal position in the firm where he worked.

Denon had recommended, almost insisted, that she accept the position of legal counsel with PERC. She thought it odd at the time that he would be willing to allow a legal associate to leave the firm. She had the experience and expertise in political matters. Parting with an asset of the law firm seemed odd, but it worked for her. HBR and the long hours, weeks, and months would be a thing of the past.

Again, she cocked her head while snippets of Owen's voice raced through her mind. Her eyes drifted to her cell. Her heartbeat stirred to a rapid pace as she pictured the word *urgent* in the e-mail.

Danielle rapidly punched in Owen's number. Then she said, "Answer, damn it. Where are you?"

# 2

*New York, New York*
*Saturday, September 1*
*8:00 a.m.*

Well, Counselor, what's the answer?" Karen asked, leaning back into her chair. A line of large pocket folders formed a border across the front of her desk. As she peered over the files that rivaled the Great Wall of China, her computer signaled an incoming e-mail.

Resting her forearms on the back of a chair, Danielle intoned in a tired voice, "I kept nodding off, only to be awakened by the honking of horns and the squealing of brakes. At four in the morning, you would think there would be some semblance of peace and quiet. But no, the sounds of vehicles droned on until I finally called it a night." She brushed a strand of her shoulder-length chestnut hair behind her ear and let out a slight yawn. "Sorry, I … I don't know what I'm thinking these days," she said, shaking her head, unhappy with her effort to harness her energy. Looking at the cappuccino in her hand, she continued, "Oh, I completely forgot; I bought this for you on my way in."

"For me? Who's the mother and who's the child here?" Karen accepted the drink and undid the lid. "Sit down—there are a few things that you should know."

Within the law firm, Karen acted as the resident mother for many of the young associates. Like a mother with little chicks, she nurtured them, if they were so inclined, through the minefields of the legal profession. At sixty years young, her unkempt strands of brown and gray hair, coupled with her heavy-set frame and a wardrobe from Walmart clearance specials, fooled most people. That was until she worked with you. She often knew more about the finer aspects of law than most lawyers. Citing from obscure precedents that she managed to find, she had a no-nonsense way of dissecting the most difficult cases.

Never having married, Karen defined law as her purpose in life. She'd offered her sage advice to associates and senior attorneys alike, but only if asked. But in Danielle's case, even when she didn't ask, the caring advice came anyway.

"Need I ask again if you've heard from Owen?"

Danielle blinked her sleepy eyes and shook her head. "No. I tried calling him several times, but there was no answer. I finally gave up." Trying to tuck his bizarre behavior, including yesterday's phone calls and messages, into the recesses of her mind, Danielle could feel her heart racing from the anxiety building within her. Karen's question only exacerbated how she felt.

"Hmmm," Karen murmured with an unspoken thought.

"He did leave a message on my answering machine," Danielle added, "but between his cell, you know, fading in and out—damn reception. The message was, well, pretty much indecipherable."

Karen was lost in thought. A brief silence filled the room, until a printer on the other side of the spacious office coughed out a sheet of paper. Her eyes were briefly averted by the sound. Then her gaze returned to Danielle.

"The message? What do you mean *message*?" Karen asked with increased interest.

"Well," Danielle said with a crooked smile, "he said, 'the books,' and like I said, there was nothing until I heard 'source code' and 'access.'"

"And what do you make of it?"

Danielle shrugged her shoulders. "Beats me. I'm not a computer techie. But he did send me two large boxes, and inside, I can't believe this myself, I found a thirty-volume treatise on Thomas Jefferson. For what reason, I don't know. Because I don't ever recall a conversation about my interest in reading Jefferson. I perused several volumes, and they were newly published."

"That's an improvement over the laws of New York." Karen said in an obvious reference to the books he sent Danielle when she passed the bar exam.

"Is there something I missed?" Danielle countered.

"No, but I find this the entire matter intriguing. You see, shortly after you left, Tony Cervasi called and wanted to speak to Denon. I asked if I could help, but his response was rather clipped no. Then he told me to find Denon, and he meant now, not later. Something must have happened."

Danielle had met Cervasi, the president and CEO of PERC, only twice. Years before she was interviewed for the position of legal counsel, she accompanied Owen to a political fund-raiser, sponsored by HBR, at the Four Seasons. It was there that Denon, the guru of political cases, introduced his team of lawyers that worked during the 2012 presidential election. Denon, who was at the forefront of the brouhaha over hanging chads and disenfranchised voters years ago, did an about-face when he saw Cervasi and walked away. It was an unintelligible encounter.

The next time she saw Cervasi, it was at an interview for the position of assistant legal counsel. Her opinion hadn't changed. He resembled a don, with his short, wavy, black hair, ragged eyebrows above deep set eyes, and cold, dark facial features. Even his demeanor, calculating and riveting, fit the part. His condescending wave of his hand after the meeting ended left her wondering whether it was an acceptance or a dismissal. But days later, she received an unconscionable salary offer.

Denon, who had a good relationship with Cervasi, put off her starting date until mid-November, maintaining her position at HBR was too important to leave during the hotly contested political elections. Ultimately, they agreed, so she was told, but Denon failed to recognize that she had accrued vacation, which she intended to take despite his irreverent protest. Now she was set to leave in late September.

Danielle snapped back from the past and concentrated on the matter at hand. "And you think this might involve Owen?"

"Earlier, I read an e-mail from Denon. He won't be in today. He's in Washington." Karen took a deep breath. "Again, here I go with my intuition, when you couple Owen's phone messages together, you …" She stopped short in her analysis and raised a questioning eyebrow.

Danielle sensed a sinking feeling. She could feel pinpricks up and down her arm. Her mouth went dry.

"Karen, yesterday you were going to say something. What was it? Is it about Owen? My new job?"

"As the saying goes, dear, politics make strange bedfellows." Karen stood, stepped around the side of her desk, and proceeded to close the door. Next she bundled several files sitting on a side chair and set them neatly on the floor. Then she sat down and locked eyes with Danielle. "I've seen some odd things over the many years I've worked here—associates, clients, and even partners, its business, strictly business. More than what I want to know, but in a way, it's my job."

*Why now?* Danielle thought. Karen had every opportunity to express her personal trepidation months ago. It was only yesterday that Karen expressed an undefined reservation.

Karen dropped her voice almost to a whisper, "I never wanted you to accept the position with that political firm. I've tried to tell you in so many ways for several months, but I didn't want to insult you."

It was Karen who had taken Danielle into her office after she lost her first case and let her cry. Then Karen gave her a swift kick and said, "Grow up. Here's a tissue—put on your face, and let's square those shoulders. I've got work to do, and so do you." Now Danielle could feel her heart thumping either from what she expected Karen to reveal or from the cappuccino she drank at Starbucks earlier that morning.

"Go ahead, I'm listening," Danielle said with an uneasiness that seemed to strangle her vocal chords.

"I can't put my finger on it. This is intuition, not fact. How am I supposed to tell you not to take a job on intuition? Maybe it's just me not wanting you to go. I've seen a lot of associates pass through this office, you know, and you'd think by now I should know not to become attached."

"It's not just intuition, is it?"

Karen frowned. "Do you remember the Sarnelli case?"

Danielle recalled Sarnelli was an alleged gangster, but you only had to meet him to know the word fit—more like mobster, really. "Denon was ecstatic when he won that case. The evidence was overwhelmingly against Sarnelli. How could I forget?"

"Exactly." Karen's eyes scanned the room, searching for words.

Danielle recalled the case was a loser. You'd have to be Houdini to pull that case out. Yet the charges were dismissed as though it never happened. At the time, she thought Denon was some type of god.

"But—."

Karen raised her forefinger, halting Danielle's objection. "Denon gets this call from Cervasi. Then moments later, mind you, *moments*, Denon emerges from his office with a wide grin—I can see it even now—and he announces that he won the case."

"Things like that happen, Karen. Denon's a shrewd attorney. Sure, he's arrogant. But I'm sure he did his homework before that case went to trial."

"Dear, you missed the point. I said Cervasi called him. No one else. He didn't get a call from the court or another attorney." Karen pressed her lips together and gave an almost imperceptible shake of her head. "The fix was in. Believe me, I know."

"What about his cell phone? Surely someone could have called him."

"No. He slipped into his office to take Cervasi's phone call, and seconds later, he announces he won the case. And there's more. Call it suspicions, okay, but Denon's taken a number of trips with your future boss to some offshore island. Did you know that Denon has a villa in the Bahamas? I just don't buy it."

Danielle wondered when and where she missed Karen's warning. Now she desperately needed to talk to Owen. What did he know about Cervasi? PERC? What could he tell her?

"You're making me think I may have rushed into something, Karen. It seemed like a good idea. More money, more opportunity. I guess it just happened." Clouded over with guilt from not thinking, Danielle tried to collect her thoughts. She was on a merry-go-round, and she wanted to get off. "Where do I go from here?"

"You need to reexamine your decision. It's that simple."

*No, it isn't.* Danielle knew she couldn't reverse course. Commitments were made to move her belongings to Washington, DC. Even Ann Burk, her roommate, depended on her being out by month's end. Ann's future husband was moving into the apartment within weeks. And what if Karen was wrong? She also said her deductions could be nothing more than intuition. And if it was totally explainable, then what?

"I can't think on a few hours of sleep," Danielle confessed to Karen. "I need a little time to myself to think this out."

"You go right ahead. Denon's in Washington, so I can stall him. And besides, we're not expecting any clients today. If you want to keep those brown eyes of yours looking bright, get some sleep, and then we'll sort this out. I can print the brief, and Denon won't be any the wiser."

Danielle hesitated. "You're right. But you promise me you'll call if you need my help?"

"Agreed."

Danielle rose swiftly from her seat, and Karen, deeply in thought, looked up to meet Danielle's gaze. Karen nodded, as though talking to herself, and then stood.

"Everything will work out," Karen said, reaching out to give Danielle a brief hug.

With that, Danielle wheeled around to exit the office. At the door, she turned and faced Karen and gave her a thumbs-up before exiting.

Retracing her steps from a short time ago, past the occupied and empty offices, Danielle began a self-examination. Why hadn't she looked into the legal position in-depth? Racked with high anxiety, she gave a lazy nod to the dark-haired receptionist seated behind an L-shaped, mahogany desk as she stepped through the double, hand-carved, teak front doors. The law firm never recognized Saturdays or Sundays as days of rest. For that matter, a holiday was another twenty-four hours of billing time.

She took an elevator to the first floor and exited into the lobby. The first three floors of the office building were dedicated to retail space, with the remainder of the floors leased to commercial establishments.

As she walked toward the entrance, she caught sight of a sign, printed in red letters, in a shop window: "Help Needed." Deep inside, she swelled with emotion, thinking she had to try one more time.

Snatching the cell hooked to her purse strap, she speed-dialed Owen, turning around to face shoppers and office personnel who were busily going about their business, when she spotted a man out of the corner of her eye. He purposely turned and ducked out of sight around a corner.

*Is he following me?* On occasion, she was the subject of flirtatious looks from men, sometimes bordering on an outright stare. *Paranoia,* she thought dismissively.

Impatiently she waited for Owen to answer, but somehow, she knew he wasn't going to. Clicking off the cell, she continued on her way, and the nagging feeling returned. Abruptly, she turned and eyed the throng of people coming and going around her. That's when she spotted him again. He had changed positions and was a little further away, but there was no doubt in her mind that he was looking directly at her.

*I'm being watched!*

# 3

*Reston, Virginia*
*Saturday, September 1*
*12:00 p.m.*

As the black Mercedes approached the mirrored glass edifice, which appeared as a brilliant diamond among the standing trees on a sunny day, Cervasi eased back in his desk chair. Amused at the sight of the approaching sedan, he knew the driver: his brother-in-law, William Parks, the general legal counsel for the company who never practiced law.

After he nosed the sedan into its assigned space, Parks, the Ivy League graduate, stepped out and retrieved his suit coat. Cervasi thought Parks had lost a step in his stately stride now that his Learjet and golf membership at the Congressional were gone, and his Potomac estate had been sold in foreclosure. And yet his underlying indifference and condescending attitude toward others hadn't changed, despite his change in social stature. Parks, nonetheless, did prove the idiom "A fool and his money are soon parted."

Cervasi laughed quietly at the financial contribution made unbeknownst by Parks to the coffers of the company. The millions had been invested in both Virginian and foreign accounts, and the revenue fueled the financial and political status of PERC. He eyed the closet with its secret wall, where he held the books and records of the investments, not to mention the cash needed to pay someone off.

Before heading for the meeting, he quickly flipped through the pictures one last time. Then he deposited them in a brown envelope, stepped out of the office, and leisurely walked down the narrow hallway past occupied offices to the boardroom.

Once there, Cervasi swung open the door to find Paul Hart and Tom Halstren at the far end of a long, oval conference table. They were hovering over Parks, who was seated, like two hawks circling, waiting for the kill.

"Problems?" Cervasi questioned.

"Hardly—some clarification, that's all," Hart said with a wrinkled brow. "You know, being out on the campaign trail sometimes leaves you out of the loop. I'm just catching up."

With a smirk, Halstren said, "Yeah … a few engaging questions posed to our esteemed legal counsel. Neither Hart nor I like to hear things secondhand."

"And what might that be?" Cervasi asked, slowly turning his attention to Parks.

"I'm not really sure."

"You better damn well know because I'm not accepting some half-assed answer." Cervasi pulled out a chair while the two hawks parted.

Parks took a deep breath and shifted in his seat. "Well, there's Roberts, for one."

With his hands on his hips, Hart shook his head. "And how did that happen? That makes two in less than three months. Milsen and now Owen. That's not going over with me—not to mention the *Feds*."

"What do the Feds have to do with this?"

"*Everything*," Hart shot back. "I, for one, don't want anyone snooping around—especially with elections around the corner. It's bad for business. Hey, we had a run-in with them a short time ago, and it wasn't pleasant, *if you remember*."

Cervasi nodded with a frown. How well he remembered the intense investigation two years ago, when a state legislator claimed that the election results were somehow altered. And an employee, who worked as a programmer at PERC, let slip to an investigative reporter some vital information about how computer software in the voting machines could be hijacked. Shortly thereafter, the programmer was found dead in the San Francisco Bay. Fortunately, that investigation ended without further incident, and a few payoffs behind the scenes snuffed out any repercussions to the company.

"And speaking of business, what's with our senatorial candidate, Philip Clarke?" Halstren probed. "The latest poll results aren't encouraging. Thomas McClay is more than twenty, and by some accounts approaching thirty, basis points ahead, and he's running a strong campaign based on family values and morality. Clarke doesn't seem in tune with his constituents."

"Don't worry, he'll win in the end, I've—" Cervasi glanced at Parks, who was examining an internal election report prepared for the meeting. The report summarized the past, present, and projected results for the candidates represented by PERC. "Counselor, how about you step out for twenty minutes or so? I need to talk to these two in private. And while you're out, tell Gina, my secretary, we're going to need coffee and some cold drinks."

"Okay," Parks said softly, with a slight head nod.

After Parks left the room, Cervasi said, "I know the guy's my brother-in-law, but I don't want McClay tipped off about this. I'm sure you already know that they're friends. And I have a sneaky suspicion that he's been talking about our campaign plans to him. I'll deal with my brother-in-law when it's appropriate." He looked at the brown envelope and a smile crept across his face.

"What do you have?" Hart prompted.

"Just this." Cervasi slid the envelope across the table to Halstren.

Undoing the flap, Halstren pulled out three pictures and thumbed through them twice. "Whoa!" He exhaled forcefully as he studied the nude photos. "Is that McClay's wife?"

There were three photos: a shot of the nude woman posing on the beach; a shot of her and McClay surrounded by three dozen long stem red roses; and McClay and her seated in a hot tub, surrounded by yellow, red, and white votive candles two glasses, and a bottle of red wine sitting on the tub's ledge.

"That's *not* his wife. Who she is, I don't care. Nor should you …" Cervasi said with intense gratification.

Halstren handed the pictures to Hart, who examined each one carefully.

"And what's this supposed to mean?" Halstren asked, exchanging glances with Hart.

For the next ten minutes, Cervasi outlined his intent to release the pictures a few days before Election Day. He maintained that McClay's followers will abandon him because his family values, which were a major part of McClay's platform, will be compromised. Cervasi believed that the pictures, if released timely and secretly to the press, would have a significant *negative impact* on McClay's campaign.

"And you *really* think this will have an impact?" Hart said, rolling his eyes.

Halstren crossed his arms and leaned back into his chair. "Extramarital affairs … it's an epidemic. I know where you're coming from, but I'm skeptical. I don't know … I think it may be a stretch. At this late date, it's a lost cause."

"How did you come across the pictures?" Hart asked, his hands gripping the back of a chair.

"Matalino," Cervasi said evenly.

"Well, that says it all." Halstren slapped the table. The sound echoed off the walls. "Knowing his venal nature, I can't say we hit the jackpot with them." He pressed forward in his seat. "You can't say Matalino's friends are the most desirable and respectable sources. Hell, for all we know, these pictures could be doctored."

"Yeah. Tony, we told you a year ago, Clarke has baggage," Hart observed. "Clarke's political machine is rusty. And you're not going to see a groundswell of support—well, not in this election. Let's just ditch him and cut our losses. He's probably ready to find a new campaign manager anyway. We've got other races."

Cervasi recalled the heated debate with Hart and Halstren, his two trusted friends and advisors, about Clarke's political and business improprieties. But Cervasi ignored their warnings, opting instead for the first chance at a senatorial race, and he had justified the risk based on Clarke's connections, which he thought could be tapped, within Washington.

"He's right," Halstren said. "The Congressman reminds me of a worn-out tire. You can recap it, but if the glue doesn't adhere to the rubber, you'll end up with a worn-out tire. He's burned too many bridges. It's plain and simple. I read the stats this morning. He's lost the teachers, young professionals, the elderly, and morally bent voters. And God knows who else. After all those years in Congress, you'd think he'd know how to campaign and when to keep his mouth shut. Right now, I can say, it stinks."

Halstren, a former prosecutor in New York, was astute, having spearheaded a number of elections for candidates, and he graduated at the top of his class at Princeton. He had that incisive instinct to cut through the issues and find a solution—if there was one.

"These photos," said Hart, ignoring Halstren's arguments, "are damaging, very damaging. But I'd have to agree, if Matalino had something to do with them, well—" He shook his head.

Cervasi interjected, knowing their mindset might be jaded by the past. "Regardless, he assures me that they're real, and I'll take his word for it." Cervasi never asked many questions when Matalino was involved; it was better he didn't know.

Cervasi knew this wasn't going to be an easy sale, but it really didn't matter what they thought. As president and CEO of the company, he could do what he damn well pleased. But he would have liked their seal of approval, in any case. "I don't want a word of this breathed outside this room. Hopefully, this might be the miracle we need." With that Cervasi got up and collected the photos and envelope.

"Miracle? Huh? That only happens at Lourdes," said Hart, who looked out over the reflecting pond in the center of the quadrangle of buildings to the rear of the complex. "Uh oh! And here comes another anomaly that we don't need." Hart looked at Cervasi. "Trouble's on the way. And it's a guy you better keep in front of you. He's headed this way. I feel confident that he's going to be fishing for information."

Silence filled the room as Cervasi joined Hart at the window. "Baker is someone I can handle." *I think*, thought Cervasi. Baker. who was confined to a wheelchair, was a thorn, and yes, he knew too much about the company, but he and Matalino decided to forego any decision until after the election. Baker seemed to know everything, which concerned him.

"For our sake, let's hope you can," Hart said, using his index finger to point at Baker. "He's a nuisance. I can't put my finger on it, but he rubs me the wrong way."

Halstren remarked, not getting up from his chair, "I give him credit for being around when you need him—the maintenance engineer. But really, he's more than that—much more. That guy makes the NSA look like the Keystone Cops. Baker's here and there … almost like … quarks. I'd get rid of him—he's nothing but trouble."

"Quarks?" Cervasi asked.

"I overhead a physicist talking about them on the flight coming in this morning. They're like here and there, everywhere. And, by the way, did you ever look into what he calls his office? Well, I've been in building three when he wasn't there. I don't know what in that room attracts him. A desk, a few chairs, and a phone in a soundproof room doesn't make sense."

Cervasi shared Halstren's assessment, thinking that there were too many unusual coincidences. But as long as Baker stayed out of the way, they didn't have anything to worry about—at least for now.

Just then, the door flew open and Denon Pierce walked in, trailed by Parks.

At age forty-six, Denon was of slender build, with a tone of voice like a grizzly. Cold, calculating, and pompous, with a steely jaw and knitted eyebrows, Denon had a permanent look of disdain. He was the New York attorney, razor sharp and arrogant, with a self-assurance that left other attorneys believing they were inferior. Denon merely nodded at each individual in the room. He wore a crisp blue shirt, a finely tailored, medium gray, patterned suit, and a pair of stylish gold wave cufflinks.

Hart said derisively, "Those threads. Didn't I see that suit in an advertisement for Sears? Or maybe, God forbid, Brioni?"

Denon was not amused as he stared with contempt. He set his leather briefcase on the table, took off his jacket, and draped it over the back of a chair.

"Things must be good. Or maybe," Hart paused, "the company is just paying you too much."

"I'm worth every penny," Denon retorted, meeting the comment head-on. "You should have stayed in New York, Paul. Although I recognize you didn't have a choice, especially when you were caught taking money under the table."

Hart grimaced and charged around the table. Before the raging bull closed the distance to Denon, Cervasi stepped between them, knowing contentious outbursts had occurred on prior occasions. "I called you for a purpose, and I want to get started. If you two have something to say to each other, you can take it up later."

"Tony," Halstren said, "I read the agenda you sent last night. I know we have a lot to discuss, but I, for one, have a plane to catch for the coast tonight."

"Noted. But you can catch another plane. We have a number of matters to discuss." Cervasi nodded several times, "We'll address them quickly."

"Wait a minute," Hart objected. "Before we start, I want clarification from highly regarded legal counsel Parks," as he stared at him, "that what is said in this meeting will not go any further than this room. I don't want McClay being a party to our discussions."

Parks looked like someone had stuck a seven iron in his stomach and knocked the wind out of him. He raised an eyebrow and said, "Tom's a friend, and he already knows we represent Clarke. Anyway, I haven't seen him in a few weeks."

"That's not what I've heard," Hart responded. "Why, only this morning, I got this call from Trevor, the nosy news reporter who inquired about the death of Roberts. He claimed he heard it from McClay, and to me, that means you."

Cervasi gritted his teeth, knowing that he had mentioned the death of Owen only hours ago.

An expression of guilt crossed Parks's face, and he dropped his pen on the table. The sound reverberated in an otherwise quiet room. All eyes focused on him.

Halstren inquired, "Getting back to Owen—what happened to him? I don't buy what I've been hearing."

"For the record, it came as a great shock to me," Cervasi said. "Real shame. Apparently, he committed suicide. Jumped off some bridge in Pittsburgh. As you know, we had our differences, but I certainly respected the work he did for our company." Cervasi's eyes drifted toward Parks, wondering what else Parks may have revealed to McClay.

"I don't want to bring this up, Tony, but where was Matalino?" Halstren pressed, his eyes riveted on Cervasi.

"He had nothing to do with it," Cervasi snapped. "He was here working out several bugs in security. You know when that dot-com company sold us this string of buildings, they ripped out the security monitoring equipment. It's his job to ensure the security of this office complex."

"Some head of security. I remember too well he had nothing to do with the guy on the West Coast, but he brought the government down on us," said Halstren. Then he mumbled, "Broken legs."

Cervasi recognized Matalino was rough around the edges, but more importantly, he was loyal and got the job done.

"The company and Matalino were cleared of any wrongdoing." Denon glared at Halstren like a recalcitrant witness on a courtroom stand. "We've been through this before. Let's not open up a can of worms. I'm not here to discuss the past, and you, of all people, shouldn't be concerned about it either."

Cervasi quickly added, "Yes, and we can thank Denon for his stellar representation when it came to the government's investigation." Cervasi knew this was not where he wanted to take the meeting, and it was all caused by his brother-in-law and his loquacious mouth.

"Just checking," Halstren said. "I wanted to make sure that Matalino and his goombahs didn't have anything to do with it. And I don't mean to make waves, but we're beyond those mobster days." Halstren returned a smug look at Denon.

With his elbow on the table and eyes studying his fingernails, Hart peered over his outstretched hand. "And what about that program Owen was developing?"

"I don't quite understand," Cervasi said with continued irritation. "Program? What do you mean?"

"You know … that special program." Halstren inquired, looking directly at Parks. "I understood it was dubbed STAR."

Cervasi, with squinted eyes, nodded ever so slightly; he now understood the import of the brouhaha that broke out earlier. He rolled up the sleeves of his shirt while he mulled over an appropriate response. "Any program developed by Owen need not concern you. We'll leave it at that. You pay attention to matters within your region. If it's something you should know about, I'll let you know," he said with vehemence.

Hart shrugged his shoulders. "No harm intended, but his program must have had some significance."

"If it had, I would have told you. And that's all you need to know. Now, let's get started; otherwise, we'll never get out of here today," Cervasi intoned angrily.

For the next several hours, Cervasi and those present studied several other political races. Cervasi purposely avoided any further discussion of the Clarke race. He was now leery about what Parks fed to Hart and Halstren. At 5:30 p.m., Cervasi adjourned the meeting.

While the others filed out of the room, Cervasi gave Parks a measured stare of anger and said, "I'd like to have a word with you." He straddled the edge of the table directly in the line of view of Parks.

"What did you say to them?" Cervasi demanded.

"I don't know what you mean."

Cervasi glared into the two vacant eyes without saying another word.

Parks looked away from Cervasi and said, "Well, I may have said something about STAR. I wondered, you know, what happened. That's all."

Cervasi lightly patted Parks's cheek, feeling his blood pressure rising. With his finger only inches from Parks's face, he said, "I've told you on more than one occasion to keep your mouth shut. Hell, I don't care if you are my brother-in-law. If it wasn't for my sister, I would have canned you over a year ago. And now I have other things in mind for you." His eyes were riveted on Parks. "If you overhear or are told anything about this company, before you say another damn word, you clear it with me." With a final glare, Cervasi picked up his papers and opened the door. He made a slitting motion across his neck. "You know what can happen." The door hinge let out a slight complaint as the door closed.

# 4

*Reston, Virginia*
*Saturday, September 1*
*7:00 p.m.*

With one hand in his pants pocket and the other holding a glass of scotch on the rocks, William Parks studied the artist's minute brushstrokes with a crooked smile. It was a masterful painting that caught the warmth of streetlights dancing off the ripples of a river against the shades of reddish hues of a sinking sun in the grasp of an evening sky. For Parks, the painting was a masterpiece, but it also reminded him of a fatal error in judgment, one that churned in his mind constantly.

From his cabin window as the plane descended into Key West, he recalled checking his watch, knowing the dinner meeting was a mere formality. He pulled from his wallet a slip of paper with the penciled routing and account numbers, beaming like a prospector who stumbled on a gold mine. A half hour later, he wired the fifteen million dollars inherited from his father for a 50 percent stake in a large oil and gas field. By sunset that fateful day, his millions were gone. So were the actors who vanished without a trace, scurrying away with his money like cockroaches. The geologist, investment banker, and driller were impostors, and so were the land leases and drilled wells.

"Is that your dinner?" asked a nearby voice that pulled him back from the nightmare.

Parks drew up his heavy eyelids and turned his head slightly, sobering up quickly upon seeing Les Baker, who was seated in a wheelchair that had already been partially maneuvered into the office.

Baker, with his beady eyes, slowly scanned the room, stopping on occasion to study a painting. His unblinking eyes focused on several original oils, and then he nodded with what seemed approval as a faint, devious smile crossed his face.

"Yeah, and it's early," Parks grunted. He didn't need someone telling him what time of day to drink; for that matter he had already drained two and was on his third. "What do you want?"

Baker toggled a small lever mounted on the arm of his chair, slowly directing the wheelchair into the room and drawing within several feet. "Tony can be quite indignant, even condescending, when you ask questions or stray into matters that don't concern you. He and Matalino don't take it in stride. Take it from one who knows—Tony's strictly sub-rosa." Baker angled the wheelchair around a table and stopped to admire another original painting.

"You didn't come into my office to tell me about Tony." Keeping an eye glued on Baker, who seemed mesmerized by the art collection, Parks sauntered across the room. As he opened the door to a bar recessed into the wall, Parks recalled Baker's half-hearted assistance in finding the perpetrators of the oil and gas scam. His brother-in-law had assigned the job to Baker, but Parks always thought deep down inside that Baker systematically stonewalled the entire investigation.

From an ice bucket, Parks grasped three ice cubes with a pair of tongs and added them to a glass. Then he grabbed the neck of a bottle of scotch, kicked the bar doors shut with his shoe, and settled into an executive chair behind an expansive mahogany desk. He plopped his feet on top and closed his eyes for a moment. Except for a collection of several unread newspapers, his desk was empty. He turned his head slightly to catch Baker's riveting stare. As they eyed each other, he could feel a growing chill run down his spine.

Baker said, "We each make choices, some good and some … not so good. You get the picture."

"What's that got to do with me? Is this some philosophical lesson? I don't need any advice from you or Tony. So why don't you just leave?" Parks undid the cap and poured himself another drink. Through his glassy-eyed stupor, he gave Baker a sideward glance.

Ignoring the entreaty, Baker slowly guided his wheelchair along the edge of the wall, stopping occasionally for a closer examination of the artwork. "I admire your taste. I see you've collected a number of American artists … Benson, Gorman. I never had money myself, you know, so I don't know what happens when—" His voice trailed off. "You've hit some hard times," he finished, raising an eyebrow and nodding at the drink.

"You can admire them all you want. They're not for sale." After what he considered a botched job in the investigation, Parks never lent the guy any credence. He intuitively believed that Baker was holding out, but he never suspected him of any complicity. His reservations were with Cervasi, who he thought could have done more for the investigation.

"There's a new attorney starting in a few weeks." Baker stopped and perused a scenic painting of a waterfall. "You know, I like this one. Simple and graceful. Kinkade?"

"Yeah," Parks sputtered, and then he looked down into his empty glass. He had to admit that his legal position at PERC was out of necessity rather than desire. For the last several years, he had searched every lead his brother-in-law uncovered, or for that matter, Baker, but they were dead ends. Even the legal authorities, with whom he and Cervasi had worked, said the trail had gone cold. Without any explanation, the internal investigation ended, and shortly afterward, the authorities closed the case. Their relationship had wilted to acrimonious feelings toward one another. Cervasi told him to write off the loss to bad judgment and move on. That was clearly unacceptable.

"Okay. The new attorney is associated with Denon. And I met her … all in all a nice person, and so forth," Parks said with a slurred sense of despair. The scotch flowed freely from the bottle, missing the glass, at first before he righted the bottle.

"When you lost all your money, Tony gave you a job. And now you're about to lose it a second time. And you know he's not the forgiving type."

"And you're some type of savior?"

"In a way," responded Baker in a playful, underhanded tone. "You know, Tony's concerned about Clarke's election. He's been less than truthful with you … questioning your friendship with the opposing party."

Naturally, thought Parks, Cervasi disliked McClay. Besides the commanding lead in the senatorial race, McClay, a former prosecutor, had lent assistance to the investigation into the scam. When McClay uncovered an actual name of an individual connected to the deal, Cervasi was dismissive, even to the point of being evasive, maintaining that McClay had unearthed nothing new. And further, as he eloquently put it, "You're not going to get a dead man to talk."

A smirk crept over Baker's face as though he knew what Parks was thinking. Or maybe it was how Parks fidgeted in his chair that accounted for Baker's snake-eyed glare.

Finally, Parks dropped both feet to the floor and stood. In his mind, and through his oblique stare, the room seemed to dizzily move around in a circle. He tried to steady himself, but his knees wanted to give underneath his weight. "You've had your fun. You weren't there. Now get out." He polished off the drink and wiped his mouth with his sleeve.

"You need me," said Baker. "I wouldn't be so hostile."

"Get out!"

For Parks, the exchange with Baker seemed more of a chess game. Parks frowned and stepped wearily to the window overlooking the stately lawn. He could feel Baker's stare pressing into his back. When he spun around, Baker was sitting ramrod straight in his wheelchair, as he usually did, and had his head cocked with a calculating facial expression.

"I know what Tony's uncovered." Baker arched his eyebrows. "McClay has made several transgressions that are less than complimentary."

"So?" said Parks, shrugging his shoulders. "There's been a number of politicians caught with their pants down. Get to the point." He had misgivings even talking to Baker. Uneasy was more like it. If Cervasi didn't send Baker, then what was he doing here?

"Yes," Baker said, "but he has a family, nice kids, and yet … that's where you come in. If McClay were aware of these photos, he might pay handsomely for the evidence." Baker dropped into his pied piper gaze.

"I don't know what you're talking about. And what's this got to do with me?" The story was too farfetched, but then again, you really don't know people.

Baker replied, "McClay might be interested in seeing them." The wheels on the wheelchair made a single revolution. "You have an opportunity here. What do you have to lose?"

"Blackmail?" Parks shook his head.

"No. This is not blackmail. It's a simple exchange. The pictures for—" Baker raised his eyebrows. "For information, that's it."

Parks resisted falling into a trap, real or imaginary. After Tony's warning earlier in the day, he didn't want any part of what was being offering. And despite his dislike for PERC, he realized that if he crossed Tony, it would be suicide.

Tony paid him well for his legal counsel, maybe too much, and, yes, he was regretfully indebted to him. After all, he and his wife would have lost everything if he wasn't offered the position. But then there was McClay, a good friend, who showed a genuine and dedicated interest during the investigation, but came up with nothing.

"I'll need a few pieces of information. That's all," Baker said as he paused at a painting. "Is this a print of a Monet? Nice. Very nice. You know, I should spend more time in a museum. Who knows? Maybe I have an artistic bent."

"Do you mind? Are you finished? I've got things to do." Parks thought Baker was a figure in the woods listening, watching, and waiting for his prey.

"Oh yes. Why, it's just a matter of time before you lose your job. You've lost plenty, haven't you? I've heard you're still looking for those con artists. They're probably on some yacht somewhere enjoying your money, or maybe they're right under your nose."

That's exactly why Parks wanted his revenge. He spent most of his waking hours rehashing the meetings leading up to his wiring the money. The trail had grown cold, but he hadn't given up.

"If those pictures, or whatever you claim that you have against McClay, are worth something, then why don't you hand them over to him? He'll be glad to deal with you," Parks suggested, thinking about the money he had lost. Parks leaned against his desk to steady himself.

Baker replied, "I wouldn't even get close. I'm an invalid. I can't chase him down in a crowd of supporters, and what am I supposed to do? Call him? If I'm lucky, I might catch him. No, I'm offering you a chance."

Parks countered, "And what makes you think I won't run to Tony?"

"You could. But you won't. You have nothing to gain. Sure, Tony will pat you on the back for a good job. Then what? In a few months all will be forgotten." With a calculated look, he said, "And so will you."

Parks looked intently into his scotch and weighed what Baker had said. "Okay, how do I know these pictures exist? And what's in this for you?"

Baker removed his wire rim glasses and pulled out a handkerchief. Cleaning the smudges from the lenses, he cracked a weak smile. "You don't need to worry about the pictures, they exist. And as for me, Tony reneged on a financial matter that doesn't concern you. Justice comes in many forms, and one never knows when to expect it."

Parks focused on the insidious expression written on Baker's face. While Baker stretched the stems of the wire rim glasses behind each ear and then neatly replaced the handkerchief in his pocket, Parks attempted to sweep the cobwebs cluttering in his mind. *There's more to this. Baker has other motivations.*

Parks asked, "Won't Tony uncover this? Once he does, you and I won't be able to walk the streets."

"I'm the only one who has access to his safe. He'll come looking for me, not you. Anyway, once this New York attorney joins PERC, you'll be history. McClay wins the election and finds you a lucrative position."

"Obviously, you want something. Money? Is that it? If McClay pays me for these alleged pictures, you want a cut?"

Baker raised a forefinger. "Nothing. But there is something that you might know. What can you tell me about Owen Roberts?"

"Is there something in particular?"

Baker pushed forward on the lever, and his wheelchair nudged closer. "STAR. That's the program."

"I don't have a damn clue. What's so important about this program?"

Baker's blank face morphed into scorn. "Do you take me for a fool? You know nothing?"

"Whatever they do over there in the IT department is none of my business. Doors are locked. And I take it, there's a reason. But I'm not one to go snooping. Anyway, I'd like to know where my money went."

Baker pulled a book from a bookcase. He opened the book and leafed through it to the middle. Then he looked up and said, "Too bad we can't start in the middle; then we could write a different beginning and end."

Parks shrugged his shoulders. "Hey, I told you what I know. You never said what this STAR does. And what's your interest?"

Baker reflected for a silent moment and then he chuckled. "We'll do it your way. You get me what I want, and I'll provide you with information you want."

"When?"

"That's up to you." Baker spun his wheelchair around and stopped at the Kinkade painting. "Light hits us in different ways, doesn't it? One never knows when the lights will be turned out." Then he turned back and said, "Do we?"

"You've made your point. I'll make some inquiries." Parks was unsure whether Matalino or Baker was a bigger threat. He always wondered why Tony never reined Baker in.

"Do that. I think we understand each other quite well." Baker spun his wheelchair to leave the room. Then he pointed to the painting. "Don't let the lights be turned out on you. Get me the information! And soon!" He never looked back as he reached out and turned the door knob.

"Hey, wait a minute," Parks called out. "Who has my money?" He attempted to gain his balance. But he fell to the floor with an empty bottle in his hand.

*Why STAR?* Parks thought before his mind slowly succumbed to the darkness that closed the curtain on his day.

# 5

*New York, New York*
*Monday, September 3*
*4:45 p.m.*

Emptiness filled her heart. Acceptance of a tragic event never comes without denial—a denial the tragedy ever happened.

For Danielle, news of Owen's suicide left her with one question: Why? Unable to absorb the shock, teary-eyed, she stared out from her fifth floor office into the light rain. She wanted to scream in anguish, but for what purpose? It wouldn't bring him back. She dabbed her eyes with a tissue, reliving the nagging feeling, the one that wouldn't leave her, from the other evening. Owen's cryptic words, perhaps, foreshadowed his own destiny and conveyed an ominous note of caution to her.

From her office window, she observed the rain-soaked sidewalks of Lexington Avenue crowded with a menagerie of open umbrellas of every size and color. Her attention was drawn to a large black-and-white paneled umbrella. At a street corner, it stopped and spun like a top, then knifed through a maze of creeping traffic. In front of her office building, the umbrella collapsed and disappeared from sight. Unaffected by the loss of the black and white, other umbrellas continued to bob up and down as though dancing to a rocking drum beat.

The ring of the telephone near a stack of legal correspondence and briefs splayed across the desktop made her jump. Danielle stepped across the room and picked up the receiver.

"Denon's on the line," said Karen. "I can—"

"No, I'd better take it." Danielle bit her lower lip. In her fragile state, she didn't want to hear from a person who showed no mercy, sympathy, understanding, or civility toward client, staff, or fellow attorney.

"I'll tell him you're out. None of us should be here anyway. It's Labor Day."

"Thanks, I should tell him," Danielle said with resignation. Pulling a clean tissue from a side drawer, she swallowed hard and pulled strength from deep inside. "Hello?"

"Things are hopping here, so I don't have a lot of time," Pierce said in his usual clear, calculating voice. "The usual problems with elections. And Parks, the worthless piece of shit, can't be bothered. Cervasi should kick his ass out of here … wait a minute." Abruptly, he interrupted the call to bark his dinner reservations at 1789, his favorite Georgetown restaurant.

"Danielle, I sent you an e-mail a few minutes ago. Besides Parks, I've got problems with Congressman Clarke. Pull out his agreement. I've sent you my objections and thoughts. I want a legal memorandum. Got it?"

PERC and Cervasi agreed to act as Clarke's campaign management team, and now, both Cervasi and Pierce concluded the situation had gone sour. That, thought Danielle, was sufficient to bail from a sinking campaign.

Danielle realized her mistake: she should have listened to Karen. Why did she take his call in the first place? She needed time to herself.

"I was about to leave," Danielle said plaintively. "You know that—" She shut her eyes tightly and winced inside. Forty-eight hours ago it was the brief—now it's Clarke's agreement.

"I need this tonight," he barked.

Pierce, a senior partner at HBR, threw his weight around more like a dictator. And he had one work idiosyncrasy: if you worked for him, your cell was on 24/7.

Danielle rubbed her forehead but didn't respond. Like a wilted flower, she was drained; the news of Owen's death took its toll.

"Are you still there?"

"Yes," she said with a definite void within her voice.

"I'll expect to see your e-mail by, say, midnight. Oh, and run a Lexus-Nexus on all the cases dealing with candidates throughout the country. I want some ammunition. Get Myers in there to help." Greg Myers aspired to become a partner with HBR, and Pierce made sure that Myers paid his dues.

Every September, Pierce left the office for Washington. A concentrated ten weeks of political gamesmanship, election upheavals, and voter discontent ensued, which required the support of Danielle and a host of other attorneys to address issues posed by PERC's offices scattered throughout the country.

"I suspect things are not going well for the congressman," Danielle observed as she attempted to regain her composure.

"That's right. And I want Tony and his corporation protected."

"Denon," Danielle said, taking a deep breath, "I don't know if you heard, but Owen has—" she couldn't finish the words without choking up, "passed away."

"Sorry ... Clarke's behind ... and sorry to hear about Owen, but you and I have work to do. And we've got little time."

Danielle winced, fighting back her tears. She recalled Karen's observation, "They're apathetic. It's strictly business, nothing more, Danielle. That's life at HBR." *Didn't Owen's death mean anything?* Danielle's eyes narrowed, feeling her blood pressure on the rise.

"We hadn't spoken in—" Danielle said.

"That's right, but it doesn't matter. Clarke's behind with virtually no chance of winning this election. But we need to make him look good. And I don't need to educate you about Tony Cervasi, who seems, at the present time, to be weathering the hurricane of downbeat political news on Clarke. PERC's credibility will suffer immensely if we lose the election."

She was about to say that she hadn't spoken to Owen in months but, as usual, Pierce only heard what he wanted to hear. "Why?" Danielle forced a half-smile, knowing the question would enrage him.

"Why? Do I need to spell it out? Clarke's going to blame someone. And it's going to be Tony Cervasi, without question. And that doesn't sit well with Tony. If Clarke's defeated, I want to muddy the waters, turn the tables. It's *got* to be Clarke's fault."

Danielle could execute that tactic. When you're in a corner and have no place to hide, make it look like it's the other guy's fault. Comb through the agreement for Pierce and find exculpatory provisions to vindicate PERC's handling of the election.

"Yes. I do know, Denon." Nothing was ever right or wrong. It was the position. Whoever paid you the most, that's the position you took.

"I'll ignore your sarcasm," Pierce said. "Your boyfriend was seeing a psychiatrist. He had mental problems. So just forget him; he wasn't your type."

"What do you mean?" His words stung like a slap to her face. But insensitivity and incendiary remarks were his bread and butter trial tactics.

"Danielle. You don't walk into a shrink's office and assault him unless there's something mentally wrong with you. You know, he was a little odd."

With a sinking feeling inside and a flushed face, Danielle said with firmness, "No ... no, that's not true. Why, I spoke to him only days ago and—"

"What did he say?" Pierce interrupted.

Danielle caught herself reaching for a bottle of aspirin in her desk. Undoing the cap, she popped two aspirin into the palm of her hand while she digested Denon's statement that Owen was seeing a psychiatrist. Was it true? "He sounded agitated. That's all."

"What did he want?"

Danielle thought, *What difference would it make?* Anger brewed inside her. Pierce was turning the knife in her back. And why should she relate the conversation with Owen? It was none of his business. "Nothing."

"Did he say anything about Tony Cervasi or the company?"

Danielle popped the two aspirin in her mouth and washed them down with a sip from a bottled water on her desk. Trying to relax and calm her emotions, she answered, "No. Is there a reason?"

Owen never said anything about what he did at work. From the time she met him, he would always change the subject or say he did computer programming. His seeing a psychiatrist made no sense. It simply wasn't true.

A silence blanketed their conversation until Pierce said, "Well, anyway, you don't go throwing yourself off a bridge unless there's something wrong."

"That's impossible. No, he wouldn't. It can't be. There's more to it. There just has to be," Danielle said. Pierce's biting rhetoric acted as a vice squeezing her lungs.

"You're wasting your time," Pierce added without any regard for her feelings. "The guy's dead. He shouldn't have—" Pierce went silent.

Danielle fired back. "Shouldn't have what?"

"Never mind. Get that project done." With a click, he was gone.

Danielle slammed the receiver into its cradle. Her eyes caught the rivulets of rain against the windowpane. No condolences. No "Can I do anything for you?" Had personal relationships become merely business transactions?

Pierce's statements tugged at her spirit, but she knew his game. She intended to prove him wrong, and his comments only fueled her desire to vindicate Owen. "Under no circumstances should you show your weak side," her father once cautioned her. "Be thick-skinned."

A tap on the door made Danielle wheel around.

"Thought you might need company," Karen said, closing the door behind her as Danielle fell into a chair. Karen seated herself across from Danielle. "He gave me an earful before I connected him to you."

"He's beyond inconsiderate," Danielle said, dabbing her eyes. "Never asked anything about Owen, and even—can you believe this—said Owen was a mental case." Her cheeks burned red, and she could feel a prickly sensation running down her arms.

"He's a pure litigator taught to undress and humiliate witnesses and then smile as though he's your friend. Overlook it. You're an attorney and a damn good one."

Danielle knew Pierce as a consummate litigator who knew all the right things to say and how to act when confronted. He had studied with the best, and juries bought his yarns. A charmer on the outside, but underneath lived a hell storm.

"He's hard core. And to think he'll make managing partner someday," Karen said, shaking her head.

Danielle nodded in agreement. "He also said Owen was seeing a psychiatrist. Mind you, a psychiatrist?"

"He didn't want to hear it when I mentioned Owen's death. Although he did brief me about Clarke's Senate campaign," Karen said, resting her arms on her thighs and leaning closer to the desk.

"Danielle, once you take your new position at PERC, he'll try to use you. Keep your distance."

"Yeah," Danielle sighed. She took a deep breath, dragging herself from her chair.

"Denon loves to debate, of course, but only on his terms. It's second nature to him. Makes them stand up and pay attention, as he would say."

"He's reprehensible." Danielle wondered whether her mother, a trial litigator, exhibited the same cold, unblinking, and unflappable character. Her mother practiced law at a time when women lawyers were in the minority. But even though women eventually filled the ranks, it remained a profession generally practiced by men. Denon believed women had no place in a law office, other than to serve as staff.

"I know what you're thinking, but Owen's death was probably accidental," Karen said.

"Yes," Danielle said, trying to convince herself.

"Why don't you get a bowl of chicken soup? It'll do you good. There's a great deli with the best hot soups tucked in a store on Fifty-First. They should be open."

"Maybe I will. I could use the walk to relieve my mind."

"That's my girl. I'd love to sit and chat," Karen said, looking at her watch, "but Jennifer, you know her, I've mentioned her on several occasions, invited me over for dinner. But if I hurry, I can cancel."

"Don't worry, I'll be fine. I need some private time after receiving the bad news from Owen's mother."

"The least I can do is walk out with you. Give me a minute."

Once she met up with Karen, Danielle said, "I'll turn out the lights and set the alarm while you catch an elevator for us." As she turned out the lights and set the security code, she looked at the receptionist's desk where a single blinking light flashed on a phone. She wondered what hapless soul would call at this hour.

For a moment, she reflected on the day she interviewed with HBR. It was Karen who came to the rescue when she accidentally stained her dress at lunch. And Karen was still offering her help after all these years. With one last look at the phone, she turned, locked the door, and hastened her pace, hearing the buzz of a cranky elevator with its door being held open. Karen was standing there with her shoulder pressed against the door.

"You know, I'm sure Jennifer wouldn't mind me bringing you to dinner. Steaks on the grill? She makes a mean cheesecake. How about it?" Karen suggested as they descended to the ground floor.

"Thanks for the invitation, but I'd rather keep working and sleep in tomorrow morning."

"Don't turn into another Pierce."

Danielle smirked. Never ending days, constant deadlines, and incessant demands from senior partners and clients were the hallmarks of an associate learning the legal trade.

"You need some time to yourself. Why don't you postpone your start date until January?" Karen suggested.

Danielle shook her head as the doors opened. "I handed in my resignation, and I need to continue with my plans, at least for now."

"Don't worry about plans; you can always change them."

They stepped out into the main lobby of the office building.

"I know I mentioned I'm staying with a good friend. She's got this wonderful townhouse in Georgetown. I can put HBR and Pierce out of my mind for a while. And I know I should never have agreed to do those special projects for Pierce, but at least it will be on my terms," Danielle said as she undid the strap to her umbrella.

"Some things happen for a reason. Anyway, you'll be long gone from this place soon. No more late nights." Karen pulled up the hood of her coat. "Pierce mentioned William Parks as being a problem. Isn't he your future boss?"

Danielle frowned. "Pierce calls him 'TW' for totally worthless. When did Pierce say a kind word about anybody?"

"Parks won't be disappointed in you." Karen put her arm around Danielle. "You're a winner. Never forget that."

Stepping through the revolving door, they exited under cover of the building. Danielle looked at her leather shoes; they were going to get wet, though the rain had lightened up. She and Karen opened their umbrellas and immediately started to dodge standing water ponds.

"Thanks again, Karen; I'll never forget you. These last several years have been trying."

"Don't stay long at the office tonight. Good luck," Karen said before they parted company at Lexington and Fifty-First Street.

Before entering the deli, Danielle lowered her umbrella and shook off the excess water. She bought a tuna salad wrap and a Coke and pulled a stool up to the window. Her thoughts returned to Owen. Could he have committed suicide? She had never seen him depressed or insecure. What could have driven him to such an act? For a time, they had traveled to see each other in Washington or New York. Then something happened. She could not describe it, but he changed, or perhaps they both did. As they drifted apart, Danielle brushed it off as the demands of her profession. She realized how death has a sobering affect when it's someone close.

By the time she finished dinner, the rain had subsided. The black, wet pavement absorbed what little light was cast from streetlights. A canopy of dark storm clouds lingered overhead and looked as though the rain would start again with a vengeance. A short distance from the deli, the figure of a man underneath a black and white umbrella hidden from her direct view limped past her. His footsteps stopped after they passed each other. With uneasiness, she strained to look over her shoulder and found the faceless man staring at her. Then he turned and continued in the opposite direction.

The brisk, twenty-minute walk back to HBR cleared her mind. Unlocking the outer office door, she stepped inside to a dimly lit lobby and threw the deadbolt before she reached for the burglar alarm. Her hand trembled when she found it unarmed. Within the scant light, she swallowed hard and wondered whether someone awaited her in the darkened hallways that fed to the lobby.

She rushed around the receptionist's desk and flipped a light switch to partially illuminate the corridor leading to her office. Taking a deep breath, she heard the faint shuffle of papers in the distance. Softly and deliberately, she edged down the corridor to its source, hearing the throbbing of her heart in her eardrums. The distant noise stopped as she approached. With her back against the wall, she waited for a moment and then made her move. She bolted into the doorway and found a fax machine light blinking. On the floor, a handful of printed documents had spewed out from the machine.

With a sense of relief, she opened her wet umbrella and set it on the floor, out of the way in her office. She removed her soaking shoes, threw them into the corner, and sat down at her desk. A flash of lightning made her stir in her chair as the thunder rolled through the canyon of high-rise buildings. Wind-driven rain pelted against the window as new flickers of light and distant thunder rumbled in the inky blackness.

Danielle typed a few commands to call up her e-mail and Clarke's contract from the server. As she waited, she reached for a tablet in a side drawer and found the books she had stacked earlier had fallen. Easing out of her chair, she discovered an empty CD jewel case at the foot of the bookcase. She examined the case and then her eyes spotted a gaping section on a shelf. There was no doubt; the missing CDs were Owen's. Trying to remember the number and titles of the CDs, she closed her eyes in an attempt to picture them.

A faint door click from outside her office made her heart race anew. She dropped the case and stepped closer to the door. Straining to hear and letting out short breaths, she heard only the whining fan from her computer. The office was quiet between the thunder rumbling and the rain. Then she edged softly forward to the doorway and waited, her eyes shifting to her desk where her cell phone sat.

With a hand on the doorknob, she quickly closed the door until the palm of a hand reached out and jammed it. Wide-eyed, with her heart pounding, she let go of the door and backpedaled to her desk with a burst of perspiration on her forehead.

"Danielle," Karen said.

Danielle landed the palm of her hand on her forehead. "Next time give me some warning," she blurted. Her heart downshifted to a slower speed.

"Sorry, but I simply couldn't let you be here alone. With Pierce hitting the panic button and Owen's death, I got off the subway at the third stop and caught a cab back here. And I'm glad I did. You shouldn't leave the lobby door unlocked."

Danielle shook her head slightly in disbelief. "I didn't."

# 6

*Pittsburgh, Pennsylvania*
*Thursday, September 13*
*10:00 a.m.*

Always makes you stop and think."

Danielle twisted abruptly to face a bespectacled, reddish-brown haired man with a trace of gray at the temples. His hands were in the pockets of his trench coat, and she made out he was wearing a tan sport coat and navy pants.

In an apologetic tone, he said, "Sorry to startle you, ma'am. I saw you gazing intently at the funeral procession. Did you know the deceased?"

"Owen … yes," Danielle said. "He was, well, a good friend."

They watched a hearse, limo, and ten vehicles creep along a narrow and windy road, cutting through a gully shrouded in fog and underneath a canopy of gnarled tree limbs. Maneuvering through a slight bend in the road, the limo slowed and parked, straddling the gravel road and the grassy shoulder, followed by the other vehicles in the procession.

"Watched him grow up, myself. Know the family. And his mother has taken it pretty hard. The name is John Shike … Detective John Shike, City of Pittsburgh Police. I'm not here on police business. I came to pay my respects."

Danielle nodded in acknowledgment, holding back her tears and reaching in her purse for a tissue. "I really wanted to be here earlier, but my flight was delayed." She gave him a thin smile.

"My wife says I'm always late. She reminds me I'll be late for my own funeral, but I always tell her that's the way I would plan it,"

Shike said in a lighter tone. Sharing her gaze at the funeral, he added, "This fog should burn off soon. We've had our share of hot, sticky weather and then those storms, high winds, and torrential downpours lately."

A short distance away, the limo driver jumped out with a black umbrella in hand and planted himself at the rear door where an older, small-featured woman stepped out. She wore a black dress and reached out for his extended arm, nodding at the huddle of friends and family nearby. With a slight nod by the driver, the pallbearers, six in number, removed the casket.

Danielle collapsed her umbrella. "He was special. A tragedy. His mother will need someone."

"Absolutely. Death, let alone suicide, is hard to accept. It's natural to question whether you missed a word or mood swing that might have given some hint."

"It just wasn't him," Danielle said.

Shike shook his head and took a deep breath. "It's one of those cases where you'd want a different answer, but I'm afraid that's what happened. Sometimes we never really know a person … until it's too late."

With the pallbearers carrying the casket in the lead, the mourners began their upward trek to a knoll underneath a large oak tree.

"I …" her words evaporated, thinking about Owen. She began again, "I followed a news account that the crew of a passing tugboat found him," Danielle said with silent tears welling inside her, believing she may have heard the tugboat's wailing horn on her answering machine.

Shike exhaled. "There's not much more to say, except for the suicide note. That … pretty much sums it up."

Danielle clutched a penny inside her coat pocket. When she first met him, he was spinning it on a table. Naturally, in his own joking way, he admitted that after learning her name, it had only taken a few taps on the keyboard until he knew where she lived and went to school, plus her age. He told her that the penny would bring her luck, but it was intended, she knew, to remind her of him.

"Is there a chance I might be able to call you after the funeral to discuss his case?" Danielle asked softly.

"Reason?" Shike cocked his head and looked directly at her.

"It's more for closure." Danielle didn't want to reveal the text message Owen had sent her before he died. "Not only am I a close friend, but I am an attorney."

"Well," Shike gave it some thought, "if I get an okay from his mother, I guess it wouldn't cause any problems. But I'll check the regulations in the meantime. That is, with what I'm permitted to disclose." From his inside pocket, he retrieved a business card and handed it to her.

"Thanks." She stuffed it in her purse.

"It was nice meeting you, Miss …?"

"Danielle Madison," she answered readily.

With that, they headed toward the funeral gathering and separated at the crest of the hill.

Danielle found a chair in the last row. There she listened to a priest recite a prayer over the casket while a few muffled cries cut through whispered prayers. Her mind was crowded with thoughts of Owen, but she kept returning to his phone call. What did he want when she had last spoken to him?

"We do not know when we are called from this earth, but …" the priest said as he moved around the coffin making a sign of the cross.

She had replayed the phone call in her mind several times. But it made no sense. What was so urgent? Her familiarity with a computer was the same as most people; she relied on the nerds to answer the questions. She never thought of computers as bits of information or even how programs worked. Owen, on the other hand, took pleasure writing computer code, the foreign language of computers, hour after hour.

At the end of the ceremony, each mourner was given a rose to place on the casket. Danielle, the last in line, closed her eyes and recalled the better times they had shared together. With a hand on the casket, she kissed the rose and placed it across the top.

"I'm so glad you came," Owen's mother whispered.

Danielle wrapped her arms around his mother. They embraced tightly for what seemed a minute. "I'm so sorry … very sorry. I would have been here yesterday, but my flight was cancelled."

Owen's mother balled a tissue in her hand. "I can't bear the thought …" She couldn't finish the sentence and began to weep gently.

Danielle intertwined her arm in his mother's as they gingerly descended the hillside, thinking that a funeral was an experience you want to forget, but it's seared in your mind.

"I just knew something was wrong," Mrs. Roberts said, looking deeply into Danielle's eyes.

"Oh? What do you mean?"

"They called him—the phone rang continually. It was like an alarm you wake up to in the morning. But he would just sit there and ignore the ringing. And he wouldn't let me answer it." She broke off her sentence and gripped Danielle's arm tighter. "What did they want?"

Danielle shook her head. "Who called him?"

Mrs. Roberts stopped and stared fixedly at her. "Why, of course, those people he worked with," she said with a sense of confusion and bewilderment.

Danielle's condolences were all she could offer. Without even an inkling what Owen was doing these many months, she had no idea who might be calling him and for what purpose.

"You know, he loved you."

Again, Danielle couldn't reconcile Owen's absence with what she was hearing. For these last several days, the sleepless nights contributed to the anxiety building within her. She had to find out what drove Owen to commit suicide, *if he actually did.*

Danielle took a deep breath and asked, "I don't mean to pry, but was he seeing ..." thinking how to say it, she finished softly, "a psychiatrist?"

"No, but a detective, he's my neighbor, asked me that same question. But I told him there was nothing wrong with Owen. Then he asked whether he ever mentioned the name Dr. James Greyson. I told him no. Apparently, my son met him on that night and died shortly thereafter." She gave Danielle a look, as though searching for answers, but Danielle had none.

Then the frail, cried-out mother began to ramble again. "Sometimes they would come to my home. Strange, though, he'd sit in my lounge chair with the oddest stare. It was almost like he was asleep, a trance ... yes, a trance. And even if his cell phone rang, he wouldn't answer. But his eyes looked vacant, like he wasn't there."

Danielle remembered his dark brown eyes with the glint of happiness and the broad smile he always wore. "Who came to see him?" Her eyes caught the rays of sun.

"Ahem," interrupted the limo driver, who appeared agitated by their talking.

Owen's mother ignored the interruption. "His name … yes, his name. Now I remember; I would bake for the church festivals, and … his name was Baker. Leslie Baker. He would come in his wheelchair. I felt sorry for him. So he would sit on the back porch, and I would make him an ice tea. He never thanked me, but I was nice to him anyway."

She paused, tilted her head, and met Danielle's eyes. "I heard Mr. Baker and Owen arguing one evening. Something about a program. And Mr. Baker left in a huff. He drove one of those handicap vans where the platform lowers the wheelchair to the ground. Owen told me once Mr. Baker was in an auto accident." She shook her head. "He never came into the house."

"Did Owen ever mention where this man worked?" The warmth of the bright sunlight suddenly peeked over the edge of a cloud.

"Why, of course, he worked at that company in Virginia. PERC. Reminds me of those executives on Wall Street."

"Did you happen to ask Owen about the program Mr. Baker talked about?"

"Yes, I most certainly did. But Owen told me I was mistaken. Then he told me that I may need to move. He was going to move me, maybe to Florida. Get out of the bad weather. I told him that I've lived here all my life. I wasn't going to leave."

"Mrs. Roberts, the day Owen died, was he home with you or at work?"

"It was like most days," Owen's mother answered. "He went to work early in the morning. But then he returned after lunch. He went upstairs to his office and closed the door. I knew not to bother him when his door was closed. For the next maybe two hours, he didn't come out. Finally, he left carrying his computer and said he'd be back later."

"Did he say where he was going?" Danielle asked.

"No, but he was in a hurry. I answered a lot of these questions for my neighbor, the detective. You know, he's a nice man."

"Did he appear agitated?"

"His door was closed, so I don't know. Although, like I said before, he wasn't himself. Maybe Mr. Baker knows. Why are you asking all these questions?"

"I just wanted … the reasons," Danielle said.

"Will you be joining us for lunch?"

Danielle patted the back of Mrs. Roberts' hand. "I would love to, but my plane leaves tonight, and I would like to check out a few things. But I'll be in touch."

"In that case, you stop by anytime you want. Maybe even call me."

"I will," Danielle said, giving Owen's mother another hug.

Returning to her vehicle, Danielle could not help but notice a lone car parked next to her rental. That wasn't out of the ordinary except for the individual seated behind the steering wheel. He wore a pair of dark sunglasses and gave her a slight wave. With a sense her every movement was being watched, she didn't look at him when she unlocked her car. Once inside she locked the car doors and took a deep breath. Starting the car, she backed up and pulled out, and as she glanced in the rearview mirror, so did the car parked next to her.

# 7

Unconsciously running his thumb and index finger down the barrel, Cervasi flipped the pencil end over end while he listened to the weather forecaster's prediction on a large, plasma screen in his office. He shifted uneasily in the soft, leather-tufted sofa when the meteorologist with the Climate Prediction Center reported the long-range forecast for colder, wet weather due to a lingering El Nino. With the former congressman behind in the race, he knew the weather factor was out of his hands, and much to his dismay, a cold weather pattern only added to the problems. This was not what he wanted to hear, with Election Day weeks away. He drove the pencil point into the tablet and snapped the pencil into two pieces.

No matter what avenue he had explored, the answer was the same: the polls confirmed Clarke would lose. Perhaps Hart and Halstren, his two collaborators, were right when they suggested that he and the company distance themselves from Clarke. Inside he boiled over with the desire to win this senatorial election, but he knew the political sands were shifting measurably toward McClay. This would be his first failure, and he wasn't going to let it happen.

The door swung open to reveal a large, lumbering figure at its threshold. Cervasi looked up and waved Carl Matalino, the director of security, into the office. Carl, with a slight nod of respect, entered and closed the door behind him.

Matalino had black, slicked-back hair with a receding hairline, and his round, doughy face, coupled with his knitted eyebrows, had the expression of a hardened scowl. His thick, beefy hands had the appearance of giant claws. He was wearing a dark suit and a white shirt that appeared a size too small, making him resemble a king penguin. His necktie, which didn't quite reach his belt, wasn't cinched to his neck.

"Gina told me to walk in," Matalino said in a thick, Sicilian accent.

"That's fine … fine," Cervasi said impatiently with a wave of his hand. "She knew I was expecting you."

Matalino seated himself in an overstuffed side chair. He was old school, a throwback to yesteryear. His family had a strong lineage for enforcement, providing muscle for the union since the twenties. Even though he had toned down his act from breaking legs to strong-arm tactics, he retained the appropriate connections.

"I attended Owen's funeral." Matalino made the sign of the cross and then rested his intertwined fingers over his expanded waistline. "And I talked with and met people, as did Luchini and Marco."

"Tell me, what did you find?"

Matalino shook his head, arching his back. "We searched the house. File drawers and the desk were empty. Checked his bedroom, but all we found were his clothes. He was either tipped off or figured we'd be coming. No computer or storage devices."

Cervasi hung his head and then motioned with his hand. "There's a bottle of homemade red wine in the bar. A paisano dropped it off. Get two glasses and pour us a drink."

Matalino slowly edged out of his seat and made his way to the bar. He poured two drinks, strode over to Cervasi, and handed him a glass. Raising his glass, as did Cervasi, he toasted, "*Salud*" with a thin smile.

Cervasi sipped his wine and examined the dark red color. "Just like my grandfather made." When he was a kid, his grandfather would hand him an empty bottle and direct him to fill it from the wine barrel in the basement. He would take a sip even though his grandfather, who stood at the top of the stairs, made him whistle to and from the barrel.

"Carl," Cervasi said as he set his glass down on the coffee table and Matalino assumed his seat. "I want you to interview his friends and neighbors, check our company records, credit cards, phone records, and check with the post office. Someone saw something or knows where we're going to find it."

Matalino nodded, his round face bobbing. "I also offered my sympathy to Mrs. Roberts and told her Owen was a fine gentleman. If there was anything I could do, she should call me. Maybe I'll pay her a visit."

"Good. Let her know we're looking for his computer, printer, and anything else that might have been in his possession. Tell her it's customary to look through his belongings. But one thing—you tell your boys I don't want any mess-ups. Do you understand?"

"Yes, I do, Mr. Cervasi," Matalino said with a slight bow of his head.

"And those pictures of McClay. We're going to need someone to leak them to the newspaper. Line someone up. They're probably our only ace."

Matalino said with a satisfied smile, "I took care of the photographer. He won't need money." He grinned, reaching out for his wine glass. "He's with—"

Cervasi dropped back in his seat and raised the palm of his right hand. "You don't need to tell me. It's better that way. That's your job. You do what you have to, *capisce*?" He lifted his glass of wine and swallowed the remainder.

"It's handled, so you don't need to worry."

No sooner did Cervasi place the empty wine glass on the table than his secretary announced that Les Baker was asking to see him. Cervasi gave his approval and then gave an annoyed look to Matalino. As Baker entered, Cervasi, with the remote, returned to the latest political news and reduced the weather station to a picture-in-picture.

Baker's attention was drawn to the screen, where a news clip on Clarke was being replayed. "You probably caught the latest blunder he made. I give the guy credit. Apparently, he lives by that quote. I think it was 'In politics, never retreat, never retract, never admit a mistake,'" he said.

Cervasi frowned. "Napoleon." But he surmised Baker wasn't there to talk about Clarke or Napoleon.

"May we have a word alone," asked Baker as he looked at Matalino.

"Give us ten minutes. There're some things I want done."

Matalino, with an understating nod, rose and then lumbered out of the room.

Baker turned, directed his attention to the flat screen, and began. "McClay is in this race to win. Why, I'll bet he is out there drumming up votes right now. And where is our candidate? Probably chasing some broad. And our reports bear out your worst fears, Tony. His congressional record will not let him ride into office on what he's done in the past."

Cervasi knew about Clarke's congressional record after his staff had put together a complete dossier on him in preparation for the charitable gala where he first met the congressman. Cervasi knew Clarke's position on political issues, beliefs, and voting record; election results past and present; when he went to work, ate lunch, and called it a day. Cervasi had even slipped the charitable planner a grand to ensure he would be seated at the congressman's table. He had figured Clarke, with his connections in the Washington political circles, would become a valuable player in the company's political plan, but now, he wasn't so sure.

"The projections show a slight loss unlike the continued slide we experienced previously," Baker said, handing Cervasi the computer run developed hours earlier by their internal polls. "Yesterday, McClay appeared with his family, discussing the need for better educational standards. And with his two daughters campaigning across the state, he continues to make inroads. He's pretty much locked up Fairfax and Loudon. His centrist views make him viable."

"I know you're here to discuss matters unrelated to politics."

"That's right," Baker said. "I recognize your dilemma with Clarke." He nudged his wheelchair forward toward the television screen. It was a ploy to get Cervasi's undivided attention. "I've been thinking quite a bit about our arrangement. Despite my efforts to get you this far, I don't see where you've made any move to make me part owner."

Drilling into Baker's eyes, Cervasi rose from his seat. In a terse, bearish voice, he said, "You listen here. I run the show. You don't have any say in my company. I decide when and if I cut someone in."

Baker countered with equal venom. "Lest you forget, we had a deal. And I'm growing impatient."

"And it's on my terms," Cervasi fired back, pointing a finger at Baker. "There's no agreement. Now I've got other business."

Baker spun around in his wheelchair and headed to the door. Then he stopped abruptly and faced Cervasi. "Before this is over, you'll want my help. And that Italian Buddha, Carl, won't save you. Have you found the program?"

Cervasi glared at Baker. "What do you know about a program?"

"Your brother-in-law mentioned it in passing. That's all." Baker shrugged his shoulders, swiveled around in his chair, and exited the room.

Cervasi picked up his phone and called his receptionist. "Find Carl and get him here fast." He slammed the receiver down.

Matalino nodded again as he entered the room, coming face to face with Cervasi.

"We've got additional problems," Cervasi said, pacing the floor. "Baker. He knows more than what we think. Now he tells me my brother-in-law was talking to him about the program." He paused for a moment and continued, "Maybe it's a coincidence. And he hasn't heard about STAR." Cervasi's anger erupted inside and his lips tightened. Parks would never learn his lesson, no matter how many times he was told to keep his mouth shut. But the bigger question was how did Parks find out? "Get Davis up here. I want a few words with him."

Richie Davis, like Owen, was a computer engineer. Davis kept PERC, founded on information technology, at the cutting edge, and he was the director of the IT department. But it was Owen whose creativity brought the program to life. And it was Davis who failed to realize Owen's efforts to halt the program's progression that undermined Clarke's election bid. Had Davis alerted Cervasi, Clarke's election would be under control.

Cervasi continued, "Oh, as for Baker, we'll have to deal with him at a later date. I don't trust him." He grabbed the latest internal poll handed to him earlier. "Do you see this?" He waved the poll vigorously in the face of Matalino. "More of the same. It should be burned, and Clarke should be hung. He's called here the last several days wanting a meeting. You and I know what he's going to say. I don't give a damn about his ideas on liberals, conservatives, moderates, or the like that he's going to throw in my face. I want this Senate seat, maybe more than him."

Cervasi, with his hands thrust on his hips, said, "You know, Carl, it was easier in the past. No computers or programs that tell us instantaneously we're on the wrong track. We owned the press, the pollsters, and the voters."

Matalino stood with his arms dangling at his side. "I already sent Silvio back to Pittsburgh to interview people like you said. He reminded me that Owen's girlfriend was at the funeral, and she was talking to a detective and Owen's mother. Her name is Danielle Madison."

Cervasi gave Matalino a sideward glance. "Isn't she the one recommended by Denon?"

"Yes. I also called HR about her. She'll be starting work here in November. We can make her talk."

Cervasi stopped his pacing and fell into his desk chair. "You better find out what a detective was doing at Owen's funeral. I thought that was taken care of."

With his arms outstretched and palms up, Matalino said, "I did what you told me. I don't have any reason to believe it wasn't done."

"You better retrace your steps, and in the meantime, I'm going to find out more from Pierce about our new employee," Cervasi grunted. "All we need is a little break." That's what had occurred to him when Senator George Montgomery announced his resignation at the charitable gala attended by both he and Clarke three years ago—that the idea of running Clarke seemed logical, maybe, a lucky break. Now all he needed to do was make sure Clarke ended up in the Senate.

# 8

A security guard peered over his glasses, nodded in the direction, and with a discreet hand motion, singled him out. Danielle jumped to her feet and gestured with a slight wave of acknowledgment. She took a deep breath and chose the angle of approach, walking briskly in order to intersect his path.

He was wearing a navy sport coat, khaki pants, and a gray turtleneck sweater. In her mind, she had pictured an older man with wire rimmed glasses, cerebral and intense looking, with dark, shaggy eyebrows. But Dr. James Greyson didn't fit her stereotype. He had a bright, cheerful demeanor, waving to several individuals inside the lobby of the office building on Fourth Avenue. He had a tan complexion and medium build, but with his thinning gray hair combed to the side, covering up his receding hairline, he appeared younger than he was.

"Jim?" Danielle asked, extending her hand and guessing he was in his early to midfifties. "I thought that was you."

Greyson turned his head and eyed her head to toe. He had a puzzled facial expression.

Clasping his hand, she said, "Danielle Madison. I met you a few years ago at the Society's meeting. You were sworn in as president." He had a questioning look as though trying to place her. "You probably don't remember me. That was in," she tilted her head to the side, thinking, "in Philadelphia. I was with a colleague who invited me to attend."

59

She wasn't going to let the moment slip away. For an hour prior to her contacting Greyson's office, she had hopped on the Internet and uncovered his educational background, specialty, and officer positions held in the local and state associations, including the Pennsylvania Psychiatric Society.

"Your speech on clinical psychiatry in the twenty-first century was visionary," Danielle said, noticing the searching glint in his eyes had softened, but he appeared to carefully weigh her words in an attempt to jog his memory.

"Why, thank you. What brings you to Pittsburgh?" Greyson asked. He nervously folded his newspaper and clutched it underneath his arm.

"I flew in early this morning. A dear friend of mine," she paused, inwardly tangled with an emotional withdraw to Owen, "died. And your name came up in the conversation. His name was Owen Roberts."

Greyson's eyes widened and the stress lines on his brow became visible. His outgoing nature now appeared strained. Then he peered over her shoulder with a distant look in a search for words.

Danielle continued, "It came as a surprise when his mother mentioned your name. You know it's really a shame to lose a patient so soon after a session."

"Yes ... ah." His words were lost in silent thought.

"Of course, I didn't divulge I knew you. And the family," she said, shaking her head, "is understandably suffering. Why, I've known Owen for such a long time. I can't imagine." She exhaled with a deep breath for effect and released the tension inside her.

Glancing at his watch, he said, "Look, I'm actually running late for an appointment with a patient who'll spend the first ten minutes of our session giving me the riot act if I'm not on time. That's hardly therapeutic; you'll understand that I don't want to undo four weeks of hard work." He added, "I don't have time to chat right now."

"I understand, Jim. But I wondered if I might ask you a few short questions, again purely from a clinician standpoint. Can you tell me anything about your meeting with Owen?"

He looked upward as though to collect his thoughts. "You have my sympathy. That was my first visit with him." He stopped, and then continued almost apologetically, "I'm sorry about your friend's death. But I'm sure you're aware of our ethical code that prevents me from revealing anything."

"Why, of course. But I thought as professionals we understand each other," Danielle observed.

Greyson frowned and said politely, "I already gave a statement to the police. There's nothing more to say." Turning his head side to side as though someone may be watching them, he continued, "I really must get to my appointment." He moved to sidestep the conversation.

Danielle blocked his angle of escape. "He was a close, personal friend," she voiced firmly.

But Greyson was unyielding as he glanced at his watch. "Like I said, I've got a patient up there that has some major problems …"

"Yes, I do. But I'll make this quick," Danielle said earnestly. "Please excuse my being rude, but I really need to talk to you." She looked at him without resignation.

Greyson said with a growing scowl, "Sorry for your loss, but you'll have to excuse me."

"What time was Owen's appointment? Had you ever met him before? What did he say to you?" she rattled off those questions and several more.

"I can't remember. Wish I could help you, but my hands are tied." Greyson slid around Danielle and headed for the elevators.

She caught up with him and matched his hurried pace. "The time. What time was it?"

Greyson fidgeted with his newspaper. "I don't know, sometime around nine-thirty. And then he left. And that's what I'm about to do."

"Just a few more questions, that's all." Danielle wasn't going to let him get away or clam up. "So he wasn't in your office very long?"

"No," Greyson said tersely, pressing the up button frantically for an elevator.

"And you never reached a conclusion about whether he had any psychiatric problems?"

"Well, I … don't need to answer your questions. The matter is closed, and that's it."

"Here's my card," Danielle said, shoving a business card in his hand. "If you have anything that might even remotely have an impact on this case, please call me. And I won't reveal the source, promise."

Greyson lowered his eyes and examined the card between his thumb and index finger as he stepped into the elevator. "Should have known."

Danielle replied, "I'm trying to find the truth."

"That's a police matter, not yours. Good day, Miss Madison."

"You're right. I apologize if I seem a little gruff. But Owen's death has had a profound impact on me."

"Perhaps you need a session or two," Greyson said, raising his eyebrows. "It helps sometimes in cases like this."

She shoved her hand in the elevator door to prevent it from closing. "Dr. Greyson, one more thing," Danielle said, raising her index finger. "It was nice meeting you." She released the door.

He smiled thinly and shook his head as the elevator doors closed.

Somewhat dispirited by the encounter with Greyson, she wondered whether her actions were actually cynical. Then she pulled out her cell phone and called her office, reaching Karen's voice mail.

"Karen. This is Danielle. Could you do a search on a Pittsburgh psychiatrist? Dr. James Greyson. No rush. I'll be back sometime tomorrow. And oh, one more thing—there was a political consultant we used sometime back in the Ranier case. See if you can find his name and number."

When Danielle entered the police station at 5:30 p.m., a twenty-year-old receptionist seated behind a desk was talking into a phone headset. She stopped long enough to point at a chair against the wall.

Danielle seated herself and set her portfolio bag on a small coffee table. As she leafed through a magazine, she shifted in her seat, thinking about the flight to New York at 8:45 p.m., which left her little time to interview Shike and clear security at the airport. By midnight, if she held to her schedule, she would be pulling back the covers and collapsing into bed.

"What can I do for you?" asked the tawdry, gum-chewing blonde seated behind the counter.

Danielle replied, "I called earlier and scheduled an appointment with Detective Shike."

The blonde picked up a clipboard and said, "Fill out this visitor sheet, and I need your driver's license."

After Danielle produced her license, the receptionist gave it a quick glance and nodded. Then she checked the visitor's sheet, which Danielle had completed by inserting Shike's name and the purpose of the visit, and said, "I'll be back in a minute."

Moments later, a side door opened and Shike appeared. "Good evening. I didn't expect to hear from you, or, for that matter, see you again. What's up?"

"Can we talk?" Danielle asked. When she didn't see an appropriate place, she added, "In private?"

"Why, sure, follow me."

With that, Shike led her down a narrow hallway past a maze of cubical offices. Overhead she saw strands of wire dangling from the ceiling and a number of missing ceiling tiles. Scaffolding reached up to the exposed steel skeleton between floors.

Danielle said, "Wealth of construction, I see. Expanding?"

"Nah. We've been in this new building for less than a year, and someone gets the bright idea to make a few room alterations. Then they examine the original building blueprints, which, of course, didn't match up with what they found when they opened the wall. Now they're thinking we need some additional building supports. What's next?" He shrugged his shoulders. "Anyway, another month and we should be back to normal. I don't mind it, though. They added a coffee bar and vending machines not far from my office. Now that's a great improvement."

Danielle said, "It's lucky you can find workers these days; they're hard to come by."

As they turned the corner, file cabinets, a copier, and several desk chairs were stored in the hallway, making the passageway narrow.

"Watch your step," Shike said, pointing to an electrical cord taped to the floor and plugged into the wall for the copier. "They were supposed to move this furniture and equipment out of here last week, but now who knows. It's been sitting here for weeks. What a mess. They've got dust and dirt all over the place."

They entered a drab room with several chairs situated around a long conference table. The chairs had worn armrests and were covered in a layer of dust. It was undoubtedly used for interrogation.

"Wait before you sit down," Shike warned. "Let me get a rag. I wouldn't want to ruin your suit."

"Sorry about holding you back," Danielle said. "I'm catching a flight tonight, so I'll make this short."

"Don't worry about it. I've got a couple of kids in college, so I can use the overtime. You know, those construction workers never clean up like they're supposed to."

Danielle unzipped her portfolio bag and pulled out a notepad. "That suicide note."

"Hold that thought. I pulled the file after I spoke to Owen's mother about you. She filled me in about you and Owen and said it was okay to discuss the matter with you. But, frankly, we don't have much here to look at."

Shike retreated from the room to the hallway and returned with a five-inch thick file secured by an outer elastic band. He retrieved a blue bound folder and opened it to an index glued to the inside. Running his finger down the index, he tabbed past newspaper clippings and found a plastic baggie where a piece of paper resided inside.

He flipped through the blue folder as he spoke. "His body was found in the river the morning after he met his psychiatrist." His eyes left the folder. "His car was found in the parking lot nearby, and inside we found a suicide note. I can't give you the details, but the note was short and to the point."

"Was it signed?"

"No, but it really doesn't matter. The car was locked, and we found the keys on the body. And—" Danielle watched as he read another entry in the folder. "Yes, he had less than a hundred bucks in his wallet, so robbery was not a motive." Then he flipped through the file to another piece of evidence. "Owen's mother said he was troubled for the last several weeks. And his employer—" Shike stopped without revealing any additional information. "No marks out of the ordinary that would indicate he was in some altercation or even a head injury." Flipping through the file, he continued, "Then we have the statements from the doc—the note and his behavior were corroborated." He peered over the file. "No eyewitnesses saw the incident." Shike closed the blue folder.

Danielle nodded. "But his mother didn't paint the same picture. She said he was agitated but not delusional."

Shike picked up a pen and began to turn it in his fingers. "Sometimes we don't know our own kids. We tend to see them through rose-colored glasses. Framed. Brainwashed. Drugged. Pick up any newspaper, and you'll find the excuses. Parents can't accept that their children are involved. The usual. I don't want to sound cold, but unfortunately, those are facts."

"Granted, I think that deep down most parents of problem children are in denial. But I knew Owen. That's the difference."

Danielle listened but refused to accept the reasoning. Owen drank socially but never got drunk. He once lived in a modest apartment in Reston. Together they took brief vacation trips to the beach. He had a new car and made monthly payments. There was nothing out of the ordinary that she recollected. And he couldn't have changed so drastically in such a short period of time. Then there was the warning in a text message to her.

"Are you saying he wasn't in need of any help?"

"I'm positive," Danielle said with conviction.

"Well, there you have it. The facts don't support you here." Shike shook his head. "I admit, though, the bridge is well traveled. You'd think someone would have seen him." He retrieved a beige folder and began to read to himself. "The coroner's report, well," he paused, "he did have a few minor contusions, but that could be explained as consistent with the fall. With passing barges, bridge abutments, and other sorts of obstructions, ah, you'd be hard-pressed to say otherwise." His eyes left whatever he was reading. "There's more, but the evidence appears rather solid."

"But that doesn't rule out if he was pushed or maybe even unconscious."

Shike closed the folder and intertwined his fingers. "So where does that leave us?"

"Well, I wanted to bring to your attention a few tidbits of—" Danielle was about to reveal her real reasons behind the visit, including the text message and the message on her answering machine.

There was a rap on the door. An older man with thinning, gray hair poked his head into the room. "Excuse me, I didn't know you had someone with you."

"It's okay," Shike responded.

"I need you for a second," replied the man, holding open the door.

Shike rose from his chair and stepped outside. He returned within a minute and said in a harried tone, "We've got a double homicide on the North Side. Looks like I'm going to be needed there. Let me see." He took a deep breath and shook his head. "Give me a few minutes, I'll see what I can do. I'm not adverse to overtime, but I didn't want to be here all night." He heaved the file under his arm. "I'll be right back." With that, Shike left the room.

Danielle got up, walked quietly to the door, and opened it. Before Shike rounded the bend, he dropped the file on top of the file cabinet. There were ringing phones and what sounded like interrogations in the distance. She figured the cabinet was maybe twenty feet away, and she became mesmerized by its close proximity.

Thoughts raced through her mind: the ethics of her profession, the words *agitated* and *irritated* from Owen's mother, the phone call from Owen, and, finally, why he was driven to this action. An elevated sense of urgency surged within her. She had to know what was in that file. Her heartbeat turned up a notch as her hand touched the file. She blinked as though in a hypnotic trance.

In the next minute, with a trembling hand, she reached for the blue folder and pulled out its contents. Then she went right for the notes and documents. Finding the half typed and half longhand investigative notes from Carl Matalino and Drs. James Greyson and Henry Milsen, she quickly realized that they were too lengthy to read. Her mouth grew dry, and she squinted under the lights.

Looking to her immediate left, she eyed the copier. Her airways constricted, and a vein in her throat throbbed as she removed a fastener to release a small handful of papers tabbed Greyson and Matalino. She loaded ten sheets in the automatic feed and, with the palm of her hand, punched copy. The copier sucked the sheets from the feeder, and Danielle, with deep breaths and beads of perspiration melting her makeup, peeled the originals from the bin and fastened them back in the folder.

She loaded the three sheets behind a tab labeled Milsen, and the copier pulled another sheet as she heard male and female voices quickly approaching. The machine was flashing the message: empty paper tray.

Fish-eyed and elastic legs giving way, she stuffed the uncopied notes in the blue folder, not fastening them. Next she shoved the blue folder in the larger file, grabbed the copies from the copy bin, and darted the short distance to the interrogation room.

Her eyes wide with fear and her heart pumping adrenaline through her veins, Danielle stuffed the copies in her portfolio bag and zipped it up. Shike threw open the door and entered with the receptionist directly behind him.

"Problems?" Shike asked. "You look flushed. Need a glass of water?"

"No. I'm fine," Danielle coughed. "The dust in the air. But I really need to go anyway. I've got to be at the airport in half hour." Her heart thundered inside, and she could feel the heavy throbbing in her eardrums. She didn't want to discuss Owen's messages; all she wanted was to leave the building.

"Where did we leave off?" Shike said absently. "Yes, you were about to tell me something."

Danielle closed her eyes and shook her head, unable to form her words.

Shike slapped the table and said, "You'll have to talk to the DA about anything else you might need. Any questions?"

Danielle bit her lower lip. "No, no, that's it," she said, swallowing hard. She told herself to take long, deep breathes. Control. Get control.

"My receptionist will show you out, if you don't mind. I've got to make several calls before I hightail it over to the murder scene. So much for going home."

Danielle nodded, stood, and walked under the watchful eyes of Shike. She passed the copier with its flashing light to load paper when she realized that one page of notes was left in the copy machine. This can't be happening to me.

Suddenly she felt a hand land on her shoulder. Now she would have to explain her actions. What would they do to her? As a professional it was unethical. Handcuff her? And what would she say? She had merely copied a few papers from a dead man's file.

Danielle turned slowly to face Shike.

"You must really be out of it. You left your bag on the floor," Shike said, holding it up to eye level.

"Thanks."

"Have a nice flight back to New York."

Danielle clutched the bag underneath her arm and walked out of the building. The fresh air only exacerbated the wrenched feeling in her stomach. She had never felt this sick since she was in college. She closed her eyes and took long, deep breaths until her heart finally settled into a normal pace.

In the distance, she heard the chime of church bells peeling out the time. Inside her rental car, with a white-knuckled grip on the steering wheel, she looked fixedly at the bag in the passenger seat, dropping her head and wondering what possessed her to take such a risk.

# 9

Seated at a table at Eleven Madison Avenue, Danielle sipped a chai tea latté and watched a red-headed pregnant mother with a blond, blue-eyed little boy, bobbing his head, enjoying a pretzel stick. A thin smile crossed her face, thinking about how she and Owen had discussed children. He had talked endlessly about having a boy, Luke, and a girl, Kim. They would live on a treed, one acre lot in a two-story house where they could play badminton like he did when he was a kid.

When they first parted, she recalled her loneliness when she saw another couple hand in hand. Strollers pushed by mothers only added to her gut-wrenching feeling of despair. Her giddy feeling about a future wedding and children were wiped away in a matter of months.

Weeks passed without a phone call or e-mail from him, which made her wonder whether their relationship was all a forgettable dream. Then the cards with sentiments of love appeared, but he never answered her phone calls or e-mails. The answer, if there was one, remained an enigma.

She closed her eyes, sinking further into reflective thought until the thread of yesterday was severed by the sound of her name.

"Danielle," said a soft voice close at hand.

She opened her eyes and found Ann Burk standing next to her. Ann was tall, and her heart-shaped face with sparkling green eyes was framed by shoulder length, wheat-colored hair. Wearing a brown plaid wool jacket and dark tan pants, Ann exuded the confidence of an up and coming woman executive on Wall Street. The waiter pulled out a chair, and she sat down.

"When I received your call, I canceled my afternoon appointments," Ann said with a dismissive gesture to the waiter, who appeared about to ask her a question. "Are you okay?"

Danielle nodded slightly. "My mind was wandering. I'm so glad you could make it. I needed to talk to someone." She set down the latté and, with her elbows on the table, interlaced her fingers.

When they were classmates, she and Ann would share their innermost secrets. They had their own mental checklists on the guys they dated and dreams they shared. It seemed like just yesterday when Ann roomed across the hallway at the University of Maryland.

Ann reached across the table and laid her hand on Danielle's arm. "I'm so sorry seems like hollow words. But what can I say? We've been friends for such a long time. I truly share in your grief. It's never easy, but I'm always here for you."

"I knew I could count on you." Danielle paused catching hold of her emotions. "I realized coming home last night that I need to make changes. These many months working and losing myself in legal cases—and now this." She picked up a glass of water, took a sip, and glanced out the window before returning her gaze to Ann.

"We've been through a lot together. You've lost both parents, and I've lost one over the years. Deep down inside, I know what you're feeling." Ann pulled her hand away, crossing her arms on the table. Leaning forward, she said, "You need to take a vacation. Maybe a sunny place this time of the year. Cancun? I'll even join you. I won't be missed at work. It'll be like old times."

Danielle managed to break a smile, thinking about spring break during their sophomore year in Cancun. They were sunning their backs late in the day when a wave washed up over them. Jumping up, their unlaced bikini tops fell to the ground and were snatched by the retreating wave. They grabbed their sunglasses and camera and wrapped themselves in waterlogged beach blankets. Later that night, they bought new tops from a sidewalk vendor.

"I really wish I could. But you're busy with the wedding, and I'm moving to Washington …" Danielle raised her head and faced Ann. "It's tempting, but I'll take a rain check for Cancun. As your maid of honor, we've got plenty to do between now and the wedding date."

"Rain check it is. And as for the wedding, before Greg left town, we visited the cathedral and met with the photographer one last time. Tonight we're having dinner at the county club. So, you are our guest, and I won't accept no."

Danielle drew a deep breath and nodded her acceptance. "I'll give you that ... but we should order lunch. That waiter has walked past us several times."

After they each ordered a chef salad and a glass of wine, Ann observed, "Greg told me that he loved LA, although he was there for business and not pleasure. And he thinks you're making the right move by joining a corporation. At times even Greg thinks the ungodly hours he works are not worth it."

"But I can tell he's going to make partner." Danielle remembered Greg's uncle once practiced at HBR and later became the managing partner. Greg's motivation for staying with the firm was different than hers.

Ann settled back in her chair and moved the fork and spoon from the left to the right side of the plate. "You may be right. A woman needs to step back and ask whether making partner is the most important thing. The price is high, and the benefits are equally as great, but you've got to balance a life with your family. Not to change the subject, but I hear that the company you're going to work for has a normal working day policy with flexible hours and working from home."

"Yeah. They'll miss me at the firm, I guess. But whoever they hire to take my place will need to deal with Denon's egotistical characteristics and tendencies. He'll be demanding briefs and petitions with deadlines on a daily basis. Maybe he or she won't have to carry Denon's briefcase like I did when I started." Danielle would never forget the uptown trips to client offices with her lugging files and briefcases on a cart in tow. And Denon had offered no help or even opened a door. That's what she was, a damn servant.

"I know Greg grumbles now and again about the deadlines, the commas, quotation marks, and his overall anal tendencies," Ann confessed, surveying the room as though someone was eavesdropping on their conversation. She caught the eye of the waiter approaching.

After he poured the glasses of wine, Danielle picked up her glass and made a toast to their health, happiness, and a spectacular wedding. They clinked glasses and drank a sip.

"I don't want it to sound like I'm talking shop, but Greg confided in me that the senatorial election in Washington has Denon in a tirade. I guess the political pundits think PERC erred in choosing a former congressman as a senatorial candidate."

Danielle had suspected from the research Denon ordered that Congressman Philip Clarke must have been a thorn in the side of the company. "I'm with you. I think he must be causing a lot of problems … from what I hear from Karen."

"Luckily it won't concern you. You're starting after the elections, aren't you?"

"I haven't moved up my start date, and if they ask me, and that includes Denon, I'll refuse."

"That's my girl. And anyway, so what if they lose a single election? Greg told me the company is growing exponentially. Why, in California they're the consultants in demand."

Danielle said in a resigned tone, "I hope they settle their problems before I start full time." Karen's warning resonated within her. Danielle knew that she hadn't thoroughly investigated PERC. Was it an oversight? Perhaps. She tried to review the thought processes that led her to the decision, but she was coming up empty. Denon had kept her busy to the point where she had no time. Now Owen's funeral was another setback.

Ann looked at Danielle quizzically. "There's something else. Isn't there?"

Danielle nodded and said in half-disbelief, not knowing where to start. "While I was in Pittsburgh, I stopped and met with a psychiatrist." Ann looked concerned and leaned across the table. Danielle blurted out, "Not for me."

Ann dropped back in her chair, relieved by the revelation. "Am I missing something?"

"Owen's obit that I shared with you the other day reported nothing about the cause of his death."

"*Danielle.*"

"Just give me a second," she said as she dabbed her eyes and then looked away. She sipped her wine before she continued, "His mother gave me the name of a psychiatrist. I never gave it too much thought, maybe it was foolish or reactionary, but I decided to meet him." She locked eyes with Ann, looking for approval.

"And?"

Danielle shrugged her shoulders and brushed her hair behind her ear. "He was less than helpful, although he's bound by ethical considerations. He can't give me any information about his patient."

"Figures. Yet you could sit in a waiting room of a doctor's office and hear all you wanted about some patient. They act as if we're all deaf."

"I had to know; maybe it was a whim." Danielle caught Ann's blank stare as though she was psychoanalyzing. "I didn't stop there. I met the detective who investigated Owen's death."

Ann arched her eyebrows.

"Before you say it, I'm confused," Danielle voiced. She took a deep breath, and with a mixture of betrayal and shock, said deadpan, "Owen was a drug addict."

Ann jerked her head backward. "Even I know that can't be true. Who told you that?"

"There's more."

"You've got my full attention."

"The personnel department at PERC provided a written statement to the police that he was on drugs for some time. And he was seeing a psychiatrist."

"I don't believe it," said Ann. "I think I'm going to change my order to a stiff drink." She shook her head in utter disbelief. "Drugs? The police? That's impossible."

"That was my knee-jerk reaction. As much as I want to think otherwise, and I do, they found drugs in his car."

Ann sat in silence, pensive and indignant.

"Ann, I suffered the initial shock. Then I considered the possibilities, and I said to myself, *No, it can't be. There's no possible way.* It raised these red flags inside me."

"And in me also. How did you find this out?"

Danielle responded, "You don't want to know." She had the police investigative reports. PERC reported that Owen was reprimanded for drug activities and was being counseled over an extended period of time. His psychiatrist was a Dr. Henry Milsen from Virginia. Dr.

James Greyson, who was the last person to speak to him, filed a report seeming to confirm the analysis. And additionally, the report mentioned he heard voices in what appeared to be in a delusional state of high anxiety.

"This is surreal. What are the police doing about it?"

"Nothing," Danielle said. "They found a suicide note in his car," she closed her eyes tightly, "and he said he loved his family. And he was sorry for them and his friends." Such a generic note struck a wrong chord within her.

Ann sat stunned, with her shoulders drooping and a vacant look on her face.

"I haven't told anyone," Danielle said hesitantly, "but I spoke to him the night of his death. It was only briefly, and he wasn't making a whole lot of sense."

"Would either of you care for another glass of wine?" the waiter interrupted as he set the salads in front of them.

Ann looked up and said, "I'll have a double martini. And she'll have one also."

Danielle was about to say no, but she followed Ann's lead. Neither of them reached for a fork. She then related in detail the conversation she had with Owen.

"Maybe he was murdered?" Danielle blurted, wondering what Ann might think.

Ann's eyes glazed over.

Danielle said, "I know it's far-fetched, maybe harebrained, but I can't buy the suicide."

"For what? Why? I think we'd better talk to Greg."

"I thought about it, but I'm just plain puzzled by it all." Danielle realized that Ann might be skeptical. But she at least wanted to put it on the table and get someone's reaction.

"Danielle," Ann said in an understanding voice, "this searching for suicide or murder—call it what you want—won't bring him back."

Danielle nodded. "I just can't … as soon as I'm settled in Washington, I'm not sure what I should do."

Ann broke in before Danielle finished. "By the way, Greg met a consultant who was formerly with PERC. The guy started his own political consulting company in LA. He's here in town for a few days. Staying at the Four Seasons, I think. I can have Greg talk to him if you're in the market for a new job. That is, if you decide to move to California."

Danielle perked up. "What's his name?"

"Leonard Wheeling. Know him?"

"Nope."

"From what I understand, he's making inroads on the political scene. He's in competition with PERC."

"I might want to talk to him." Danielle wondered whether Wheeling could shed some light on PERC. It was a tantalizing proposition.

"Good. You can discuss it with Greg tonight. And he'll pick up the tab. After all, he's going to miss your going away party."

Danielle gave the idea more thought. She could also discuss her murder theory with Greg.

The waiter arrived with the double martinis and brought a forced smile to Danielle. Drug addiction? She wouldn't believe it today, tomorrow, or yesterday. And Owen's mother would call the personnel file a total fabrication.

# 10

*McLean, Virginia*
*Friday, September 14*
*9:00 p.m.*

William Parks emerged from his Mercedes uneasy about the upcoming meeting. Instinctively, he handed the keys to the valet at the Ritz-Carlton in McLean and deposited the claim check in his wallet. He massaged his forehead with the tips of his fingers both to relieve the tension and to partially shield his face. With no one near the hotel entrance, he strode inside quickly, not wanting anyone to catch a glimpse of him.

Having attended legal conferences and entertained politicians at the hotel, Parks knew the lobby and the layout of the ground floor quite well. As he stepped inside, he skated across the granite floor, cradling his head between his thumb and forefinger. Glances to either side gave him only a limited perspective of the lobby. His objective was to reach an elevator before a lingering member of the news media caught him in his crosshairs. If that were to occur, he had no idea where to hide.

He could hear the news reporters asking questions of his brother-in-law. What was William Parks doing at the Ritz-Carlton the other night? Doesn't McClay stay at the same hotel? Does your attorney support McClay? And so forth. There would be plenty of stinging questions, and the answers would be opaque and evasive.

Parks gave a fleeting thought to climbing the fifteen floors up the stairwell, but he questioned whether he could make it. With each step, not hearing someone call his name or express a passing interest in him, he reached his objective, relieved. He hung his head low and pressed the elevator call button.

He paced expectantly, and he did not wait long. Once the elevator car arrived he dashed in, selected the floor, and pushed the close door button several times as though it would shut sooner if he kept up the repetition. As the doors began to close, a hand reached in and then pulled back, all within in what seemed like less than a second. Parks nervously continued to press the floor button. Finally, the car shot upward without an intervening stop. His head throbbed, and he could feel a mist of sweat on his forehead.

It was too late to turn around. Satisfied with his course of action, he trudged down the corridor, leaving a heavy foot imprint in the thickly piled carpet. Before he rounded the corner, he closed his eyes and pictured an auction where the highest bid was five million dollars. Enough, yes, if he watched how he spent it. But friendship was the overriding consideration.

Inwardly, he knew that he had made the correct decision, and without any further rumination, he rounded the corner and came face-to-face with a security guard, who supported his upright body against a wall. The guard, almost a foot taller than Parks, blocked his advance with threatening eyes. Now joined by an equally towering backup, Parks produced an ID, and after a call to someone within the campaign suite, he was cleared. The second guard escorted him inside the suite and directed him toward the main room.

The narrow foyer of the suite opened up into an expansive room previously used as a combined living and dining area but was now converted into a tactical support room. A long conference table, a group of wall-mounted plasma monitors, and a whiteboard were on one side. The opposite side had several desks with desktop computers resting against the wall. A sofa and lounge chairs finished the room.

A cabal of seven studied an electronic map of Virginia pinned with colored markers for polls, conferences, and rallies for the upcoming week as projected on a plasma monitor. At the forefront was Thomas McClay, the former UVA professor, engaged in a lengthy discourse with his political advisors about moving and then positioning volunteers within Loudon County for the upcoming election.

McClay, tall and slender with wavy, black hair and a wide, toothy smile, was a dynamic speaker who had the ability to draw a partisan crowd to his way of thinking. He could associate names and faces months after he initially met them. And even though his campaign manager told him to lose it, he refused to remove the small gold earring, shaped from a part of his deceased father's wedding band, in his left ear. Parks remembered him saying the earring was a part of his life, and he could hear his father speaking.

McClay imprinted his campaign with the idea that he would engage voters to find answers similar to a professor who challenges his students. He theorized government cannot solve all problems; rather, his constituents must work with those elected to direct resources toward the common good. His platform was built around asking questions and seeking ideas from ordinary people, unlike Clarke, who wined and dined representatives of big business.

"What do you think?" Dan Goodwin asked, putting his hand on Parks shoulder.

"Looks like the place is still humming," Parks said nervously.

When McClay ran for the state legislature, Goodwin, a longtime friend and Princeton classmate, collaborated with him to write his speeches. Now that McClay stepped into a senatorial race, he tapped Goodwin again for his expertise in writing.

"We're actually running late. We should have been out of here a few hours ago, but we're tying up a few loose ends for tomorrow."

"With the campaign ramping up, I'm sure it's been trying," Parks said in a vacant voice, wondering whether he should fade into the background and slip out the door. McClay had assured him the place was secure, but he was growing increasingly uneasy.

"Speech writing, reviewing updated demographic studies, voter trends, the usual. Campaign fever has become infectious, and it goes without saying that the demands are higher."

After breaking off from the group standing near the candidate, a young man with brown, spiked hair made his way toward the conference table. He took a lightning glance at Parks as he snatched a tablet off the table.

Parks looked away instinctively after he met the staffer's gaze. For a minute, he recalled seeing the man previously, but had no recollection where.

Goodwin pointed out the advances the campaign had made over the last few weeks. "These modern communications systems allow us to receive instantaneous feedback from the field. Yes, speeches from our supporters and, need I say, from our opponents. We can analyze and readily counter what Clarke says in his speeches. Our feed comes from our campaign headquarters in Richmond."

Parks only nodded, half-listening to what Goodwin said, racking his brain about the young man who had now rejoined the group. "That guy in the gray turtleneck standing next to Tom. Do you know who he is?"

"Not exactly. He joined our team several weeks ago. We were looking for an advisor to assist in the southwest region." Goodwin ran his fingers through his hair and massaged his neck. "It's been a long day. Bradley. Russ Bradley. That's the guy's name. Somebody you know?"

"No, I thought it was someone I may have met, but I don't recognize the name. If Tom's busy, maybe we can meet up on another day."

"Nonsense. He told me you were going to stop by. They shouldn't be too much longer. Let's join them. Maybe we can learn something."

"That's okay," Parks motioned with a dismissive hand gesture. "I'd rather not, what with me working for ... PERC."

Goodwin frowned as though he remembered. "You're right. Follow me."

They retreated in the direction of the suite's entrance and continued down a corridor past a small conference room, where a striking blonde with soft facial features was seated at a table. She looked up, gave a furtive smile, and raised her hand in acknowledgment.

"Who's she?" Parks asked as Goodwin led him deeper into the suite.

"Press secretary. Jill Hillard. She and I were finalizing a few press releases before I received an urgent call from security."

Goodwin opened a door revealing a small anteroom. It was connected to the master bedroom suite. A Chippendale sofa, a pair of Queen Anne chairs, and a coffee table were situated on one side and an entertainment system in a large, cherry cabinet on the other side. A mini wet bar, an executive writing table, and a computer with a flat-panel monitor completed the room.

"Make yourself at home. I'll let Tom know you're here," Goodwin said, closing the door.

Parks found a remote and flipped on a news channel. With his hands in his pants pockets, he paced the room, watching the evening news. When it came to the political news, the anchorman pointed out another straw poll showing Clarke behind McClay.

Within minutes McClay walked through the door and gripped Parks's hand, shaking it. "Sorry about the holdup. There's no time to think. It's run, run, run." He caught his breath and dropped onto the sofa. "There's a bar over there—why don't you have a drink?"

Parks shook his head. "Thanks, I think I'll pass. It's late, and I should be heading home. Another time."

"Okay. After the election, we'll sit down and have one together," McClay said, whose attention was drawn to the news. "I was in Blacksburg this afternoon," he said, pointing to the television, "talking to college students. You know, it's been a number of years since I taught at a university, and it's really great to meet up with inquisitive young people. That's one thing about campaigning—you meet a lot of good people."

"I'm sure you're right." Although Parks, like McClay, knew a number of people they would like to forget.

"Now what's this about?"

"You know, I shouldn't be seen here." Parks exhaled with tension. "I'm already on the outs with Tony. If he knew, well—" Parks recalled Tony's scowl and the dire warning.

McClay shook his head. "I can understand. But you've been a good friend over the years. Once I'm elected, we'll find a position for you on our team. That's if you're so inclined."

"I may need one." Parks looked for a way to break into why he was there without tarnishing his image of Tom. "How's Jen?"

McClay's wife, Jenny, was petite and slightly younger than McClay. Attractive, well-spoken, and good humored. Her pleasant countenance and reserved style made her a vote-getter for him.

"She's fine. She's in Charlottesville tonight doing several TV interviews. And my daughters, Lyn and Michele, I left in Blacksburg. They're working the college and young voters' scene," he said, "and it's paying off."

"You're doing a great job. Another few weeks, it will be all over," Parks responded as he shifted his weight and surveyed the room.

McClay grabbed the remote and shut off the TV.

"Tom, I wouldn't be here if there wasn't some urgency to your election bid." Parks clutched the top of the Queen Anne chair with both hands and squeezed the leather.

"I know," McClay said, leaning back into the sofa. "Tony's had a change of heart." He lightened up. "I'll bet Tony is questioning why he decided to throw his weight behind my opponent. I could never figure why he made that decision. Hell, both he and I could be cleaning up," McClay mused. Then he added in a derisive tone, "He's probably thinking of how he could undermine my campaign, but he underestimated my supporters."

Parks recognized McClay had correctly diagnosed Tony's mistake, but McClay had underestimated Tony's relentless desire to win this election. And in this case Tony had a fervent goal to win the senatorial seat, which meant Tony would do anything.

"Tom, despite what I say, remember, I came here as your friend." He and McClay met each other at a Virginia Conservation District banquet, where they shared thoughts about the future of conservation and politics. McClay had announced his intent to run for state office only days before. Parks financially supported McClay in his successful bid for state legislator.

"Okay, fire away."

Parks winced. "Tony's got these photos, and—"

"What do you mean?" McClay cocked his head, pinching his eyebrows.

Parks hesitated. "I haven't seen them, but they have you with—" Stopping in midsentence, he cleared his throat. Baker had never produced the photos, and even if Parks took possession of them, he didn't want to actually examine them. What McClay did behind closed doors was his business.

"What?" McClay frowned. The color drained from his face, and he wrung his hands.

"I had a conversation with Tony's assistant the other day, and he started to blab about compromising photos." He shifted in his stance, and his mouth felt bone dry. "Anyway, he related how these photos are worth money. Loads." The revelation seemed to sink into McClay as he interlaced his fingers and began tapping his foot.

McClay lowered his head in pensive thought. "What's he want me to do, rollover? Play dead?"

"No."

Standing abruptly and heading for the wet bar, McClay said, "Did Tony send you? You tell him I won't play ball. Got it?"

"It's nothing like that," Parks said solemnly, arching his eyebrows and tightening his lips.

McClay poured himself a scotch on the rocks and stood upright, leaning against the mini bar. "Yeah, maybe I do have this all wrong. Months ago, you came here flying off the handle about some oddball program—yes, that's it. You were all concerned. We ended up investing time and money into some harebrained idea. We were paranoid. We didn't know what it did, if it worked, or what it was." McClay took a short drink. "So now you're back again about another idea. Don't you think Tony's misleading you in an attempt to rile me? Get me off the campaign trail?"

Parks wondered how McClay might receive the information. "But the photos do exist."

"You said you haven't seen them," McClay retorted.

"No, not exactly."

"You see what I mean," McClay said, taking another swallow. "Tony will resort to anything. We're in the homestretch of this campaign, and he has to pull out all the stops. He's a one man wrecking crew. And I'm not buying it."

Parks reconsidered having a drink but pressed on. "What happens if the photos do exist?"

McClay said with rich sarcasm, "I think Tony doesn't know what to do. Wait and see. Tony's good at what he does, but I think we'll see more of these wild goose chases."

Parks could feel his heartbeat pounding in his head. He hadn't seen or heard anything more about a computer program for months. And yes, he didn't actually know that it did exist. The IT department occasionally dropped a word or two about an experiment until the leaks were plugged. As for the pictures, Baker had broken the news, and he had a reputation for being nosy. But Parks doubted whether Baker was the type who surrendered misinformation lightly.

"But—"

"Forget it, Bill. Tony's pulling your chain. There aren't any photos." McClay swallowed the remainder of his drink and set the empty glass down on the counter. "Now, I've got to get back to business."

A knock at the door interrupted their conversation.

"Sorry to interrupt," Jill said, "but everyone has left. Will you need me any longer?"

Parks noticed the glint in her greenish-blue eyes as she stared intently at McClay with her pouty lips and slightly raised eyebrows.

McClay fleetingly eyed Parks before he locked eyes with her. "We're almost finished. If you could wait a few more minutes, I'd like to go over what you and Dan decided."

"Okay," Jill said softly, giving Parks a wry smile.

The door closed, leaving Parks to examine the sheepish expression on McClay's face.

"I've really learned to count on her. Hard-working. Knowledgeable," McClay said, as though he was defending her. "She's dedicated."

Parks now recognized another problem. One he couldn't solve. It also didn't seem to coincide with the pictures that Baker said existed. He continued to stare at McClay in silence.

"Is there anything else?" McClay asked.

"No. Nothing. I think I better leave now." Parks opened the door, with McClay following behind him. As they passed the small conference room, Parks looked in, but Jill was not there.

At the door, McClay turned and said, "If you find those so-called pictures, call me."

"Yeah, sure. I'll stay in touch."

# 11

Unlike the usual business attire she was accustomed to wearing at the law firm, Danielle was dressed in a charcoal button-down jacket over a gray T-shirt imprinted with Georgetown Law in blue and a pair of black jeans. But this time, neither Denon Pierce nor any other partner had any grounds to make a fuss about what she wore. She was officially a former employee.

Wanting to end the relationship on a positive note, she agreed to wind down a number of cases in progress, including several last-minute, strident demands made by Denon. Her problem was that she couldn't recall when her head hit the pillow last night. And then she'd regretfully remembered her acceptance of an invitation to meet him in Washington on Monday to discuss her research on the Clarke agreement.

Danielle looked up from her desk when Karen, with straggly hair, stumbled into the office and oozed herself in a high-back chair. Karen's eyes were half shuttered behind the oversized glasses sitting on the bridge of her nose. She excused herself when she yawned, but it was understandable after the party last evening.

"We're doing something wrong," Danielle said. She tapped on a few keys to boot up her computer. "After a night of partying, neither of us look ready for another legal marathon." A mixture of resignation and disbelief filtered through her voice. Logging into the network, she pulled up her e-mail.

"I don't know about you, but I didn't get to sleep until four o'clock. That's late for this body. When I was younger, I could do it. Now I feel it sooner and longer the next day. And this is the next day."

Danielle shifted her gaze from the monitor to Karen. "You're only as old as you feel. That's what they say."

Karen settled back in the armchair, slowly opening her eyes. "And this body has answered," she yawned. "As soon as we get that damn legal memo put together, I'm headed home. That's if I haven't already collapsed on the sofa in the lounge. Tomorrow's another day."

Somewhat sluggishly, Danielle cracked a grin. "You really pulled it off last night, luring me into Carmine's. That's one place I couldn't refuse, and then to find my friends and colleagues. I was truly moved," she said in earnest. Her attention was averted by an e-mail from Ann Burk.

Leonard Wheeling leaving for LA tomorrow. Don't have his cell. Remember, dinner's on Greg tonight.

Dismayed by the thought that Wheeling would be off to California before she could ask him a few questions, she needed another plan. She didn't want Wheeling, who had previously worked for PERC, leaving the city before she could ask a few questions.

With a slight smile, Danielle tapped her fingers on the desk, thinking about Higgins, the patriarch of the law firm, who had always had legal gems of wisdom for the young associates. Roadblocks, he'd say, are mere challenges; a lawyer could meet them head-on or find another way. She was always up for a challenge.

"At least you won't be writing any legal memos," Karen said as she rose from her chair and lumbered over to the window ledge. "By this time next week, you'll be sleeping in. I don't know the last time I did that."

Half listening, Danielle swiveled in her chair and asked inquisitively, "Do we have any contacts at the Four Seasons?"

"Ah, let me think about it," Karen said with a pensive look but droopy eyes. Then, with arched eyebrows, she said unenthusiastically, "You know, I have the perfect candidate."

In New York, it pays to know people, and Karen was quite knowledgeable, having worked under Biggs, a former assistant attorney general, and Reed, a former member of the House of Representatives, both founding partners of HBR. Danielle knew Karen had connections with executives of major corporations, governmental heads, and professionals throughout the state. Her database was better than any phone book with home and cell numbers.

"There's a guy in town who formerly worked for PERC," Danielle said, pausing for a moment. "Leonard Wheeling. He's a political consultant. Staying at the Four Seasons. Only problem, he's leaving town tomorrow."

"Never heard of him, but that's not a problem," Karen said with bravado. "Leave it to me. What do you want to know?"

"How about his room number?"

"That's it?" Karen said, shaking her head. "No-brainer. I need a meatier problem. I'll tell you what—give me a couple of hours, and I'll have the number of his plane flight and where he's having dinner."

"You're on," Danielle quipped. Her mind raced ahead to the questions she might ask if she had the chance. Without a doubt, her interest was rooted in the nature of the relationship between Wheeling and PERC—and also Cervasi.

"What's with this Wheeling character?"

"Ann told me Greg met him in LA, and Wheeling worked formerly for PERC, so I thought I might strike up a conversation about the company. I'm doing the due diligence I should have done before I accepted the job." She chided herself on not having investigated her future employer long ago, but as her father drilled into her, it was better late than never.

"In that case, I'll find out what brand of underpants the guy wears, if that makes a difference." Looking out the window toward Lexington Avenue, Karen said, "After Labor Day, it's all downhill until Thanksgiving and Christmas. And, unfortunately, you won't be here." Her voice trailed off before she turned abruptly toward Danielle, "Oh, one more thing; I've dug up some information on your Dr. James Greyson."

"You did?" Danielle said, sitting bolt upright. "He's the psychiatrist Owen saw immediately before he died." She looked away but caught her emotions before she broke down.

"I've started a short dossier on him. But here's the skinny: in addition to his office in Pittsburgh, he has an office in Reston, Virginia."

"Reston is where PERC has its headquarters."

"Yep," Karen said. "I thought you might be surprised. But that's not all." She sauntered across the room and leaned her arms on the top of a guest chair. "In Reston, you've got to have money, and he sifts through his appointments to determine, I guess, whether he wants you as a patient." She extended her hand, rubbing her thumb across her middle and index fingers. "It's all private pay, rather exclusive. Like a country club. He's normally there every other weekend."

Danielle's adrenaline flowed freely; the fatigue from the prior day had left her. Mesmerized by what Karen had to say, Danielle clasped her hands together with her elbows resting on the desk.

Karen continued, "I know where he did his undergraduate and graduate work. And, he spent some time working for the government— *the CIA*. But I don't know where or for how long; it's classified. And he's written several articles and lectured on psychiatry. I didn't know if you had an interest, but I've requested copies of recent articles."

"Sure, anything might help. That is, it might give me at least some insight."

"Okay, could you let me in on what you're after, and what this all means?"

"When I was in Pittsburgh, a few things made me think, what if Owen was trying to alert me about a matter that was imminent?" Danielle filled Karen in on Greyson and Milsen, the two psychiatrists who prepared reports that were submitted to the police. "And I don't believe those medical reports. Lastly, why would Owen tell me that my life is in danger? That statement has haunted me every time I hit the sack each night."

"I'll give you this," Karen said. "When you and Owen split, I was perplexed by what you told me about his conduct. Those cards he'd send now and then …" Karen bit the inside of her lower lip. "Something was amiss, all right. What was he thinking about?"

"Yeah," Danielle breathed with some resignation. "And then I never quite understood why someone would want those CDs." She peered over her monitor to a spot where a number of CDs once held a space. "It's as though they held some significance."

"I forgot about them. You may be right," Karen said, looking intently at the shelf. "They just didn't walk out of here. And it was only music, right?"

"Well, at least, I think so. That's what's odd. Whoever it was could've taken anything. Money, files, laptops, monitors. But no, they wanted those CDs." She crossed her arms on the desk and mumbled, "For what reason?"

"Huh. Are you thinking that whoever it was might be looking for something?"

"Agreed. But Karen, you and I need to move on to the memo."

"Yes. What are your thoughts on this memo that Pierce wants?"

Danielle weighed the question. "On one hand, you've got PERC, which endorses a candidate for Senate and then wants to find a way out. From what I've heard, representing Clarke is a challenge you wouldn't want to undertake. They're probably feeling the heat about the representations in the contract. But, hey, that's politics."

"Politics is like the stock market; one day you're up, can't do anything wrong, and then the next … well, who knows?" Karen shrugged her shoulders, and walked to the doorway. "I just don't get it. But, in any case, you've got me thinking about Leonard Wheeling. Time's wasting. *I'll be back*," she finished with a wry smile.

"Sure," Danielle murmured. If someone didn't ask the right questions or push hard enough, then what was false became true. But what happens if there are multiple answers to the same question? If someone doesn't want you to know something, then he covers it up with blankets of false information. And an answer, not the correct one, might stick if you accepted it at face value. She was unwilling to accept that Owen took drugs.

For the next several minutes, Danielle reflected on the choices a person makes during any given day. As an attorney, she was trained to keep an open mind, look for answers, and offer solutions. Now she had to find answers, pick through them, sort the real from the imaginary, and piece the puzzle together. And it *was* a puzzle. She wondered whether Owen made the wrong choice, met the wrong person, or chose the wrong company.

She rubbed the back of her neck with her hand and looked around an office devoid of the pictures and degrees that once adorned the walls. The bookcases were partially emptied of her personal effects.

Her imprint on HBR was about to close like the end of a chapter of life. It was time to move on. She wondered whether anyone ever gave Karen that same advice.

After all, Karen led a solitary life, never married, and never depended on anyone. Whatever the reason she stayed on, Danielle didn't know, but at the same time, she didn't want to get caught in the vortex of a life dedicated to a job.

The next hour passed slowly. She reexamined the contract between PERC and Philip Clarke. While she searched West Law, Karen pitched in and ran LexisNexis. By midmorning, Karen bookmarked a number of legal cases for Danielle to read and incorporate into the legal memo. Karen conducted legal searches on precedents for representation of candidates and whether the factual situation was similar to the PERC contract. Then they hammered out legal defense arguments for Denon.

At 11:30 a.m., Karen stood in the doorway and beamed. "Well, I've got your Wheeling answers," she said, handing Danielle the room number, the flight departure time and flight number, and the time and place for dinner reservations.

"You never cease to amaze me," Danielle said, holding a typed sheet with the information. "You always come through."

"I wouldn't go that far. But do me a favor," Karen responded, peering into Danielle's eyes. "You don't remember where or how you got this. And one more favor—keep me apprised."

"It's a deal, and don't forget we're going out for calamari when I return from Washington in a few weeks," Danielle said, looking at the time on her monitor. "I'll tell you what, I can see you're worn out. How about I finish up this research, and I'll dictate what I've got. Then all you need to do is combine our research, send me an e-mail, and I'll read it on Monday morning before I meet Pierce for lunch."

"Now that's music to these tin ears. But I hate to leave you all alone."

"Thanks for all your help. I already feel better. I'll have the dictation done for this memo in an hour."

"Good," Karen said, talking through another wide yawn. "And by the way, your plane leaves Sunday night at eight o'clock from LaGuardia. I've arranged for a rental car. You've got no worries."

"Thanks," Danielle said, getting up and walking around her desk to give Karen a hug. "I won't say good-bye because I'll be back here sooner than you think."

Karen held up her arms. "If you need anything, you just call me. No matter the time. Call here first and then call my home and cell. You promise?"

"Promise. And I'll lock up the place and reset the alarm when I leave."

Karen let go and blotted her tears. She gave a hearty wave as she left the office. Danielle thought Karen would never leave the practice of law; she was married to the characters in every legal case she worked.

For the next hour, the proverbial dropped pin could not be heard. Now and then the overhead air conditioning system kicked on, interrupting her thoughts. The contract between PERC and Clarke read like most contracts, but it included a liquidated damage clause, which she found quite unusual. Clarke had the right to seek retribution against PERC, but the terms were referenced to a letter. Denon never gave the letter to her, and a quick check of the file revealed nothing. She dictated a note for Karen to e-mail him about a missing letter. That was the last piece of business for the day; now she had her own mission to accomplish.

Snatching her laptop and purse, she flicked off the light and wended her way through the hallways and doors until she found herself at the elevator. For the next several weeks, her assignment was to act as a legal consultant. To her, the practice of law was a merry-go-round, and the ride was coming to an end.

As the elevator door opened, Danielle came face to face with a delivery man with a FedEx emblem emblazoned on his shirt. He had light, closely cropped hair and was dark skinned.

"Delivery. Anybody still working?"

Danielle looked at him askance, although she had seen him before at the office delivering packages. "No, they're gone for the weekend. I'm the last one."

Perplexed by his dilemma, the delivery man scratched the side of his head and then ran his fingers through his hair.

"I'll tell you what; I'm an attorney with the firm, so I'll sign for it. I'll make sure it gets into the right hands," Danielle said, looking into vacant eyes.

He thought it over for a moment. "Gee, thanks. You can have it, sign here." He pulled a pen from his inner pocket and handed the digital pad to her. After she signed, he right-sided the express envelope and said, "It's addressed to Denon Pierce," handing it to her.

"I'll make sure he gets it."

"Thanks, I should have been here earlier, but I was caught up in traffic."

Danielle and the delivery man boarded the elevator and returned to the ground floor. Exiting the elevator, the delivery man skirted around her and flew through the door, running down the sidewalk to a large FedEx truck with blinking lights along Lexington.

Danielle checked her watch and figured she had just enough time to change and get ready for her dinner engagement at the Four Seasons. Knowing that she could deliver the envelope to Pierce in person on the next business day, she pulled up the flap on her laptop case to stuff the envelope inside. She froze when she saw the sender of the package: Owen Roberts.

# 12

In the lobby of the headquarters for PERC, the receptionist's desk, made out of volcanic rock, was partially framed by exotic fan ferns and palms that tickled the three-story, vaulted ceiling. Black granite floors with flecks of white and tan meandered through the garden, which was filled with a cacophony of sounds from caged exotic birds, and continued over a footbridge to a rugged rock formation where a waterfall lazily fed a small reservoir.

The outdoor amenities were equal in grandeur to the lobby. There was a small pond on the front lawn, which was sprinkled with American dogwood trees, and behind the main building, nature trails led outward from the three rear buildings that formed part of the courtyard. A series of patio homes available for overnight guests were situated on the outer perimeter of the campus. This was the pride and joy of Tony Cervasi, who purchased the property, replete with its lavish excesses, from a defunct dot-com company.

Sweeping a piece of lint from the sleeve of his dark Italian suit jacket designed by Baroni, Tony strode past the receptionist, who gestured with a slight wave and nod. With a crooked smile, he gave her a passing glance as he continued to the reception area with its set of lounge chairs, a sofa, and coffee table. He bent over and picked up a political news magazine, where he found an article exploring the future of politics in a melting pot of cultures and Spanish-speaking Americans.

But his reading was interrupted by a distinct feeling of another presence nearby. His eyes wandered from the page and surveyed the room until he uncovered the reason. Les Baker sat in his wheelchair like a hawk about to pounce on an unsuspecting prey. Cervasi looked away when he heard the approach of dragging heels over the granite floor and dropped the magazine on the table.

Cervasi jerked his head ever so slightly to warn Matalino about Baker's presence above them. In a lowered voice, Cervasi voice said, "He should be here soon. Hart warned me about Clarke's propensity for unexpected visits—nothing but bitch sessions. That's why Hart threw his hands up in the pejorative sense. But I'm not putting up with Clarke's antics; no congressman is going to tell me how to run a campaign." Hart was not only right about Clarke's drifting eye and moves toward women on the campaign trail, but also the candidate's desire to draw in special interest groups to grease his palm. The subjects were broached on several occasions, but to no avail. And it didn't end there; Clarke's wife was disgruntled, and her rumblings were becoming more pronounced.

Matalino nodded. "We have uncovered no new clues about STAR."

"I figured as much." Cervasi had a recalcitrant congressman whose indifference and hutzpah threatened to torpedo the senatorial election. Then a screw-up caused the death of a computer scientist and in turn the company lost its potent political weapon. Despite the probable outcome of the election, he had not weighed the financial repercussions and his reputation. And to further add to his pressing problems was Baker, a person to whom he owed a debt.

With his arms dangling at his side and a long face, Matalino stood for what seemed minutes. His bulk resembled a football player in a business suit.

"If we catch some luck at the polls, we might have a fighting chance," Cervasi said, shaking his head in disgust. "At this late date, the election may be out of our reach. At the very most, maybe ten points, that's it. And will it stick? We need to close the gap, and soon. I spoke to Hart and Halstren by phone this morning, and they had nothing to offer, other than reporting solid gains in their elections." Cervasi had orchestrated congressional races in California, New Mexico, and Nevada, but Clarke's election proved more than challenging. A failure to elect Clarke would jeopardize his goal to head a presidential election.

Looking for some inspiration, Cervasi again noted the presence of Baker overhead. Baker never moved—he merely trained his eyes on both of them.

With an almost imperceptible head bob, Cervasi made Matalino aware of Baker's continued presence.

"He's one person we need to address maybe sooner than later," Cervasi said in a conspiratorial tone. "He's up to something."

"No messes, I promise." Matalino made a guttural noise and wrung his hands as though wringing a wet towel.

"Not yet," Cervasi said. "We may need him. The rat has played his last hand." Cervasi had heard from Richie Davis, the IT director, about discrete inquiries made by Baker. "We'll need to discuss this later." Cervasi chided himself for not having dealt with Baker years ago when he had the chance.

"Mr. Cervasi," the receptionist said, standing a few feet away, "excuse me for interrupting again, but Congressman Clarke would like to see you prior to the meeting."

"Fine," Cervasi said, brushing off his jacket unconsciously as he turned to Matalino. "Keep an eye on Baker, and find out what he's up to."

Cervasi stepped out into the afternoon sunshine and spotted Clarke's entourage—a black, tinted window limo and a lead vehicle—wending their way down the drive. A slight breeze with a discernible chill was in the air as he waited across from the entrance. He rubbed his hands together to warm them.

When the limo came to a stop, the attendant opened the rear door and Clarke stepped out. He was of medium height with short, salt and pepper hair. At fifty-six, he was a head taller than Cervasi and had a condescending expression. And his persona demanded respect. He was known to play to a crowd and give impromptu news conferences, but only to raise himself on a pedestal.

"Congressman," Cervasi said in an upbeat tone, "if you're in town this evening, I've made dinner reservations at The Hay-Adams."

Clarke waived Cervasi off and said laconically, "I'll get right to the matter."

Cervasi had read the latest polls figures earlier, and nothing seemed to work to pull Clarke's numbers up in any corner of the state. Intense newspaper and televised ads and appearances had yielded very little progress.

"Have you seen the latest polls?" Clarke asked, taking a hard line. He pulled his suit coat taut, took a handkerchief from his pocket, and, lifting his loafer onto a planter, bent over to clean the dust from his shoes.

"Yes," Cervasi said, knowing he had to keep control of the conversation before it ended in a shouting match. Clarke was stuck with PERC as much as PERC was stuck with him.

"Let's walk," Clarke said, pointing to a path that would take them to the pond where a column of water gushed from a fountain. "What do you intend to do about it?" He halted and folded his handkerchief before depositing it in his jacket pocket.

Cervasi said, undeterred by what he knew had to come, "We're studying the results."

With riveted eyes boring into Cervasi, Clarke barked, "Studying. I heard that the last time. I want more than some flunky studying results. Get those so-called experts off their asses."

"Now wait a minute."

"No, you wait a minute," Clarke snarled, his eyes mere slits and his neck muscles popping. "You made promises. I'm going to hold you and everyone on this so-called campus to the fire. Got it?"

"Yeah, I get it," Cervasi said, not backing down. "You do your job, and I'll do mine. We've invested more than what you've paid us. And don't call my staff with your complaints like you did the other day. If you've got any gripes, you address them to me," he said with conviction. PERC prided itself on presenting the consummate candidate. A team of analysts studied and analyzed a candidate's physical characteristics from hairstyle to clothes and the tone of voice and articulation of words. Then the recommendations were implemented. Facial mannerisms were even choreographed.

Clarke scowled, "You need to make changes … all I see is more of the same. McClay has the press and television eating out of his hands. You'd think that he's running for president. Why, a reporter asked me whether I'd consider running for governor when I lose." He was not about to let go. "Where are those media people? Have them dig up some dirt. Surely, we can find something on McClay?"

"Mudslinging won't do much good. He's too far ahead. We have to contend with your credibility." Cervasi took a breath. "And that's more than what we bargained for. Unsupported statements will not get you elected this time around." Cervasi understood the political process too well, and even he had to admit that perhaps Clarke deserved to be defeated.

Pointing his finger in Cervasi's face, Clarke said arrogantly. "I really don't give a damn about your lame excuses. You've got only days—time's running short. I want results."

"You'll get results," Cervasi said snidely. "But it's my way, not yours. You hired me. I'm tired of hearing about what we failed to do. All you've done is make our job harder. We had to retract your comments about McClay's voting record in the state legislature, your endorsements by unions proved false, and then you attributing statements to McClay, again false. Not to mention your womanizing. Need I say more?"

Clarke stammered, "Don't you lecture me. If I'm not voted into office, you'll never see another election. I'll make sure of it." Before Clarke could say anything further, his cell phone rang. He yanked the phone from its holster. He looked at the caller ID and said, "We'll take this up shortly. I need a few minutes."

Cervasi walked ahead. He meandered along the walkway, mesmerized by the fine mist of the fountain. Mudslinging. Statements true or untrue, in or out of context, twisted or turned. It all had a stinging effect. Spinning was Cervasi's forte, but this election was out of control—a train wreck waiting to happen. And to think that he and Clarke grew up in Detroit. But Clarke would not admit he grew up in the poor district. Clarke's father picked up the family and moved to Virginia where he had their name legally changed from Clemenzi to Clarke—a move to rid themselves of their Italian heritage.

Clarke approached Cervasi and said with a sneer, "Where's this special plan you promised me? 'Don't worry, you'll win. I have a foolproof plan.' Hollow words."

Cervasi said with equal venom, "I'll keep my part of the bargain."

"Where's this computer software engineer, or genius? You told me you needed a telecommunications company. So I pulled a few strings and delivered Shannon Telecom. Well, now I'm here to collect. Do you understand me?"

"I can hear, and I understand English," Cervasi said, thinking he had paid Clarke in full for Shannon as they made their way back to the building. "We've had a slight setback with the program, but we're working on it."

Clarke said, "I don't give a damn about computers and how they operate. I know politics. Are you telling me you don't have this program? After all the grandiose statements about how it will change the political landscape?"

"The program does work," Cervasi said with renewed conviction. "We have leads, and we're tracking them down."

"*Leads*. What the hell do you mean?" Clarke shook his head with disdain. "I should have handed my election to AMRE Media Group. But no, I decided to let you handle it." Clarke sat down at a bench along the pond.

Cervasi steeled himself. "It took us five years to get this program to work. And we've had some problems with a disgruntled employee. But that's our problem, not yours." Cervasi hoped Clarke wouldn't pick up on the misstatement. Davis explained the problem to Cervasi by pointing out that each program has algorithms, and each programmer writes them differently. A program and its progression are not easily replicated.

"You don't have *five* years. You've got weeks with or without that program."

"We'll do whatever it takes. But—" Cervasi did not want to reveal the possible solution to the dilemma.

"But what?" Clarke took long strides as they headed back to the main building. "You can't find it. That's it, isn't it? Your employee ripped you off, and now you can't get the program. Right?"

Keeping pace with Clarke, Cervasi said, "No, that's not it." But that *was* it, and Clarke knew.

"I'll give you one last chance, Tony," said Clarke in a more civilized tone. "We grew up together, so you say, back in Detroit. If we did, I don't remember. I don't care what you've got to do. But if your employee did rip you off, I'm going to get some help—John Candecki."

Cervasi frowned, not understanding how Clarke made the connection to a lost program.

As they entered the main building, Clarke said, "I want all the particulars. I'll have Candecki call you. He'll do the job, but you're going to pay his bill."

After he showed Clarke into the campaign meeting, Cervasi promptly excused himself and stepped out. Then he punched in a number on his cell and connected to Matalino. "Carl, I'm headed to my office. Be there in five." He hastily strode into his office.

Matalino barged through the door unannounced and pulled up a chair.

"Clarke's flying Candecki in from the coast."

"Candecki? Why?"

"Clarke knows we don't have the program. But how?" Cervasi said, searching for an answer in his mind.

"That's impossible."

"Somebody tipped him off. Not only do we need to contend with Clarke, we're about to have Candecki. And now a snitch."

Matalino crossed his arms.

Cervasi continued, "We don't have much choice right now. More importantly, if they find out the significance of the program, we'll be working for Clarke and Candecki. And every time I turn the corner, I've got Baker in my face."

Matalino offered, "Do you think Baker has something to do with it?"

"I don't know. But we've got to move fast." Cervasi put his hands on his hips and looking out the window, murmured, "We've got to find that program."

# 13

*New York, New York*
*Saturday, September 15*
*7:00 p.m.*

At the corner of Park and Madison Avenues, Danielle emerged from a cab, pulled up the collar of her jacket against a cool breeze, and strode half a block to the entrance of the Four Seasons. As she entered the foyer, a sudden case of queasiness, the kind she always associated with addressing a jury for the first time, flared up inside her. She stepped back and had a second thought about meeting with Leonard Wheeling. After all, what did she hope to accomplish?

Considering the medical examiner ruled Owen's death a suicide, she questioned whether her little crusade was hopeless. Her hunches were mere ideas stripped of substance and inadmissible as evidence in a court of law. She sounded out the arguments to herself for fear of being chastised for incredulous suppositions. But deep within her, feelings of suspicion and disbelief overshadowed her despondency and stirred her conviction.

To compound her uncertainty was the thought Wheeling would summarily dismiss her. For that matter, she had little time to consider the quintessential questions about the company or Owen. The more she thought about it, the more perturbed she became. Usually she had days to prepare for a cross-examination, but in this instance, she only had the cab ride. Relying on the gritty instinct of a trial attorney, she took several deep, controlled breaths and managed to regain her composure.

After passing through the lobby with its geometrically designed concrete columns, she made a quick left near a newsstand and strolled down the corridor to the Fifty-Seven Fifty-Seven bar, where, if Karen's sources were right about the credit card charges for the past two evenings, Danielle would find Wheeling. In addition, his dinner reservations for three were made at the hotel's restaurant. But another aspect of finding Wheeling unsettled her. Ann had never answered her phone, leaving Danielle in a quandary about how to recognize him in a throng of people.

At the coatroom, she received a claim check and then slipped into the ladies room where she brushed her hair, applied a peach lip gloss, and touched up her eye shadow and eyebrows. With one examining look, she stared at the likeness of her mother in her brown eyes, high cheekbones, and pouty lips. Even her olive skin tones and the small chin favored her mother's European descent.

Unlike her mother, who had the mettle of a tank firing a barrage of ordinance against an adversary in court, Danielle remained wary about whether she had the same stamina and fortitude. Possibly, it was the outcome of having spent her formative childhood and teenage years inside a courtroom where an adversarial relationship was always present. Deep down inside she loved the law, but not enough to become inextricably tied to the profession.

With one last look in the mirror, she swept a strand of hair behind her ear. Then she exited. She slipped her bag strap over her shoulder and walked into the warm, ambient-lighted lounge, feeling the mahogany floor underfoot and admiring the richness of the red mahogany paneled walls. For an early Saturday evening, waiters and waitresses buzzed through the room with drinks, unaffected by the clamor of voices, which, at times, drowned out the notes struck by a pianist on a grand piano. With little to go on, smiling occasionally at the furtive glance of a gentleman, she wormed her way through the patrons surrounding the bar. She ordered a California cabernet and sipped it while her eyes scanned the room, hoping to spot someone or something that might jog her memory of what Ann had said about Wheeling.

Seated at most of the tables were four or more people, several tables had two, but no table had three, which lead her to believe that either Karen's information was incorrect, or Wheeling and his party had not arrived. She retrieved her cell phone and punched in directory assistance. After some prodding, the hotel's operator forwarded the call to the lounge where she made an urgent request to talk to Leonard Wheeling.

Danielle swiveled around in her bar stool to watch a short, balding bartender motion with his index finger to a college-aged waiter with spiked blonde hair. Their animated conversation was brief, and then the waiter nodded approvingly and scurried off to a round table where five men were seated. The waiter leaned over and whispered into the ear of a clean-shaven individual with short, light-brown hair and a ruddy complexion. Wheeling, she surmised, nodded and checked his watch through his wire rim glasses.

He stood and pushed his chair away from the table. Before he left, he leaned over between the two faceless individuals, seated with their backs to her, and patted them on the backs. Then he followed the waiter to a telephone at the other end of the bar. As he slapped the receiver to his ear, Danielle hung up, managing to read the expletives from his lips. For a second, he cocked his head, and then he slammed the receiver into the cradle before he retraced his steps hurriedly.

Now there were only three seated at the table, the other two having slipped away without being noticed by her. As he returned, Wheeling snapped a cell to his ear. About a minute later, he returned the phone to his pocket and waved to someone on his way out of the etched cut-glass doors. Danielle caught a fleeting glimpse of a medium-built man wearing a light-colored jacket and noticed he walked lamely.

For the next twenty minutes, Danielle sipped her drink and stared intermittently at Wheeling and his party as they downed another round of drinks. A thick-fleshed individual seated to the left of Wheeling raised his glass and gestured for another round to their waiter. Once the waiter had the drinks on his serving tray, she threw down her credit card to pay.

As the waiter told Wheeling and his party the drinks were compliments of Danielle, she raised the stem of her wine glass and winked. Judging from Wheeling's expression, he was nonplussed, as were the others seated at the table, but each nodded their appreciation and approval to her.

"To what do we owe this pleasure?" Wheeling asked with an examining look.

"We have a common friend ... isn't anyone going to offer me a seat?" With a wry smile, Danielle settled on the one with a lecherous gaze and gave him a slight nod. He was in his midfifties, and from what she observed from the bar, his flailing hands were those of an intoxicated person. He sprung to his feet and offered her a chair. After she seated herself, the alcohol vapors he expelled were so potent that it made her turn toward Wheeling for fresh air.

"Anyone that buys me a drink is a friend of mine. Isn't that right, Leonard?"

Wheeling frowned with obvious annoyance.

"If Leonard won't introduce you, call me Harry. Harry Mitchell," he said in a slurred voice and cocked his head backward. "And this here," gesturing toward the individual seated to his right with day-old stubble and penetrating eyes, "is Carmen Vittorio."

Danielle introduced herself and extended her hand to Mitchell, who grasped it in a gentle but firm grip. Then she shook hands with Wheeling, and, in turn, Vittorio, whose hand was cold and rough. The dark-haired Vittorio, in his late thirties, was muscular, as evidenced by the bulging biceps underneath his dress shirt.

Wheeling exchanged glances with Vittorio before he asked, "And who might be our common friend?" he asked in bewilderment. He appeared to search nearby tables for someone who might have pointed him out.

"Actually, Greg Myers. I was waiting for a friend and happened to overhear your name. And I just had to say hello," she answered, catching Mitchell's gaze at her cleavage. "I hope I'm not interrupting anything," she continued in an apologetic tone.

Mitchell slammed his drink down on the table. "Nonsense, what are friends for? Any time you want to interrupt, don't hesitate," he said, downing nearly half of his drink with one gulp. With a toothy smile, he looked for approval from his compatriots. With his elbows on the arms of the chair and his fingertips touching each other as though in prayer, Vittorio gave a slight nod as he continued to stare at her with unblinking eyes.

Wheeling responded, "And what's the nature of your business?"

"Let's not talk business. That's later. This young lady," Mitchell said, "is from ...?"

Danielle finished the sentence, "New York."

"I believe the young lady has other plans for the evening," Leonard said in a jaded tone.

She could feel Vittorio's edginess and, more importantly, his obvious suspicion and dissatisfaction. He had a stony expression and stared fixedly at her.

"Yes," Mitchell said, "and she's visiting with us." His head bobbed a few times. "Carmy here is from Chicago, and I'm from Boston. Leonard's the outsider—He's from L A." Mitchell took another pull of his drink.

"Harry, she's not here to discuss where we're from," Leonard said in a raised voice over the burst of laugher at another table.

Oblivious to Wheeling's sarcasm, Mitchell cupped his head in his hand. "What do you want to know?" His mouth dropped open a bit before he took another slug.

From the corner of her eye, Danielle caught the finger gesture by Vittorio to Wheeling that Mitchell had too many and might reveal something that he shouldn't. She proceeded to explain her acceptance of a position with PERC and how she wanted to know more about the company.

Ignoring the intoxicated Mitchell, Wheeling leaned forward. "You said Myers?"

Danielle said, "I work with him at Higgins, Biggs and Reed. And you, I believe, were a former employee of PERC."

"Yes," Wheeling said, whose frown turned to a scowl. He volunteered, "Years ago. Like the weather, the personnel have turned over, but that won't change my opinion of the company or its president, Tony Cervasi," he said in a venomous tone.

Mitchell, with one hand on his drink, loosened his tie, swaying back and forth in his chair Vittorio shifted in his chair, but his eyes remained locked on Danielle.

Vittorio intertwined his fingers. "Then you know Denon Pierce."

"Know him? I work for him," Danielle responded. She had never heard Leonard Wheeling's name until the meeting with Ann Burk. With numerous offices and clients throughout the country, it was impossible to know every client, although she thought it strange, especially when Wheeling was a political consultant. "I take it you gentlemen work for the same company."

"Not exactly," Mitchell said, dropping his empty glass on the table. "We're all political consultants and—"

"And we had business in New York, kind of a small get-together among old friends. Isn't that right, Harry?" Wheeling looked at Mitchell with a piercing gaze and a furrowed brow.

"Yeah, I guess so." Mitchell looked for the waiter and added, "If you want the lowdown on Tony Cervasi, you came to the right place. Why, Leonard and Tony were partners at one time. That was some time ago, though." Mitchell dropped his head and peered upward at Leonard.

"We'll be late for our dinner reservations," Vittorio said with a sudden raised concern.

"Nah, we've got time. I'm not going just yet," Mitchell said, crossing his arms. "And I'll tell you, dear, if you get mixed up with Tony. Well." He motioned to the waiter, pointing down into an empty glass and a circular gesture for the table. The waiter nodded and headed back to the bar.

"Well, what?" Danielle asked.

Wheeling butted in, "What he's saying is," nodding his head, "Tony's hard to work for. You a lawyer?"

"Sure. I've worked on political and tax matters for HBR these last several years," said Danielle, wondering whether Owen, who never commented much about his employer, had run-ins with Tony.

"If you're going to work for Tony, you've got problems." Mitchell leaned closer to the table and said in a hushed tone, "Anyone connected with Tony has problems. I've heard it before." Neither Wheeling nor Vittorio said anything. "Tony doesn't play by the book. We all know it. He's been in and out of trouble over the years." Mitchell smiled at both Wheeling and Vittorio.

"If all you want to know is about Tony, I'll tell you, and then, I must beg your pardon, we have dinner reservations," Wheeling said. He turned and raised his eyebrows almost imperceptibly at Vittorio. "Tony and I had a falling out several years ago over the usual, you know, the money aspect of the business. I worked with him a number of years. We split, and he moved his main operations to DC. And that's all there is to it."

Danielle was no Girl Scout; she knew there was more. "But I understand," she nodded toward Harry, "that Tony has problems. What kind of problems?"

Vittorio, with a dark look and menacing eyes, braced his hands against the end of the table and said tersely, "You should be addressing your questions to Denon, not us."

Wheeling gave Vittorio a sideways glance, "Miss, PERC does a fine job. Politics is like any other field—difficult."

Mitchell dropped his head and shook it. He wiped his mouth with his sleeve after his drink missed its mark. "They are very well connected. You know, with his father and grandfather in the business. A lot of political favors. Unions and the like. One thing's for sure, you don't cross Tony. He's … well … he's not afraid of anything or anyone. He can fix an election." Silence engulfed the table. "It's his way."

"Or else." Wheeling interrupted. "What my friend is saying is that we've all had dealings with Tony. He's a likeable guy, but more or less he's a politician himself. End of interview."

Wheeling rose from his chair without hesitation and Vittorio followed.

Vittorio leaned over Mitchell and said, "Let's go, Harry," gripping Harry's shoulder.

Mitchell slid back in his seat. "I'm coming, don't worry." Vittorio and Wheeling began to wind their way through the tables. Mitchell, shaking off the effects of the alcohol, cocked his head sideward toward Danielle. "The candidates they put into office, well, there's a reason they remain loyal. He keeps them on a tight leash. Call it blackmail, I really don't know. Like Leonard said, he's not someone to cross. A lot of good firms out there." He cupped his fingers together, and moving his hand in a hinge-like fashion, he said, "You're a nice girl. Mind my words. Find another job."

Danielle showed a thin smile.

"You got a card with a cell?" Mitchell winked.

"Sure," she replied, taking a card from her purse and writing down a fake cell number.

"See you later." With one last swallow of his drink, Mitchell pulled up his pants and trudged off.

# 14

*New York, New York*
*Sunday, September 16*
*8:00 a.m.*

Danielle, where are you?" Karen asked anxiously. Without waiting for an answer, she blurted, "You better get over here. And make it as soon as possible."

"Something wrong?"

"Plenty. I've got to make a phone call. Just get here."

It was unlike Karen to be so terse and enigmatic. And the anxiety in Karen's voice, coupled with the abruptness, triggered a sense of foreboding.

She quickly slipped into a pair of designer blue jeans, pulled on a light wool sweater, and brushed her hair into a ponytail before pulling it through the opening in the back of her NY ball cap. Then she strapped on a wristwatch, the one Owen had given her. Like the hardcover legal books, which became dust collectors, the digital, illuminated wristwatch was rather impractical save for its keeping excellent time. She could hardly forget opening messages on the LCD screen and seeing the words "I love you." And neatly folded and integrated into the wristband was a USB drive. He reminded her, "No need to lug those books—you can store and send whatever you want." But with the improvements in digital technology and increased storage devices, the wristwatch was relegated to an obsolete timepiece, more a novelty.

Finding her way around shipping boxes that were half-filled with her personal belongings, Danielle emerged from her bedroom into a hallway stacked with sealed boxes. She scooted into the kitchen where a whiteboard was magnetically attached to the refrigerator. On it she wrote a short note to Ann about having to make a quick trip to the office. Then she poured her latte into a travel mug and bolted down the hallway.

A group of boxes angled toward the opposite wall halted her advance. The bottom box had partially collapsed from the weight of the others. With her shoulder, she gave the upper boxes a shove.

She took no more than five steps when a loud thud made her grimace. Letting out a deep breath of despair, she turned to find two boxes pinched against the opposite wall, with the contents of another two strewn on the floor. Setting her purse and her coffee mug on an end table, she resigned herself to straightening out the mess.

Cutting through the living room around the blocked hallway, she retrieved packing tape from her bedroom. On her knees, she righted the first split box, replaced its contents, and taped the box securely, along with reinforcing two others.

The final box had books protruding from its side. It was one of the boxes Owen sent. Breaking through the top flaps, she began to withdraw the treatise of twelve volumes on the early writings of Thomas Jefferson. He had a deep interest in the history of the writer of the Declaration of Independence. Together they had often visited the Jefferson Monument, and sometimes Monticello, like pilgrims seeking personal renewal at a shine. After removing several volumes in order to tape the side, she fished out a thinner book hidden underneath. It was titled *Nerds 2.0.1: Brief History of the Internet*. She set it aside and replaced the volumes before she taped the outside of the box.

For a moment, she stared at the book's cover, and then she smiled. She shelved it in a bookcase found within her bedroom among the outdated computer software books. In college, her interests were initially in computer science until she decided on a pre-law major. Right now, she had no time to leaf through the treatise, what with the office emergency. Tomorrow the movers were scheduled to pick up the boxes and furniture for shipment to a storage unit in Virginia.

At 8:30 a.m., Danielle walked out of the building, flipped down her shades from the cap, and shivered slightly from a cool breeze. At the edge of the apartment complex, she sipped her latte, in need of a shot of adrenaline. She waited no more than five minutes before she hailed a cab trawling for a fare. With one last swallow, she jumped inside and belted out the street address.

As they approached her office building, the driver slowed, but what she saw made her pat the driver on the shoulder and demand a drop off down the street. In passing she caught a glimpse of Greg Myers and Harry Mitchell engaged in an animated conversation next to a waiting black sedan with its motor running. By the time she rounded the corner, they were gone.

Pausing for a moment to consider the implications, Danielle could not fathom the apparent cordiality they shared. She flashed her ID at the security guard and rushed across the granite floor to the elevator. Inside, she impulsively pressed the floor button several times. On the fifth floor, in a partially lit corridor, she scrambled to the office and dashed through the main door.

Perched on the edge of the receptionist's desk was Greg with a grim facial expression and his arms crossed. Karen was seated in a lounge chair with her glasses perched atop her head.

"Well, what's the problem?" Danielle voiced slightly winded, thinking about what she stumbled across outside.

She picked up Karen's surreptitious glance at Greg, who remained steadfast in his stance. Feeling flushed, Danielle wasn't going to wait. "Will someone please tell me what's this all about?"

He exchanged glances with Karen again. "We had a break-in last night. From what we can tell, your office was the only one affected. Any reason you can think why someone chose your office?"

Danielle met his gaze. "No," although she wondered whether her encounter with Wheeling and his cohorts may have triggered the intrusion. If anyone should be called to the witness stand, it was Greg. But for now, she would wait until the picture became clearer.

Karen abruptly rose to her feet and intertwined her arm with Danielle's. "Come with me." Greg followed closely behind.

Thinking their actions pointed the finger at her, Danielle became more mystified. Where are the police? What about the night security?

Karen opened the office door and stepped aside, leaving Danielle an unobstructed view.

"God," Danielle uttered, raising her hand to cover her mouth and feeling a heated flush. She swept the room with her eyes in disbelief, trying to spot anything that might offer an explanation. The question why ran through her mind.

A muted, white light poured from the computer monitor like a beacon off the coast. Book spines were separated. Guest chairs were overturned with the lining ripped out from underneath. The desk chair laid on its back. Pictures were separated from their frames. With a flip of the wall switch, Karen turned on the overhead florescent light and illuminated the extent of the damage.

"We hoped you might shed some light on this," Greg said dryly, almost with an air of disbelief.

Once the shock wore off, Danielle turned to him. "Me? I don't know what you mean. I have nothing to do with this." She surveyed the damage again. "I really don't know what anyone would have wanted." Her voice quivered. "I just don't know." She shrugged her shoulders as two pairs of eyes watched solemnly. "I suppose someone … maybe was looking for something. But what?" She shook her head, recalling the incident several days ago, with the disappearance of Owen's CDs. "No. And I can't answer it. Are the police on their way?"

"Not exactly." Karen replied.

"What do you mean?"

Greg rolled up his sleeves. "Well, that's why we called you. The incident occurred around midnight. That's when security admitted a female matching your description. The register was signed: Danielle Madison."

"I swear it wasn't me."

With his hands on his hips and never making eye contact, he confessed, "We didn't call the police. Nor do we want our clients to know. This matter can be handled internally." He leaned forward and stared her down. "The partners wouldn't want the firm's name muddied on the street, especially with the sensitive files and data in our possession."

*Well, it's not about me,* Danielle thought. It was for the protection of the firm and confidentiality. Inside she could feel her heart rapidly tapping, her mind racing—who did this, and what did they want? She had become the victim, but Greg and the firm didn't want an investigation.

Greg's poker face left her uneasy. She couldn't explain her visceral feelings, but she sensed it wasn't good. Something bothered him. And what about Ann, her roommate? *I'm in your wedding*! And surely it wasn't like Karen, in whom she had confided her deepest secrets.

Feeling betrayed, she turned away and gingerly stepped deeper into the room, trying to avoid stepping on open books and the client files emptied on the floor. Her computer monitor screen displayed an e-mail sent yesterday to Denon. She shook off the thought about failing to close the mail program. The question why ruminated in her mind.

Karen voiced her reservations, "I have to confess … I'm as confused as you. Someone … targeted you, or—"

Danielle thought, *That makes two of us.* A clammy feeling ran up and down her arms.

"I've arranged for a cleanup tonight. I don't want anyone knowing about this, except for the three of us. It never happened," Greg said, turning and walking away.

*It's as though he's turning his back on me*, Danielle thought. Pressing her fingers against her temples, she could feel blood flowing through her veins. She wanted to scream at him and didn't know why she couldn't. Her thoughts were riddled with how she became a person of interest. It made absolutely no sense.

Leaning against the door frame, Karen shrugged her shoulders. With an almost imperceptible shake of her head, she said, "I know what you're thinking."

"You do?" *Really*, she thought, Karen had no idea unless she was a mind reader. If she did, then she'd be in for a dark surprise. Karen fixed that years ago, and Danielle wasn't going to revert to what she was years ago. She was stronger and could withstand any verbal abuse, she told herself, although she couldn't explain Greg's untoward actions.

"Danielle," Karen confessed, "Greg has the tape."

"Tape? What tape?"

"Of course, Greg shied away at first from revealing it to me. But supposedly they caught you in the act of coming in and leaving the firm last night."

"Karen, please believe me. I didn't have anything to do with the break-in." Mystified by what she was hearing, Danielle wondered why her paralegal, and even Greg, would consider her the culprit. Unless, they thought she was having a nervous breakdown.

"I believe you, I truly do. But the tape … I've seen it. It is you… unless you have an identical twin."

"And I don't"

"Exactly."

Danielle was unfazed. For her, the game was in the first inning, and she'd have more innings to prove herself.

*Richmond, Virginia*
*4:30 p.m.*

"How did you get in here?" Clarke growled as he barreled through the solid oak door. "Who do you think you are? You got a lot of nerve breaking into my house." Clarke's flared nostrils and protruding chin made him look like a charging animal.

John Candecki raised his hands. "Whoa. Wait a minute. I didn't break in. I came through the front door." Absent was the toothy-grinned congressman that he saw on TV news conferences and ads.

Clarke raged on. "Get out of my chair," he demanded as he stampeded across the library. His footfalls rattled the glass curio. His face hardened red with veins popping out of his neck.

"Relax, you'll blow a gasket," Candecki said, sweeping his running shoes off of the desktop and relinquishing the executive chair.

"Someone gave you the security code. Who was it?"

"Stress is a killer. You'll have a heart attack." He snatched a brandy snifter from the large mahogany desk. "Oh, this brandy's not too bad. I see you're buying top-shelf. Why don't you make yourself at home?"

Clarke stopped short of the desk and took deep, controlled breaths. "This is my home," he said in a gnashing tone. "I called you to do a job. You were to call me."

Candecki frowned, unaffected by the tirade. "I did call, but you were out campaigning. What was I supposed to do? You said it was urgent." He noticed that the years had taken a toll on the congressman. What once was a black mane now was mostly gray. His choir boy face was marked by stress-lined scars across his forehead. His reputation, actions, and temper were anything but that of a choir boy.

"And what if my wife were home?" Clarke asked in a calmer but pressured tone.

"But she wasn't. You and I both know she's on the other side of the state campaigning while you're here in Richmond all by your lonesome. Now isn't that right?" Clarke's wife, Christina, was pressing for votes but only half-heartedly, which, according to the newsprint, was due to an unspoken rift with her husband.

Throwing his blue suit coat on the back of the sofa, Clarke did an about-face and retreated to the bar, filled a glass with cubes, and poured himself a scotch. He took a large gulp. He loosened his tie and stomped across the room to his desk chair.

Looking at the honors and awards hung on the wall, Candecki sipped his drink. Concerned Citizens for a Better Government had recognized Clarke's accomplishments for honesty in government. Clipped newspaper articles showed Clarke receiving the keys to Richmond, Fairfax, and Williamsburg.

Silence filled the library until Clarke said, with his heavy breathing subsiding, "I called you for a reason. But let's get something straight; I don't want you in my house again."

"Relax, Congressman." Candecki raised his glass as though in a toast. "You hired a professional, not some two-bit burglar. That's no way to treat a person who flew more than twenty-five hundred miles on a moment's notice. All I want is some gratitude. By the way, I'm impressed with your friends. You probably think I don't know them, but I do. There's Tony Blair with you and the president. And then the Clintons. Ah, politics. I should have become a politician."

With a penetrating gaze, Clarke said, "My campaign manager or adviser, whatever you want to call him, has a program. A computer program. I've been told the company, that's PERC and Tony Cervasi, lost track of it. That's where you come in. I want you to find it."

Candecki's laughter came in spurts. "You want me to track down a program? Are you joking? I flew all this distance for a computer program? I don't get to whack someone? My, aren't we getting civilized. What's with this program?"

Clarke took another gulp of his drink. "For me, it may mean the difference between winning and losing. Find it. And fast. After the election it's meaningless."

"So there's no one I need to kill? Well, there's no fun in that. You should have told me. This case may be out of my league. You need a Boy Scout, not a professional."

"I want that program, and I intend to get it. Now either you can help, or if you are not interested, you can catch the next plane back home."

"A computer program? Well," Candecki said, shaking his head, "if there's money, and a lot of it, I'm interested."

"Twenty-five down and twenty-five on delivery."

Candecki looked into the snifter and then looked up to meet Clarke's inquisitive eyes. "You drive a hard bargain. But its plus expenses and fifty on delivery."

Clarke dropped his drink on the bar. "Nonsense."

"Do you want to win or not?"

For a moment, Clarke thought about the proposition. "You get it here soon, and I'll give you what you want. I assume you have an overseas account."

"Yep. You get the money in my account, and I'll start immediately." Candecki set down his glass on the bar. He grabbed a cigar from the humidor. "I'll need this for the road," he said as he walked to the library door.

"Where's your vehicle? I didn't see it in the driveway."

"Congressman, don't you remember that I was an army ranger? I run five miles a day. But for your information, I left my car a few miles down the road. You see, Congressman, no one's going to stop a jogger. They're relieving tension, you know? You should try it." As a ranger, he was put through a series of mental and physical tests, and he maintained his routine to keep up with his professional job.

"Don't you want to know where to get started?"

Candecki turned with a laugh. "I already know. That's why you're paying a professional. I know Cervasi and his company. Talk to you soon."

# 15

*Reston, Virginia*
*Sunday, September 16*
*9:00 p.m.*

From the overhead luggage compartment of United Flight 7328, Danielle retrieved her laptop computer and made her way into the terminal's concourse. As she headed to baggage claim, she stopped at a storefront and bought a bottle of water. Glancing at an election news headline in the *Washington Post*, she snatched a copy from the counter and leafed through the sections until she found the article. There she read that the Virginia senatorial election had turned ugly. Clarke had begun a mudslinging campaign directed at his opponent. The article examined the unsupported accusations of corruption. After paying for the paper, she unzipped her case and tucked it next to the envelope.

With the last forty-eight hours being anything but normal, she absently followed a bevy of passengers headed toward baggage claim and transportation. As she did, her thoughts wandered from her ransacked former office to the overnight envelope addressed to Denon. And, even more disturbing, she recalled that the envelope had been sent the day *after* Owen was buried. She had half a mind to rip it open and read the contents, but with building anxiety, she decided to give the honor to Denon. Besides, she wanted to watch his reaction—she had become an unwitting participant in a web spun by someone.

By the time she reached the baggage carousel, a number of passengers had already staked out positions along the serpentine-shaped belt. She could wait until the crowd, now two deep, dispersed.

She wasn't in any hurry, and her overnight accommodations were at the nearby Hyatt Dulles.

In the morning, after making arrangements to store her luggage at the hotel for the day, she'd catch a cab to downtown Washington in time to meet Denon for lunch. Later, she planned a dinner with Brooklyn Lang, her old roomy in the South Campus Commons at the University of Maryland, who offered a room in her townhouse to Danielle. It would be like old times.

The chatter of disgruntled and impatient travelers had modulated to a louder tone when the belt stuttered several times and then fell silent. Finally, the yawl of an overhead buzzer triggered a cheer from several passengers as the conveyor started in earnest. Through a parting in the crowd, she caught a glimpse of her bag and waited for the next go around.

Moments later, she yanked the luggage piece from the trough, kicked out the wheels, and extracted the handle. Before she took a step, a well-dressed man with a rugged face blocked her path. A thick gold chain with a gold cross dangled from his neck.

"Miss Madison," he said in a suave voice beneath closely-cropped, reddish-blonde hair. His blue eyes met hers. "Jonathan Lansel."

"Pardon me," she said warily as she retreated a step.

"I apologize, Miss Madison. It is Miss?"

"Why … yes."

"I should've known you wouldn't get the message. With electronics, you know, answering machines, e-mails, and cells, there's still no foolproof method of making sure a person gets the message." He shook his head and a faint smile swept across his face. "I know what you're thinking. Who is this guy?"

*Exactly*, Danielle thought, studying his facial expression. Underneath his angelic face, he showed a genuine regard for her apparent confusion. And she sensed honesty in the pitch of his voice.

"Go on," Danielle said, her suspicion melting.

"I got a call earlier. Luckily, it was after the Redskins drove down the field for a touchdown before the half. Naturally, I thought, this is my day off, and now I'm being called to act as an escort. Go figure. Anyway, the Redskins beat Dallas, twenty-four to fourteen," Lansel said with a wide grin.

"And who called you?"

"Security. You know, I thought it was odd myself. After all, you're living in a civilized country. But I guess they had their reasons. What could happen in broad daylight?"

*Plenty.* But Danielle wasn't going to answer that question.

Lansel added, "Your plane did arrive late. And," he shrugged his shoulders, "you can't be too sure at this late hour."

Despite his explanation, she was never met by an escort on previous trips to Washington. "And who sent you?"

"Why, of course, PERC. See, I work for the same company, like you, and I'm told what to do. And that was to pick up you at the airport."

Again, it was odd. She wasn't scheduled to start her new job until November. But Denon did ask—no, he demanded that she be in Washington for a luncheon to discuss sensitive matters. And possibly he had learned about the incident at the law offices, raising the need for her security. "How did you recognize me?"

Lansel patted the holstered cell on his belt. "Digital picture," he said, raising an eyebrow. "Plus, I knew your flight number. Give me a few details, general vicinity, and I'll pick out the person every time. And your initials on the side of your laptop case—DM—were a dead giveaway."

For anxious moments, Danielle juggled his answers in her mind, and he had a good answer for every question. He was dressed sharply, with a blue turtleneck sweater, khaki trousers, and a bluish-gray, checked sport coat. She guessed he was in his early thirties.

"Still have doubts? Let me put you at ease." He reached into his back pocket and pulled out a wallet. After he retrieved his ID, he handed it to her.

She studied it, issued by PERC, and sheepishly looked up at his smile. The ID looked the same as the one held by Owen. She handed it back to him.

"Satisfied? Hey, I would be hesitant too. You never know." He reached out and latched onto the handle of her suitcase. Then he said, with an extended hand, "Here, let me carry your computer."

"No thanks. I can handle it."

"Nonsense. Let me carry it for you. Don't worry, I'm not running off with it. Hey, when it comes to computers, I'm still learning. And that PowerPoint program, it remains a mystery to me. The other day, I bought this dummy book. Who would think I'd have to buy a book for dummies." He reached out for the laptop with a choir boy expression.

"Well—"

"It's entirely up to you. We've got a walk before we get to the car. Just thought, you know, I'd be of some help. And if you still have any reservations, I'll get you a cab. At least, I can report I put you in a cab. Right?"

"I guess so." She was already exhausted by the flight and packing all day in preparation for the moving company.

He strapped the laptop case over his shoulder and placed his hand on the suitcase as they recommenced their stride toward the exit. "Care for something to eat? They don't feed you anymore on those planes. I know of a small restaurant not far from here that might accommodate us. We can stop on our way to the Hyatt."

"Well," Danielle said with relaxed hesitation. She hadn't eaten since morning, but she didn't know whether she was more hungry than tired.

"Excuse me for saying, and I don't want you to take this the wrong way, but did anyone ever tell you that you have the most beautiful eyes?" He winked at her.

And the answer was yes, she had heard that line before. Inwardly, she cringed and ignored his unwanted advance. "I grabbed a bite to eat before I boarded the plane, but thanks for the invite."

Danielle pulled a strand of hair behind her ear. "How long have you been with the company?"

"Oh, PERC. I've been with them …" he looked upward as though calculating the time, "for around six years. They keep me busy. The pay's good and so are the hours." He fished out a business card from his breast pocket and handed it to her.

Danielle squinted and read "Senior Security Consultant—PERC" underneath his name. Her mind filled with whirling concerns. How long had he been watching her? For five, maybe ten minutes, she had been under the spying eyes of a stranger. The thought sent a sudden chill through her. The surveillance game didn't sit well. After the dinner meeting at the Four Seasons, the break-in at the firm, and Karen's admonition, she had reason to look closer at the company.

While they inexorably continued to walk toward the outer doors of the terminal, he removed his cell from his side and read a text message He shook his head and smiled before he returned the phone to its holder.

"Problem?" Danielle asked.

"No. A friend of mine wondered what I was doing. If he only knew I was with a New York lawyer. And a good-looking one."

Danielle had to admit he was handsome, but she was not in any mood for pick-up lines. She had heard enough in her lifetime. "You know, I can't fathom why I rate this special privilege. That is, you coming here to pick me up."

"I've accompanied employees on overseas trips. Met them at airports. Driven them around town. Shown them the sights. Are you new to Washington?"

"Not really. I attended the University of Maryland and interned at a Washington law firm before I landed in New York. And you?"

"Worked for a number of security companies. Then PERC came along. I've been with them ever since, but I must admit this is one of the better assignments. Oh, by the way, what time are you leaving for the office tomorrow?"

"I've a luncheon engagement with a partner of the law firm where I worked."

"Forget it, I'll pick you up," he insisted with a little boy smirk. "I'll have you at the downtown office with time to spare."

For a second, his charm caught her off guard. He seemed legit, with good intentions, but it didn't add up in her mind. Then why, she argued with herself, was blood rushing to her face? Why was there a lump in her throat? Why were there red flags all over the field?

As she spotted a ladies room from the corner of her eye, she studied his grip on her suitcase and the laptop swinging from his shoulder. "I've got to remove these contacts. I'm sorry, but could we make a little side trip? If you don't mind, I think what I need to freshen up is in my bag."

He shifted the weight of the suitcase in his hands; his eyes never left it. She didn't care about the suitcase, but leaving the laptop in his hands made her feel as though she had handed over her purse to a stranger.

"You know—lady stuff." She nodded toward the laptop.

He took a deep breath. "If I haven't convinced you, then I'll be glad to hand over your suitcase and laptop."

"I guess," she said hesitantly, "it won't take long."

He let go of the suitcase with a thud, his hands clenching the strap of her laptop bag for dear life. "I'll be right here," he said with a broad smile.

"I'll be just a minute. Honest." As she reached for her bag, he clenched anew.

"Don't worry. Where am I going to go, this is an airport, with all those cameras?" he stammered as he let out an audible sigh.

Danielle turned and bolted to the ladies room. She thought about Owen, how he used to tease her that although she was one of the most intelligent women he had ever met, she could be a downright ninny at times.

Once inside the ladies room, she exited through the opposite door and began to mingle with a few travelers. She rummaged through her purse for her cell. The first person she thought about was Karen—she could check to see if Lansel was legit. Fumbling with the cell, she punched in the number, praying that Karen would answer. But she didn't.

Danielle craned her head around the corner. *Gone.* He was gone. She stepped out into the main corridor and hastened her pace to where she entered the ladies room. Again, she didn't spot him. *Where could he have gone?* That's it, as she turned frantically in search of a men's room. Then it occurred to her in a flash. *Don't tell me that someone did it again.*

Minutes passed as she paced, thinking that this was not happening to her. Owen would say, "Calm yourself down. There's a simple explanation."

"No, it's not that, Owen. I saw my mother deal with death threats when she practiced law. It pays to think the worst. You're too trusting," she remembered saying.

By her watch, twenty minutes had passed. If there was an explanation, it was simple: Lansel had hooked her and reeled her in.

When she found a police officer and related what had occurred, the officer raised the palm of his hand toward her and pressed the send lever on the black microphone clipped to his shirt. "I need a page," he said in a calm and collected voice as he read from his notebook, "for a Jonathan Lansel."

Within seconds, an overhead speaker pitched loudly, "Mr. Jonathan Lansel, please pick up a courtesy phone for a message."

"Maybe he's outside waiting to pick you up," the guard suggested.

"Yeah, maybe," Danielle said with a sense of frustration.

Together, they traversed the walkway and stopped occasionally where cars were temporarily parked. She heard the announcement several more times from overhead speakers.

The guard faced Danielle. "Sorry, miss. There's nothing more I can do here."

"Doesn't it just grate you?"

Indignant, she reported the incident to the police station within the terminal. An hour later, she booked a room at the Hilton, thinking Lansel knew too much of her itinerary. How could she fall for a scam artist? She had arrived in Washington to take a job, not to play a role in some offbeat mystery.

As she stepped into a cab outside the terminal, her eyes caught the reflection of a small object stuck in the side of her purse. With her thumb and index finger, she extracted what looked like a straight pin with a small, almost microscopic pinhead. As she examined the object in the shallow light from passing traffic, her thoughts returned to Lansel.

Where did he get her picture? And he had an ID and knew everything about her.

Within minutes, her cab pulled underneath the portico. Tipping the driver, she headed to the front desk and handed the desk clerk the bug. "I think someone may have dropped this."

Finding a waitress at the bar inside the hotel, she ordered a drink and asked, "Where can I find an exit other than the front entrance?"

The waitress, in her twenties, understood. "Follow me."

Staying close behind the waitress, Danielle was led through the kitchen where she did attract a few stares from the kitchen help.

At a door, marked by an exit sign, the waitress said, "Outside, you'll find a walkway to the side of the building. Make a right. Follow it. You can find your way from there."

Danielle said, "Thanks," as she stepped into a pitch-black parking lot. The night sky was clear, and the cool air helped her regain her composure. She made her way to the ramp leading to the Hilton and found a lone cab with its driver dozing. She opened the rear door and jumped in.

The sleepy-eyed driver was startled as he craned his head over the seat.

"Georgetown. O Street," Danielle bellowed.

"But lady, we're pretty far from there."

"Drive!" She said firmly.

She had had enough. All she wanted now was peace of mind. Whoever stuck the tracking device in her purse would only find an empty room. Her eyes closed as the cab blended into the night with a thousand other cars.

# 16

With his feet perched on the side of his desk, Alex Preston underlined a sentence and then stopped to jot a note in the margin of a report cradled in his lap. As he read the weekend election quotes and news around the Washington Beltway, he reached for a steaming cup of Starbuck's coffee. Most of the campaign rhetoric was the usual fare about a candidate's past records and positions, which he believed belonged on the back pages of the newspaper. But he read the election reports, nevertheless, in search of an angle for a fresh news story.

On his desk amid stacks of books on political gamesmanship and the art of campaigning, newspaper clippings found a nestled spot between the dual computer monitors. His keyboard was layered over by newspapers set aside during his morning read and discarded tablet paper scattered the floor next to a garbage can a short distance away. When he heard the muffled jingle, Alex pulled on the handle of the middle desk drawer, snatched the receiver, and pressed it to his ear.

"Yeah, go ahead," Alex said, annoyed at being disturbed while he gathered his ideas for the day and especially when he hadn't finished drinking a cup of coffee.

"Alex?"

"Yes, who's this?" He ran his fingers through his hair, wondering how someone reached him on his private line. He pulled the remainder of the phone from the drawer, looked around, and then finally set it on the floor where he found a void.

"It's Danielle … Danielle Madison. Do you remember me?"

Alex dropped his feet to the floor and caught the report before it fell. "Of course. How are you?" he asked, surprised. Then he toned it down. "I mean, I was sorry to hear about Owen."

He and Danielle had grown up together in a small town outside of Pittsburgh. He was several years older than her and never paid much attention to the little girl who cheered at his high school baseball games. Years later, when he was in graduate school and she in college, they met at a mutual friend's birthday party. Only then, after becoming reacquainted, did he recall the cheerleader with the alluring brown eyes and forceful voice. But she was already thick with his frat brother, Roberts.

"Thanks. It was a shock, and I'm still—" Danielle paused. A few seconds passed before he heard her voice crack. "Ahem, I didn't want to bother you, but Brooke insisted I call. I wondered if you might answer a few quick questions."

Not wanting to pry into Owen's death, Alex decided to let her lead the conversation. He could hear her muted cry, for a moment, and then she cleared her throat.

"Go ahead."

"Well, I've taken a job in Virginia. And I'm staying here in Georgetown until I find a place."

Alex interjected. "If I can be of any help, please let me know. And maybe we could get together sometime; that is, when you feel up to it." He pictured her as starry-eyed, with a smooth, unblemished complexion.

"That would be nice," she said softly.

"We could catch up. I wouldn't mind hearing about your law practice in the Big Apple."

"It's different," she said with some hesitation. "Exciting. Challenging. But the cases stack up. It's twenty-four seven. When you're done with one case, there's another waiting for you. And that brings me to … but I really don't want to hold you back from your work."

"I'd be glad to answer your questions, with one exception: I hope you won't hammer me like a witness on the stand," Alex said, trying to lighten the conversation.

Danielle related her recent encounter with Wheeling, Mitchell, and Vittorio and her feeling of foreboding now that she had accepted a position with PERC. And then Cervasi, who seemed, from her understanding, to be egotistical, ruthless, and volatile.

Alex was aware of the company, hearing about their election tactics—some good and, naturally, some bad. "They're actually new to the DC area. I've heard Tony Cervasi is somewhat temperamental. Will do anything to win. But that's basically what you would expect from most political consultants. Though he's considered a good spinner." He pulled out a clipping from between the monitors. "And then you have the Clarke/McClay race in Virginia. Clarke, that's who your new employer supports, is far behind in the political race. He's been taken out to the woodshed, so to speak."

"So he's going to lose?"

"By a wide margin, but hey, that's politics. Even Cervasi knows that." Alex thought for a moment and then added, "And when it comes to blemishes, I don't think you'll find any consultant without a few skeletons in the closet. You mentioned Wheeling and Mitchell. What a pair. Like the same poles on a magnet. They really don't like each other."

"But they were drinking at the same table, and I didn't get the impression they were at odds with one another."

"That's my point. It's out of context, like sitting across from unflinching and opposing terrorists." He thought out loud. "That's politics for you."

"From what I understand, Wheeling was associated with Cervasi at one time."

"I've been covering politics for years. You get to know the players, the major and, on occasion, the minor leaguers. And that's true; they were a team on the West Coast. But you and I know it always boils down to money. I haven't seen Wheeling in years. Cervasi, though, has been surfacing here and there. Nothing out of the ordinary."

"What about Mitchell?"

"Your Honor, Counsel is prying into matters that are hearsay. How's that?" Alex asked. "I thought it sounded pretty good."

"Your honor, this is not hearsay. I'm asking whether the witness knows the person, and if he does, he should so state."

Alex retorted, "I think I remember. He's a political consultant in Boston. Does a good job, well respected, a player. He works between Boston and Chicago. That's all I know. Oh, one more thing—he likes to drink. I remember one time when I was covering a political election, and, well, never mind, maybe that's a story for another day."

"You? Now that's not the Alex I remember."

Alex studied his worn-out loafer, the one with the blown side, as he sat in his chair. "Well, let's just say that a journalist has to do what a journalist has to do."

"Is that right?" She paused for a moment. "And Carmen Vittorio?"

"While we've been talking, I've checked our internal political database, but nothing comes up. The only thing I can say is he must be Irish with a name like that." He raised his eyebrows. "That's it," he said as he jotted down the names.

"Can you do lunch?" Danielle asked.

"Fine. I'll make reservations for Friday night. I'll pick you up at six o'clock." When she didn't raise any objections, Alex said, "See you then." He hung up the phone and removed the sheet of paper from the tablet. He never considered for a moment whether he should have told Danielle that Wheeling, Mitchell, and Cervasi are cousins. He leaned on the desk and folded his arms onto the mess of strewn papers. He scratched his head. He didn't know if that fact held any significance.

Danielle set the receiver in its cradle and strolled to the window. Eight hours ago, she had arrived in a panic. But Brooke, like always, with her soothing advice similar to college, managed to ease the anxiety. And even Alex was receptive, although she hadn't spoken to him in years. To her, he was the handsome guy next door who was the consummate high school athlete and every girl wanted to walk hand in hand with him. She took comfort, and even was somewhat relieved, knowing that he lived nearby and was from her hometown.

With one tug on the chord, a burst of sunlight streamed through the Venetian blinds of the second floor bedroom window, making her squint until her eyes adjusted to the light. Unlike the view from her apartment in New York, she appreciated the blend of brown colors and shapes forming the cobblestone road and sidewalk, the wisp of mist coating vehicles, and the dry leaves from a hot summer clinging to an oak. The gentleness of early fall gripped her as she peered through the paned window.

Then, like a drop of water hitting a sun-drenched sidewalk, her inner smile melted. Across the street, a man wearing dark sunglasses stared brazenly at her. Instinctively, her hand covered her chest as she dropped back a step. Minutes later, he turned and sauntered down the sidewalk. She focused on his every step until he was out of sight.

Closing her eyes, she took a deep breath, feeling her veins racing with a mixture of fear and shock. Her luggage and laptop were gone. And now her nemesis was back, wanting something she could only guess at. Her attention was drawn to the bedroom door by a muted tapping sound that emanated from the hallway outside her room. She expected to hear a rap on the door, but she was greeted only by silence interrupted by the sounds of a grandfather clock chiming the hour from a downstairs room.

Gingerly, she returned to the window at a sharp angle. There, her eyes roamed in both directions, but she found only parked vehicles along the tranquil street. Then she heard the tapping again. It was coming from the attic. She breathed faintly, with her heart ramping up. Peripherally, she caught the curtain moving ever so slightly. The bedroom window shook. *The wind*, she thought, as she peered out the window to find trees swaying. When the wind stopped, so did the tapping. She realized that it was a branch from the oak hitting against the roof.

She found herself at the bedroom door, her sweaty palm curled around the doorknob. As she turned it, she heard the release of the latch and stepped into the hallway. There she called out for Brooke, but there wasn't any answer.

Walking down the old oak hallway, past the brass candle sconces, she stepped on a loose floorboard that caused a muted banging sound, and her anxiety climbed a notch. She placed her hand on the wall, carefully placing her foot on each wooden step as she descended the creaky staircase into the living room. To her immediate right was the kitchen, where she spotted a scribbled note on the table.

The note was written by Brooke. She was attending a conference for the day, but she left a phone number where she could be found. Brooke was in medical residency at George Washington University Hospital and kept odd hours. Danielle remembered how excited Brooke was when she found a townhouse within walking distance from the hospital. The high cost of the living accommodations did not deter her as she came from a wealthy family.

Danielle glanced at the side door to find a smiley face taped on the window. She half smiled until she realized it was taped from the outside. *Unusual.* She wondered about its significance, but instinctively she looked out the front window to the street. Finding nothing out of the ordinary, she shrugged and glanced at her watch.

"Wow," she said to herself, "this house has some serious hiccups. Since Owen's death, I can't believe how squeamish I've become." She heard another rafter ping overhead. "I don't know how I'm going to get use to this. In New York, it was sirens; here it's creaking." She shook her head. "There's got to be an answer to all this." As she swept the curtain aside, it seemed as though she was back home peering through the window at the birdfeeder.

But it was the eerie feeling of being alone in an old, strange house and the taunting by someone that increasingly unsettled her. She considered the possibility that the person who stood earlier across the street might have been a sightseer. That was not illogical, but she remained unsure. She seated herself at the kitchen table and imagined Owen. He'd walk into the room and sit next to her.

At ten o'clock, she realized she had little time to waste if she were to meet Denon on time. She used hair spray to hold a stray hair in place and then seated herself in a chair to squeeze into a pair of Brooke's heels, a half-size too small. Under her breath, she cursed whoever took her bag and laptop.

As she shambled toward a computer, situated on a slant-top secretary desk in the family room, she wondered whether her circulation had been cut off to her feet. She winced anew until she seated herself in front of the computer. There she typed in her password and accessed her e-mail. Karen had sent her the latest draft of the memo. Within minutes, she printed two copies.

Running out of time, she strapped her purse over her shoulder on the way out. On the stoop outside, she stood and rubbed her foot before she set off in the direction of Wisconsin Avenue.

She didn't get far before a man with a dark navy jacket exited a black sedan. He was parked around the corner but within clear sight of the house. Flashes of last evening reverberated in her mind. She made a dash for the main artery in Georgetown rather than waiting for a passerby to ask for help or retreating to the house.

Danielle bolted to the other side of the street, scraping her heel on the cobblestone and cleanly breaking the high heel off. She broke into an uneven jog, craning her head over her shoulder as the distance closed between them. Her gait was up and down, dragging her left foot on occasion. She darted onto Wisconsin Avenue into the path of a yellow cab. The driver jammed on the horn, slamming his brakes.

Without much thought, she opened the front passenger door and stretched her foot across the floor, ramming the gas pedal to the floor. The wide-eyed driver spit out a number of profanities before he got the cab under the control. By that time, they were a half a block away. Danielle glanced at the side mirror and didn't see anyone giving chase. But she wasn't taking any chances.

"Foggy Bottom. And make it fast." she barked at the driver, whose expression turned from one of outright shock to acute fear.

Her heart pumped double time, which made her grimace in pain. She looked over the back seat to find an elderly couple who wore expressions of panic. She gave them a short smile and looked through the rear window to find no vehicle giving chase.

"Don't worry, I'm …" Danielle said, gasping for air, "trying to catch the metro." Neither the wide-eyed driver nor the gasping passengers said anything, but she pointed to an intersection. "Drop me off there," she demanded after they had already traversed nearly a mile. While the driver found a clear spot, Danielle pulled fifty dollars from her wallet and handed it to him. "That's from the folks and me." Turning around, she said, "Thanks for sharing the cab. Have a great day." She jumped out but slowed at a nearby bench.

There she sat down and calmly took a deep breath. For a moment, it seemed passersby were staring at her, but the group of students merely followed a tour guide.

No one had chased her across the street or even attempted to catch the cab. Had she become a victim of severe paranoia? As her anxiety dissipated, she wondered whether she was in need of a shrink.

# 17

*Washington, DC*
*Monday, September 17*
*12:30 p.m.*

With time to spare, Danielle entered the Lafayette at The Hay-Adams hotel and waited for a hostess engaged in a heady conversation with a waiter about a snafu related to the seating of a party of nine. Although Danielle had made numerous business trips to Washington, she had never had the occasion to dine at the restaurant. Naturally, she would have preferred to experience this restaurant with someone other than Pierce.

As Danielle's patience and understanding had worn thin, so did the line of guests who muttered under their breaths about what was taking so long. Taking in the richly appointed room with its crystal chandeliers, her thoughts were interrupted by the polyphonic chime of her cell. She retrieved it from her purse but heard only a soft, static-filled phone line.

Another dropped call, and now her nerves sat on a razor's edge. Impatiently, she checked her watch and could feel redness in her face. "Owen's computer," she said absently as the words faded in her mind. She turned abruptly, but she recognized no one in the crowd.

"I'll be right with you," the hostess said.

"Excuse me," said Danielle in a firm but gentle voice. "Could you tell me whether Mr. Denon Pierce has been seated?"

Without looking up, the hostess pressed her lips together while she flipped through the page of reservations. Using her index finger, she ran down the list. "Yes, he's here," she said, relieved. "It's been one of those days. I'm sorry." Then she gestured to a waitress standing several feet away. "Please show this young lady to table thirty-five."

The waitress nodded approvingly and grabbed a menu. "Follow me."

Danielle pedaled awkwardly with the mismatched shoes as she picked her way around tables, avoiding waiters, in the growing cacophony of diners. She kept up, but she noticed a few stares at her gait and heard the muffled chuckles as she passed.

Seated at a white linen-covered table, framed by a large gridded window, Pierce was dressed in a herringbone suit and a red-stripped rep tie. From the half-eaten slice of buttered French bread and splayed files on the table, she surmised he had arrived much earlier. A double vodka on the rocks, his favorite drink, was nearly empty. He had a pleasant, almost alluring smile, the kind he used in trials. But it was a façade. And he had an uncanny ability to read a face—a twitch, a blink, a lip lick—as he looked for a weakness. Once he had it, then he would undress a witness.

She seated herself across from him, and he gave her a half smile while he spoke on his cell. Before long, he finished his conversation and flipped the cell shut. When he reached for his drink, she noticed his initials stitched into the starched white shirt and his gold cufflinks.

"How was your trip?" he asked as he ate the remaining buttered bread and then reached in the basket for a section of flatbread.

"An adventure."

"I can imagine with the way you walked in here." He raised his eyes from the memo while spreading butter over the cracker like bread. "Oh, before I forget. Karen called this morning to say your luggage and computer are at the airport. You didn't answer your cell phone." He swept the crumbs off the paper he was reading and onto the floor.

*Understandably*, Danielle thought, w*hen you're running for life, you react instinctively and block distractions.* Leaning partially over the table, she said in a raised whisper, "Denon, could you give me a minute of your professional time?"

Denon, not making eye contact with her, placed his bread on a side dish, pulled the napkin from his lap, and dabbed the sides of his mouth. He intertwined his fingers, and then with an icy stare and taut facial muscles, said, "I want you to know that we have pressing legal problems in various races. Not to mention the problems associated with the senatorial race. I suggest we defer your so-called problems to a later time."

For her, deferral was not an option, and she was not going to budge. "Listen, I took a job with this … this political firm on your recommendation. Since that time my best friend was murdered, my *luggage and computer* were stolen, and I was chased through a neighborhood by some lunatic. All because I came to Washington for a job."

With his face leaving nothing to the imagination, he retorted with a high degree of sarcasm, "Quite obviously, your personal possessions were not stolen. Owen's death was ruled a suicide—not a murder. And knowing that you're a runner, I hardly believe that a lunatic could catch you. I can't offer you advice except that you're stressed out. See a doctor." With an air of disgust, he leaned back into his chair.

She had seen Denon handle an unfriendly witness. He would dance around the subject, pointing out the inconsistencies, offer his view, and then coldly stare at you as though you're mistaken—the art of intimidation. Who better to learn this art than from one of the best? She locked eyes with him; she wasn't going to blink.

In a calm and collected voice, she broke the silence between them. "I know what happened. I'm not changing my mind. And by the way," she added in a revealing voice, "I met Leonard Wheeling— I'm sure you know him—and he had a lot to say. And it wasn't complimentary."

A calculating smile crept over his face, "Danielle, if you insist on talking to strangers, I can't help you. All I can tell you is that if you're not inclined to help, just say so. I'll call the office and have another lawyer assigned." He held up his hand as a waiter passed. "I'll need another drink, and the lady will have?"

"The same." She was not going to back down. Not much had really changed since her mother worked the courtroom. She knew she'd have to drink it slow, very slow. If she didn't, she'd need a seatbelt to ensure that she would not fall off the chair.

With a disarming smile, he said, "You continue to surprise me."

She had to agree that sometimes she even surprised herself. Her mother's fire rose within her, and she hadn't even noticed. She was being tested at every turn.

Denon turned his attention to the waiter. "Could you bring us an appetizer? Possibly a cheese, or make that a shrimp and cheese dip. Tell the chef to be creative. Make sure to put some bread wedges and chips on the side. And, oh, throw in more of that wheat flatbread." Once the waiter left, he joined her gaze of the White House and said, "Beautiful view. Instills a sense of pride, warmth, and power. Yes, ah, you were saying something about this Wheeling fellow. What did he say?"

She knew he'd dismiss her skirmishes as though they held no significance. When it came to power, it was what he thrived on. "Nothing. Nothing at all," she said pensively and with deep suspicion. Why should she reveal anything to him? "Do you know a Jonathan Lansel?"

"No, should I?" Pierce grunted. "Is this another one of those characters you met?"

"Merely asking. He is supposedly a security officer with PERC who was sent to pick me up at the airport. But instead he took my luggage and computer."

He arched an eyebrow. "Contact the airport. Need I make myself any clearer?"

"I don't buy your bullshit. And one more thing—Wheeling worked with Cervasi." She recognized that he had reverted to toying with her.

Denon picked up his pen and jotted a few notes in the margin. "I'll have to check into the matter with Tony." He shrugged his shoulders. "Right now, I really can't help you." He pulled a slip of paper from his jacket pocket. "Here's a name and number at Dulles. Call them to claim your possessions."

"One other thing," she snapped sarcastically, stuffing the notepaper in her purse. "On Saturday, FedEx delivered an express mail envelope addressed to you. It was from Owen." She studied his face, but it was blank—not even an eye flicker or a nervous twitch.

"Well … where is it, Danielle?"

"It was with my luggage."

"Now, let's go over your version of the facts. This Lansel fellow, who allegedly works for Tony, was supposed to pick you up and transport you from Dulles, but instead he steals your luggage and computer. Yet we now know you'll find them. Within your luggage is an envelope addressed to me and sent by Owen. Did I miss anything?"

"*No.*"

"So Lansel takes your luggage, and miraculously it shows up at the airport."

She shook her head. "No, I'm telling you this guy had identification that … that places him with PERC. I'm sure."

"Well, at least we know where your possessions can be found. Then all you need to do is hand me the letter when you retrieve them. It's plain and simple."

"Have it your way. But I'm sure it won't be there."

Denon muttered, "If it ever existed." A thin smile crossed his face. "Fine. Moving on, and before I forget, Tony wanted to know if you know anything about Owen's computer?"

"And why would I? And the answer is *no,*" said Danielle, barely holding her temper. "What's the interest?"

"Nothing, merely asking."

She retorted, "So am I."

Denon shook his head as the waiter showed up with the appetizer. He picked up a chip, and before dipping it, he said, "Danielle, these matters really seem bizarre," with a derisive chuckle. "You sure it's not your imagination?"

She realized the man had absolutely no understanding or sense of compassion. He often said that women didn't belong in the legal profession, that they gave it a bad name. She was not about to give him a chance to make up.

"Danielle, you've got to try this dip. You'll love it."

"No, thanks. I've lost my appetite." She wasn't going to let him rattle her. She could take the hits like a demo derby driver, but she could also wield punishment when the time came. A time would come, she knew, when his arrogance would be his own undoing.

Karen picked up the phone on the second ring. "Well, how did the meeting go?"

"Denon was his usual arrogant self. And to think he's going to make managing partner. He'll hack and claw his way to the top. All with that one thought: power. Enough with my epiphany. We're done with his research." Looking around her with rising paranoia as she stood lopsided on the platform at McPherson station, she confessed, "I don't know what's going on with PERC, or even Denon." With antidotal evidence mounting, she relayed the events of the past twenty-four hours to her.

"I wish I could have spent more time with my ear to the ground. Lately," Karen paused, "I've noticed he keeps the deck of cards closer to the vest. Meetings with names I don't recognize, phone calls with no caller ID, and he's even changed the password on his private e-mail account. Sometimes he'd give me access privileges to it. But now it's protected by a password, although I have my guesses what it might be. And then he hands off only the mundane matters to you and Greg. Mind you, I can't say he's hiding anything. Yet, deep down, I feel there's been a change. It's like a skipped heartbeat and then another. Nothing to give anyone alarm, but there nonetheless. If I had to say when, it probably started a little more than a year ago."

Danielle listened intently, but she held her mixed beliefs at bay given what had happened to her office. "If you ask me, he's gotten worse. Demeaning. Demanding. And I don't know why I put up with him. He forgot I put in my last day with the firm. I should have never said I'd stay on to help clean up the open projects. Sorry for the outburst, but he upset me." She shook her head in disgust. Then she continued in a calmer voice, "Right now all I can think about is my luggage and laptop. Who called, and where can I pick up my belongings?"

"A woman from baggage claim left a message with our answering service. Apparently, a passenger on your plane picked up your luggage and computer in error. She didn't identify herself, but she said to check with United Airlines baggage claim."

Danielle remarked, "Sure. Bogus. Plain and simple. That guy knew what he was doing."

"With all these mishaps, maybe you want to return to New York."

"Not yet." she answered without much thought. Her mind was on Denon and Cervasi. Was their relationship more than attorney-client?

"Oh, and one more item. That psychiatrist, ah, Dr. Greyson, called you. But he didn't leave a message." Silence filled the airwaves. "Did you know that he has a psychiatric practice for professionals and politicians? The reason is simple: they don't want to submit documentation to their health care providers for reimbursement. And I figure those patients in Washington are not in favor of having their personal lives under the microscope, if word ever got out."

"I'm not surprised at their not wanting the media to dissect their personal lives. My train is the next one, so I don't have long before I lose the connection." An older man brushed against her as he bolted for the train. *The nerve of some people*, she thought. *Access.* Then she whispered into her phone, "Access?"

Danielle pondered the question, which made her somewhat uneasy. "Never mind. I've lost my train of thought." She turned to find the train pulling into the station. "Before I forget, did Greg hand you the security tape—you know, the tape the night of the break-in?"

"No, he took it with him."

"I would assume security would time stamp each tape."

"You would think. What are you getting at?"

"Maybe it was me, and security gave the wrong tape to him. Why? I don't know. This whole thing makes no sense." Why would Greg want her to believe that she had something to do with the ransacked office?

"Danielle, you still there?"

She stared fixedly, oblivious to the train that had stopped. "I've got to go. My train's here. Call you later." She flipped the phone shut, slipped into the train as the doors were closing, and found a seat next to an elderly lady reading a book. The train lurched and then revved up to speed into a tunnel, with lights blinking ever so slightly. The squeal of wheels pressed against the rails jostled them at a curve, making her lean into the elderly woman, who smiled at the intrusion.

Danielle grappled with how Lansel, or whoever he was, would have known her flight number. And what about the tracking device? She was sure now that's what it was.

"Farragut West," pitched the overhead speaker as the train slowed to the station. At the station, her eyes swept those individuals hovering over her, looking for anyone whose gaze might have stayed too long. But no one seemed the least bit interested. The woman seated next to her marked the page in her book, *Positive Thinking*.

Once the train started, the woman removed her bookmark and began reading. Danielle skimmed a passage and read:

> We know the studies made to effect change … It
> starts with our conscious mind and the need to change
> our subconscious way of thinking. To effectuate
> change, you must place a seed in the subconscious

and nurture it through constant repetition. The subconscious mind remains an unexplored world.

Danielle lifted her eyes from the page to meet the elderly woman's extended frown. The woman shut the book and retrieved her metro pass. On reaching the destination, Danielle rose and waited for the doors to open. That's when she felt a tap on her back; it was the elderly woman.

"Your shoe's broken. There's a nice shoemaker not far from here on M Street. He might help you. Think positive."

Danielle nodded in agreement and pressed on into the early evening. "Access," she said to herself. "But access what?"

# 18

*Reston, Virginia*
*Wednesday, September 19*
*7:30 a.m.*

After meeting with McClay, Parks avoided the offices for the next few days. Surely his absence wouldn't cause a stir after his brother-in-law made it quite clear that all legal decisions reverted to Denon. That left only one concern—whether his meeting with the senatorial candidate went undetected. Not having received any phone calls or messages from his secretary or from his estranged wife, who always called if there was trouble, he felt at ease.

As he wended the tree-lined drive before the sun burned off the mist, Parks immediately caught sight of Clarke's black limo parked outside the main entrance. After reading the morning newspaper, he surmised the candidate's presence spelled trouble.

Parks thought an election could be engineered to an extent, but when a questionable congressman linked himself to whatever issue or special interest group that would slingshot his political agenda, it undermined the honesty and integrity of the person. And surely, when one considered Clark's voting record along with the media revelation that he'd received political contributions allegedly for his vote, it became obvious why he was perceived by the public as shady.

After pulling into his assigned parking space, Parks crossed the lot to a sidewalk that wrapped around the front of the building. When he came to the limo, he stopped to recall days when he arrived at nightclubs in San Francisco in a white limo. That was before he sunk his entire fortune in a fake investment.

He took a deep breath and gritted his teeth as he entered through the glass doors into the lobby. As he entered, Clarke, with a cell phone slapped to his ear, passed him at a heightened pace and gave him a curt nod. Parks exchanged glances with the receptionist, who rolled her eyes. With an understanding smile, he knew the congressman wouldn't mince words—he was hot.

It wasn't unusual to find candidates coming and going from their offices, but Parks, reading the same political polls, whether conducted by the media or undertaken internally by the company, wondered why Cervasi invested an inordinate amount of time in a losing campaign. Plus, they had hundreds of clients, but none seemed to receive the personal attention accorded Clarke.

Word, though, did leak out about a brouhaha between them several months earlier. Shortly thereafter, Cervasi called a meeting of his advisors to discuss the implications of the congressional race. Then, as Parks recalled, his brother-in-law had a lengthy meeting with Davis, a computer software engineer assigned to the IT department. Out of the ordinary, but a move made undoubtedly for a reason, and the reason had to do with a computer program kept under wraps.

There were times when an array of marketers, psychologists, strategists, and computer programmers descended onto the campus. At the time, Parks misattributed the visits to the development of a new advertising campaign. The flurry of activity continued for weeks, with late night meetings and programmers working around the clock. At one meeting, he recalled seeing Owen and Davis having a heated discussion. Then, as though they had settled their differences, the two of them parted ways. Thereafter, Owen could not be found on the premises, and all seemed quiet until his death.

A new spate of computer programmers scrambled into existence, taking up residence in the IT department. Parks could pinpoint two reasons: Owen's death, and Clarke's election bid.

Not wanting to wait for an elevator, Parks took the steps to the second floor. As he did, his thoughts returned to McClay. Would his brother-in-law leak pictures of immoral behavior of McClay, if they truly existed? Undeniably, the answer was in the affirmative. The pictures must exist, and if he knew Tony, it was only a matter of time before they would surface in some tabloid at the grocery checkout counter.

As he pulled on the stairwell door, Parks found Davis bounding down the hallway.

"Hey, Richie," Parks called.

Upon reaching the casually dressed programmer, who was wearing a wrinkled shirt, blue jeans, running shoes and a silver USB stick dangling from a gray lanyard rope hung around his neck, the wizard asked, "What's up?"

"Hey, I see the lights on every night. Do you guys come up for air?" No one got close to the department with its finger identification systems; it was a virtual fortress comprised of passionate overachievers.

Davis pursed his lips tightly. "We do what we have to." Then in a demeaning tone, he said, "I never see you lawyer types work hard. We've got deadlines."

In an attempt to diffuse the remark, Parks commented, "I understand it hasn't been easy without Owen."

Now Davis didn't remain stoic. "Between now and Election Day, we've got a lot of work. Is there anything else you would like to discuss?" With that he turned and continued down the hallway.

Parks kept pace. "Have you found a replacement for Owen?"

Annoyed, Davis stopped in his tracks. "If you want to recommend someone, have him send his resume to HR. He'll be screened. I don't have a whole lot of time. I've got a meeting to attend."

Parks wasn't invited to any meeting. "I'll walk with you. I'm headed upstairs."

"Suit yourself," Davis said smugly, choosing a faster pace.

Davis, midthirtyish, sporting a short, spiked haircut, never had time to talk. He was always on the go.

"I'll bet that storage device holds plenty of data," Parks suggested, referring to the silver USB stick.

With a deep frown and narrowed eyes, Davis answered, "Without a doubt, it holds plenty of data. If you need additional instruction, I'll arrange it. And no, I don't miss Owen. He was an employee, not the man in charge. You're looking at the brains of the IT department. I hope that sets you straight."

Parks nodded, thinking the guy had a complex. "I never meant to suggest that Owen ran your department or rivaled the expertise you bring to STAR."

With an expression of obvious concern at the mention of STAR, Davis said, "Good. I don't know where some people get off."

"Know what you mean. I always thought your direction was instrumental to the program, you know."

Davis hesitated with what appeared reflection, and then geared down to the subject at hand. "Yeah, it is. The program is on a need-to-know basis."

"Do you think the bugs will be removed in time?" Parks knew he was probing into a dark room, not knowing whether anything would be revealed. If it hadn't been for his encounter with Baker, Parks would have forgotten about STAR.

"If they would have listened to me, we wouldn't … never mind. Tony makes the decisions."

"They should have listened to you. Time is of the essence. I saw Clarke leaving the building only minutes ago, and he didn't look happy." Parks had no idea what to ask next. He was merely taking any avenue that might lead him somewhere.

"You got that right," Davis said, nodding with a smirk.

"But I didn't think Owen's absence impacted the development of the program that much?"

"From what I understand, Denon has already blessed what we're doing. Besides, I'm sure if Tony wanted your opinion, he would have asked."

"When's its introduction?" Parks probed, increasing his confidence.

"I told Tony, and I'm going to tell you. We're going as fast as we can. I've got the data files and the program with me. There won't be any more slip ups." Davis glanced down at the drive dangling from the lanyard around his neck.

Parks imagined Owen was the slip up. "How effective is this program? I mean, will this happen overnight?"

"Are you kidding? We were scheduled to start over Labor Day, but that never happened. Now we've got to make up for lost time. I think it should have the impact as promised. Changing a person's mind isn't easy." Davis glared. "Tony wouldn't listen to me," he said as he flipped the watch on his wrist into sight. "We're going to be a few minutes early."

Parks sighed, "Oh brother," hitting his forehead with the palm of his hand. "I need to tend to another matter. Thanks for jogging my memory. I almost completely forgot." He wheeled around and headed in the opposite direction.

"Do you want me to tell Tony you'll be late?"

That was the last thing he wanted his brother-in-law to know. "Don't worry about it. He wanted me to ..." He hastened his pace, never looking back, never completing his thought. Parks now had received confirmation that STAR was going forward. McClay needed to know.

When he unlocked the door, Parks heard, "Well, what did he say?" He flinched. Then his body stiffened, searching for the deep voice within the darkened room. His hand shook while he fumbled for the light switch. Finding it, he said, "What are you doing in here?"

Baker pulled on the chord that opened the blinds, letting streams of light into the room. "You've got a nice view from this office."

"You didn't answer my question," Parks stammered with his hands on his hips.

Baker spun around in his wheelchair, "I've got keys. Nothing goes unnoticed by me." His steely look turned to a grin.

Parks opened the bar doors in disgust. He dropped a few cubes into a glass and poured himself a Johnny Walker Black. Taking a deep breath, he positioned himself in his chair and propped a leg up on his desk. "So what's your angle? Money? Revenge? Obviously, you know everything that goes on around here." He raised his glass. "Drink?"

Baker shook his head, and with a wide grin, he said, "Motives are not your concern. Rather, it's you who should take care. And did Davis enlighten you at all?" Baker slowly moved in his wheelchair past the paintings. "These pictures truly stir one's imagination. No new additions?"

"To answer your questions, no," Parks said, studying Baker.

Then Baker wheeled abruptly around. "In the top drawer of your desk, you'll find two keys and a piece of paper in a white envelope. One key fits Tony's outside door. The other fits the inner door to the side room." For the next five minutes, he detailed the wine closet and the steel vault. "Inside, you will find what may surprise you. Do it before he changes the combination."

"What makes you think I'd do such a thing? That's a suicide mission." He hammered down the remainder of the drink. Dropping his leg to the floor, he pulled opened the drawer and grabbed the envelope.

Baker raised his eyebrows. "You surprise me. What one thing does Tony want?"

"That's easy. He'd do anything to get a senator elected," Parks retorted without hesitation.

"And what do you want? A job? No. Your money. Well, now we're closer. I think it's worth repeating that 'A picture's worth a thousand words.' For you, it's worth millions. Your money. Where do you think Tony got all the money? Look around you—this is your money."

Parks listened intently to what Baker was saying. Tony never had money before, but somehow he was able to purchase their business offices and the adjacent vacant grounds, which Cervasi referred to as the political campus. "Tony stole my money? Hardly."

"Who orchestrated the investigation? When the fox is in charge of the henhouse, there's bound to be no answer."

With a strong jolt of skepticism, Parks said, "Hard to believe." But the more he thought about it, the clearer it became. Tony took it upon himself to head up the investigation, and he also found nothing. Parks could feel the blood vessels in his throat begin to constrict, and his breathing became heavy. Could his brother-in-law have orchestrated the whole scam?

Baker opened the door. "Those records do exist, and you're not going to find them easily. Think about it. In California, Tony paid off people to gain a reputation as a political consultant. Without your money, he wouldn't be where he is today. He hit the lottery. And you are looking for someone you will not find. The clock's ticking."

The door closed, and Parks looked at the keys and the combination.

Standing next to the black BMW M6, Candecki donned a sand-brown jacket over a blue glen plaid shirt. When he traveled out of town on business, he always treated himself to luxury, and he especially liked the vehicle's responsive handling.

Pausing in the midafternoon sun, he admired the lush green lawn that reached from the glass façade building to Route 7 around a small pond where a fountain shot sprays of mist on a windy day.

The picturesque site reminded him of a country club like Pinehurst where warmth and beauty of nature blended with the surroundings.

Candecki thought that Tony Cervasi, catering to politicians throughout the country, had done very well over the years; better than he'd initially believed. He knew politicians had a boatload of money, and he obviously maneuvered himself into a position to receive the fruit of others.

At the front door, Candecki pocketed his Ray Ban sunglasses and entered. The exotic garden inside a cavernous lobby was breathtaking, and he imagined politicians being swept away by the splendor and, in the end, the price. Of course, Tony had his share of successes on the West Coast, and Candecki had heard the company was making slow inroads in the east.

"You must be Mr. Candecki," the brunette said, approaching him while he studied the cantilevered ceiling.

He turned his head to meet her gaze. "Yes," he said with a half-smile.

"Mr. Matalino is expecting you. If you'll follow me."

He took one last look around and shook his head in wonder. He followed her to a conference room connected to the lobby. The small room had a solid oak conference table, six leather chairs, and pictures of morning sunrises identified as lookout points in Virginia. The room faced the back of the main building where interlocking, edged sidewalks led to three other smaller buildings with glass facades.

Looking out over the courtyard, he heard Matalino enter the room with his strained breathing, a virtue of being overweight and a heavy smoker.

"It's been a long time," Candecki said, wheeling around and reaching out to shake Carl's beefy hand. But Matalino kept his hand to his side, and Candecki quickly withdrew his. Matalino hadn't changed over the years, although he had added considerable girth.

"Quite. Business not so good that you have to come this far?"

"If the price is right, I can travel." Candecki noticed the sour look on the dark-skinned, fleshy-faced Italian who once was his boss. Matalino was never one to quibble. His strong arm tactics were a thing of the past. Now more sophisticated methods for getting the job done existed. That's where he and Matalino differed. Candecki prided himself on using intellect and technology.

Matalino looked at him with disdain.

"Aren't you going to ask me to sit down?" Candecki asked, placing his briefcase on the table.

"You can sit anywhere you'd like."

Candecki raised his eyebrows and smirked inwardly, taking a seat at the opposite end of the table.

"Why are you here?" Matalino asked in a raspy voice.

"I was in town and thought I would stop in and say hello."

Matalino intertwined his fingers as though in prayer. "Obviously you want information. I know Clarke sent for you. We can handle our own business. We don't need or want your help."

"Her name is Madison. She's a New York attorney who's supposed to start working for the company in a few weeks. Her boyfriend committed suicide," he said, clearing his throat, "and he developed a program. And Tony wants it back. Need I say more?"

Matalino sat bolt upright in his chair. "What do you want?"

"My, my. That's no way to treat a guest. I may have information for you. Information you might find helpful."

"Go ahead."

"Ah, but we failed to talk about price."

Matalino slammed his hands on the table. "You don't have anything," he sneered.

Candecki broke into a wide smile. "That's where you're wrong. Things haven't improved very much since the last time we worked together. But this job is like taking candy from a baby."

The last comment knitted Matalino's eyebrows. "It doesn't belong to you."

Candecki tilted his head. "You're right. But if I find it first. Well, the price will go up. That is if you want it back."

"You can't use the program."

"Maybe so, but there might be someone who can."

Matalino's face reddened with anger.

"Carl, you don't need to get mad. I came here as a guest. Remember? I called you and asked if you might be interested in learning something. You hold your temper, and we'll get along just fine. The difference between us is that I bring professionalism to the job."

"Where's the program?"

"A demand?" Candecki brushed his coat with the back of his hand. "Now let's get something straight. Either you cooperate with me, or I'll take my business elsewhere."

"And what about your client, Philip Clarke?"

"Him? Well, he wants to get elected. He doesn't want the program. He called me to do your job. And since you can't, I thought Tony might offer me an incentive to find what you're after. And I assume, maybe, the computer where it's installed."

Matalino raised his head like a raging bull. "Where is it?"

"Not so fast. That's why I wanted to have this conversation. I understand Tony couldn't make this meeting. We could have solidified our deal. But I'm willing to let bygones be bygones. I know Tony's busy with campaigns throughout the country. So here's my proposition. You or Tony can call and leave an amount on my answering service. If I think it's reasonable, then I'll call you back."

"How much is that?"

"A hundred thousand would be nice."

"It's not worth that."

"It's worth whatever a senatorial election might be. And if it's worth money to Tony, then it must be worth something to someone else."

Matalino clenched his jaw. "Tony won't pay."

"That's Tony's decision. I was prepared," Candecki said, picking up his briefcase and tapping the side of it. "You tell Tony to leave a message. And don't make it too late."

Matalino opened the door and stared into Candecki's dark, arrogant eyes. "Watch your back, you never know."

Candecki grinned. "Same old Carl. And by the way, this is a fancy place. Did you rob a bank?"

"Investors."

"I'll bet," Candecki said with a sly smile. "That's why Tony can afford to pay me. I can find my way out." He extended a business card, but Matalino ignored the gesture.

# 19

Leaving work before 5:00 p.m. on a Friday was unusual for Alex, but a dinner date with Danielle Madison was special. A week ago, he scheduled a dinner with her, but she later cancelled. Thinking she had brushed him off, he was actually surprised by her phone call earlier in the week. Although he had heard that she handled a number of political cases that ranged from influence-peddling to political corruption when she worked the New York law firm, he resisted any thought to call her. His interest in her went far deeper than a professional contact.

As he exited his Nissan, he thought that the night had already started on the right foot. After all, he found a parking space with ease on the crowded streets in Georgetown. And he avoided another chicken banquet and political speech, which was a plus, when he considered Danielle and the candlelight dinner he had planned.

Standing on the red brick stoop lit by lanterns on either side of the front door, Alex reached for the black iron lion's head knocker and rapped several times. As he waited, he pondered whether the passage of time had changed her. When he last saw her, she had shoulder length hair, shapely lips, and dazzling brown eyes. Lost in thought, he didn't notice the door had opened widely.

"Are you going to stay out there?" Brooke asked in a witty voice. He stepped in, and she closed the door and threw the deadbolt. Wearing a pair of blue jeans, an oversized sweater with an insignia of Georgetown in black, and barefooted, she resembled a teenager rather

146

than a first year medical resident. "You can join me. I'm chilling out, watching TV between cleaning up from dinner. Danielle's running about a half hour late."

Clearing his throat and forcing a smile as he seated himself, he felt as if he were under the microscope of Brooke's gaze. He shifted his weight in the chair and blurted out, "Nice day. At least it didn't rain." Similar to a college student seeking the approval of a roommate before meeting his date, the awkwardness showed as he took a short breath and let it out.

"Are you nervous, Alex? You look a little pale." Brooke threw the dish towel over her shoulder and set down the glass she was drying on the end table.

"No, not really." He shook his head, but who was he kidding. This was a blind date. And what would he say if she had changed drastically? Her voice, at least, sounded like the girl he remembered.

"Sure," Brooke said satirically, "I understand. Danielle's a nice person, so let's keep it that way." Seated in a chair opposite him, she continued to stare fixedly.

"Very funny," Alex said, shaking his head.

"On a more serious note, I wanted to share this with you. If she seems ... uneasy, just be empathetic. I'm sure everything will pass in due time. A little bit ago she was rifling through her laptop case and mumbled something about a stolen letter. And how is she going to face her boss without it? She buried her head in her hands. And said something like 'why's this happening to me?'"

"Is there something wrong with her?" Alex questioned.

"No—at least, I hope not." She stood, picked up the glass, and walked around the chair in which she had been seated. "I wouldn't be telling you this if I didn't trust you." For the next few minutes, she described how Danielle related the incident at the airport; the tracking device at the hotel; the tail outside the house; and now the return of her supposedly lost luggage and computer without the envelope. She arched her eyebrows. "Considering Owen's death, she's been through a lot. But I'm not ready to say it's delusional. If she's right, then it's all very suspicious. And that leads me to my concern."

Wide-eyed, he could feel his mouth going dry. This was certainly not what he had expected.

"And what's the worst. All these episodes might represent an early manifestation of chronic stress or the onslaught of a nervous breakdown. It might be repressive conduct related to Owen's death, which, by the way, she steadfastly maintains was not a suicide. But I lack sufficient clinical information and observable symptoms to place a specific diagnostic label on her condition."

"Thanks for the words of wisdom. You're a real confidence builder," he replied. He recalled Danielle's call about Wheeling, Cervasi, and Mitchell, making him wonder whether there was more than she revealed to Brooke or him.

Brooke continued her mini-epiphany. "You see, the application of the term nervous breakdown constitutes a label for a number of symptomatic disorders—for example, clinical depression, panic disorder, or an anxiety attack, just to name a few. These traumatic events can have an effect on a person, leaving him or her with lasting mental scars. And ..."

Tuning out Brooke, he replayed his conversation with Danielle in his mind. He never had a chance to further investigate the names she mentioned, but now he wished he had. From his distant thoughts of the other day, he looked up to find Brooke studying him. "I've heard enough. I get the picture." Hearing a creak at the top of the steps leading to the second floor, his attention was directed toward the staircase, and the butterflies returned to flap inside him.

He saw the black suede heels attached to legs in black stockings, draped in a black dress with a pleated skirt and a halter top. Her hair, parted to the side with a slight bang, giving her a peekaboo style, framed a face with a clean and faultless complexion.

Danielle reached the bottom of the steps and examined him. "You haven't changed." The twinkle in her eyes and her alluring smile caught him speechless for a moment.

"Nor have you," he complimented. He couldn't fathom how this small-framed individual with a sensuous smile could have an aggressive and antagonistic bend in her like a trial attorney. Quite frankly, he didn't mind being tethered to her for the evening even if she did exhibit unusual behavior as described by Brooke. "I've made reservations at 1789, which is not far from here; the restaurant is known ... for just about anything that peaks your palate."

"That's fine. I know where it's located, and I think the walk might do me good," she said with a sheepish glance at him and then Brooke.

"Good." He checked his watch. "We should get started." With a broad smile, he winked at Brooke. "I'll bring her home early."

"I'll catch up with you later. Have fun." Brooke gave a responsive wink.

Alex took Danielle's arm and escorted her out the door. They descended the steps to the sidewalk. As they made their way across O Street toward Thirty-Sixth, she abruptly slowed her pace.

"Something the matter?" Alex questioned.

"Did you see him?"

He strained his eyes in an attempt to catch a shadowy figure in the wisp of light cast by the row houses.

"There behind the tree," she said in a voice coated with fear.

He turned and couldn't make anything out. "If you'd like, I can drive. My car's not far from here." Maybe she was a little paranoid. Either his eyesight was bad, or her night vision was keen. All that he could make out were tree trunks and cars shaped by the specs of light from indoor lamps and outdoor lights. "Let's cross here. My memory tells me that the sidewalk is in better shape, and we should have better footing. Crossing the cobblestone street, she continued to glance now and then over her shoulder.

He kept a watchful eye and occasionally listened for footsteps behind them, but he couldn't confirm what she was saying. Trying to make her feel at ease, he said, "Now, tell me about what you've been doing in New York, and when do you start your new job?" He didn't want to rehash Owen's death or the relationship she had with him.

Warming up, but with an air of caution as she involuntarily looked over her shoulder, Danielle said, "I'm scheduled to start in November. I'm meeting with an HR representative on Monday. We're going over the benefits and the usual employee matters. But for now, I'm acting as a consultant to my old law firm." They walked a few steps before she said, "Ann Burk, I don't know if you remember her, was in my sorority. I lived with her in New York. She's engaged to Greg Myers, who's also a lawyer." She turned and faced him, "Ann was the one who put me onto Wheeling. I don't know if you had the time to investigate him."

He searched for words. "Sorry to disappoint you, but I had a number of deadlines this week, so my information is sketchy at best. Years ago, according to what I've uncovered, Wheeling and Mitchell were indicted for a host of election violations in California. The allegations included, among other things, false statements, election fraud, and graft. You get the picture. Anyway the buzz on the street was Tony Cervasi was involved. Apparently the only witness met his death when the SUV in which he was riding lost its brakes and plunged off a canyon road. The matter was eventually dropped." His attention was drawn to a car that parked on the opposite side of the street, but the occupants never emerged.

At the corner, rather than taking a direct route to the restaurant, he decided to take a longer, out-of-the-way route just in case. He didn't want to alarm her, but he did pick up the pace. "And then Cervasi formed PERC," Alex reported, "and he seems to have made it. In the world of politics, a lot of horse trading goes on. Deals we don't want to know about. Wheeling is a player, but now he stays under the radar. And Mitchell, he's quite loud and loquacious. But one thing's for sure, there's bad blood among all three."

"From my standpoint, it makes me wonder."

"Sure. When I heard you were with those two, I asked the same questions. Rumor has it that they were the scapegoats. Cervasi set them up. But in the end, they all walked away innocent of any charges. After they separated, each went on to establish his own company. But only Cervasi seems successful."

"That evening, when I met up with them, I recall Mitchell made the comment that Tony can fix an election. And it wasn't said in jest."

Danielle ran through the timeline from the date of her recommendation for the job to the date she accepted it. "With Owen's death, I'm not sure it was the right move."

Alex replied, "I can't say whether it's good or bad. But one thing's for sure, Cervasi wines and dines a number of top-notch candidates. And from outward appearances, his firm seems to have done a good job; that is, up until now." Outside the restaurant, he said, "Vittorio remains a mystery." Although Alex sensed, without any basis, that the guy might be a lieutenant in an undefined organization.

"And that's the way he came across, saying if I want answers I should talk to Denon Pierce."

As Danielle entered the restaurant, Alex turned and spotted a camera lens emerging from the passenger side of a sedan parked in the middle of the street. He strained his eyes for a glimpse of the photographer, but the sedan slowly pulled ahead with its lights off. "I think we'll take a cab back."

After dinner, Danielle said, "I'm not in the mood for dessert. There's a matter more pressing that I've got to tend to." She explained to Alex what Owen had sent to her New York apartment.

"*Tonight?*"

At 1:00 a.m., they pulled into the driveway leading to a storage warehouse on the outskirts of Manassas. The large warehouse was fenced in and blanketed in yellowish-gold lights. Within view were security cameras mounted on the roofline, light poles, and the high chain-link fence.

Alex pressed the buzzer on the outside of the building, and he and Danielle were admitted. An Asian woman who was reading a book on how to speak English sat behind a thick pane of glass. Sitting amid a room full of black and white monitors, she seemed enthused to find something else to do during the wee hours of the morning.

Danielle said, "I spoke to Lisa this afternoon. She told me they were unloading the truck with my personal belongings this evening. I wanted to remove two cartons from storage."

The woman nodded again. She reached out and pulled a note pinned to a board hung on the wall. "I need copy of driver's license. Fill out form." She slid the form on a clipboard through an opening in the window.

After Danielle followed the instructions and submitted the documentation, the Asian woman stated, "I buzz you in. I take you."

As she and Alex entered the warehouse, the small woman waved for them to follow. Only minimal light from the few overhead florescent fixtures provided a sense of where they were, or for that matter, where they were headed.

Danielle remarked to Alex, "I don't know why I never gave more than a cursory exam of the books in those boxes."

"You take with you?" the Asian woman asked as they turned the corner. Through a glass-paned door they emerged into a larger room, where a number of storage lockers were stacked in the three-story building.

"Yes. I think we'll need to," Danielle said.

"You have combination for goods shipped to you?"

Danielle nodded and flipped through her purse for the combination. The large storage locker, the size of a small room, was lowered to the floor. Danielle entered the combination on the lock mounted on the outside. Within seconds, the large door turned on its squeaky hinges and the contents were revealed. She and Alex managed to remove a number of shipping boxes while the Asian woman stood and watched. Finally, they found the cartons and placed them on a dolly.

After Danielle signed the papers, which evidenced her removal of the property from the premises, Alex loaded the boxes into the rear of the Nissan.

"Now what?" Alex asked.

Danielle raised a pair of scissors. "We're not going to wait. I'll open the boxes now." Under the vehicle's courtesy light, she ran the scissors through the tape over the tops and sides of the cartons freeing the flaps. She looked at Alex before she pushed backed the flaps.

"Well?"

"We're going to examine each book."

"And what are we looking for?"

Danielle shrugged. "I'm not sure, but there must be something in these books."

# 20

*Reston, Virginia*
*Friday, October 5*
*1:00 p.m.*

With marked trepidation, Danielle resigned herself to the scheduled appointment made earlier in the morning with the director of human resources, Reanne Morgan. Coursing within her was a mixture of emotions. At the forefront was a mental picture of Owen when she had first exchanged glances with him at a conference where she sat in for Denon. That quickly faded to her standing at Owen's gravesite. Then she was yanked back to reality as she headed west on Route 7 to PERC, a company she now realized she knew little about.

Though she was mindful of Alex's preconceived notion expressed at dinner about the difficulty of working for a political consulting company with its wayward electioneering activities, she was unwilling to concede—at least not yet. Plus inside, she had the feeling of being in the crosshairs of the impostor who had rifled through her personal possessions. Her heightened sense of resolve to uncover the meaning of the intrusion had led her to keep the appointment.

Danielle strode into the foyer where a receptionist in her thirties with red painted fingernails sat behind a computer monitor busily pounding out a message on a keyboard. "Pardon me," Danielle said to the inattentive receptionist, "I have an appointment with Ms. Morgan."

The receptionist, with a glance of annoyance, said dryly, "Sign your name on the guest register and take a seat. I'll tell her you're here." She motioned with the back of her hand in the general direction of a waiting area.

Surprised initially by the inhospitable response, she spun around and retraced her steps to a black leather sofa, chairs, and tables across from an atrium. After taking a seat, she pictured Owen as he entered the lobby smartly dressed and clutching a paperback book. With a Bluetooth ear receiver and a smartphone holstered to his belt, he was eerily wired to technology. And it wasn't unusual to find him with his nose in a book, reading something about computers.

While waiting, she found a political magazine splayed out on the mahogany and smoked-glass coffee table. The décor of the lobby was quite unusual, with its exotic birds perched in cages nestled among tall ferns and palm trees. From what Owen had told her, it was designed by the chairman and CEO of a dot-com company that had formerly occupied the building. As she sat, the soothing sound of a waterfall similar to a brook in the woods relaxed her raw nerves.

Her attention was drawn away by a petite, prim-looking woman emerging from a corridor leading into the lobby with a notepad in her hand. She had gray hair with wisps of black and wore a houndstooth suit. Walking at a hastened pace, she approached the receptionist, who nodded in Danielle's direction.

As the woman closed the distance between them, she said, "Ms. Madison," in a timbre similar to a schoolmarm, "You're early for our appointment. I'm running between meetings. If you'll follow me."

"And you are Ms. Morgan?" Danielle asked in an attempt to slow the agitated woman.

"Right," she replied as she stepped smartly across the lobby to the elevators. She impatiently pushed the elevator call button several times and glanced at her watch. "You can wait in your new office until I call for you. It shouldn't be too long." Entering the elevator, Reanne closed her eyes and massaged her forehead. The ascent to the third floor took less than a minute. As they emerged from the elevator, she scurried down the corridor. "We can take up your questions when we meet later."

Between the receptionist and Reanne, Danielle wondered whether their insensitive attitude was contagious. She didn't say anything, hoping to discuss her employment at a later point.

Reanne barged through the outer door to the legal department, startling the secretary seated behind the L-shaped secretarial desk.

"New hire. I don't have time to talk. Show Ms. Madison her office and give her a tour." She turned abruptly and headed out of the room.

Danielle smiled appreciatively at the receptionist, who had a transcription headset draped around her neck.

"Call me Candy, but my real name is Cadance," she said as she extended her hand. She had shoulder length hair coiled in strands of brown and was in her early thirties. "I didn't expect to meet you until after the upcoming elections," she said with her head slightly tilted to one side and a questioning look.

"Well, I don't actually start until then, but I thought about getting a heads-up while I'm in Washington looking for an apartment." Danielle's interest in Owen's activities leading up to his death pervaded all other thoughts. "I hope I didn't cause Ms. Morgan any unnecessary stress. And call me Danielle."

Candy shook her head. "Morgan's that way. If she's pulled out of her daily routine," she said, rolling her eyes, "she can't be bothered. Don't worry. She'll get over it." She shrugged her shoulders. "You never know what mood she's in. I ignore her, or maybe I am accustomed to her habits. She gets her orders from the powers above. But welcome aboard—I'm looking forward to working with you." She put on a pair of magenta rim glasses.

"Don't let me interfere with what you're doing."

"Not a problem, in fact, I needed a break. Mr. Parks sent me several lengthy voice memorandums by e-mail, which I need to transcribe. Gives me something to do with him flying in and out of the office. He's gone now." Candy edged around her desk.

"He's probably busy around this time of the year," Danielle suggested, in an attempt to learn more about her future boss.

"Hardly, I've been here for the last two years, and he doesn't work that much. But lately he's been doing a lot of research, making all these calls checking the registry of corporations and tracking down individuals. And he's been so busy, it's actually not like him. Come on, I'll show you to your office."

"Oh, by the way, where is the IT department located?"

"They're upstairs. Why? Is there something you want to know?"

"No, just wondering. Owen Roberts was a good friend of mine; I don't know if you knew him."

"Shame about his death."

"Yes."

"You just never know, do you?" She glanced over her shoulder at the phone planted on her desk. "If anyone calls, the answering machine will pick up. Come on."

As they sauntered down a short hallway, Danielle turned and admired the stunning artwork of hot air balloons in flight depicted against varied backgrounds of sunrises and sunsets. For a moment, she imagined a free-spirited glide across the greenery of forests and open fields on a crisp, early morning flight, losing herself in silence.

"Not bad. What do you think?" Candy asked, referring to a piece of artwork captioned as a hot air balloon race.

"I'm impressed. You do get a soaring feeling. It's almost like you could touch the treetops in a few pictures."

"Yeah, but that's not what they say about the legal department."

"Oh?"

"This collection of artwork," Candy gestured, "came from a dot-com company. You'll find other collections in other departments, but this one somehow becomes the butt of a joke upstairs in the boardroom. Well," she chuckled, "someone failed to tell the interior designer this suite was going to be occupied by lawyers."

They walked around the corner and past two smaller, unoccupied offices until she stopped and pushed opened an oak door. She allowed Danielle to cross the threshold first. Inside the spacious office, carpeted in a plush emerald green, was a large, mahogany desk with a matching bookcase extending the width of the room. Three deep, green leather guest chairs, with mahogany wood features, were pulled up to the front of the desk.

"Why don't you make yourself at home? I've got to clear my desk of a few things. Then I'll take you on that tour before Morgan returns. If you need anything, just call me. You'll see my name on your phone," Candy instructed. "And one more thing—don't let Morgan get to you. I think she was thrust into the position without knowing a damn thing. I mean about human relationships. See you in a little bit."

"Thanks." Danielle walked around the room, admiring the lavish accommodations. Running her hand over the finely polished desktop, she wondered about the executive from the dot-com company who occupied the office before the implosion of the industry. The office overlooked a vast courtyard. She was somewhat aware of the plush office suites from talking to Owen, and now she occupied an office comparable to the head partner at HBR.

"Hello," said a deep voice from behind her.

Danielle jerked around suddenly and found a bespectacled man, seated in a wheelchair, with a steely jaw and an expressionless face.

"Sorry, I didn't mean to startle you. I should have knocked." After he reached the center of the room, he extended his hand. "The name's Les Baker. You must be … Miss Danielle Madison. I had heard you might be visiting with us today. And I wanted to welcome you."

"Why, thank you." Danielle shook his hand with a firm grip.

"Make sure that you take time to get outside and smell the roses, that's what they say. And from this view, well, I'm sure you'll be out there quite often." He maneuvered over to the window.

"It reminds me of McKelvin Mall at the University of Maryland."

"Know the place, and you're right. It actually does have an uncanny resemblance," Baker said, turning his head to look at Danielle. "I was sorry to hear about Owen. Denon filled me in. I had the pleasure of working with him on several occasions. The loss makes me think how vulnerable we can be," he said, shaking his head.

Danielle stared vacantly at the courtyard, feeling the ebb and flow of the loss inside her. "It's always nice to hear he was appreciated." Funny though, she never recalled Owen mention working with a Les Baker. His voice rang rather hollow. And the exchange of pleasantries seemed more mechanical than sincere.

"I also have a deep interest in computers—" Baker paused. "He spoke so highly of you. I was under the impression, from the way he spoke, of course, that the two of you would be married." He exchanged glances with her. "What a great loss to lose your best friend and confidant. I've had such experiences in my life."

Danielle inventoried his face, the deep brown eyes and the furrowed brow. "Do you know what he was working on?" She chided herself for speaking before she thought. She barely knew him, much less if she could trust him.

Baker furrowed his eyebrows. "To take one from you legal eagles, I'm not sure I understand your question," he said in a matter-of-fact way. "Although I use those damn computers every day, I'm not sure how they work with those bits of data formulated in 0s and 1s."

She hesitated, thinking that she had no other choice but to inquire about a program. "On some type of computer program?"

"Huh? Not exactly. I leave the programming to the IT department. I really can't answer your question. They're always working on computer programs in there."

Baker removed a tablet from a pouch on the side of his wheelchair and jotted down a few words. Then he shoved it across the desk. The cryptic note read: "Meet me at the Reston Towne Center, Mercury Fountain, 8:30 p.m. They're listening." Danielle reread the note and was about to ask what he meant when he raised his index finger to his pursed lips. He pointed to the vents, the lights, and the phone and then nodded. She placed the tablet into his outstretched hand.

"I have a couple of matters to tie up before this afternoon. If you need anything, ask Cadance to track me down." He tore off the top sheet of paper and stuffed it inside his shirt pocket. Then he pivoted the wheelchair and headed out of the room, stopping to say, "See you later."

Danielle froze as her eyes examined the room with a new purpose, thinking her apprehension about the company was confirmed. She stepped across the room and closed the door. Next, she kicked off her shoes, and her feet sank into the thick carpeting as she approached her desk. Overhead her eyes were trained on a vent, and using a chair as a step, she climbed to the top of her desk. On tiptoes, she tried to peer into the air vent. Nothing. What did he mean they're listening?

"Do you have a problem?" asked Candy, who was standing in the doorway.

"No," Danielle said, startled. "I was sitting at my desk, and I thought there might be some type of control to limit the flow of air." She jumped and managed to land firmly on her feet.

"I'll get maintenance up here to check it out for you."

"That will be fine."

Candy glanced at the air vent and then said, "I got a call from Morgan. She wants you in her office in five minutes. We'll take that tour later."

"Great," Danielle said, wondering if they would pass by the IT department.

As they exited the legal department, Candy asked, "Isn't Les Baker a little odd?"

"He seemed fine. Does he work in the legal department?"

"Heck, no. He's the maintenance engineer—so they say—but it's odd. He seems to opine on various matters like elections, politics, financial, and he's sharp. And if you ask me, he knows too much. You know the type. Seems to have an answer for anything and everything. What did he want?"

"Nothing, really. I guess he wanted to welcome me aboard."

Candy raised an eyebrow. "Fat chance. He's quiet, but he's like a cat with his ear to the ground, if you know what I mean. Like I said, he knows everything that goes on around here. Sometimes I start early in the morning to get out of here sooner. I see his van parked outside. Other times, I work late into the evening if someone wants to push something out. He's still here. He's always wandering around. I really don't know what he does. Don't underestimate him. He has Cervasi's ear—you know, he knows about surveillance, security, and who knows what else—sometimes I wonder who's running this place. I try to stay clear of him." She opened the stairwell door, and they descended to the next floor.

Danielle's attention was drawn to a security camera mounted on an overhead wall bracket. "They must have tight security around here."

Cadance chuckled. "If you're referring to that camera, it's not connected; none of the cameras are in working order. The security connections were stripped from the premises before PERC bought the building. That is, except for the wiring in the walls, with all those RJ45 and fiber hookups, so you know what was important: the computers. But we're slowly getting around to security. A few months ago, Mr. Matalino, wait until you meet him, he's a piece of work, had a company install a key card system. They're still working out the bugs. Maybe in a few months. Who knows?" She opened the door to the second floor. Halfway down the hall, she said, "Here's Morgan's office. I'll tell her secretary to call me when you're done."

As Danielle stepped into the personnel office, she found Morgan engaged in a heated conversation. "Get him on the phone for me." Quite obviously, Morgan was in a huff like a pressure cooker about to let out steam. Her foot was tapping, and she wore a scowl on her face. She turned toward Danielle and gave her a fleeting smile.

The receptionist nodded and dialed the number. When Danielle walked into the personnel department's office, she immediately recognized the floor plan. It was very similar to the legal department except for the artwork dedicated to flowering trees.

Morgan spun around and marched down a corridor presumably to her office. "Are you coming?" She half barked.

Danielle caught up, and Morgan recommenced her pace. Her office was rather plain. She had two beige, metal, lateral file cabinets, bookshelves of reference materials on payroll and personnel binders, with each book standing straight upright, a desk, a credenza, and a small, oval conference table with seating for four at the other end of the room. On her desk was a notepad and a stack of papers neatly arranged, a computer, and phone.

Morgan pointed to a chair across from her and then picked up the ringing phone. "Morgan," she proceeded in a deep authoritative voice. "Last night, your cleaning people failed to clean one wing of our building. My assistant told me you were short workers, but that's no excuse. Either you do your job, or I'll find another cleaning company." She thanked the person and then replaced the phone in its cradle. "I swear he deals in illegal immigrants. They can't even speak English."

Without saying another word, she opened the center drawer, retrieved a set of keys, and walked over to a filing cabinet. There she unlocked the drawer, retrieved a file, and returned to her chair. After putting the keys away, she opened the file and said to Danielle, "I've got a number of papers for you to complete, including medical and insurance plan applications and state and federal tax forms. Also, our company requires your signature on a confidentiality agreement, but as you know, being an attorney, we want you to review the agreement with an attorney before signing it. Is that clear?"

Danielle nodded, thinking about Owen's personnel file. The medical report issued by PERC said Owen was being treated for drugs, and he was seeing a shrink. She could only wonder what was in his file.

Morgan secured an envelope from a desk drawer and stuffed the applications and tax forms inside. Next, with her head high and her back ramrod straight, she accessed her computer. But it soon became apparent she was having trouble. With knitted eyebrows and tightly pressed lips, she jammed her fingers into the keys. Then she pulled open a side drawer and snatched a file. Laying it out on the desk, she then mouthed the password in a whisper. Once the computer responded, the redness drained from her face, and she replaced the file in her desk.

"I've printed out the confidentiality agreement, and you can pick it up at my receptionist's desk on your way out. Do you have any questions?"

"No."

"Good." Morgan checked her watch. "Cadance will now give you a tour of the complex." With that she rose from her chair, extended her hand, and said, "Thank you for coming. Have a pleasant day."


"What do you think?" Cervasi asked.

Matalino sat, fingers intertwined, with a cold, calculating stare. Moments passed before he spoke. "I think she's on to us, Mr. Cervasi. The other night we found her with a newspaper reporter. And it was Alex Preston, the one who's covering the senatorial race. What other reason would she have to be with him?"

"Yes, you may be right. I never liked Denon asking her about Owen's computer. He has a way with words and can be confrontational." Cervasi removed the stopper from a wine decanter and poured himself a glass of red wine. He took a sip and then replaced the stopper. "She denied having it, but I wouldn't expect any less."

Matalino sat impassively.

Cervasi continued, trying to rationalize her actions. "Odd. And she left no tracks on her computer, no e-mails, letters, or memos even referring to it. She's here for a reason. I checked with Denon, and she never said anything to him at lunch about coming to our office. She's not due to start for another few weeks." He drummed his fingers on the desk. "We're missing something, but I hope Denon didn't raise her suspicions."

Matalino cleared his throat. "And what about that letter you received? Maybe it was her who sent it?"

Cervasi picked up the FedEx envelope and read the return address: Owen Roberts, PERC Headquarters, Reston, Virginia. "Could be.

Someone wanted to put the fear of God in me. If it's her, she's not going to get away with it."

"I'm thinking maybe she's working with that news guy," Matalino suggested. "They're putting a story together."

Cervasi glanced at the outside of the envelope. "Find out how these two know each other. I don't recall a whole lot about this Preston fellow." He got up out of his chair and grabbed his glass of wine. While his mind churned through the facts, he watched the free-flowing water in the fountain on the lawn. Then he turned to face Matalino. "And if we didn't have Candecki breathing down our necks, or Clarke, that SOB, making all these demands on our staff, we would know who's behind this."

From a basket of Italian cookies at center table, Matalino grabbed an Italian wine cookie, broke off a piece, and dunked it in his wine glass. Wiping his hands on his pants, he said, while munching, "If I could have her for thirty minutes, I believe she would break."

"That's why you can't. We don't operate that way anymore, *capisce?*" Cervasi said firmly, knowing they didn't need the Feds snooping around.

"But we should because we're running out of time."

"We don't need more problems. We'll keep up the pressure. Get those answers, and if you need more help, you have my permission to call a few other boys in to lend support."

Matalino nodded. "It will be done," he said, and then he stood and made his way out of the room.

Cervasi looked at his glass of wine. Finally, he muttered to himself the words from the letter: "I know what you're doing."

# 21

*Reston, Virginia*
*Friday, October 5*
*5:00 p.m.*

Heading east on Leesburg Pike toward Washington, Danielle adjusted her rearview mirror and flipped on the radio. Switching between stations, a layer of jagged noise faded in and out, compromising the broadcast similar to the recent cell phone reception she experienced upon her arrival in Washington. Although disturbed by the dropped phone calls, she found it equally disturbing that Reanne Morgan, with whom she had made an appointment, seemed quite uneasy about a matter that concerned her.

After making a right onto Reston Parkway, Danielle slowed in order to merge into traffic. Glancing in the rearview mirror, she spotted a black BMW several car lengths behind her. For the next few miles, she weaved in and out of traffic, sped up and slowed down. The BMW stayed with her, but kept its distance.

She shifted in her seat, gripped the wheel tighter, and glanced frequently in the mirror before she pulled onto the gravel shoulder. The BMW slowed measurably, as though the driver was undecided based upon her decision to pull off, and then he sped off into the distance.

With the engine running and the air conditioning pushing out a rush of cool air, she considered her options. Ahead, she could find a suitable place to turn around and head the car in another direction, or she could wait there for an hour, maybe two. She cut the engine and slipped her cell from her purse. Linking up with Brooke's answering service proved rather easy. Danielle left the message that she had made arrangements for dinner with a person of interest at Towne Center.

Next, she punched in the number for HBR and was immediately connected. "Karen, did Dr. Greyson ever call back?"

"No. But Denon called and wanted to know with whom you were staying. Inadvertently, I told him Brooke Lang, a former classmate, and that you were both living in a Georgetown townhouse. I know that I shouldn't have told him, but either he asked the right questions, or his tongue wagging actually undressed the information. Sorry."

"That's okay. I don't think it's a problem." Danielle was a bit unnerved, questioning why Denon didn't ask her, and why he wanted to know, but that would have to wait. "I thought I'd pay Dr. Greyson a visit. I'm not far from Reston."

"Let me put you on hold for a second." A moment later, Karen said, "Got him. He's on Foundation Street. Here's the telephone number."

"I don't need it. I'm going to stop whether he's there or not."

"Then I'll send you a text message with detailed instructions."

Listening to Karen tapping on her keyboard, Danielle shut her eyes and leaned back into the seat. In a dreamy haze, her thoughts were drawn back to STAR and Owen's computer. Then she heard a thumping sound. She opened her eyes with a start. Standing outside her door was a tan-faced man with dark sunglasses and high cheekbones. His face was nearly pressed against the window. With an immediate jolt of fear flowing through her veins, she pressed back into the seat. And with a quick glance, she checked the door locks. He was wearing a navy blazer, blue pinstripe shirt, and khaki pants.

"Are you having car trouble?" the stranger asked in a loud voice.

Danielle could faintly hear him over the whiz of cars passing. She replied no in a startled voice, shaking her head.

He nodded with an impish smirk, gave her an examining look, and retraced his steps.

Danielle watched him open the door of the BMW in her side view mirror. He didn't budge as her eyes darted between the side and rearview mirrors. For what seemed like minutes, he remained parked, obviously waiting for her to make a move.

Karen asked, "Hey, you still there? Did you get the message?"

Danielle keyed the ignition, and the car came to life. "I got it." Danielle's eyes were glued to the driver, who stared into her rearview mirror. Finally, the BMW spun out into heavy traffic and barreled down the road. She wiped the light perspiration from her forehead and took a deep breath. "I'm meeting Les Baker for dinner. He's a guy I met at the office this afternoon." Her heartbeat peaked and then ratcheted down to a normal pace.

"Know the name, he's spoken to Denon on a number of occasions. Though he hasn't called lately. I'd say maybe several weeks ago, he and Denon had a lengthy conversation." She paused and then added, "Did he ask you out?"

Danielle's hands trembled. "Not exactly. Not my type, and he's a bit older. I've got to run now; I'll call you later." With that, she shut off her cell phone. She muttered, "Access file. STAR." The words danced in her mind and flitted away as she stared vacantly. Awakened by the blast of a horn from a passing auto, her mind switched to why Baker would call Denon.

Her mind jockeyed between the past and the present, rehashing the events: no, she didn't have Owen's computer or the program, nor did she have a preconceived idea where she might find them. As for those books Owen had sent, neither she nor Alex found any messages, notes, or maps that might yield a clue. But they did find a thank-you note for the personal gift of the Jefferson treatise from the university's library. She had previously donated the first set of legal books he had sent her years ago to a public library. At the time, he told her if she didn't make use of the books he would donate them. And he did.

With a quick glance over her shoulder, Danielle found an open spot in heavy traffic and peeled out, leaving gravel in her wake. For the next twenty minutes, she searched in vain for the BMW in the parade of traffic until she arrived at her destination, Democracy Drive. Dismissing the encounter to overreaction since she hadn't seen her tail, she parked the car and moments later found herself reading the marquee inside a multi-storied complex.

Hurriedly, she found an open elevator, but before she boarded, she bumped into a person who exited the next elevator, only to identify him as the root of her quest.

"Oh, it's you." Greyson's eyes narrowed, and he appeared unsettled by her presence.

Danielle smiled inwardly; she had the element of surprise. "I thought I would save you a phone call."

Greyson hesitated, eyed her, and then, as though he had second thoughts, recommenced his stride.

"Hey, wait a minute," Danielle called out, but Greyson power walked to the door and was outside before she caught him. Now shoulder to shoulder, she said, "Let me refresh your recollection. You wrote that he appeared normal but exhibited tendencies of a drug addict. What was it, the shaking hands? The eyes? A staggered walk? Or was it something he said? Did he confess? Because I don't believe a word that was written."

Greyson stopped, cocked his head, and then without even a flinch or blink of an eye, started anew across the street.

"I know what you wrote. What did you mean he may need further consultation?" Danielle asked, feeling the adrenaline feeding on itself.

Greyson frowned, never looking at her. "I don't know what you mean." Raising a hand, he summoned a nearby cab, which did a three-sixty in the middle of the street and inched up to the curb. He opened the back door and gave her an unwelcome stare.

"Are you hiding something, Dr. Greyson? Why did you call my office? Did you have a change of heart? Did someone put you up to it? Which is it? And what about STAR?"

But Greyson, with one foot in the cab, said, "Don't tread where you may find answers you don't want to know, for you might find your life in danger. Leave it. We can't change the past." With that, he ducked his head and seated himself inside, locking the door. As the cab pulled out, he shook his head.

With her head spinning from the pain of reality and a sense of frustration, Danielle fiddled with her cocktail napkin at a table along the promenade of shops and cafes lining Market Street. *This,* she thought, *is coming together in some bizarre way.*

A waiter spirited out of a small Italian restaurant café and suggested, with an Italian accent, a fine imported cabernet wine from the Abruzzi province. She nodded, saying, "That will be fine." In what seemed only a minute, the waiter, with a white towel draped over his arm, reappeared carrying a full glass of wine.

At 8:15 p.m., her cell phone rang, and she answered only to hear a slight whistling noise like metronomic static. She slammed the cell down on the table. She knew that the caller ID would read unavailable, restricted, or private. This was not the first; there had been several other calls during the day. Intuitively, she began to consider the distinct possibility that she had attracted a stalker.

As daylight faded and the shop lights grew brighter, she could feel the emptiness inside her. She was caught in a web, and it all pointed to Owen. Her fingers ran around the rim of the wine glass, and absently she pondered STAR. *What did it mean?* Owen never said anything to her. True, he loved to experiment with algorithms and discuss bits of code ad nauseam with fellow programmers, but she had no inkling that he could be engaged in anything diabolical. But it was just like Owen to take chances and be a nonconformist.

"Would madam care for another?" the waiter asked as he lit a candle on the table.

Danielle looked up and said, "Yes, that'll be fine." She looked up and down the street, coming to rest on a shadowy figure. A clock chimed half past the hour, her patience had worn thin, and she stood up out of boredom.

From behind, a voice asked, "Going somewhere?"

A wheelchair emerged from the shadows as if drawn to the beacon of candlelight and maneuvered around a table until Baker parked it. "Sorry, I'm late. I had several business matters to tend to. I see you have already ordered." He raised his hand and caught the attention of the waiter.

After ordering a Manhattan, he continued, "I'm glad you came." His eyes strayed from her as he observed the patrons sitting around them. Leaning forward, with his elbows on the wheelchair's armrests, he whispered, "Within your office, there's a device to record your every word."

"And why would anyone do that?"

"Danielle—" he shifted in his chair. "When I heard about Owen, I was shocked. Saddened by his death. We were good friends, colleagues ... but he ... he took one too many chances, and I warned him. I couldn't change his mind."

A cold shiver ran down her spine. It was something she didn't want to hear, but she knew it was somehow true. "About what?"

Danielle's head was spinning with questions. *Why? What did he do? What does this all mean?*

"Have a drink, my dear," Baker said in a soothing voice. "Owen's project was shrouded in secrecy. I can't go into it here. This is far too public. But believe me when I say, we need to work together on this. We've got to stop them." He reached across the table and patted her hand.

Danielle looked down and slowly withdrew from his sudden grasp.

"You can't escape them."

"Who? What do you mean?" Danielle asked with increasing anxiety.

"They think you're hiding it. That's why I'm here to help. You've got to trust me," Baker said with a glint in his eyes. "I was working with Owen, and then—"

With a jolt of skepticism, Danielle recalled her conversation with Owen's mother about a heated exchange between Owen and Baker. But it was the vague recollections of an elderly woman who may have misinterpreted the incident. With examining eyes, Danielle focused on his facial expressions. He seemed genuinely interested in helping, with a sensitive demeanor, and making an effort to define the impending peril she faced.

"What do they have?" Danielle asked.

He paused and intertwined his fingers. "You know, Owen was protecting you. Danielle, I'm trying to help you. We need to trust each other. Please believe me, I beg you. Remember, I came to you, but," he said softly, "you need to give me his computer."

Between clenched teeth and short breaths, Danielle said adamantly, "I don't have it. That's the truth."

"He sent you the computer, the file, and I'm sure, the code." The flicker of light reflected in his eyes. "You hid them. Let's be honest with each other. I'm trying my best to assure you that we have the same interest—your safety," Baker said with a brazen and scornful chuckle. "Isn't that so?"

"No. No," Danielle protested. "He sent me books, a treatise. I don't have what you want. Believe me." She began to hyperventilate.

"Okay, have it your way. You've got STAR," Baker said.

Danielle grabbed her purse.

Baker grabbed her arm in a vice-like grip and leaned forward until she saw his penetrating eyes. He continued, tilting his head and leaning closer to her. "STAR. Access file? You've got it." Then, in a soft, hypnotizing voice, he continued, "*Source code*. Where is it? Tell me ... tell me."

Her eyes glazed over, staring at Baker in silence. Her eyes wanted to close, but they couldn't. She could hear the echoes of the voice deep within her. The words resonated, stirring in her mind the command: *Source code. Owen said, "Source code."*

"Did you hear what I said?" growled Baker with a glowering expression.

The sounds of shattering glass drew her attention. She snapped to attention and saw the stem of a wine glass resting at her feet.

"I'm so sorry." The waiter pulled the towel from his arm and handed it to her. "I'll get you another drink. It's on the house." The waiter picked up two shards of the wine glass. "It slipped out of my hand."

Baker frowned at the waiter. "You idiot," he murmured.

"Sorry, sir. Here's your drink. I'll be right back."

Baker tried again. "STAR. You'll remember. *Think*."

"I don't—" Her mind was fuzzy. She struggled to focus. *What the hell is going on with me*, she wondered.

He said with a devious smile, "I can help you only if you tell me." He tightly curled his hand around her arm.

His almost imperceptive nod to an outline of a figure lurking in the darkness made her recoil in fear. Wrenching out of his grip, she ran toward the café's entrance, hearing his words cut through the darkness. "You're not going anywhere."

Before she entered, she stole a glance over her shoulder only to find Baker had vanished. Retrieving her cell from her purse, she read the display: *no service. Damn,* she thought, *why don't they build more towers?* Her adrenaline was pushed to the limit. She shoved the phone back into her purse.

Looking side to side, her heart pounding, she spotted a bartender. Racing to the bar, she breathlessly asked, "Excuse me, do you have any public phones?"

Without looking up, he pointed with his index finger. "Behind the bar, lady."

As a waitress balanced a tray of empty beer bottles and dirty dishes over her shoulder, Danielle slid in behind her down the narrow, darkened hallway. The waitress slipped into the kitchen while Danielle closed in on a pay phone. Resting her purse against her leg, she punched in her credit card number and Brooke's cell number. "Come on, pick up," she said quietly.

A nervous twitch started in her left eye. Stay calm. Her heart was in her throat. Hurry! Answer! But no one did. Out of the corner of her eye, she caught the steady gaze of a person in black pants, a dark shirt, and rather muscular build leaning against a wall facing her direction. The feeling of being boxed in sunk into her. Danielle could feel the dampness of fear crawling down her arms. She dropped the receiver and headed directly for her pursuer, who blocked her retreat; she ducked into the kitchen to the surprise of the cooks and waiters.

Her eyes scanned the room in frenzy until she found it. And then she bolted out the fire door into a causeway. She ran until she stepped out onto Freedom Street. The footfalls of someone giving chase were unmistakable. She glanced over her shoulder, oblivious to the men and women seated for dinner. It was him—like a thundering bull, he was barreling down on her.

A cold rain began to fall, making the sidewalk and roadway like slippery, black onyx. Danielle felt a shortness of breath. Ahead, rounding the corner, was Baker. She was being herded. Stopping abruptly, she looked in panic for another direction, but there was none.

"Help!" A low, guttural cry from her gasping lungs, which cried for air, went unheard.

"I'm here, my dear. What's the problem?" Baker said.

"You know, don't you," she said, trembling and shaking. Then she caught Baker's face in a different light. *I've seen you before*, rambled through her head. She turned around and no one was there. Not one person was within close proximity to her. Across the street, she noticed a few people gawking.

Baker said in a controlled, almost hypnotic voice. "I'm here to help. May my assistant and I give you a lift? Trust me."

Danielle ran abruptly out into the street, coming face to face with the headlights of a car. She stepped aside and the car screeched to a stop. The door swung open. Then she heard, "Get in."

# 22

*Reston, Virginia*
*Friday, October 5*
*9:30 p.m.*

What was that all about?" Alex asked as Danielle collapsed into the seat with her head hitting the headrest. He pulled straight away until he stopped at a traffic light.

Danielle exhaled a heavy breath and answered with an edge in her voice, "That was … I will … just give me a minute. Lock the doors." In the blue LED light cast from the dials of the Nissan, Alex found her arms wrapped around her purse in a stranglehold. With glistening beads of perspiration, her face was marked by pained anxiety.

"You sure you're okay?" Alex wanted to reach out and squeeze her hand in comfort but dismissed the thought. Once the traffic light changed, he slowly made his way through the intersection.

Danielle fidgeted in her seat, peering over her shoulder through the rear window and then glancing at the side mirror.

"I'll be fine," she said, pausing in an effort to control her breathing. She thrust the palm of her hand over her forehead. "I parked my car around the corner in a lot. You'll need to drop me off, and you can follow me from there."

"I don't think you're in any state to drive," Alex said as he patted her clammy hand. At the next red light, he hung a right and turned on a soft music radio station. "I'll tell you what—I know of a nice, quaint Thai restaurant not far from here. We can grab a drink and pick up your car later. And you can tell me what happened." She was now breathing at a steady rate. "Have you had dinner?"

Danielle shook her head. "I've lost my appetite."

"Nonsense. We'll grab an appetizer, at least." But he didn't want to seem pushy. She was an attorney with a mind of her own.

She seemed to weigh what he had said. Then she tuned and faced him . . . took a breath and smiled.

For the next ten minutes, Danielle sat quietly. Seated next to him was a striking woman who had charm, wit, and beauty. But he also pictured her as an aggressive, unrelenting courtroom attorney capturing a jury in her spell. As he had learned more about her in the last few weeks, arguably she was a mixture of spark and tenderness.

Danielle asked, turning her head toward him, "How'd you know where to find me?"

"Apparently, your friend Karen from New York was quite worried from your telephone call. She managed to contact Brooke, and in turn, she called me. I've been cruising around for the last half hour hoping to spot you. I tried your cell several times, but I couldn't reach you."

"Thank you for not giving up. The next time I'll be prepared."

"What next time?"

"Expect the unexpected, my father always said. But I seemed to have forgotten the principle. Throw your car into reverse, cut between heaps of disabled vehicles, and run over fenders and bumpers in an effort to remain the last vehicle. You learn quickly, but sometimes the hard way. I remembered those when I drove."

He vaguely remembered her father's hobby was to customize autos to compete in demolition derbies, and an article in the newspaper mentioned she tried driving a few times. "Sorry, but we don't drive that way in Washington. Demo derbies—now that's something I haven't seen in years. Tongues of fire belching out of engines and noxious fumes filling my lungs with smoke ... those were the days." It was a weekend event, but he always thought it was an event more for guys.

She reminisced, "How we're shaped by things we do while we're growing up."

Alex raised his eyebrows, glanced at her, and said, "Now that's a side I would have never expected from you."

"That's a part of me. I'm sure it was a combination of my mother and father. A latent, gutsy side." She closed her eyes.

Alex said, "Danielle, I don't know what you're up to, but—"

Danielle cut him off. "When I competed, I didn't have much time to think. Instinct, quick reaction, and a plan. And, of course, you didn't want to get pushed around. I won several events." She smiled. "That's why it will be my turn next."

Alex could hear her inner resolve. "You know the saying that politics make strange bedfellows? Don't forget the break-in at Watergate and President Nixon. Or the presidential aide that shot himself. There was brouhaha over that incident."

"What are you saying?"

"Only that politicians sometimes believe they are above the law. They play for keeps."

"So do I. My father always said, 'Danny, it's good to be defensive to a point, but then you will need to be offensive when they least expect it.'"

"It's one thing for the derby, but it's another for politics. It's no secret that politics can be caught up in kickbacks, back-scratching, and political favors. And despite all the laws and watchdogs, it still goes on. And then there are those individuals who get in their way. You can read that any way you want to."

Danielle sat in silence for the next minute before she responded, "You make a valid point. I'll keep it in mind."

"Just be careful."

"I will. Now where's this restaurant?"

Alex chose not to alarm her, but he had seen it before. She may already know too much.


As he leaned back in the wing chair at his desk, Parks studied the two ringed keys. Those keys, worth no more than a dollar a piece, had the potential to determine the outcome of a senatorial race. Let alone the thousands of dollars in campaign contributions and untold political favors worth, perhaps, millions over the span of a political career. And yet if the pictures were removed, Tony would consider him a suspect since their relationship already strained.

And if Baker were correct about the implication that his brother-in law was the person who conspiratorially set him up with the bogus oil and gas field investment, there would be a price to be paid. But the loss of the senatorial race was not enough justice for what he had been through the last several years. No. He wanted his life and his money back.

Parks took a long drink of scotch and swallowed it slowly. He never would have suspected Tony; after all, Tony was his brother-in-law. But Tony had the motive and the opportunity. It was shortly after his investment disappeared that Tony had purchased the property in Reston and expanded his operations in the western states. Why he hadn't seen it before? Of course, it had to be Tony. Who else?

The company never existed, and the investors were impostors. It was a pure sham. An offshore company where his investment would yield millions, with no taxes and beyond the reach of creditors, was the centerpiece of the strategy. Tony knew he wouldn't loan the money or buy into PERC. So it had to be another way: deception. And Parks confided in Tony, telegraphing every move during the fraud investigation.

Parks knew how they set the trap and how he fell for greed. He was wined and dined in the Bahamas, flew in for conferences with top level management, and asked to opine on various strategic investments. Drilling rigs represented by dots on a map for regional operations in Canada, the United States, and Caribbean and drilling contracts for closed deals with hugely profitable rates of return were represented to him. And he was being cut into the corporation for a huge stake of the profit. A haven, as he recalled, for the super-rich. So he invested his entire inheritance from his parents, encumbered his residence, and pledged his stock and bond funds.

Parks wondered how many others were involved as the scotch had the desired effect and the anger began to flow through his veins. Carl Matalino, next to Tony, had to have known, and probably set up the players. But Carl wasn't the shrewd type with his old style of handling people. And Tony, in his own manipulative ways, may not have been the mastermind, although he had the intelligence to orchestrate the deal. Tony was the head of the corporation and stepped on people like they were ants underfoot.

He walked over to the bar, dropped ice cubes into his glass, and replenished the scotch. Then there were the physical assets of the oil and gas company. But he had failed to investigate or undertake the necessary due diligence. The company was a shell with no assets and no contracts. Within hours after he had wired the funds, the money was gone. The plotters had folded their tents and scattered like cockroaches.

And it was Tony who came to the rescue, tapping sources for information on the whereabouts of the perpetrators. Yet with every turn, his investigation yielded nothing. And it was Tony, when the remainder of his money dwindled, who graciously offered him a job as corporate counsel.

Then there was Baker, who left a trail of intrigue. Tied to a wheelchair, Baker motored around the place, and no one questioned his authority. Parks thought Baker's loyalties, if that's what you would call them, were not beyond reproach. In fact, he classified Baker as a cynic.

After swallowing the remainder of his drink, he grasped the keys and examined their cut ridges. For him they unlocked secrets that he didn't want to know. Those cut ridges would tear into what Tony Cervasi desired most. He shoved the keys into his pocket. It was late, and he knew the building would now be empty. With one last look around his office, he turned out the light and, at a leisurely pace, headed down the corridor.

In dimly lit hallways, he made his way to Tony's office, where he had attended meetings on numerous occasions. With a tinge of trepidation, he selected the outer door key and inserted it, looking side to side. Meeting utter silence, he turned it to the right and heard the tumblers fall inside the door lock. He pushed on the door, and it opened with ease. He retrieved a small flashlight from a jacket pocket and cupped his hand over the beacon of light, allowing just enough to find his way to the interior door.

There he retrieved the longer of the two keys. He keyed the door lock and slowly nudged the door open with his shoulder. Behind the wine rack was the safe, and he wondered whether the grave robbers of the pyramids had the same chill of fear and excitement over what secrets lay within. The thought briefly crossed his mind that it was too easy.

He threw open the wine racks, gaining access to the safe as described by Baker. With his adrenaline pumping, he opened the door with little effort and found the envelope. And for a single moment, he sensed the rope tightening around his brother-in-law's neck tighter and tighter. The thought of gasping for air was similar to the feeling he had experienced when he learned that his fortune was gone, and it gave him a sense of satisfaction to think his brother-in-law would suffer the same fate.

Unfolding the clasp, he opened the envelope with fumbling hands. The moment he did not want to see was at hand. Parks had second thoughts for an instant about whether he wanted to view the photos. He prepared himself, thinking what he might see. And to think he and McClay went hunting, fishing, and golfing without even a hint. It was as though he didn't know McClay.

He reached in and pulled out the pictures. He turned over the first, then the second, and finally the third to reveal three sheets of blank photographic paper. With a pained grimace, the idea of a double cross echoed within him.

"Did you find what you were looking for?"

Parks recognized Cervasi's voice. He went rigid, not having heard the door open behind him. He reached for the Glock on the shelf inside the safe. "Yeah, I found it. And I discovered more than I expected."

Cervasi recoiled slightly, and a derisive smile crossed his face. "You think you're going to use that?"

Parks could feel his hand trembling. "I will."

"Put it away." Cervasi sauntered to a chair at a small table and seated himself. "We can work out your problems."

"Sure, like you did before. You took my life ... my money!" Parks seethed.

"Is this about you or your friend, Thomas McClay?"

"It's about me." Parks made his way over to the door in order to face Cervasi. "You cut me off at the knees."

"No. I didn't take *your* money. If I recall, you inherited it, and I didn't really take it. Look around you; you aren't suffering. We're family. You're married to my sister. I know we have our differences but, hey, that's life. I never intended to cheat you. Why, we're partners. You're the silent one, and I'm the one that gets all the grief."

Parks moved slightly to his left to meet Cervasi, who had repositioned himself. "No. I can't believe you. How could you do this?"

Cervasi frowned and leaned forward slightly. "William," he said, shaking his head, "that's why I'm in charge. This is politics. We can't let our personal feelings get in the way."

"You're wrong." Parks steadied his hands. Although inwardly he knew what Cervasi could do, the scotch filled him with the courage to see this through. "No matter what the price or the justification, you can't do what you've done and get away with it."

Cervasi rose and leaned against the table. "That's where you're wrong. Phil Clarke will be the next senator. Tom is merely noise in the background. But we're different, and that's why we're going to make great partners."

"You'll never change, Tony. You're a good strategist, but—"

"Thank you."

"But you won't get away with it this time."

Cervasi settled back into the chair. "So it was you who sent the letter to Denon?"

"Letter?"

"How much do you know?"

"Enough for the authorities. I never thought you would murder Owen. He's the one who developed the program. Then there's Carl and his family of thugs."

"Very good, but that proves nothing. What do you have?"

"It doesn't prove anything, but it might be enough for the authorities to investigate. Then the photographs."

Cervasi asked with a grin. "Where's your evidence, Prosecutor?"

"You set me up, you bastard. I should have known. I told you about the investigation step by step. You knew how to cover your tracks. But the police will figure it out. The files are here, I know it."

"Is that any way to address your brother, William?" Cervasi leaned forward, resting his forearms on his legs. "You've got nothing. And you're wrong about one thing. I didn't set you up. But it really doesn't matter," Cervasi said with a prophetic smile. They locked gazes.

Parks felt a sharp pain crease the side of his head. It knocked him sideward, and he reached for the back of a chair. But the next blow was to his back, knocking the wind out of him. His stare was glued on Cervasi, who sat there with a tilted head and a frown on his face. The next hit came at the base of his neck. Now he could taste blood, and he had a hard time keeping his eyes open. His eyes closed and then reopened to see his brother-in-law before his legs buckled and his head bounced on the floor. Then he tried to say something, but it came out garbled with a gush of blood.

# 23

*Reston, Virginia*
*Thursday, October 11*
*4:30 p.m.*

It was late afternoon when Danielle learned the IT department at HBR had already removed and archived all of her e-mails. And although their retrieval should take minutes, once she received the nod from two partners, which Karen had managed to obtain, IT dragged their feet on the project.

For Danielle, the actions of Reanne Morgan typing a password frantically into an unresponsive computer had triggered an idea. But Danielle had failed to recognize its significance until now. Whoever trashed her office had left a calling card, and it was unmistakable: the monitor with an e-mail displayed on the screen. Someone had used her username and password to open her e-mail, and she doubted an outsider had hacked into the computer systems only to retrieve her e-mails. That meant that the password had been compromised. Now she became increasingly curious whether an e-mail held an answer.

"Are you still there?" Karen asked.

"Yes," Danielle said as she peered through her bedroom window, still unwinding from the confrontation with Les Baker.

"I thought I lost you. Sorry for the hold up, but there's this new lawyer, Jonathan, who's bright and sociable but lacks common sense. I had to show him where the men's room is located. Anyway, getting back to your question, Ann is calling here demanding more time from Greg with the wedding creeping up. Meanwhile, Denon has been on the phone with Greg virtually every day. But I've got to say, Greg helped out immensely to get those e-mails released for you."

Danielle knew she couldn't determine what e-mails had been read, or if they were all there. Her intent was to ascertain whether Owen had left a clue, possibly, about STAR.

Karen declared, "I think IT didn't get the right message. They've restored more than twenty-one thousand e-mails for you to review."

Danielle ran the math in her head. That's more than 4,000 a year, and at a mere two minutes per e-mail, she had spent more than a few weeks of every year reading and writing words, phrases and sentences, answers, remarks, comments and ideas; it was mind-boggling. After receiving the gateway to remotely open the e-mails, she learned HBR would tag each read e-mail to prevent her from making any changes or deleting them.

"You better make a strong pot of coffee before you begin," Karen suggested. "Because it's going to take a lot of time. Do you know what you're looking for?"

"Not exactly. I'm hoping I'll spot it right away." With that Danielle signed off. After dinner, she sat in a side chair, propped her legs on the bed, set the laptop on her lap, and placed a tablet and pen on an end table.

After an hour, the e-mails proved harder for her to read. With dry eyes and a headache that inched across her forehead, it occurred to her that whoever had examined the e-mails may have had the same problem. That's when she hit upon the idea to examine the e-mails sent rather than received.

She opened the file for sent messages and found what she was looking for. The last five messages were sent to owr@perc.com. The initials were Owen W. Roberts, and more importantly, it established that the trail led to PERC. Attached to those five e-mails were a series of older e-mails of Owen's attached to the outgoing messages. She paused and swept a few strands of hair behind her ear. She closed her laptop with a mixture of thoughts—Owen, the e-mails, and STAR. Now she had to find the program or the computer. "And I need the access file," she said, as though the answer would be forthcoming.

Getting up for a stretch, her attention was drawn to an older woman sweeping the sidewalk. Within seconds, she rummaged through the closet, finding an old pair of jeans, a baseball cap, and a sweatshirt. Minutes later, she went downstairs and found Brooke sipping a chocolate latte and seated at the kitchen table with her nose in a thick medical book.

Brooke raised an eyebrow as she eyed her from head to foot. "Where are you going dressed like that?"

"I've found a new job, cleaning." Danielle replied. "What do you think? Do I fit the part?"

"There's something to be said for it. Old lady Miller is out there every night sweeping the sidewalk in front of her house. That's her exercise. And for ninety-five, she's in great shape."

"Where I'm headed I won't need a broom. They'll supply it. All I need is a set of wheels and some luck."

"The keys are on the counter. I'm in for the night." Brooke shook her head and returned to her reading. Without looking up, she said, "Do me a favor and stay out of trouble. Oh, and good luck."

"Thanks." Danielle gave a half-smile and bolted out of the house. She waved to the woman across the street and jumped into the black Acura TL. Minutes later she found herself crossing the Key Bridge onto the George Washington Memorial Parkway. If she timed it right, she might make it before her fellow coworkers started.

But her grin turned to a gritty resolve when she glanced in her the rearview mirror. A late model sedan seemed to follow every lane change. At Tysons Corner, she dropped into the parking garage and took each corner with squealing tires to the second floor. There she angled the car into a parking space and jumped out. Inside the nearby stairwell, she took the steps two at time to the next upper floor and waited. Hearing the footfalls of her pursuer as he descended the stairwell, she retraced her steps to the TL and wasted no time speeding out of the garage.

On International Drive, she dropped into the far right lane and made her way to the intersection where she blended into traffic. She continued with her plan with the knowledge that the answer to the conundrum was buried deep within corporate headquarters.

Miles down the road, she pulled into PERC's parking lot, took a deep breath, and found a space at the rear of the building. Patience was not one of her virtues; perhaps it was the demolition derby days when grit, oil, and gas flowed through her veins before an event. With her hair pulled back and tucked under a black and gold cap, Danielle patted the armrest as she read the news headlines from a smart phone.

At 7:40 p.m., a steady flow of headlights entered the parking lot. The cleaning brigade, a group of men and women in all shapes and sizes, trudged to the side entrance. Her heart dropped when she noticed the purple shirt uniform. A few stranglers arrived closer to the hour, and she decided it was now or never.

The parking lot was bathed in near darkness except for beacons of ambient light from atop light poles. She swallowed hard and pressed her lips tightly together. The chirp of crickets near the sidewalk was her only encouragement. Approaching the entrance, Danielle joined the tail end of a knot of workers.

A young woman with long, black hair gave her a thin smile. Clutching a paper lunch sack and wearing a purple shirt emblazoned with B & B Janitorial, the woman said in a Spanish accent while pinching her shirt, "You have?"

Danielle shook her head. "First day."

"You don't need to worry. They'll get you a shirt, but you don't want to get in trouble, so make sure you wear it. And wash it every night. They want you to look nice."

"Thank you. I'll remember."

They drew within eight feet of the door when a guard angled himself out from a desk. He eyed each worker, handing out a blue security badge. When it came to Danielle, he gave her a once over, knitted his eyebrows in disgust, and then shook his head.

But before she was ten feet away, she heard him say, "Hey you, Steeler."

Danielle turned to meet his gaze. "Yes?"

The wide-waisted guard who had his hand inside a bag of potato chips, said, "We're Redskin fans around here. You better get your priorities straight." With a derisive chuckle, he backed away and returned to his desk.

Danielle murmured, "Love those Steelers." She pinned the badge to her lapel and caught up with her newfound friend.

"Have you been in this country long?" Danielle asked before she realized the woman may have grown up in the states.

"No, maybe several months." The woman admitted and then proudly added, "I came here for work and my son. I'm a hard worker. I want to stay."

"What's your name?"

"Maria. And my son, Juan, he's five," she said, warming to the conversation. "I had to leave my country. So did many others.

Someday, I want to become a citizen. They said if I work hard, they could help me become a citizen."

Danielle smiled and pulled a pen from her pocket. "Do you have a napkin in your lunch?"

Maria nodded and handed Danielle the napkin.

"Let me give you the name of a good immigration lawyer. He'll help you. Make sure you give him a call." Danielle wrote down the name and number of a DC lawyer she knew. "Tell him Madison told you to call. Remember my name, Madison."

Maria smiled broadly as they rounded the corner. They came to an office where a number of people lingered outside. "We have to report," Maria said, walking into the office.

The cleaning manager, a stern-faced woman who appeared to be in her early forties with unkempt, brown, stringy hair peered over her clipboard and caught Danielle's eye. "And where's your shirt?"

"I was told to report tonight. I guess they didn't have time to give me one," Danielle said sheepishly.

"Figures. I'm not going to be blamed for this. What's your name?"

"Olivia … Roberts."

"Olivia, huh," the woman said, writing down her name. "Let's get this straight. No work. No pay. And if you do a poor job, I'll fire you in an instant."

"I understand."

"You go with Maria here and get started. All I want is a clean office. I assume you know how to clean?"

"Yes, I do." When her mother was in court, the duties of cleaning the house fell to her. She never minded the polishing and vacuuming, but she didn't like doing the bathrooms.

"Good. Just because you're a woman doesn't mean you know how to. We sign in and out. So sign your first and last name and the time. You'll report here before you leave. We're out by 1:00 a.m. And another thing—take that cap off. We frown on those things."

Danielle nodded, taking off the cap and looping it through her belt. She signed the sign-in sheet as Olivia Roberts. For the next few hours, Danielle worked with Maria cleaning offices and learned how and why Maria came to America: her mother and father depended on her meager income for support in Mexico, and now that she had a son, it became increasingly difficult. At the evening break, Danielle slipped away with a utility cart, throwing a towel over her shoulder, and turned the corner not far from a small vending area with tables and chairs where the workers congregated.

Exit signs at both ends and in the center were the only hints of light in the darkened hallway. Her running shoes gave a squeaky whimper against the polished floor as she made her way to the HR department. Wrapping her hand around the doorknob, she turned it—locked. She pondered her next move, but a finger dug into her shoulder. She froze. Her heart thumped, and she could feel a mist of sweat quickly glaze her body.

"Did you need to go in?"

"I forgot the furniture polish," Danielle said, knowing it sounded like a lame excuse even to her. But Maria never questioned it.

Calmly, Maria held up her index finger and whispered, "Wait." She retreated around the bend to where they had left their fellow workers. A few minutes passed before she returned with a set of passkeys and unlocked the door, and then she abruptly retreated.

Danielle entered the pitch black office, locking the door. She pulled out a small penlight and surveyed the room. Glancing at her watch, she realized that she had only one hour before quitting. The small footprint of light made it difficult to weave through the office.

As the minutes ticked off, she found Morgan's room and gingerly made her way to the window. Feeling the wall and the sides of the window frame, she found the chord for the blinds and lowered them before pulling the drapes shut. Then she tabbed the penlight to the on position and swept the room before seating herself at Morgan's desk.

Once there, she booted up the computer. While counting down the agonizing seconds until the network connections were made, she opened a side drawer and focused the light. There she found a job application for a position. The applicant, who had a master's degree in psychology, answered an ad in the *Boston Globe* for studying behavioral conditioning. She replaced the job application and made her way through the other drawers, but found nothing of interest.

The monitor drenched the room in an eerie blue glow. Addressing the computer, Danielle spotted the program: HR Resources—PERC. She clicked on the icon and a screen called for a username and password. With no hesitation, she typed it, having remembered Morgan mouth the password as she fumbled with the keyboard. But now there was the username, which she didn't know.

Reanne Morgan. But the computer failed to launch the program. Then she tried Reanne and Morgan separately, upper and lowercase, with no response. She could feel her body heat rising. Cradling her head in her hands, she never recalled Morgan typing in a username, but there it was. She had come this far and hit a dead end.

Twelve fifteen. She began to sift through the desk drawers once again. She stared at the computer monitor, curling her fingers in the palm of her hands in a vain attempt to recall something she may have missed. Then she recalled Morgan opening the center drawer before she started to type. She opened the drawer and immediately noticed a small, metal plate marking the inventory number for the desk. She smiled inwardly as she typed the number. The program launched with a click of the mouse.

Her stomach felt queasy, a sensation from not eating and her anxiety. Twelve thirty-five. Her heart raced. Under the tools menu of the program, she moved down to search the desktop. She squirmed in the chair and closed her eyes tightly, considering what information to locate first.

Twelve forty-one. She punched in STAR. The computer whirred for few seconds before ten names appeared on the screen. Then she clicked the print icon, and the printer menu wanted a printer. There were five printers, and she had no idea where they were located. After she cancelled the print job, she pulled the pen from her pocket and jotted down Dr. Henry Milsen and Mary Simes, including their addresses and phone numbers, on a notepad on the desk. She folded the paper and stuffed it in her pants pocket.

Twelve forty-seven. She typed in OWR, and for a moment she hesitated, thinking about whether to continue. Then she caved, knowing it would take time to catch up with her fellow workers. Hurriedly, she shut down the computer, undid the drapes and blinds, and closed the door. She flipped on the penlight and flew, bumping into a desk on her way out.

Danielle remembered the manager saying, "We're out of here at one o'clock." Sucking in air, she bolted down the darkened hallway to the exit sign and then down the stairwell. On the first floor, she got her bearings and headed for the main corridor. Once there, she listened but heard nothing.

"There you are," said a gruff voice. "Where have you been?"

"I … I got lost."

"Lost. You were to stay with Maria."

"Well?"

"Follow me," the woman growled.

Danielle, flushed from the sprint, wiped away the sweat in her sleeve and followed the straggly haired woman.

When they returned to the staging office, the manager said, with her head slightly askance, "I don't tolerate insubordination. You can't just walk around the halls any time you damn well please. This is your first and last warning, girl. You either follow instructions like the others, or you're out of here. Sit yourself down."

"Yes ma'am." Danielle rubbed her eyes and gave a wide yawn.

"The others left here fifteen minutes ago. You held me over. There's just no excuse. I won't put up with it. Where were you, anyway?"

"I was cleaning the floor, and the next thing I know they moved, and I sort of got lost." Danielle thought if this woman buys this flimsy excuse, she'll buy anything.

"Huh. You were probably sleeping somewhere. There's no sleeping on the job. Do you understand?"

"Yes, sorry."

"I'll let you go tonight, but I don't put up with shenanigans."

Danielle nodded.

"I already signed you out, so make sure you hand in your badge to the guard at the end of the hallway. And one more thing—get here fifteen minutes earlier tomorrow night. I'll make sure you get a shirt. I don't know why the company keeps me in the dark about new hires. They just show up."

"Sorry to inconvenience you," apologized Danielle as she rose from the chair and walked to the door.

"And by the way, Maria told me you did a good job. If you keep it up, someday maybe you'll make something of yourself."

Danielle smirked and exited the building.

# 24

*Rockville, Maryland*
*Friday, October 12*
*10:00 a.m.*

You must've gotten in late last night. For me, these last few days have been hectic, so I climbed into bed early. Alex called several times trying to get in touch with you. And then he proceeded to fill me in on all the details of what happened at Towne Center. My first reaction is you better look for another job. From what I've heard these last several weeks, it doesn't sound like your type of company," Brooke said.

"You may be right, but I'm going to see this to the end. And I've got several more weeks to decide." Even Danielle admitted to herself that the job was no longer enticing, but neither was the thought that she had become a target.

"Believe me, with your legal credentials, you won't have any trouble finding a position in Washington. I've got friends who practice with the big firms. From what I hear, they're always looking for a politically savvy person." Brooke glanced at the side mirror, and seeing no vehicle within two car lengths, she swerved into the outside lane. "Now what's this about a computer program ... I mean, there are thousands of programs."

"Yes, but this one's extra-special for some reason. STAR. And they want it so desperately, even if it means ... well, maybe murder." With a fleeting glance at her vibrating phone, she noticed the display read private. She refused to answer it.

"Murder? And who might *they* be? For that matter, you're not one hundred percent sure Owen was murdered, are you?"

"No, I'm not exactly sure, but obviously something's amiss. And Les Baker, that's the guy at Towne Center, meant business. His tactics were blunt and … I wouldn't put anything past him."

Brooke turned sharply from the outer to the inner lane when the driver in front of them hit his brakes. She frowned with a head shake, as if her tailgating was acceptable. "Some people can't drive." Annoyed, her eyes darted between the rear and side mirrors, looking for an opportune time to switch lanes.

At the next red light, Danielle proceeded to explain how she obtained the lead to Mary Simes from the personnel department.

"Danielle, I'm sure you know that breaking and entering is a criminal offense. With you being a lawyer, ah, I think you've crossed the line," Brooke said with alarm. "What were you thinking?" On a straight stretch of road, Brooke turned to Danielle in complete astonishment, taking her eyes off the roadway for a second.

"Don't worry. I didn't get caught, and besides, for all they know, I was another cleaning person doing her job." She glanced at Brooke, who appeared taken aback by the confession.

"Murder. Breaking and entering. Okay. That's not your ordinary, everyday life, or is it? What's next?"

"You're right. I'm not above the law." At Maryland, both Brooke and she once broke into a fraternity, posing as maids hired to clean up a fraternity house. But actually they were writing a story for the campus paper on underage and binge drinking.

For the next quarter mile, Brooke obeyed the speed limit, appearing to be deep in thought. "Rifling through the files in someone's office? Whoa. Maybe you should talk to the police?"

"About what? Somebody chasing me? That's lame. And here's what they would do: take the facts and then say we'll look into it. Meanwhile, they're out searching for murderers, rapists, burglars, terrorists, and the like. By the time they look into it, the trail will have gone cold. When I reported my luggage was stolen, did the police look into it? I doubt it."

Shaking her head in disbelief, Brooke appeared to be coming to grips with Danielle's surreptitious conduct. "Well, in that case … what did you find?"

"Dr. Henry Milsen. He was linked to STAR. When I tried to reach him by phone, his calls were being referred to a Dr. David Bateman. And guess what, he's a psychiatrist."

Brooke turned off the radio as her interest seemed piqued by the mention of two doctors. "Huh," she said, thinking. "It's a long shot, but I could ask the docs at the hospital if that would help."

"Pieces. That's all I've got," Danielle said as she ticked off the several landmarks depicted on Google maps. "Now, I wondered—and don't read anything into it—but why hasn't anyone latched on to Alex?"

Looking in the rearview mirror, Brooke turned on the radio and fumbled for a station before she peeled around the car in front of her. "I wondered when you were going to ask that question. And the answer is simple: he's been busy pursuing a career. Like the rest of us. Though, he *was* engaged more than a year ago. They broke it off. I never thought it would work." She rounded the bend hard, pressing Danielle into the passenger door. "She ran off with another guy who had loads of money. Since that time he's been dating, but nothing serious."

"Oh?"

"He's perfect for you."

"Thanks, but—"

"Don't answer. Just think about it."

"You sound like Karen. She's been preaching to me. And just the same, I'd rather not encourage him."

"Why?"

"Right now, I've got other things on my mind. There—" she said, pointing to a housing development on the left side of the road. Towering oak and maple trees and oversized shrubbery bordered the one and two-story homes. Slowly, they passed a number of streets until they found the point on the map where to turn.

"Danielle, does this Mary Simes know we're coming?" Brooke slowed while Danielle watched the house numbers.

"Not exactly. I thought we'd take a chance." Danielle had interviewed hundreds of plaintiffs and defendants both inside and outside the office. Her preference was the element of surprise. "Third house on the left ... we merely have a few questions. No harm in that." She pointed to a two-story, brown brick colonial with its lawn and shrubbery neatly manicured. A mixture of trees in the backyard towered above the house.

Brooke pulled into the driveway where a pink tricycle sat.

For a moment, Danielle was back riding her own tricycle on a paved road when her mother called out to watch for cars. But she wanted to impress her father and show him how much she learned while he was at work. He would say, "Danny, you were born to ride." And he would stand patiently with a broad grin on his face until she showed him.

"Somebody must be home. I don't think her parents would leave that tricycle on the driveway," Brooke said, and shut off the engine.

"Agreed." Danielle opened her door and stepped out onto the driveway. She strolled up the winding stone sidewalk to the front door.

With a knock on the windowed door, a little girl with blue eyes and dark hair pulled back by abalone barrettes answered. She wore purple shorts and a white blouse adorned with pink daisies. Her left arm was tightly wrapped around a brown teddy bear with a red bow tie.

Danielle crouched down to come face-to-face with the girl. "Hi, honey. Is your mommy at home?" she asked softly.

The little girl glanced at her teddy bear as if for advice. Without warning, she retreated into the recesses of the house and started yelling for her mother. A petite woman in her midthirties, slender in appearance, with auburn hair swept into a ponytail, answered the door, with the little girl burying her face in the side of her mother's leg.

"I'm sorry to bother you. Mary Simes?" Danielle asked, looking into the stunned eyes of the woman.

"Yes?" Simes's voice was muffled by the windowed door.

Danielle pressed her driver's license and business card from HBR against the window. "I wondered if I might ask you a few questions." Before Mary could answer, Danielle offered, "I'm an attorney, and this is a good friend of mine, Brooke Lang. Rest assured we're not here collecting donations. But long story short, I accepted a position with political firm where you previously—"

"How did you get my name?" Simes asked, wrinkling her forehead into a full-blown scowl.

Brooke said, "Believe me, this will take less than five minutes. Actually it was my fault, I was supposed to call you and," she looked sheepishly at Danielle, "anyway … I forgot."

"What do you want?" Simes looked slowly over her shoulder and then back to face them.

"Answers to a few questions, that all, and then we'll be gone," Brooke added.

Simes put her arm around her daughter and squeezed her.

Danielle stated, "You worked in the IT department. So did a good friend of mine, Owen Roberts. Did you know him?"

Simes froze for an instant before she responded. "Sure … but I don't work there anymore. He died." She bit her upper lip and glanced over her shoulder again.

"What can you tell me about STAR?"

Simes stared wide-eyed and then said, as though the question struck a chord, "Why, I … I can't tell you. I really can't help you. If you don't mind, that was some time ago."

"You don't remember STAR?" Danielle asked, "or maybe a program developed by Owen?"

Simes blanched and her expression went vacant, as though she wouldn't or maybe couldn't answer. She released her daughter and reached for the knob on the main door.

Danielle pressed, "But your name was associated with STAR."

"You're mistaken. I had nothing to do with it. Nothing," Simes said, becoming defensive as her daughter tugged at her skirt. She bent over and listened to what the little girl whispered into her ear. "I've got other things to do. I don't have the time."

Brooke interjected, "Do you know when you—" but she stopped.

Simes shook her head and glared at them. "Good-bye," she stammered and began to close the door.

"Wait! How about somebody else in the department who might know?"

"I wouldn't know."

"What was your job? Why did you quit?" Danielle asked, feeling impatient.

Simes merely shook her head and slowly closed the door.

Danielle pulled a business card from her purse. "I have several more questions, but I'll call you and arrange a more convenient time, if I may. I've marked my cell number on the back."

Simes waved if off. "Good day." The door slammed shut.

Danielle turned to Brooke and said, "I guess we got our answer," arching her eyebrows and dropping the card on a porch chair.

"And that was?" Brooke asked as they retraced their steps to the car.

"Everyone becomes tightlipped when I mention STAR." Danielle looked back and saw a curtain pulled slightly askew as if someone was watching.

Brooke dropped into the driver's seat, and Danielle pulled her sunglasses from the top of her visor without saying a word. Finally, Brooke broke the silence as they headed back to the Capital Beltway. "Did you happen to notice how she kept looking over her shoulder?"

Danielle nodded. "Yes, I certainly did. Nervous habit or, maybe someone was there. From the time I arrived in Washington, it's been an adventure. Still, the more I try to piece the puzzle together, the more the pieces just don't fit."

Brooke looked at Danielle as she shifted through the gears. "One thing's for sure—that visit was short and sweet. Anything else you want to do out here in Rockville? We've got some time."

Shaking her head, Danielle murmured, "She definitely had a frightened look. You could see it in her eyes." She pulled an envelope from her purse. "No, I think we should grab a bite to eat. You know, this whole thing reminds me of a chess game, and I'm being pushed around like a chess piece on a board designed to look like Washington."

Cervasi lifted his eyes from the notepad and waved Matalino into the office, penning a few details. Faced with weekly reports stacked almost a foot thick filed by the directors of the various regions where the company had a presence, it would take hours to process the data. Covering a large-sized conference table, the detailed reports included an analysis of strategies from internal and independent political polls. Within the coming weeks, the company would allocate its political muscle moving demographic, advertising, and speech strategists, as well as print, radio, and television analysts, around the country to waning campaigns with a conceivable chance of being turned into a winner.

After he penned his last sentence, Cervasi found Matalino waiting with fingers intertwined and head pressed back into the chair. "Well, Carl, based upon the preliminary polls, I'm pleased to announce we're having a great year. We have a carry-through rate of approximately ninety-five percent. That's the good news." His smile turned to a frown as he slapped the table with his hand. "Then there's the senatorial election. Now that's a thorn in my side, but," he said with a faint smile, "we're making a little, mind you, a little progress," holding his index finger and thumb almost together for emphasis.

Matalino pursed his lips, and with a slight head nod, stared expressionless.

Cervasi continued, "We eked out a few percentage points. Richie Davis reported he's made some progress at Shannon Telecom. He's figured on a Band-Aid approach until we find the access file to unlock the full potential of the program. From what I gather, they're feeding the channels, but it's awfully slow. And they can't increase the burst rate of the message. If we only had the access file or could find Owen's computer, we would be sitting pretty." He tilted his head and sighed. "On another front, I've already discretely lined up the release of McClay's photos." He got up from his chair and arched his back to release the kinks. "I need a massage; I've been sitting here all morning."

Matalino sat impassively, his steely eyes glued to him.

Cervasi chose to continue rather than ask what the problem was. "And it'll take McClay time to pitch the idea that it wasn't him. Timing." He landed his fist in the palm of his other hand. "If we release too soon, the impact might read as sour grapes." Finally, with his hands on his hips, he gave a single nod in approval for Matalino to speak.

"I know who has the computer," Matalino said, deadpan. He held a sheet of paper in his hand. "A shipper's invoice the day before Owen was iced. He FedExed two boxes to Danielle Madison. We've learned part of her property is in storage here in Virginia."

Cervasi barked between clenched teeth. "Get someone over there immediately."

"I did. And that's not all." Matalino handed him a black onyx pen.

Cervasi unscrewed the cap and examined the stainless steel nib. Then he scribbled his name on a sheet of paper before he replaced the cap. "A fountain pen," he said, examining the initials HBR printed on its side. "Higgins, Biggs, and Reed."

"Exactly! Reanne Morgan stopped earlier by my office and said she found this pen on her desk. And she's positive she cleared her desk before leaving. That means Madison was there in her office after hours."

"But how?" Cervasi could feel the tension building inside and blood rushing to his face.

Matalino looked toward the ceiling before he locked eyes with Cervasi. "The manager of the cleaning service confirmed they had a new person on board, except they hadn't employed any new staff. She signed her name as Olivia W. Roberts."

"That bitch. We get rid of one problem, and now we have another. Too bad we didn't know because we could have taken her and Parks out at the same time."

"What's missing?" Cervasi snapped. He began to pace the floor.

Matalino explained that Danielle apparently accessed the files of two former employees and did a search on STAR.

"Well, one thing's for sure. She won't get anything out of Milsen," Cervasi observed in a heated tone.

Matalino nodded in agreement and then added, "I paid Mary Simes, our former employee, a visit this morning. And who shows up? None other than Madison."

Cervasi could feel the muscles tightening in his face. "And?"

"She wanted information on STAR. I don't know what to make of it. Oddly, she doesn't appear to know what she's got."

"Are you sure? How do you know?"

"Yeah, Simes assured me that Danielle was on a search mission. Dumb broad."

"But you can't be sure enough. Need I tell you this?" Cervasi eyed him. "We better get on this before Candecki."

"Mr. Cervasi, we haven't run across Candecki. And he doesn't know where she lives."

"How do you know that?"

Matalino's smile broke into a hearty laugh, "Because he was asking some of my paisanos. He's a fly on a horse's ass."

Cervasi didn't crack a smile. "I wouldn't underestimate him."

Matalino said, spinning a gold bracelet around his wrist, "Just let me handle this. Richie will have his program. In a week or, maybe two, Clarke will be back in contention, and he'll be asking you for forgiveness."

Cervasi slowly bowed his head with approval. "It's in your hands."

After the introduction by Danielle and Brooke, Eleanor Davis, a young lady with brown eyes framed by black, rectangular glasses and shoulder length, brown hair, escorted them into a spacious office with a view overlooking McKelvin Mall at the University of Maryland. The librarian directed Brooke and Danielle to an espresso leather sofa while she seated herself in a matching chair.

Danielle handed her a letter she found among the volume of books by Thomas Jefferson.

Davis smiled and exchanged glances with both Danielle and Brooke. "Yes. I wrote Mr. Roberts about the proposed donation of a set of books to our permanent library collection. Of course, when I spoke to him, I expressed our sincere gratitude that he would consider the university."

Brooke said, "Unfortunately, Mr. Roberts recently met an untimely death, and Danielle and I wanted to fulfill his intention to make the donation."

Davis expressed her deepest sympathy to them. "We will, of course, appropriately label the books in his memory." After Danielle provided the address of Owen's mother, where a formal letter of acceptance would be sent, Davis said, "Mr. Roberts instructed me to deliver a letter, which I have kept in my desk, to the person or persons who delivered the books to the library. Unusual, I must say, considering the many gifts we receive, but I agreed to comply with his wishes." Davis rose and walked over to her desk, where she retrieved a sealed, white envelope from a slightly larger, stamped, brown one.

Danielle reached for the envelope and opened it. The letter read: "Two words define the keys to success." A broad smile crossed her face as she twisted in her seat to face Brooke. "We have one more place to visit before we leave."

At the university's chapel, Danielle, who had remembered the simple words, found Father Tom, with the ebullient smile and personality from her days at Maryland, outside next to a flower garden. With a lilting voice, he greeted them as he swept the crumbly dirt from his pant legs and rested the rake next to the shovel along the chapel wall.

Danielle said, "Two words define the keys to success."

"Indeed, and I pray they have served you well." Once Danielle explained how she and Brooke were led to the chapel and their relationship to Owen, he shook his head upon hearing of Owen's death. And then he responded, "Ah," nodding his head and raising his index finger. "I have what you're looking for. And he told me to dispose of the item if he or another person didn't claim it within a year … wait here. I'll help you."

Brooke turned to Danielle and asked, "And what's the key?"

"No matter the degree you're awarded, if you remember these two words, they'll open many doors for you: 'thank you.'"

# 25

A grandfather clock ticked loudly, piercing the silence in the room as they faced one another, each lost in her own ruminations, tight-lipped but with eyes flitting from ceiling to floor. A floor lamp with a muted light bathed a portion of the room, leaving the remainder steeped in darkness.

"I think it's time," Danielle said, with her hand gripping her cell phone.

Brooke sat pensively with her hands settled on the arms of a chair. "Do you think you can handle it?"

"It's bulky, a little clumsy, and just a tad heavy, but I think so. Alex will meet me at the university. Besides, his friend is doing him a favor, meeting us at this time of night. I thought it could wait until tomorrow, but Alex was insistent. And I was as equally insistent that we could handle this without his help."

Wearing jeans and sitting with her legs folded underneath her, Brooke declared, "I've walked the block several times within the hour, and unless they're related to Houdini, I didn't see anyone watching our place."

"I still think we should stick to the plan," Danielle responded, remembering the other night when she was followed. "I didn't see him until the Key Bridge, and then he stuck like glue."

Brooke glanced at her watch and shifted in her seat. "When will this computer expert do the analysis?"

"I understand it'll take a few days, although I doubt whether he'll find anything." She and Brooke had thought they would only have to boot up the computer and examine the programs and files, but that turned up nothing. There were no unusual files. The programs were normal, off the store shelf. But Alex had convinced her that techies have an uncanny way of disguising and hiding what they don't want found. He pointed to Trojan horses, viruses, worms, and macros operating in the background but readily present.

Danielle crouched, drew a deep breath, and picked up the computer. "Wow, this is a little heavy, but I'll manage," she stated, exhaling a deep breath. She stepped out into the darkness of night, where only the diffused light from a door lamp splayed across the sidewalk. Her gait was tentative on the uneven brick pavement. Brooke opened the car door, and Danielle angled the computer onto the front passenger seat. With her heart thumping, she turned and said, "When I settle down, I'm going to make it a point to get in better shape."

Brooke looked over her shoulder and then down the street. "Give me a few minutes to lock the house, and I'll follow you."

Danielle eased in behind the wheel. For a moment, she weighed the fleeting thought that the computer was valuable, maybe priceless. But why? She had to know what it all meant.

After she adjusted the mirror, Danielle started the vehicle and inched out onto the one-way street. Behind her, the headlights of another vehicle came to life. She took some comfort knowing that Brooke was close by. At the end of O Street, she turned left onto Wisconsin, which would, after she wound her way through Chevy Chase, connect to the Capital Beltway. There were shorter routes to the university, but at night, this was a direct route.

For the next few miles, with Brooke pulling up the rear and always staying a few car lengths behind, Danielle weaved through traffic, sometimes light and then heavy on Wisconsin. In the bluish glow of instrument panel, she caught a glimpse of a red, blinking light on the passenger seat. She knew instinctively it was her failure to switch the cell from vibrate to ring.

Snapping it to her ear, Danielle heard, "Where are you? I've been frantically trying to reach you." She glanced in the rearview mirror and drew a bead on the vehicle she presumed was Brooke. Her adrenaline kicked up a notch. "What do you mean?"

"I had the wrong set of keys. By the time I got the right set, you were gone."

"I think I have someone on my tail again." Danielle checked off the two headlights in the rear mirror.

"Let's not panic; you can't be more than five to ten minutes ahead of me. Slow down, and I'll catch you. And don't hang up."

As they chatted for the next fifteen minutes, Danielle played cat and mouse games with the driver behind her until Brooke caught them. Her thoughts turned to a dizzying play over and over of the words STAR and access file. Her fingers gripped the steering wheel tighter, and her head was now pounding with the words. What did it mean? The thoughts stuck in her mind like gum to a shoe.

"Know anyone with a black BMW?" Brooke asked.

Danielle shook off the dazed feeling. "Yes," she said, pausing to rethink about the incident the other day. "Well, not exactly. But a guy did stop and offer assistance after I had pulled onto the shoulder of the road."

"Did you get his license plate number?"

"Hardly." Danielle had erroneously dismissed the chance encounter. "I wasn't thinking."

"We can talk about that later. We're approaching Chevy Chase Club. You'll find it's a long stretch of road bordering a golf course." For a minute, Brooke detailed their plan of action and where Danielle could park without being seen.

Stepping on the gas, she pulled away as they agreed and saw Brooke crossing lanes to cut off the BMW in the rearview mirror. At one point, the BMW swerved into oncoming traffic before it settled back into the outer lane where Brooke cut him off. The circus became a blur of headlights as she followed Brooke's instructions on the stretch of road. Twenty minutes passed before her cell phone rang.

Brooke said, "You won't have to worry. The police pulled him over. What can you say when you weave and cross the centerline one too many times. *Reckless driver*. Talk to you later."

Danielle shut off the phone and paused. "Yes, I've got to hand over the computer to … to …" she muttered. But to whom? A car honked its horn behind her. She stepped on the gas and continued on her way. But the thought was strong, and she could almost articulate what he wanted.

At the University of Maryland, the A. V. Williams Building houses the College of Computer, Mathematical, and Physical Sciences. Alex had arranged a meeting with his college roommate, Mark Rand, an electrical and computer hardware professor.

After finding a parking space off Paint Branch Drive, Danielle managed to lug the computer to the main entrance, where, winded, she leaned against the wall. Finally, she trudged onward, but this time she took intermittent breaks. She was an hour late, and without much thought, she presumed Alex was already at Rand's office. Passing a number of darkened classrooms in the half-lighted hallway, she found a beehive of activity in two labs where a few trashcans, parked outside, reeked from empty boxes of tomato, cheese, and pepperoni pizza. She held her breath, but the stale odor seemed to follow her. As she rounded the bend, Danielle found Alex midway down the corridor, talking on his cell.

Upon seeing her, he ended his call. "You made it. Ah, I think you need some help."

Danielle handed over the computer and took a deep breath.

"Glad you made it safely." He shook his head more in disbelief. "Brooke called and filled me in. I called Mark and told him we'd be late. I tried calling you, but all I got was an answering service."

"When I reached to turn off the radio, my cell dropped between the seats," Danielle said, exasperated. "What time are we meeting Mark?" Before he answered, Danielle spotted a man with a briefcase striding hurriedly in their direction.

Alex turned abruptly. "That's him." As Mark approached, Rand switched the briefcase to his left hand, grabbed Alex's extended hand, and shook it.

"Sorry, I'm a little late. Errands," said Rand. He was about thirty-five years of age, had brownish-blonde hair, and wore a designer sport coat, a tan sweater, blue jeans, and running shoes. "And who's this beautiful lady?"

Danielle smiled faintly, feeling tired and ragged from her ordeal. She looped her hair behind her ear.

Alex introduced Danielle and added, "A New York attorney. So choose your words wisely."

Danielle extended her hand. "Glad to meet you, Professor Rand."

"Call me Mark. And I'll be sure to watch what I say. Let's head into my office, and we can chat a bit." He unlocked the office door, flipped on a light, and escorted them into a cramped office. Alex snatched the computer and followed behind Danielle into Mark's office.

On a credenza behind his desk, which was stacked with papers, sat half-open books propped on magazines. Three chairs, pressed up against his desk, were filled with another series of books and papers. Neatly stacked piles of documents lined the floor, making passage an exercise in walking across a stream on stepping-stones.

While Rand cleared away the books and papers from the chairs, Danielle studied a shadow box with an IBM data card, an eight-inch floppy disk, a five-and-a-quarter-inch disk, a three-and-a-half-inch disk, a compact disk, and a postage-sized memory card. Hung on the wall next to the shadow box was a series of awards for excellence in computer programming and hardware design with signature photos from Gates and Jobs.

Danielle, who seated herself in a now empty chair next to Alex, leaned over and whispered, "Is this guy for real? I wouldn't be surprised if you could find a few lunches buried in this mess."

Alex merely nodded and said, "Don't worry—if anything's on that computer, he'll find it."

Rand threw his jacket on the credenza, covering up half of the clutter. He caught his breath, laced his fingers as if in prayer, and said, "Is this the mysterious computer?"

"Yes," Alex said.

"What can you tell me?" Rand looked inquisitively at Alex and Danielle for an answer.

Danielle shrugged her shoulders and settled back in her chair. For the next hour, she related the incidents leading up to meeting with him and lastly why she believed the computer held something of significance. "I think a person I knew may have been murdered for this computer. And yes, this is my take on the matter."

Rand, who had reclined in his chair during her story, straightened up and patted the desk. "Murder? So we shouldn't take this lightly. Hmm … and you say this program is called STAR." He cradled his face with his thumb and index finger. "There was a virus program called STAR a few years back. I don't recall all the specifics, but

I believe it was a spyware program. That's it. Didn't amount to anything."

"I wouldn't know the purpose of the program except to say there's more than a general interest," Danielle said.

"By who?"

"By a political consulting firm, I think."

"That doesn't seem to offer us much. Speculative, huh?"

Alex offered, "Danielle and I think that this political organization has a distinct reason to want this computer. And we want to know why."

Rand tilted his head slightly and furrowed his brow. "I haven't heard anything that offers any semblance of a computer virus. Let's head to the lab." He sprung out of his seat and picked up the computer.

Danielle pulled herself out of the chair, followed by Alex. Together, they stepped down the corridor to a room marked Private Lab.

The lab was quiet, with only a few students: one with thick eyeglasses and another with a ponytail who seemed in control, lingering around a computer at a table a short distance away. They looked up and returned to their work, disinterested in the three of them.

Rand placed the computer on the counter and connected a monitor, keyboard, and mouse. Then he booted up the computer. As they waited, he unscrewed a side access panel and pinched the latches holding the panel in place. From a drawer underneath the counter, he snagged a small pen-sized flashlight. Then he focused on the hieroglyphics written on the various boards and internal written hints within the computer.

After Rand pressed the power button, the computer whirred and beeped a couple of times. Electricity flowed through its circuits as the computer stirred to life. The monitor displayed a number of responses as programs flashed across the screen with system checks.

Rubbing his hands together, Rand placed them on the computer keyboard. "Okay, girl, show me what you've got." He punched in a few commands and said, "I'm checking out the system." He proceeded to examine directories and program files, stopping now and then without saying a word before he checked the system profile, ram, hard drives, various peripheral cards, and protocols.

Rand turned and faced them. "Nothing unusual … but it's odd that I couldn't find any data. No letters, memos, e-mails, calendar, tasks, or notes. You know, it's similar to driving into a ghost town; everything appears normal until you realize there are no people. Maybe your friend cleaned the computer. He could have stored the data on a CD or on a thumb drive, but the data is missing," he said with a perplexed look on his face.

He slowly tapped his index finger on the counter. "Wait a minute." He again resorted to his penlight to survey the innards of the computer. "A-huh."

"Find something?" Alex asked.

"Do you see it?" Rand pointed to a metal object inside the computer.

Danielle and Alex peered into the computer and then turned and shook their heads in unison.

Rand patted the top of the computer cabinet. "This computer has three hard drives, but only the first and second ones are being accessed. The third is not. Then there's a docking station, although the actual unit is missing. So ..."

"What does that mean?" Danielle inquired.

"Well, what we're seeing is what somebody wants us to see. It's like viewing a screen that is a pure façade."

"I'm lost." Danielle tried to glean something from the monitor while Alex seemed unfazed by Rand's discovery.

Rand swiveled around on his chair and addressed them. "In every theatrical performance, you have a main stage. And behind every presentation on center stage is a series of stagehands preparing the props and assisting the actors for the next scene. It's like having two main stages, but one is hidden by a curtain. We're only seeing one and not the other. The other program has not been queued to perform."

Danielle asked, exhaling deeply, "And?"

"It's equivalent to another dimension, but our eyes trick us into believing there is nothing else there. In Owen's case, he must have hidden the data and special instructions behind the curtain. In other words, we are seeing a show, but not the real show."

Alex scratched his head. "Where do we go from here?"

"Right. We need to find the key to unlock it. Owen must have placed a backdoor somewhere on the computer. It could be a combination of keystrokes or accessing computer programs in a certain manner." He stroked his chin with index finger and thumb again. "Surely, he left some type of key to access it. And we don't know if it means something. But certainly he wants to hide something."

"This is like the *Wizard of Oz*."

Danielle ignored Alex's comment and asked, "Do you think you can find it?"

Rand screwed up his face, deep in thought. "I'd like to try. And based upon what you've told me, apparently he wanted you to find it. That makes me think it's possible."

Danielle shook her head. "But Brooke and I tried earlier. And it seems to me you could find the answer."

"Obviously," he continued, "he must have said or written something for you to find, otherwise why would he lead you to the computer?"

"He said 'source code' and 'access.'"

Alex and Rand began exchanging ideas about the depths of computer security and hacking into computers and then the Internet and the ability to access a computer from great distances. Danielle, with her eyes glued to the computer, raised her eyes and faintly smiled. "Besides the set of books, he did kind of … mixed in with the books, oddly, was a book titled *Nerds 2.01: A Brief History of the Internet*. I shelved it with my books on computers back in New York." She furrowed her brow, searching Rand's eyes for some eureka expression, but he remained expressionless.

She knew, for her, the sands of time were running out.

# 26

*Georgetown, Washington, DC*
*Friday, October 12*
*10:00 p.m.*

In the grip of darkness, with threads of light streaming through paned windows in the academic schools of thought lining McKeldin Mall, Danielle and Alex strode underneath the gnarled branches of willow and oak trees. The broken silence of dried, paper-thin leaves crackling underneath their feet resembled the sound she had heard on her cell.

"Danielle," Alex said, "these last several weeks, and I don't want you to take this the wrong way, made me consider how I've spent my life poring over political reports, reading investigative pieces, and writing newsworthy articles. Never did I think I might have a chance of ... of meeting you again."

Years ago, when she had first seen Alex at Maryland, her heart leapt with a warm feeling of home when life had been talking about boys endlessly on the phone. As a teenager, he was a mere crush and a heartthrob. Alex, she realized, had always had a place in her heart. And seeing him brought back those pleasant memories. But love was more complex than a childhood attraction.

She didn't quite know Alex in the same vein as Owen, but nevertheless she had caught Alex's alluring gaze. Owen had no pretenses. He could show up with a single rose or a dandelion with the same sense of pleasure and pride. At the door, with his treasures in hand, he had an unending smile and bright eyes. Alex appeared to show the same caring and understanding qualities as Owen, but it seemed to her that their relationship was developing too fast. Perhaps it was simply because he showed a genuine and deep interest in what she viewed as important. She wasn't sure if she was ready.

Alex grabbed her hand and squeezed it. At first, Danielle's reaction was slow, with a gentle but noncommittal squeeze in return. His hand felt warm.

Danielle said in a solemn tone, "Owen was dear to me. We shared many fond memories, the kind you don't easily forget. I need a little time." Her mind seesawed between thoughts of Owen and Alex, and the current state of affairs accentuated her commitment to what triggered Owen's death.

"I understand, but don't count me out. And hey, maybe you can teach me something about a demolition derby." He stopped on the walk, letting go of her hand and putting his arm around her. "I know you came into my life unexpectedly. And I'm glad that you did. I wouldn't want anything to happen to you."

Although she couldn't see his face clearly in the darkness, she could feel the resonance within his voice as heartfelt warmth and concern. Yet she still found it hard to accept Owen's death, and she had mixed emotions about meeting someone so soon. A feeling of betrayal gripped her.

Alex asked, "Could you tell me what happened earlier tonight?"

As they strode toward the library, Danielle related the details about leaving the townhouse and the pursuit. Her thoughts wandered to whether the driver was the same person who had offered help earlier in the day. It could be a mere coincidence, she hoped, but deep inside, she knew differently

"Why don't we go to the source? We'll simply ask Tony Cervasi. What's the interest in STAR, or, for that matter, Owen's computer?"

She stopped in midstride and swept her hair from her eyes. "Do really think he would answer that question? I doubt it. But Owen had to have a reason to lead me to the computer."

"So you think there's something Cervasi's hiding?"

"Maybe. Call me stubborn, if you like. But I want to know what's on that computer," Danielle said in a clipped voice. "And besides, I'd be interested to know everything about STAR. Wouldn't you? And maybe more importantly whether the program was the cause of Owen's death."

"What can I do to help?"

"You've helped already by connecting me with Mark Rand. But—" Danielle didn't want to confess her other concerns for fear she might be looked at differently. Although she had to admit, even to herself, there were other problems. Every time she wanted to bring up the subject to Brooke, she shied away for fear her roommate would immediately diagnose the problem as delusional. Her emotions flitted in one direction or another, and she needed to confide in someone.

They recommenced their stride when she made the decision to tackle the problem from another perspective. "There is something else." She was concerned that Alex might form the wrong impression of her, but she decided to press on. "Where do I start? Okay ... there's a song you like. And every time you hear it you find yourself singing the lyrics. It's like osmosis."

"Yep, it resonates within you. "Living on a Prayer" or "Piano Man" surely do the trick for me. The lyrics, the music, stay with me."

"And something might remind you of the song—maybe a word or musical note." As they stepped through the first set of doors into McKeldin Library, a bunch of *Diamondback* newspapers, with the signature picture of a terrapin emblazoned on the front page, were stacked in two piles on the floor, and flyers with a myriad of announcements of dances, fraternity and sorority pledges, and tutors were taped to the wall. She grabbed a newspaper before they entered the library amid a flurry of student activity.

"Yes, I get the picture. So what you're saying is this image or song has become a part of you, so to speak." He led her into a Starbucks tucked in a small room to the right where they could sit down.

"I can't explain this, but I hear the words: code and source code. But it doesn't stop there. There's also access file and STAR. It's like a numbing repetition."

Alex looked at her, with raised eyebrows "You're asking yourself: Why am I hearing those words?"

"Exactly."

"Danielle, there's nothing wrong with you. This whole matter about would prey on anyone's mind. Don't give it a second thought."

"And one other thing." She scanned the area so no one could overhear her. "Call it weird, but it's as though I can hear a voice."

"And, like the flu, it will ultimately run its course," Alex offered as they seated themselves at an oval table. "I wouldn't worry about it. Now, what's your pleasure? Coffee? Tea?"

Danielle ordered iced green tea lemonade, looking down at several articles on the front page. Her eye caught the announcement of a seminar being held at the university. None other than Dr. Greyson was a scheduled speaker. She peered over the top of the newspaper.

Alex set the drinks on the table. "Anything of interest?"

"That psychiatrist with whom Owen had an appointment the night he died is speaking here at the Union. And the subject is," dropping the top of the newspaper in half toward him, "psychological manipulation. That's a talk I'm not going to miss."

Alex walked behind her chair and, over her shoulder, read the announcement of a seminar on Business Management and Advertising to the Masses sponsored by the Departments of Business and Psychology. He said, "Sounds like a thought-provoking seminar when you put those departments together. But I thought this psychiatrist was located in Pittsburgh."

Danielle spun around in her chair and looked up to meet Alex's inquisitive facial expression. "He has an office in Reston also. And I understand he meets only those who want their name kept anonymous. No medical insurance submissions; it's solely a cash business. Strictly quiet, underneath the radar, so no one knows."

"How did you find that out?"

"Karen, my paralegal. And it seems to me that Owen showing up at Greyson's office was no accident."

Alex frowned and asked with full skepticism, "You think this guy has something to do with his death?"

"I haven't received a straight answer from him, and his office is in close proximity to PERC. Oh, and when I met him the other day, he told me to leave the past in the past." Danielle looked into Alex's questioning eyes and decided she should spell out what happened before she met up with Baker the other evening.

Alex was shaking his head in disbelief when his cell rang. He set his coffee on the table and removed the phone from his pocket. Looking at the caller ID, he said, "Did you solve this one already?"

She sipped on her tea, sitting on the edge of her seat. She powered up her cell and found a text message. It read: meet me at the Smithsonian Air and Space Museum, IMAX Theatre, Sunday, 2:00. Mary.

"Right," Alex said into his cell, bobbing his head, "I understand." He cocked his head and stared distantly as though cobbling several thoughts together.

"What gives?" Danielle asked when Alex closed the phone.

"You know, you may be onto something. Mark said he managed to gain access to PERC's computers. He was rather surprised someone didn't think to block him. Anyway, he didn't want to get too nosy so he shut down the connection."

Danielle heard, but her interest lay with Mary. "It's getting late, we better go."

"You're right, I've got a story to write for tomorrow's newspaper. But I'm going to follow you home ... so don't drive too fast."

With that, Danielle ripped out the ad and pitched the remainder of the newspaper in a trash can. It was late, and tomorrow would be a busy day. She intended to look for an apartment, but now she had another matter to add to her list. She needed to call Ann about the business seminar.

John Candecki, seated at a bar stool, drowned out the din of a boisterous crowd at Clyde's in Georgetown. The handwritten phone message, which had been handed to him earlier at the hotel, told him a mistake had been made. As he sipped on his vodka martini with a twist of lemon and two drops of vermouth, the way he always ordered it, he dismissed his encounter with another aggressive driver who had boxed him out as misfortune. However, he had not forgotten the taunting driver with a Maryland license number he could not forget.

Though he has been ticketed for reckless driving, a charge he'd rather pay than being fingered for identity theft, he had a more pressing conundrum to deal with. He had lost Danielle Madison in traffic, along with the computer she had removed under the cover of darkness from the townhouse.

His eyes met a blonde, who gave him a faint smile. He raised his eyebrows and returned her inviting smile. She was the type he always liked when he was in the mood. She had high cheekbones and a pouty mouth. On several occasions her roving eyes danced across the room before locking on him. With a turn of his head, he ended the flirtatious eye contact. After he finished his job, he would have time for an evening of pleasure. Right now he needed rest, knowing that tomorrow he had to find Madison. He laid down a twenty, spun out of his stool, and winked at the blonde before he departed.

Once he returned to his hotel room, he pulled out his luggage and laid it across the bed. He entered the security code and unlocked the case. With a slight push on the latches, the lid released to reveal a smaller, zippered case. At a table, he unzipped the case, removing a badge and identification as a special agent for the FBI. He smirked when he examined his photo, which was purposely touched up for hair color, narrower eyes, and a rounder face. Then there was the alias: Benjamin DeFore.

A small shop located outside Los Angles specialized in police identification. In less than forty-eight hours after he placed the call, he also had an identification card, badge, and driver's licenses for Virginia and Maryland. He never asked how the shop made the items. "Strictly cash," he recalled the wiry woman saying with a smile of uneven and missing teeth. On one occasion in the past he compared the fake ID with a genuine one. Not even a trained, discriminating eye could tell the difference. Wherever he was called on a job, he'd order a new one purely as a precaution, making sure that he had the latest ID whether he intended to use it or not. The ID came in handy, especially when he needed information or access, and more importantly, it bailed him out of a few close calls.

He placed the ID on the phone message, having removed it from his inside pocket. Satisfied, he turned out the light and went to bed.

# 27

Y̶ou better get down here," Davis said, "we've got a visitor. And they're using Owen's computer."

Tony Cervasi didn't respond, slamming the phone into its cradle. He launched his chair away from the table, jumped to his feet, and blazed through the office. On the way out, he shouted to his secretary, who snapped to attention, "Call Carl and tell him Davis has a fish on the hook."

With that, Cervasi thundered down the corridor to the stairwell door, which he swung open with such force it that jammed against the doorstop. "Out of my way," he barked at an employee who was making her way to the next floor as he clamored down the steps. Within five minutes, he reached the IT department only to find himself trying to open a locked door that was marked private and only for authorized personnel. At first he rapped on the door, although his patience was spent, what with the stress from elections and the days counting down quickly. His anxiety level had reached overload. That's when he pounded on the door, triggering a series of flashing, red lights and a shrill siren.

The IT department had settled into the same office space held by the technology department of the dot-com company. Similar to the previous occupant, which Cervasi believed had its own dark secrets to hide, the security surrounding the department was tight but not foolproof, especially when Owen Roberts walked out of the department with STAR.

For the most part, Richie Davis was charged with the responsibility of developing software and running the back office programs. That was until STAR was developed, and its broad implications became apparent. Cervasi watched the program from the concept stage to development through testing. He was now fully aware of its potential in a political race and the need to keep it under wraps.

When the door was unlocked electronically, he continued his rampage through a second set of doors into a large room that had no windows and a double wall to prevent unwanted listening by competitors and, especially, the government. The room was sterile white, arranged in three levels similar to a classroom, with the computer techs facing a central computer whiteboard where a series of flashing geometric lines showed connections between locations. It was similar to a war room. Davis had insisted on a command center due to the various offices feeding data on a 24/7 basis as races heated up throughout the country.

Cervasi spotted Davis, who sported an unshaven look of several days, a scowl on his face, and crossed arms. Standing next to the physically fit Davis stood Matalino, who had joined them. Cervasi said, "We think it's the computer. Owen's computer."

Matalino wiped the sweat from his brow with a paper towel pulled from his pocket. "Where is it?" He grabbed a nearby chair and drew it closer, using its back as his support.

"Earlier this morning, we had a problem with M5 flashing a red light as though an unauthorized user was attempting access to our systems. So we switched to a different access code. Within an hour, our visitor was back. Presumably, Owen left a number of backdoors hidden within our systems in case he was shut out. At that point, we sat and watched, but it soon became apparent that the individual was merely probing our systems and didn't know where to go," said Davis.

"Yeah … yeah. Tell me where I can find—" Matalino demanded.

"Madison," Cervasi finished, knowing that he had turned Matalino loose within limits, and the results so far were dismal. And when she snuck into corporate headquarters and interviewed Simes, he strongly believed that she was keeping the computer under wraps. "By now she has someone working with her."

Davis turned with his hands on his hips. "Carl, to answer your question, we never equipped our computers with a GPS tracking device. A hacker can cover his tracks from where he's actually accessing the network. A computer can latch on to the Internet through a provider at a location, and an hour later, even minutes, they've moved to another place—maybe even a different provider. We could have a moving target."

"Okay," Cervasi said in a hardened voice, "you can cut through the mumbo jumbo. How long has she or they been accessing our systems? And where can we find them?"

Davis looked as though he was caught in a tangled mess. "To answer your first question, we immediately ran a list of users on our systems for the last fourteen days. It seems, based upon what we can tell, that everything checks out. But apparently whoever it is only has made one other venture into our systems, last night."

Matalino popped an antacid in his mouth.

With his wrist turning in a circling motion, Cervasi said, "Go on," remembering Davis had a penchant for explaining the workings of computer systems in detail. But he was in no mood for a lecture on systems, programs, or networks. He had had a tour of the IT department several times, learning Davis called the computers by code names like they were a bunch of kids. "You mean to tell me that this person, hacker, or whatever, broke into our computer systems?"

Matalino ran the palm of his hand over his face, pinching his chin as Davis explained that the computer systems had not been compromised.

"This person was testing our systems," said Davis. "Like sending out a ping and waiting for an answer. It's a probing technique. But he did manage to take a quick glance at the directories and did a search for the word STAR."

Cervasi could feel his blood pressure rising. "STAR, huh. Did they get into it?" His eyes bulged at Matalino.

Davis studied the monitor with increased concern. "No, not exactly. Our visitor apparently searched our systems, but from what we can tell nothing was accessed. That tells me they don't know what they're after. For that matter, they may be sitting on the program without their knowledge."

"How so?" Matalino asked.

Cool and collected as he surveyed the monitor, Davis said, "It's obvious they've got Owen's computer or that a hacker circumvented our firewall. But I lean to the former reason. The person was looking for STAR."

Cervasi questioned, "Didn't we move STAR, at least, what we could access, to another computer? Does this mean we've lost the use of STAR?"

"Tony, if you remember, we can only use the beta version of STAR for a limited number of times. Owen built the limitation into the program. And I don't think whoever accessed our computers will affect STAR—at least I hope not."

"Yeah, yeah. I remember," Cervasi growled.

"I wouldn't worry just yet. Our engineers at Shannon Telecom are using it like I told you, but I wanted you to know someone may have another agenda."

Cervasi remembered that the beta version gave them limited access to the program's functions. The beta version was experimental. That is, fully workable but with bugs. Owen had ironed out the bugs, increased its reliability, and then took the program and the access file.

Matalino shoved a cigar in his mouth. "You know, my doc told me not to smoke if I wanted to live longer. Well, he died yesterday. When I find her—"

"Hey, you can't light that in here. You'll screw up my kids," Davis gripped.

Matalino glared at him. "STAR is going to kill me before my cigars have a chance." He pulled the cigar out of his mouth and looked at it. He shook his head and shoved the cigar into his breast pocket.

Cervasi looked around and noticed a number of techs from a distance had their eyes on them. "Conference room. I'd like a few words with you."

Matalino said as he turned to Davis, "Tell one of your boys to keep that intruder on ice until we get back."

Davis rolled his eyes, and within a minute, joined Matalino and Cervasi.

With his hands clasped behind his back, Cervasi paced the floor. "We should never have hired that bitch from New York. Pierce assured us that she'd be an asset and one he could control. I knew it would only be a matter of time before she connected the dots. Not only does she know about us, but she has the computer and, undoubtedly, the access file."

"She's probably a good attorney, but we'll never know." Matalino grimaced, slipping another antacid into his mouth.

"Our best bet is to let this person, whoever she has working for her, believe he hasn't been discovered," said Davis. "I'm confident we could get a fix."

"But that's only if they won't cause more problems," Cervasi suggested, addressing Davis's concerns.

"Leave that to me ... as soon as I pinpoint her, or whoever she's working with ... I'll let you know. In the meantime, I'll warn Shannon Telecom about our little visitor so they're not caught off guard."

"Then do it," snapped Cervasi. Turning to Matalino, he said, "I want a blanket on our campus. No one gets in or out without proper identification! Put guards at every door. She may be back," he said with sarcasm. "If she shows up, she won't live to tell about it."

Matalino nodded. "I'll see to it."


As she approached Foggy Bottom metro station, Danielle hesitated, abruptly ducking through a double set of doors into the lobby at GW Hospital. From there, she could immediately observe if someone had followed her. Her discomfort had eased but was not erased by taking a vantage point at a public place. An ID must be quick and precise if she wanted police involvement.

After Brooke's incident with the BMW, Danielle called the police about a possible stalker. But without a concrete description of the person, the times, and places at a minimum, which she had none, the police gave her lip service. They agreed to send a cruiser more frequently through the neighborhood. Even she had to admit that a black BMW, without more details, sounded like hundreds of cars, and besides, she'd be the first to admit her paranoia. That didn't help either, but she was unsure what more she could lend to a complete description of her stalker.

Peering through a smoked glass window in the hospital lobby, she focused on pedestrians approaching the metro station, processing facial features and body language. She would recognize Jonathan Lansel since she had an extended conversation with him at the airport. That meant finding him quickly in a throng of people hurriedly passing before her.

After ten minutes, the many faces blended together and became a blur. She realized that even if she snapped photos of groups of pedestrians, it would take too much time to analyze—not to mention the continual movement of people. With a sense of resignation, she exited the lobby and headed toward the metro station's escalators. It took less than five minutes from the surface to reach the station's boarding platform.

Boarding a metro car, she latched on to a pole, giving her a panoramic view of the passengers. She renewed her search in the crowded car, but this time she had a finite number of faces. Three stood out.

A man in his late twenties with sandy hair and a few-days-old facial hair was slouched in an aisle seat. His head rested on his shoulder as though he was sleeping. A newspaper lay on his lap, and he wore a brown polo shirt and a beige jacket with a turned-up collar. She could not define the reason for her interest in him. His sunglasses covered part of his face, making it difficult for her to connect the stranger to someone she may have met or seen at one time.

The next curious passenger who piqued her interest had a dark complexion and blondish-brown, curly hair. A pair of earphones draped from his pierced ears, he straddled a briefcase between his legs, and his sunglasses were perched atop his head. His furtive glances in Danielle's direction made her wonder about him. A girl whose blouse was unbuttoned nearly to her navel also seemed to attract him.

The third possibility braced himself against a pole, like her, at the opposite end of the car. She exchanged repeated glances with him in a space of ten minutes. His sideward glances made her think that he was some type of detective. And he seemed to fit the description dressed in a blue shirt, charcoal pants, and sport coat. He was in his early thirties and had a cold, calculated facial expression and piercing eyes. And he'd always look away the instant she looked his way and shift his stance behind another passenger. She made a mental image of him.

But none of them confirmed her suspicion. As the car swayed ever so slightly, rumbling toward the next metro stop, her thoughts returned to STAR. Although Denon first approached her, it was Les Baker who confirmed the program's significance. Their questions and actions only spiked her interest, causing her to display one of her father's traits: thick-headed stubbornness.

Rounding the curve inside an underground tunnel, the train's wheels squealed as it headed into the next station. She tightened her hold on the pole as the train came to a screeching halt.

"McPherson Square," a nasally voice said over the loudspeaker.

Danielle blinked and looked up to find the man holding the pole was gone. Her eyes raced throughout the car since the doors hadn't opened yet. Then she saw he had merely changed positions. He was standing behind two other passengers. The other characters of interest had remained in their positions and seemed genuinely disinterested in her. When the car stopped, her prime suspect opened a cell phone, gave her a wink, and exited.

The curly haired man with a Hollywood smile stood and assumed the position of her prime suspect. The girl with the unbuttoned blouse, no bra, and little to show had exited at McPherson, leaving him, Danielle believed, in search of another attraction. Her vain attempt to spot someone with a special look had only yielded vacant faces and two men whom she now concluded were no different than the others who had boarded afterward.

At the Smithsonian metro station, she resigned herself to paranoia as the root of her suspicions. She waited until passengers boarded and others dodged out of the car at the last second. As she walked away, she spotted Hollywood, who had his briefcase caught in the grip of the closing doors of the train.

Danielle skipped the escalator, choosing the stairs instead, which she took two at a time. Rays of sunlight filtered through the clouds and made her squint when she reached the sidewalk. But menacing rain clouds in the distance foretold that her umbrella would be used sooner or later.

Putting distance between herself and the metro station, she caught the distinct aroma of hot dogs, steak and cheese, and potato fries wafting from the grills of sidewalk vendors. The food purveyors were joined by the con artists engaged in the selling of knock off neckwear and watches.

"Can I help you, ma'am?" a peppered-gray-haired man asked. He was wearing a dark pair of sunglasses and white apron and stood behind a leaf-hinged panel truck. A rudimentary sign that read,

"Health foods for those who want to live longer" was painted red on the aluminum door.

Danielle quickly surveyed the menu. "Tuna wrap and a lemonade." As the proprietor made her wrap, she spotted Hollywood seated on a bench across the street. She dropped her head and inwardly congratulated herself on a job well done.

"Somethin' a matter, miss?"

Danielle smiled faintly and brushed the hair out of her eyes. "There's this guy with sunglasses who's been following me." She shook nervously and could feel her pulse quicken.

"In about five minutes, four busses will be comin' up the street. Young adults on the early afternoon tour. Come here about this time almost every day this time of the year. They always drop off directly in front of the place where the guy is sittin'. You slip away under those trees." He nodded to his right. "He's not gonna find you."

Danielle unwrapped the sandwich, leaving her drink on the counter as the busses lazily approached. She grabbed her drink and sipped it as though nothing was wrong. As soon as the lead bus stopped in front of him, she made her move. From her vantage point, she saw him dart from between the busses to her side of the street with his newspaper in hand. Looking up and down, he appeared exasperated, not knowing which way to run. He finally threw his newspaper down in disgust. And he began to backtrack toward the metro with his briefcase bouncing against his knee.

Five minutes, later she emerged from her hiding place and nodded to the vendor.

"Have to watch yourself in a big city," he said, wiping the counter with a rag.

Danielle, with a self-confident smile of mission accomplished, murmured, "Gotcha."

# 28

*Washington, DC*
*Sunday, October 14*
*1:15 p.m.*

At the intersection of Seventh and Jefferson, Danielle glanced over one shoulder and then the other, swallowing hard and exhaling deeply despite her sense of unwavering confidence. He could be anyone on the crowded sidewalk: young, old, tall, or short. Lose one tail, pick up another. She shuddered to think that she was someone's mark.

Her question was simple: why? She presumed Owen was the root of the intense interest over the computer program. It was as though he was leading a covert life. It was a side of him that she had never known. And somehow she had been drawn into it by association.

When she worked for HBR, the older partners spoke on occasion about their predecessor and founding partner, Ben Higgins, who searched out witnesses in the dead of night. Higgins, so they said, had the instinct of a hound dog. Give him a case, and he'd unrelentingly hunt down witnesses until he unearthed the last morsel of evidence. Then he'd research the law and case decisions in the same dogged way. He never stopped, or even slowed his work pace, and it was said that he never lost a case because he was always better prepared than the other side.

Like Higgins, Danielle was known for her sleuthing skills, searching underneath the proverbial rock, if need be, to uncover what someone didn't want her to find. She remained undaunted by obstacles, which she considered challenges. She'd merely go around them in her search for an answer. And, in this case, those who shadowed her were challenges, but not insurmountable.

A pedestrian sign across the busy thoroughfare signaled "Walk," in white letters, but she waited at the curb for a group of camera-laden tourists headed in her direction. Finally, the tourists pushed past her in a surge, hypnotized by a triangular yellow flag taped to a flexible whip carried by their tour guide, a short fellow who barked directions in three languages. Danielle joined the middle of the pack.

On Independence Avenue, with the wind beginning to kick up, the leading edge of a dark storm cloud crawled over the top of a building across the street that housed the U. S. Department of Education. With less than a quarter of a block to the museum, the group hastily resorted to a half jog like a horse stampede as marble-sized drops of rain fell. At its entrance, the crowd, some covering the tops of their heads with plastic bags and cradling their cameras underneath their arms, jockeyed for position, quickly funneling through several outer doors.

After she wormed her way in, Danielle collapsed the wet umbrella, allowing a puddle of water to form at her feet. She raked one side of her hair behind her ear and stamped her wet feet on the granite floor. At a display rack nearby, she pulled out a brochure and thumbed through the show times for the IMAX theater. With time to spare, she made her way through the crowd to purchase a ticket for the 2:00 p.m. showing and called Alex on her cell phone.

"What are you up to?" Alex asked, who seemed quite disturbed by her absence. "I've been trying to reach you all day."

"Busy dodging stalkers," Danielle said in a half-serious tone, although she was wary. She heard his heavy sigh. "I'll fill you in later." She confidently scanned the atrium, which became seemingly impassable with those exiting from and entering into the museum.

A museum employee bellowed over the babble of the crowd, "This way to the Golden Age of Flight." Another one cried out, "Lunar Exploration Vehicles, today and tomorrow," in an attempt to lure visitors, who were shoulder to shoulder, away from the main doors.

Danielle pressed her cell firmly against her ear to hear Alex say, "I spoke to Mark earlier, and he wants to meet with us. He'll be there tonight. I thought we might grab a quick bite and then run over to the university."

"That'll be fine. As soon as I meet this person who left a message for me, I'll call you." On guard, Danielle scanned her surroundings, taking in the multitude of patrons, looking for a familiar face.

There was silence before Alex spoke. "Danielle, I know you want to find answers, but I'd feel a whole lot better if you'd call and at least tell me where you're headed and who you're meeting."

"Don't be so serious. I'm a big girl. I've been in courtrooms with murderers, rapists, burglars, and the like. You've got to watch yourself, and that's pretty much all you can do. And I don't mean to diminish your thoughtful concern." Owen would've likewise objected, but she had a mind of her own. Plus, how was she going to unravel this case unless she could move around freely?

"You're not in a courtroom," Alex retorted with a heightened anxiety. "Right now, from what you've told me, I think you've raised someone's attention. And whoever it is will eventually run out of patience. Remember, you can't outrun them. And then—"

"Nothing's going to happen," Danielle said dismissively as her eyes roamed the crowd. "Alex, I'm in the middle of a public place. Nobody's going to reel me in. Besides, the guy who just passed winked." Frankly, she was both amused and complemented by Alex's concern and interest in her safety.

"Where are you?"

"National Air and Space Museum," Danielle responded, hearing the worry in Alex's question. Thinking that she should change the subject, she asked, "How's your research going on political races?"

Alex resigned. "Fine … promise me, though, you'll call me if you run into any problems."

"Agreed."

"Good. You should know that those names you gave me, Wheeling and Mitchell, don't give me any peace of mind. They're not up for an Academy Award for best star and costar in a G-rated movie."

Danielle, sobered by his admission, could feel a knot forming in her stomach. Her flippancy had retreated. "Alex, your concern is duly noted. And I thank you. Now tell me what's going on with the Clarke-McClay race."

"Clarke is picking up some momentum. And that's bizarre."

"Reason?" Danielle thought about the legal memo she and Karen had prepared for Denon.

"Because he's been behind since the day he announced his candidacy. He's been in the House for such a long time. His ratings, platform, and speeches are stale, but that's my opinion, and not necessarily his constituents'. He's continually alienated his party, and it shows in the polls. But that's up until now. It's as though he's been resurrected from the dead. This could be a mere blip on a cardiac monitor."

"Pardon me," a short, dark-haired woman said in a harried, shrill tone to Danielle. The woman was pushing a wheelchair with a frightened girl who was white-knuckling the wheelchair arms. She was about seven years old, and her leg was in a cast.

Danielle nodded with an understanding smile and stepped aside, allowing them to pass but keeping the phone pressed to her ear. For a moment, she watched the little girl in the wheelchair as the sea of patrons parted. Looking away, Danielle began to wend her way toward the box office. That's when she spotted him. She was being jostled in his direction. But the double-earring man with curly hair and Hollywood smile from the subway craned his head in another direction.

Like a lighthouse beacon, he turned slowly and deliberately in search of her. She dropped to her knees as if she lost something. A wave of people angled around her. "I can't talk now. Later. Bye."

A solicitous security guard offered his hand, pursing his lips in surprise. "Lose something?"

"STAR," Danielle said without thinking. That's why she came to the Smithsonian, to return Owen's program. She locked eyes with the guard, who looked at her, puzzled. She blinked several times and shook her head. "Access file … I mean. Actually, I don't know what I mean. Let me think," she said, taking his hand and standing. A rush of blood to her head made her dizzy as she popped up. Her mind was flooded with a symphony of thoughts that she should return Owen's computer, access file, or source code to PERC. She closed her eyes tightly and then opened them in an instant. "No, I actually don't need your help."

The pudgy guard cocked his head. "Do you have a problem, young lady?"

"Ah, yes, a little too much excitement, getting out of the rain. I was pressed by the crowd when I dropped my phone. Then I heard it ringing." She pointed to the phone in the palm of her hand. "Found it," she said with a half-smile.

The guard rolled his eyes and said, "Please be careful. You don't want to be trampled."

"Will do," she said, smiling, and did an about-face and headed in the opposite direction away from where she last saw Hollywood. She took several steps, turned in an attempt to locate him, and stood on her toes checking in every direction. It looked like he was gone, although she remained unconvinced.

After she purchased her ticket for a movie of the space shuttle launch in the IMAX theater, Danielle headed quickly for the theater doors. Waiting until the doors opened, she was among the first to enter. Inside, she climbed two steps at a time to the top of the cavernous, eight-story screen theater until she reached the last row, where she grabbed a seat and waited.

At 1:55 p.m., the theater was three-quarters full when the doors closed and the lights dimmed as the movie was about to begin. Danielle's immediate thoughts were Mary Simes wasn't going to show, or worse, it was a setup. With minutes before the launch of the space shuttle, a theater door cracked open and a fan of light found its way in. A few stragglers entered, but they were immediately ushered to seats several rows in front of her.

"Danielle," an amorphous voice said from behind. The scant light in the theater was cast by the immense screen, where the space shuttle parked on the launch pad sat gleaming, white and majestic, with tongues of billowing white gas escaping from its sides.

Danielle turned abruptly, making out a silhouetted shadow against the back wall. Her eyes adjusted to find a woman, who gestured with her hand. Rising from her aisle seat, Danielle climbed the last few steps to an exit ramp. She approached the woman, who shielded her face with her hand.

"You weren't followed?" Simes asked in a disturbed voice. "If they find out, they might do something to my daughter."

The launch director keyed a mic between the shuttle and the astronauts, ticking off last minute details, with the launch countdown already in progress.

"There was a guy who followed me, but I lost him." Mary suddenly reeled around and took a short step before Danielle tugged at Mary's arm. "Wait—"

"Why'd you pick me?" Mary asked, continuing to shield her face, almost shouting above the growing roar.

"You're name came up in the personnel department's database under the word STAR."

"I couldn't talk the other day. They know."

"Who does?"

"Carl Matalino. He's security at the company, and don't double cross him. That's why I couldn't say anything. For your own sake, give them what they want."

"And what is it?" Danielle's voice rose above the growing din.

"Owen … he's the one," Simes said in a louder, exasperated voice. "If he had never divulged what he discovered, then he'd still be alive. I knew it from the beginning. I caught wind of what they were planning. I wanted no part of it."

Liquid hydrogen fuel lines had been disconnected from the space shuttle, and the vehicle was now operating on internal power. The countdown was less than two minutes until launch. The shuttle expelled a steady hiss of gas.

Simes said, with hand animation, "But Dr. Milsen and Owen stayed on. For God knows what reason."

Danielle stiffened for a moment. "Let's sit down, we'll talk this out."

"I just don't know," Simes said, rubbing her forehead in a nervous way. "Oh—this shouldn't take long, but I'm leaving shortly."

Simes tried to speak above the engine growling from the surround sound speakers. "There was this secret project … you didn't ask questions … it was just there … oh, sure, I heard people talking, but I minded my own business."

The launch director narrated, "One minute and counting; the bird looks good."

Danielle pulled out a stick of gum and handed it to Mary. "I always chew a stick of gum when I'm nervous. It calms me down."

Simes nodded and waved it off. "Promise me this," she said. "You'll never contact me again. My daughter is all I've got. And if you tell anyone, including the police, about STAR, I'll deny it." Her head moved side to side. She even hunched down at times as though she was ducking. "Owen was a good programmer, maybe too good for his own sake. And if they knew about you, they would have threatened him. The first time they mentioned my daughter, I quit. But I made them think it was for medical reasons."

Like a thunderbolt had hit her, Danielle surmised Owen had broken off their relationship because he was protecting her. Owen told her not to contact him, but he kept sending those cards. He never called, and he wouldn't take her phone calls. But he never warned her about taking the job with PERC. It was Denon who convinced her. The money, perks, and freedom were enticing. She may have been a pawn.

Danielle momentarily glanced at whitish-red fireflies sparking and turning into balls of fire and flame from the bottom of the shuttle. "I wouldn't want any harm to come to you or your daughter. Believe me." Danielle spoke above the whining sound rattling through the speakers. "Tell me about STAR. What is it? You've got to tell me."

"You've got Owen's computer, don't you? And the access file. Without it they're sunk."

"Wait a minute, slow down."

Mary fidgeted in her seat and covered her forehead with the palm of her hand. "I know a person who I can trust. He told me what happened. In fact, he pleaded with me to convince you to hand it over when I told him I was meeting you."

"Who?"

"He can help. All we need is the computer and the file. It could be used as a bargaining chip to buy protection."

"Nine. We have main engine start," the director said amid the three engines ignition, which appeared like lighted torches, "booster ignition … two … one." The shuttle lurched upward slowly at first, and then in a blast of awesome power, it cleared the launch tower. The roar was deafening.

"Les Baker," Simes said.

"Who?"

"Les Baker, he'll help."

Although she did not have the vast experience of many practicing lawyers, Danielle never forgot words of advice about trial practice when it came to examining a witness. Look for a facial answer—it could be a nervous twitch, hand movement, the raising or a lowering of a person's voice, the inflection, head bobbing, or body movement. Greg Myers had once said, in the practice of law, you can smell them.

You know if the witness is telling the truth. For Danielle, the jury had handed her the verdict on Baker. Questions were now racing through her mind.

"It can't be. He's—" Danielle's sentence broke off as she thought, *That's the last person to stake your life on.*

"You can trust him, Danielle. He always did favors for me. He bought birthday presents for my daughter, and he'd buy her gifts when he went out of town. I guess she was like his adopted daughter because he never had a family. He's not like the others."

"I don't understand. What do they have?" Danielle's voice had risen several decibels to match the growing sound.

"They can … can get into their people's minds … manipulate, no, maybe sear into their minds a message. I don't know why I'm telling you this. The less I know the better. So … so I don't have to be involved," Simes stuttered, opening a red, flashing cell phone she held in her hand. She lifted the cell to her ear and covered her other ear with her hand. She didn't say anything, but she slowly cocked her head to the side. She bounded out of her seat and began to run wildly to the end of the row.

"Houston now in control … with shuttle beginning its roll," the speakers broadcast.

Danielle called out, "Mary … Mary," but it was covered by the deafening roar.

Halfway down the row, Simes spun around and slumped, falling dizzily backward, with arms flailing, and landed across two seats. Danielle rose until she heard a "pfft" sound whiz by her, and then she hit the floor. With her heart thumping, she crawled on her hands and knees toward Simes, who was now lying in a pool of blood.

From the exit ramp, Danielle heard the footfalls of ushers passing by hurriedly. A voice from behind yelled, "Call an attendant," and then another yelled into a two-way, "Send up security."

Looking down at her blood-covered hand, she wiped it on a seat before she stood and raced toward an illuminated red exit sign. Outside, she braced herself against the railing. Her stomach was churning, and her legs were weak. Quickly pulling herself together, her attention was drawn to a man with a perceptible limp who was moving at a hastened pace toward the exit door.

With her pulse racing, she took the steps to the first floor, not wanting to look behind, and scampered out of the museum into a soft rain shower. She looked up and down the street, hearing police sirens blaring, and then she spotted an outstretched black and white umbrella. It was angled overtop of the backdoor of the cab, obstructing its owner. He shook it free of rain from his seat and closed the door. All she could do was watch as the cab sped away.

# 29

*Washington, DC*
*Sunday, October 14*
*2:30 p.m.*

Catch that cab," belted out Danielle as she jumped into the rear seat and extended her arm over the driver's shoulder with her finger pointed at a cab a quarter of a block away.

The driver of Middle Eastern descent raised his dark eyes to find her in the rearview mirror, giving her a scowling look before he shot out into the knot of traffic, pressing her against the backseat. With the cab's horn blaring, it was as though his passenger was a mother about to give birth.

A prickly sensation blanketed her head to toe as though she was embraced by a briar bush. It was the sudden realization that she was as much a target as Mary. With beads of perspiration on her forehead and a tightness across her shoulders, her thoughts wandered between whether to confront her pursuer or drop out of sight. Whether she had the choice was problematic; how long could she remain obscure before he would find her?

The driver's wild, animated actions drew her back. His slamming hands on the steering wheel and epitaphs in a foreign tongue, coupled with the horror that she experienced inside the museum, unhinged her—life was spinning her out of control. She needed time to reconsider her options and plan a course of action.

A torrential downpour brewed by Mother Nature put an abrupt end to the driver's cat and mouse chase. Storm drains spouted water like fountains, which flooded the sides of the street. A thick cascade of pelting rain was too much for the windshield wipers, and suddenly the cab slowed to a screeching halt.

Danielle said in a harried voice into her cell, "Alex, I need your help!"

"Are you still at the muscum?"

"She was murdered. It was awful," Danielle said in a muffled, anxious tone. Looking up, she exchanged glances with the driver in the rearview mirror.

"Danielle, where can I meet you? *Answer me.*"

She edged herself closer to the right rear door out of the driver's direct vision. "I'm. I'm—" A blinding flash of lighting and, seconds later, a rolling thunder shook the car, making her cringe. *Pull yourself together. Focus. You're a fighter.* "I'm near … ah," wiping the mist from the window with the back of her hand, she strained her eyes to read the National Museum. The glazed eyes of a man inches away from her face sent her reeling in shock. She dropped the cell and instinctively reached out and locked the front and rear doors on the passenger side and then on the driver's.

"Don't open the doors!" she yelled at the driver, who mumbled something in a foreign tongue. Buffeted by the wind, the car swayed like a rowboat in a rough sea.

"Alex," she took a deep breath, retrieving the phone. Her heart hammering, she kept an eye on the doors and didn't dare look out. Feeling numb, she clenched the cell in a vice-like grip out of fear. That's when she heard a distinct beep announcing another caller, which she ignored.

"Meet me at the Old Ebbitt Grill. You're not far away. And Danielle, if you get there first, don't move."

"Yeah, okay." She knew the restaurant; it was several blocks away. Then she leaned forward and tapped on the driver's shoulder. Giving him the address, he didn't acknowledge her, but she met his scornful look in the mirror. Exasperated, she touched the receive button on her cell for the next caller. But there wasn't anyone, merely a vibrating hum, which lasted for fifteen seconds before the call was disconnected.

Her mind filled with heartfelt thoughts of Mary and her daughter. She had told Mary not to worry. She dropped her head and closed her eyes tightly, thinking someone would need to explain why the little girl's mother was not coming home. This was not how she planned to spend the weeks before she started her new job. Waves of grief kept rolling over her.

Then she focused on Hollywood, from the metro, before she moved to the man with the limp. What did he look like? How tall and approximate age? Any distinguishing characteristics? What did he wear? She rifled through the material questions, trying to remember. The police would ask those and plenty more. Pulling a notepad from her purse, she tried to vividly catch the flashback of the man with the limp.

With pen to pad, she formed the letter S. Then she scrawled the letter T and several more. Before she realized it, she had spelled out the word STAR. Fixated by the word, in the flashes of headlights breaking through the rear window, she began to scribble A and then an incomplete circle for a C. She stumbled over the letters C, E, S, and S. "*Access file*," she mumbled to herself. I need to find the file and hand it over. Within the parade of thoughts from this afternoon, a single thought drummed to the forefront of her mind—it was the urgency to relinquish the program and the file, but to whom was unclear.

The driver laid on the shrill horn, stirring Danielle from a flurry of demands. She brushed them aside, tapped on the driver's shoulder again, and said, "Take me to the nearest police station."

*5:30 p.m.*
"Now let me go over this one last time," Detective Ed Rosen said. With his elbow on the desk, he ran his hand through his thinning, gray hair, stopping to massage the nape of his neck. He moved his head in a circular motion and alternately stretched each shoulder forward until he heard a slight crack in his back.

Danielle stared fixedly at the detective sitting across from her in the interrogation room. He resembled Sam Reed, the former partner of HBR. Sam would rub the side of his face with his hand and stroke his chin, and his eyes would wander from ceiling to floor as though lobbing ideas back and forth as he phrased the next several questions. Then he would sit upright and fire away from the edge of his seat.

"Miss Madison," Rosen said in his hard voice as he rubbed the side of his stubbled face. He dropped his head and looked up, drilling into her eyes as he rolled a pen in his massive hands.

Danielle met his stare and pictured his churning mind. "Yes."

Rosen accentuated each word. "So you meet this Mary, who you don't really know, at the Smithsonian." Smacking his lips together, he continued, "And there she begins to relate the problems she had with your new employer, including a veiled threat by a Carl Matalino. You're both seated in the last row, and for some unknown reason, she gets up and races off. And you didn't see the shooter or hear the shot because you were glued to the space shuttle launch." He arched his eyebrows, looking for an answer.

Her eyes became temporally glued to the ceiling, saying inwardly, *We've been through this several times.* The story wasn't going to change now or tomorrow. Her primary motive was to seek justice and find the killer. But justice, she realized, could be elusive and, at times, excruciatingly slow. Feeling the anxiety within her, she was becoming wary.

When she failed to respond, the detective added, "Who claims she has a problem with her leaving and revealing company secrets." He rubbed his upper lip with his index finger. "And you don't know this Matalino character. And a man, wearing earrings, followed you from the metro to the museum; you don't know who he was or where he went. And you ran after a man with a gimpy leg, but he wasn't the guy who followed you." He drew in a breath with a questioning look on his face.

"That's right." Danielle knew it sounded farfetched, but it was the truth.

"Oh, and I left out that this may have something to do with a computer software engineer who wrote a program, but we can't ask him questions because he's … dead?" Rosen dropped back into his chair.

"Detective, I've told you what I know. That's all. There's nothing more to say." Danielle shrugged her shoulders. The incredulity of her story would strike most with questions not only about the incident, but whether she was mentally competent. Whoever it was knew enough to press the right buttons but stay far enough away to watch. It was as though they were toying with her psyche. She was the hunted, and she had no idea who was the hunter.

"This might take a few more hours before you can leave tonight, you know. The lieutenant assigned to this case may want to ask you a question or two." He took a gulp from his coffee cup, and she could see he was in no hurry.

"Listen, I've given you my statement. If there's anything else, I can't help you. Now I've got a splitting headache, my feet ache, I'm starved, and I'm in no mood to spend another several hours rehashing the same facts. As a member of the New York Bar, I give you my word that I'll return to sign my statement when you call. Now, if you'll kindly show me the way out. I know my rights."

"But—" The detective raised his hand like a traffic cop at an intersection.

"No buts."

Rosen lumbered out of his seat. "Okay. You're free to go," he said as he dropped his chin to his chest.

She grabbed her purse and headed for the door. "And one more thing … it was nice meeting you."

Rosen grinned. He angled himself around the corner of the table and left the room with her. It was a short distance down a corridor to the main exit doors. He held the door open and said, "Good night, Miss Madison."

She gave him a quick smile and strode quickly into the main lobby, where she spotted Alex engaged in an animated discussion with a police officer. She was partially relieved, but her hair looked like a wrung-out mop, her makeup had been swept away by the humidity and the rain, and her outfit was rumpled. There was no way to present herself in the best light. And she was irritable and tired, not having had anything to eat for hours. Her eyes roamed the lobby for a ladies room, but her search went unfulfilled. Inside her the tautness of a piano wire had been building, and now seeing him, she wondered if it would break.

Facing her, he broke off the conversation and approached. She closed her eyes, wondering what he would think.

Alex put his arm around her shoulder. In a soothing voice, he said, "You had me worried. I'm so glad to see you. But I was surprised you'd elected to stop at a police station. When I got your message, I sped over as fast as I could. I even tried to call a criminal attorney I know. Why didn't we meet at the restaurant?"

"Second thoughts, I guess. I shouldn't have dashed from a murder scene in the first place. I called you because I didn't want you to worry."

"I was downright frantic."

"I didn't commit the murder," Danielle said, looking into his soft, understanding eyes. A piano tuner he was not, but his comforting embrace and understanding voice eased the tension. "Let's get out of here; I need some fresh air." Aside from CSI death scenes on television, she had never seen a dead body. Greg Myers had once shared with her black and whites of murder victims, but photographs were not the same. Even color snapshots never evoked the stupefaction she felt. Her rain-soaked clothes had dried, although sweat and dirt clung to her, making her wish she had a hot shower.

"You look emotionally drained, but I'm here now. My car is parked a block away. Stay here and I'll swing around to pick you up."

"No, thanks; I'd rather walk with you." After they exited the station, moments of silence passed as they followed the lighted sidewalk before she said, "You know, I don't think that detective believed me."

"What makes you think that?"

"He had this questioning look … one of disbelief. It was like what other story can this broad make up."

Alex fumbled for words and gave her a gentle squeeze. "I'm sure they'll take what you said into consideration when they do their investigation. Don't be hard on yourself. Everyone reacts differently to a stressful situation." He intertwined his fingers with hers.

"I didn't see the person that shot her. It was dark, and I couldn't see from where the shot was fired. But I ran out of fear. Desperation. I don't know what made me look over that balcony. Maybe a reflexive reaction. I know I'm not making sense." She studied his face, but he seemed to weigh her version of what had occurred. She decided not tell him about the shot that missed her. Almost as a conditioned response, she noticed she was holding his hand.

Alex yanked on the door handle of his Nissan, letting Danielle in. "I wouldn't worry. It's in the hands of the police. They'll get to the bottom of this."

*But it sounds like a dead end*, thought Danielle, *because the officer failed to even concern himself over Carl Matalino.* Maybe her judgment was clouded, but even the interrogation seemed on the level of a matter-of-fact conversation. Her throat was seared from not having had anything to drink.

"And what about Mark Rand?" Danielle asked after Alex seated himself in the driver's seat.

"I didn't get a chance to call him to cancel. But I'm sure he'll understand. We can do it another day this week."

"I would rather do it tonight instead of waiting until tomorrow. I'm exhausted, though that won't stop me. I've got to hear what he found." Mary's death seemed surreal; they were talking and then she ran. That someone had known they were meeting and didn't know what Mary would say. For a moment, Danielle thought that possibly she had misjudged Baker. On second thought, he seemed like a different person from Mary's viewpoint.

"Okay, if you're up to it. I'll call him and ask whether he'll wait for us."

Danielle dropped her head against the headrest and closed her dry eyes. The air conditioning unit blew a steady stream of cool air, allowing her to relax and wash away the myriad of thoughts crowding her mind, from the street vendor to the sound of a bullet. "Thanks, Alex." She reached out and squeezed his hand. Collecting her thoughts, she could almost feel Alex's warm embrace as she dozed off, only to awake with a start. Her eyes shot open wide. She mumbled the word *brainwashed*.

"Benjamin DeFore, FBI," Candecki said firmly to the curvaceous young woman with electric bluish-green eyes and ash-blonde hair pulled back in a clip. He held his credentials an arm's length from her, pulling them away before she had an opportunity to read them. "I'm looking for a Miss Danielle Madison." Then he folded the creds in a snap and stashed them in his jacket pocket.

"Yes, she's a friend of mine, but she's not here," Brooke said, who guardedly left the door partially open. She was petite and wore a white starched lab coat, the type worn by a doctor. Her gold chandelier earrings blended with her facial tones.

"Do you know where I might find her?"

"Why … no," she said haltingly, with an immediate air of distrust. "Is there a reason you're looking for her?" Looking over his shoulder, her eyes drifted up and down the street as though looking for someone.

"It's like this, Dr. …"

"Lang. It's Dr. Brooklyn Lang," she said, ruffled, but he continued to fire off the pointed questions.

"How long have you known her?"

"Maybe eight years or so. Now—"

"So you've known her for a number of years. And where does she work?"

Brooke knitted her eyebrows before she answered heatedly. "Actually, she was working in New York for a law firm. Is there some point to all these questions? And how did you know where to find her? Like, coming to this address."

He ignored the question. "It's imperative I talk to her soon."

"Is she in trouble?"

"Can't say. Does she own a computer?"

"Computer? Doesn't everybody?" she responded flippantly with a furrowed brow.

"I know this must be somewhat annoying to you. Hey, I get a call from a higher-up, and he says get over here." Candecki shrugged his shoulders. "I do what I'm told," he said in an attempt to placate the young woman. "That's about it. Someone asks whether she has a computer, and I merely jot it down. I don't know why they are asking, or if it holds some significance."

With knitted eyebrows, Brooke said, "I think you should talk to her."

"What about later tonight?" Candecki hadn't seen Danielle since the night he was in hot pursuit, lending more pressure to find her soon.

"You'll have to leave a phone number where you can be reached."

Candecki sensed she wasn't going to be of any help. "Okay, Miss Lang, I'll give you this much. We want to talk to her as a material witness in a homicide."

Brooke's eyes widened.

"The Washington Bureau got a call from New York. Her life may be in danger. Now you can help or stonewall. That's up to you."

Brooke looked away before she returned his gaze. "Well … there was an incident the other night. And you can't be too careful in this crazy world. She was being pursued in her car by some lunatic, but I managed to cut off the jerk unceremoniously."

Candecki's trigger finger became itchy, knowing he had found the person that cut him off. He would settle up with Dr. Lang at a later time. What he really needed to know was where he could find Danielle.

"I'll bet he's pissed," Brooke smiled satisfactorily. "Yeah, he was almost caught in a head-on when he tried to swerve around me. He was staring at an oncoming bus." She shrugged her shoulders and shook her head. "You meet these morons on the road now and then."

"I'll bet you do." Candecki had a notion to wait inside the townhouse. Although more than a few people had walked by, and he could be easily identified.

Brooke asked, "Does this have something to do with Owen Roberts?"

"Ma'am, I can't really say. But about this computer—" Candecki glared at her and then smiled inwardly with satisfaction. He wondered how she would react to a loaded gun barrel in her face.

"Danielle called the police to report the incident. Of course, they didn't do anything except have a squad car sail through the neighborhood. I don't recall her saying anything about a homicide."

"Like I said, I'm here to help. Do you know where she was going the other evening?"

The last question seemed to rub her the wrong way. The thought again crossed his mind about beating the information out of her. Someone was bound to hear her scream if he pushed his way in. And if she was right, a squad car could wander by at any time.

Candecki fished out a calling card and handed it to her. "Tell her to leave a message with the answering service. I'll get back to her as soon as possible." He had used the answering service before. If someone traced the number to his cell, he had used another alias to open the account. It didn't really matter.

"I'll do that," she said, closing the door. The sound of a deadbolt and the slight sway of a curtain in the downstairs window made him wonder whether she bought his story.

As he turned, Candecki drew a bead on a young man of athletic build, whose button-down shirt appeared too small for his body, with boulder-hard arms and an expansive chest. He was twenty-five to thirty years of age, with a shadow from not shaving. He carried an open map in his hand and stopped on occasion presumably to find his bearings. But his attention was always drawn back to the townhouse. His frequent walks back and forth, at regular intervals, were obvious attempts to keep a tab on its occupants.

The athlete's behavior lent itself to a surveillance operation. For the last several days, Candecki noticed the subversive actions of the stubble-faced individual, particularly when he finished his rounds. His home was a Jeep Cherokee, silver in color, parked half a block away.

And he wasn't a cop. Cherokees are not for stakeouts. Nor would a cop have magazines and newspapers lining the backseat or a license tag framed in a plate cover imprinted with Washington Redskins. This individual, when not stretching his legs, would sit in the driver's seat pitching sunflower seeds out the window or talking on a cell phone.

"Rank amateur," Candecki mouthed, thinking Matalino must be scraping the bottom of a wine barrel to hire someone of that caliber. As Candecki watched intently, a pearl-colored AMG sports car slowed as it passed him, eventually finding an empty parking space.

A short, stocky man with a thick mane of dark brown hair of brush-like texture emerged. Reaching into the vehicle, he pulled out a bony, brown cane. With a slight lean into it, he made his way to the sidewalk. His long sleeved blue shirt hung loosely over his belt, giving him a disheveled appearance.

The athlete pumped the stocky man's hand as though they were old friends. Minutes later, the man driving the AMG patted the individual on his back in a congratulatory gesture. They were engaged in an arresting conversation, turning occasionally in the direction of the townhouse. Laughing, the athlete seemed pleased and nodded his head profusely. Then he opened the book and scrolled a note on the back cover, showing what he had written to the stocky man, who nodded with approval.

After they parted ways, the athlete jogged ahead to his Cherokee. The stocky man, now settled in the driver's seat of the AMG, pulled out and slowly made his way down the street. A hand protruded from the driver's side window of the Cherokee, motioning the AMG to pass. As it did, the Cherokee pulled in behind.

# 30

*Washington, DC*
*Sunday, October 14*
*6:30 p.m.*

With an unflinching eye on the AMG, John Candecki shoved the BMW into first gear and swerved around the corner, wondering whether he had second-guessed himself. After all, his first instinct was to wait for Madison, who undoubtedly, from what he confirmed, had the computer. And yet the anecdotal exchange between the athlete and the older man heightened his intuition that the sentry had been recalled for a reason, which was of greater significance than Madison and her roommate. He had no choice.

For the next half hour, the two vehicles, with Candecki in tow, switched from Wisconsin Avenue to Nebraska before tearing onto a two lane back road. As the road meandered past a series of housing developments and convenience stores, he maintained his distance. Ahead, in the direction they were headed, dark blue-gray clouds were bearing down. Tree branches swayed, kicking up autumn leaves with the gusts of wind. He switched on the halogen headlights and eyeballed the taillights of the AMG as he expected the clouds to unleash their well of rain. With one hand on the wheel, he retrieved his cell from the passenger seat and called up GPS for a location and a map.

The road finally emptied onto Route 410 as triangulated by GPS. Dime-sized drops of rain fell, and the wind skimmed across the car. Candecki soon saw florescent lights from a string of office buildings, shops, and hotels that lined both sides of the thoroughfare.

While stopped, he checked for text messages, but there were none. He had actually expected Clarke to call for a status report, especially after what he had heard earlier about the Senate race. Though he had to admit, Clarke had improved his chances. That didn't equate to winning except in horse races, where being close was enough to win.

Out of the corner of his eye, he watched three youths, anywhere from fifteen to twenty years of age, dressed in cargo jean shorts and pixilated t-shirts, walking with a decided slant of their shoulders in a seesaw motion. One character, with a silver-studded rhino on his black shirt, was swinging an aluminum baseball bat before it came to rest on his shoulder. *Doesn't he know*, thought Candecki, *a bolt of lightning could strike?* Drawn back, Candecki recalled when a friend had been struck by lightning during a pick-up baseball game. The kid lived but never played ball again; he was blind.

A mile later, the AMG and Cherokee slowed and made a quick right off the main road between a litter of yellow blinking road signs that read: "Danger Construction Site." Candecki broke off the pursuit, curving around a bank to a rear parking lot. Cutting the headlights while the engine revved down, he considered the implications. With little thought, he pulled out his Glock and laid it on the passenger seat. In the distance, framed by gnarled branches of lighting, he could barely make out the taillights of the vehicles, which appeared to have made a course adjustment before being swallowed by the dark.

With his prey little more than a quarter mile away, he mashed the gas pedal, bisected the lot, and spun onto the back road, flicking on the headlights. He was immediately jarred in his seat by crater-sized potholes. His headlights caught a billboard announcing a future office and residential complex with a completion date set for next year amid a pile of rubble. Thrown by winds, the distant flashes of lightning grew closer. Vestiges of windowless, rundown, multi-storied edifices, which he surmised was a former housing project, crowded his field of vision.

With the glow of the business strip fading fast behind him, he pressed forward, slowing at the bend in the road before he stopped abruptly where barricades marked the road's end. As he made a right turn, he flipped on the high beams, then off, to catch a featureless figure being absorbed by the darkness. Against the blackened sky, the silhouette of a towering crane, illuminated by a toggle switch of lighting, resembled a metal dinosaur behind a chain link fence.

At a slow, measured pace farther down the road, he read the warning, "Road Ends Five Hundred Feet." With no sign of the vehicles, he circled back. That's when he spotted the side panel reflector of the Cherokee, which was angled behind a paneled fence.

A glance of the GPS coordinates on his cell pinpointed the location. For him, this was no different than gathering intelligence when he was an army ranger. Answers and discoveries were developed in the battlefield, not from a distance. He retreated back to a parking lot less than a half mile from the main road.

In ambient light cast by an overhead parking lamp, he retrieved a duffle bag from his trunk. After he slipped out of his dress clothes, he removed his running gear. Years of training in the military and instinct came into play in undercover operations. It boiled down to knowing your surroundings and studying your enemy, but most of all keeping a sharp mind. And in this case, he wasn't enamored with going out into a rainstorm, but it was better than wading through alligator-infested rivers in a jungle.

Minutes later, he found himself at the chain link fence, checking the GPS coordinates again. With his Glock holstered to the small of his back, he found a Cadillac SUV with diplomatic plates, the Cherokee, the AMG, and a light-colored sedan. Using the lightning to check his footing, he jogged the fence line in search of a rear entrance. Between flashes of the storm, he made mental snippets of the former brick building, which was about four stories and largely intact. As he jogged some hundred yards down the road past a host of demolition equipment that sprinkled the property, he found a gate.

Inside, as he approached the rear of the building, he dodged piles of bricks, wiring, and steel. A Dumpster with wiring and scrap metal draped over its side, two dump trucks, and a bulldozer were parked nearby. He cautiously stepped around the equipment and trash, wondering about the building's structural integrity in a storm.

At a clearing, he caught a glimpse of an excavated area the size of a football field. A fluorescent orange plastic fence was erected near the perimeter. The depth of the pit, with forms for the pillars and foundation already in place, lent itself to be the start of a new building.

Making his way to where he saw the parked vehicles, he rounded the building and was knocked to the ground. With his face pressed against the rocky soil, he raised his head and shook it. He soon realized that he was pinned. The back of his neck was caught in a grip of teeth and saliva oozed down his neck. As he moved his hand carefully, he could hear the threatening growl of a dog in his ear and its hot breath against his skin.

A commanding voice snapped, "Off, Satan."

The dog loosened its grip and retreated, but not before a knee landed in the square of his back. Bathed in the wide beam of a flashlight, he gasped at the hit. He could feel the individual patting him down and removing the Glock from his holster.

"You won't need this," the voice said in a heavy Italian accent. The clang of the gun hitting the inside of a barrel rang out.

"And if you make one false move, I'll drill you right here. Spread your hands out, and make it quick," another voice said, moderately accented, holding the flashlight.

With his face turned to the side, Candecki made out varicose flashes of lighting arching overhead and the form of a Doberman watching from a few feet away. The dog was panting as though it was waiting for its next meal, while pellets of rain bit into the side of Candecki's face.

"He's clean."

"Okay. Rocco, hold this flashlight. I'm going to ask the boss for instructions. But if he makes a move, shoot him … and don't hesitate."

"Right."

"Come on, Satan. You've been a good boy. You'll have to watch this place while we're gone."

*The dog's name is Satan?* Candecki thought. As the lightning subsided, he said, "Hey, Rocco, still there?"

"Yeah, and don't get funny. You're not going anywhere," Rocco said, his dark silhouette coming into focus. "No need to get your head blown off. You wouldn't want your head separated from your body."

"Ah, Rocco, holding that gun might be a little dangerous, don't you think? I mean, lightning is attracted to metal objects." Candecki found himself shouting above the rain. Rocco didn't respond. "I've heard once you're hit, your belt buckle will brand you first. Then the metal turns to a hot liquid that oozes down your pants."

A thunderclap made the beam flicker. Candecki leapt to his feet. He plunged into the darkness as the flashlight's beam waved aimlessly, and he heard a gunshot. A strong gust of wind sent a chunk of concrete and glass crashing to the ground harmlessly yards away.

Candecki stumbled in the drenching rain, trying to get his bearings during bursts of lightning. He could hear Rocco swearing a short distance away. Low to the ground, he made his way to the building and through a window opening only to come face-to-face with growling and teeth-baring Satan. Freezing in his tracks, he saw two beams of light headed in his direction.

"You're lucky, Rocco," the voice shouted above the claps of thunder and driving rain. "I was about to tie him up for the night when I heard the shot. I'll take this guy to the trailer, and you take the dog. And make sure you latch his chain because I don't want him roaming the premises. He caused enough problems this morning."

"Sure thing."

As Rocco leashed Satan, he said, "You're lucky he didn't chomp on your leg. Let's go. And nothing funny—I've got a gun pointed on the bulls-eye painted with this flashlight on your back."

Candecki coughed and grimaced in pain, trying to remember how he didn't see anything before he was struck down. Then he heard the distinct growl of an SUV engine. Halogen headlights flickered on as the vehicle pulled out.

At the construction trailer, the door flung inward and Candecki stepped into a generously sized, comfortable-looking anteroom. It had a whiteboard, a large table for drawings, a midsized desk and office chairs, a sofa and lounge chairs, and a corridor branching off to back rooms. A series of architectural drawings were splayed across two separate tables. And a drawing of the nine-story building with offices on the lower floors and luxury apartments on the upper floors was nailed to the wall.

"Sit down," the athletic figure said.

Candecki remembered him from Georgetown. A few moments passed before a large bulk of a figure strode into the room with two dark-haired individuals a step behind.

"Aha," Tony Matalino said with a derisive smirk, "to what do we owe this visit? Why didn't you call and tell us you were coming? I would have made preparations." He looked at his goombahs, who nodded approvingly. "What happened to your sport coat and sweater? Out running in this kind of weather?" Taking a seat behind the desk with a look of disdain, he folded his hands in front of him.

Candecki exchanged glances with the others in the room before his eyes came to rest on Matalino.

Matalino smacked his lips together a few times. "Excuse me, I forgot to introduce you. These are my *caporegimes*," he said, nodding in the direction of the man dressed in a black blazer with a black shirt underneath and a frown. "Jimmy Salvatore." Then he nodded toward the guy who drove the AMG. "Joseph Alonzo." Then Matalino said with an angry expression, "And this here, my cousins, is John Candecki."

Candecki had been offered a job as a lieutenant years ago, but he refused. He was his own man, never wanting to report to anyone.

The storm outside rocked the trailer and the lights blinked for a second. Then, almost as though someone threw a switch, the thunderous pounding on the roof stopped.

Salvatore threw a towel from the mini bar in the direction of the individual who escorted Candecki into the trailer. "I see you already met Lanny. Where's Rocco?"

Lanny reported, "He's putting Satan in for the night." With that, Rocco opened the trailer door and stepped in.

Alonzo threw him a towel too and said, "Wipe off."

"This," Matalino said, grinning to the men in the room, "is the professional hired by our distinguished client, Philip Clarke." His wide grin burst into a chuckle with the others before his eyes narrowed and his facial expression turned grim. "What are we to do with you when you interrupt our business transactions?"

"Carl, we're on two sides of the fence, but we're working for the same candidate. This is about an election for U. S. Senate. And that's," nodding to those who were watching him, "my job. We may have our differences, though we respect each other."

Salvatore pulled a bottle of dark red wine from the mini bar and poured himself a glass. "*Salud,*" he said, and gestured to Matalino.

Alonzo jerked his head around, hearing a knock on the door. He nodded to Rocco, and Lanny grabbed a package from a cabinet drawer and exited the trailer. "A little business transaction."

Matalino nodded with satisfaction and waved his hand around the room. "We're becoming legitimate businessmen. We're closing those less savory businesses like gambling, protection, prostitutes, and drugs. But now we're into political races and real estate. We're becoming respectable."

"Yeah, we're builders," Alonzo joined in.

"You'll get to see our construction up close. We don't break legs and arms anymore," Matalino said with a smirk, looking at Alonzo. "But you'll get a firsthand inspection, eh?" With a grin, Matalino nodded to Lanny.

"Thanks for the invitation, but I think I'll pass." Candecki glanced at Salvatore and Alonzo before he turned his attention to Matalino. "You and me have come a long way. We're no longer mobsters. And we go way back as *paisanos*."

"Do you have some business you want to conduct?" Matalino asked.

"You know it was simply a coincidence. We both have the same interest."

"That's right, we are in the computer business. But we don't need you," Matalino chuckled. "We don't want competitors. We've got what we want." He exchanged glances with Salvatore. "Our property was stolen, and we didn't take kindly to your offering it back to us for a price." He slowly turned his head and looked to Salvatore. "Isn't that right?"

Salvatore raised his glass and swallowed the remainder of his drink. "I don't want to break up old friends, but we've got a meeting and dinner tonight yet."

"Our computer program is worth millions," Matalino said. "But no one is going to steal it from us. Why, tonight we've already entered into our first licensing contract. And we're going out to celebrate. Sorry you can't join us. You understand."

Candecki knew he had to make his move, and soon. "And what's so important about this program?"

Matalino paused as a grin washed across his face. "If you lived long enough, we'd change your way of thinking. Maybe you'd come to understand our ways. Oh, and you're timing is quite good," he said, shaking his head. "You'll be joined by another. The two of you can share stories." Throwing his head back in amusement, his snorting echoed like a bull in a cavern. Then he abruptly stopped, and his demeanor was all business. He turned to Rocco and said, "You and Lanny get Mr. Candecki's companion." Matalino threw a set of keys to Lanny. "We'll wait while you get him. The concrete should be here early tomorrow morning."

"Hey, Carl," Alonzo called, "we've got to move if we are going to meet our next set of investors."

Five minutes later, Rocco opened the door. "All's clear. We can take him now."

"What can I say to you, John? You're out of time. I'll tell Tony you send your regards," Matalino said, and snorted a laugh. "So … chow."

# 31

*Georgetown, Washington, DC*
*Sunday, October 14*
*8:20 p.m.*

The rain had all but stopped as Candecki was herded to the rear of the construction site where his fate was to be sealed.

"Don't you think you're forgetting something?" Candecki asked.

"Oh, we haven't forgotten. He's already on ice. But don't you go and worry, you'll have an eternity to talk to each other. Isn't that right, Lanny?" Rocco said sarcastically.

"Yeah ... we've prepared a final resting place for you two. At dawn, we're going to fill the forms. And when they pour that concrete, I guess you'll be considered a pillar of the garage, not of society."

A youthful voice rose from the depths of darkness inside the vacant building. "Where's our snow?"

Rocco twisted around with the flashlight in hand. "Who's that?"

Out came two youths that Candecki recognized as two of the three walking the main shopping artery. In the fanned light, he recognized Deadhead shirt and Spider shirt.

"You know, man, we paid ya the bills for a trip. Now we want our money or the white stuff," demanded Deadhead.

"We've got business," Rocco said. "If you don't get out of here, I'll charge you extra. And you're trespassing."

"We don't deal like that," Spider replied. Without warning, he lunged at Rocco, knocking the flashlight from his hand.

Lanny froze and said, "Hey, you!" The diffused light from his flashlight poured wildly into the building in search of Deadhead. Pulling a gun from his holster, he tried to get off a shot at the youth who wrestled with Rocco.

Candecki said, "I think you better help."

Lanny stretched out his arm, waving the gun erratically. But before he did, a figure shot out from behind, hitting Lanny in the midsection and pinning him.

Candecki wasn't going to wait to find out who was the victor. He wheeled around and was about to bolt when two gunshots buzzed past his head. He stopped midstride.

"One more step and I'll drill you in the back," Rocco snapped and turned his attention to the tussle on the ground. With a brick in hand, Deadhead was about to deliver a menacing blow to Lanny. Another shot rang out, "I wouldn't," Rocco barked, "Get up. Did you hear me?"

Rocco waved his gun at Deadhead. "Get your friend," who was nursing a bloody nose, "and get your asses out of here." Rocco never saw the flash that shattered the darkness. He merely dropped to the ground. A whistling sound erupted from his chest as he gasped for air.

Deadhead grabbed Rocco's dropped flashlight and flung it at Lanny.

Candecki picked up the flashlight and found the source of Rocco's pain. The third kid, with the Rhino-imprinted shirt, was brandishing a baseball bat and swinging it wildly. With a swoosh, the bat swept over Candecki's head as the juvenile swung for the fences. He could feel the rush of air as the batter missed his target. As it did, he landed a punch to the groin of the batter, sending him reeling.

Next Candecki pivoted and landed a kick in the side of Deadhead's chest. Grabbing Lanny's gun, Candecki blinded Lanny's eyes with the light. "We've got some unfinished business."

But Rhino had other ideas. This time he flicked open a switchblade. Candecki didn't hesitate and shot him in the thigh. The youth grimaced in pain, holding his leg with both hands. Candecki said, "Next time, I won't miss." He then grabbed the bat and flung it into the pit. With Rocco moaning on the ground, Candecki said, "Now I'm going to find my gun."

"And as for you—" Candecki dragged Lanny to the edge of the precipice. "Here's your view," he said as he shoved Lanny, despite his protests, over the edge.

As he stepped over Rocco, Candecki heard him gurgling like a clogged drain from the vomit he was swallowing. The youths had disappeared into the night, leaving Candecki to find his gun. Finding the garbage, he stumbled across a long, plastic bag, which he immediately identified as a body bag. Unzipping the bag, he uncovered a middle-aged man, grayish in color, with a shot to his head. Leaving the bag, he retrieved his gun.

As he passed the Cherokee, he shined the flashlight through the front window. There on the front seat was the paperback book next to a wallet. He snatched both, shoved the book into his pocket, and opened the wallet. In the billfold, he found two hundred dollars, which he quickly removed, and a license. The driver's license belonged to a William Parks.

Satan was barking up a storm. Candecki smiled as he spirited away into the night.

*9:45 p.m.*

With his chair tilted slightly back and stockinged feet perched on the desktop, Mark was engrossed with the book in his lap until he looked up from the printed page.

"Can I help you?" Mark asked with a frown.

"Dr. Mark Rand?"

"That's me." Rand sat up and tore a slip of paper from a newspaper to mark his place in the textbook.

Candecki, who had cleaned himself from his frolic in the darkness, had held out little hope that he would find Rand at this time of night. "Benjamin DeFore, FBI," he said, throwing open his credentials for Rand to read for a moment. "I'll get right to the point, Doctor, seeing as you're busy. Several weeks ago, a computer containing highly sensitive data was stolen. From our investigation, we've learned that the computer may be here in your department. Would you happen to know anything about this? You know, student, professor, or staff, it really makes no difference." Candecki examined the room, thinking he could never find a program in a room filled with what he considered absolute clutter.

"No." Rand struggled with his shoes parked alongside of his desk. "What appears on the surface may point here, but I assure you, we don't have any stolen computers."

Candecki recalled that hackers generally hide their identity and location through other surrogate computers; at least, that's what he read in newspapers. All he had to go on was a note scrawled on a flap of a book.

Rand added rhetorically, "The university computer network handles a continuous flow of data from computers connected to the network. That means someone could conceivably plug into the network and make it look like it's coming from here. In order for me to be of any assistance, I'll need more information."

Candecki eyed Rand with suspicion. "That won't be necessary. Thanks, anyway." He strode to the door, and with a hand on the door, he heard Rand's question.

"How do I get in touch with you?"

Candecki fished a card from his jacket and dropped it on a nearby shelf. "If you stumble onto anything, call and leave a message."

"Will do, have a nice evening."

Hearing the words, Candecki walked out and ambled down the corridor, wondering why Lanny wrote Dr. Rand's name on the flap of a paperback book.


*10:15 p.m.*

As he rounded the bend, Alex spotted Mark in the middle of the hallway, facing the opposite direction, with his hands in his pockets.

"Something the matter?" Alex questioned as he approached.

Mark wheeled around and said, "What have you got there?"

"Danielle and I stopped for pizza on our way here. We've got plain and pepperoni. Anchovies on the side. I hope you have an appetite."

"Why, sure, I'll take a slice. By the way, you didn't pass a guy dressed in a navy sport coat, gray pants, a definite scowl, unfriendly demeanor?"

"Can't say that I did."

"I'm a bit nonplussed. The guy said he was with the FBI. Gave me his card and said the number was his private line. I just called and got an answering service. You'd think they'd answer Federal Bureau of Investigation or FBI." He shrugged his shoulders.

"What's his name?"

"Benjamin DeFore. Said he traced stolen computer equipment to the university," Rand acknowledged. "Students stealing laptops isn't unusual. Happens every day." He dropped the card in his shirt pocket and asked, "Where's Danielle?"

"She'll be here in a second. Stopped in the ladies room to freshen up. Sorry about being so late. Danielle had her own share of problems this afternoon. I won't go into it, but the incident ended with her talking to the police."

Rand raised his eyebrows. "Fill me in."

"She was pretty shaken up." When he received her frantic phone call, Alex wondered if she was suffering from a paranoid hallucination.

Rand shook his head. "Let's head over to the lab. We'll grab a few sodas from a vending machine along the way. We'll leave the door open. I'm sure she'll find us." As they meandered down the sparsely lit hallway, Rand said, "Things are hopping around here with school in session. But I've managed to open the program and its … well, you'll see."

As they approached the lab entrance, Danielle caught up with them. "Mark, I want to apologize. I insisted, if you were up to it, that I preferred meeting tonight."

"Not a problem," Rand replied. "I'll make this short. I'll run through what I've got, and if you think of any questions, call or send me an e-mail." After they grabbed the sodas, they walked the short distance back to the lab. Rand retrieved his ID from his wallet and slid it through the card reader. A pea-sized light flashed green as Rand grasped the door handle and pulled the door open.

Rand dragged stools over for each of them to sit closer to the counter. He unlocked a metal storage locker underneath the counter and shimmied out the computer. Then he connected it to a monitor before feeding the electricity.

As the computer ran through its boot up protocol, Rand said, taking a bite from a slice of pizza and wiping his lips with a napkin, "To refresh your recollection, we've already established the concept of front and back stage doors. It's similar to a false perspective in the movies. And in this case, Owen partitioned one of the hard drives into two sections. He wrote a short program called a false directory command with a rogue directory code." Once the computer was booted, his fingers glided over the keyboard with the finesse of a concert pianist.

Alex cocked his head and caught Danielle's confused look.

"Never mind," Rand said with apparent recognition that both of them were lost by his explanation. "Suffice it to say that in order to enter the backdoor, Owen cut a few corners, but he gave you, Danielle, the key to unlock the door." He exchanged glances with both of them before he continued. "I had to reset the computer's real time clock."

Confused, Danielle asked, "So the key to the backdoor was the date?"

Rand looked at her with a wide grin. "Well, not exactly. As a safety precaution, Owen added another password to prevent you from entering … more like a secondary key. Changing the date essentially gave me access to the door."

Alex butted in. "Wait … wait … but why that date?"

"Danielle actually spelled it out for me when she gave me Owen's date of birth and mentioned the book *Nerds 2.01*. Actually, it took me longer than you would think to figure it out. That book is packed with dates, names, places, universities, and acronyms. So in a way, I was shooting in the dark. But," he sighed, "the password had to be subtle and yet obvious. I took Owen's month and day and added a different year, namely, 1969. That gave me October 1, 1969. Supposedly, the first true computer network test occurred on that date between UCLA and Stanford. The date unlocked the backdoor. Now I needed a password to unlock the program. Again, I reverted to the first word transmitted on the test date: login." Rand said with a clever smile.

Alex shook his head and noticed Danielle's puzzled expression. Now he knew why she would never have discovered the existence of the backdoor on her own.

"Login?" Alex said jokingly, forking several anchovies onto a slice of pizza.

"Hey," Rand replied with amusement, "no one said it had to be some complex set of numbers and letters. And Danielle, you aptly pegged Owen as a computer nerd." Rand took a swallow from his drink.

Rand gained access to the secret passageway and opened the program to reveal a screen parsed into boxes with the titles of name, address, phone, date, and message. A series of electronic icons were labeled play, stop, forward, and backward, and an icon in red was labeled send.

Rand folded his arms and said, "Well, there it is."

As the three of them stared at the screen for what seemed minutes, Alex settled back in his seat. "I assume this is STAR. So what's it do?"

"That's the million dollar question." Rand leaned over the countertop and drew attention to parts of the information with his pen. "The other evening, I tinkered with it. I typed my name, a bogus address and phone number, and then used one of the e-mail addresses I use for a listserv in the message box. When I connected to the Internet, that's when things became interesting. This computer must have an internal program to automatically connect to a host computer in cyberspace. When I connected, a message flashed on the screen, 'Do you wish to send?' And I replied yes."

Rand exchanged glances with both of them. "I checked my e-mail and found no message. I probed the host computer for a couple of minutes … well, maybe a little longer … but I didn't really find anything of value. It's like entering a cave. You need more time to explore."

Danielle observed, "If you ask me, it resembles a text messaging request form."

Rand raised his hands, palms up. "Those were my sentiments also."

Alex pointed to a section on the monitor. "I take it those audio icon commands are to listen and record messages?"

With her eyes glued to the monitor, Danielle said, "I'd have to agree."

Rand asked, "Danielle, did Owen hint to you what he was working on?"

"No. He was not the type, and besides, based on the explanations that you just gave, I wouldn't know what he said anyway. Sorry."

"What about the source code?" Alex set forth. "Would that give you any idea what this program does?"

"Maybe, but that will take time. I'll need to read the code and figure out what it's attempting to do. Even then, I'm not sure I'll be able to get the program to work. I think there's an access file that either unlocks another program or has an executable file built into it that triggers the program. Right now, I'm not sure. As soon as I return from my trip, I'll work with it a little more."

Alex looked at Danielle for confirmation, but her expression was one of bewilderment. "Danielle, did you hear what he said?"

Her eyes roamed the room, darting between the examining gazes of both Alex and Mark. She appeared torn on how to respond—not suspicious, but stuck in neutral between leaving the computer or taking it.

"Do you have a problem, Danielle?" Alex asked. Her eyes focused on him as though her words were frozen. In an unblinking stare, she attempted to open her mouth, but it seemed glued shut.

Finally, Danielle caved. "I ... I," she stammered, swallowing hard and peering into Rand's eyes, "yes, you keep it."

"Good," Alex said, satisfied but nonplussed by Danielle's obvious reservation to let Mark keep the computer. "We'll leave it with Mark, and he'll call us."

After Rand shut down the computer, he retrieved a cart from a storage closet and banded the computer to it. "Where did you park?"

"At this time of night, we didn't have any problems parking near the entrance." Alex noted Danielle's silence.

"Let me grab my jacket, and I'll walk out with you," Rand said.

While Mark strode to his office, Alex questioned Danielle, "What's wrong?"

Danielle shook her head unconvincingly.

With his arm around her, he gave her a squeeze. "Don't worry, we'll get to the bottom of this," Alex said. But she remained uncharacteristically quiet, which he dismissed considering her ordeal and a long day. The shock of Mary being shot, examining Owen's computer, and answering questions at the police station would be unsettling for anyone. Her color was almost ashen.

"Are you ready?" Rand inquired.

"Let's go," Alex responded, firmly gripping Danielle's hand, and she responded in kind. She remained stone-faced, as though her mind was miles away.

For the next few minutes, they discussed the scheduled Redskins and Steelers game. Danielle kept her head lowered and walked in a normal gait to Alex's car.

"Mark, I can give you a lift to your car," Alex offered.

"That won't be necessary. I need the exercise. Plus, the fresh air will do me wonders. I'll give you a call next week. On Tuesday, I have a morning flight to San Fran, and I'll be returning in several days on the redeye. I'll call ahead before I return."

Alex said, "Have a great trip."

Rand turned to Danielle and extended his hand. She shook his hand and smiled thinly. "Good luck. I'm a bit fatigued."

Alex watched until Rand walked beyond the reach of the floodlights mounted on the building. Once Rand was swallowed by the abyss of darkness, Alex got into the driver's seat.

*10:45 p.m.*

"Don't know anything, huh?" a voice pierced the darkness beneath the overhang of tree limbs.

Rand swiveled around abruptly, straining to pinpoint its location.

"I know you have what I want. I figured you had it when I saw those two characters."

# 32

Have a seat," Alex said, pointing to an L-shaped, brown sofa with large, contrasting, fluffy throw pillows that framed a matching granite coffee table. A candlestick cloisonné lamp in the corner lent a soft hue to the butter-toned room. "The house recommends a California merlot. I don't keep many other wines in stock since I spend so little time here. You know, you had me worried when we met Mark. If you don't mind me saying, your complexion was rather pale, and you seemed quite disturbed. Maybe you expected more, but he did have some answers." He poured two glasses of wine, handed her a glass, and seated himself in a leather chair across from her.

Danielle took a deep breath. "No, not at all. I don't know what happened; suddenly something came over me." Relieved and closing her eyes briefly, she said, "I'm not sure if it was what he said or merely fatigue." She took a deep breath. "From everything that I've encountered these last several weeks, being on pins and needles, wondering what Owen was doing, and now having to question my own involvement, maybe sanity, I guess everything has weighed down on me. Something just didn't click. I was strangely detached; it's a feeling hard to express. I … oh, I really don't know what to think. But thanks for hearing me out."

"Not a problem, I'm thankful we hooked up," he said, looking deep into her tired eyes. "Sorry if the place looks messy, but I don't get much company. You may be my first visitor in several months. I try to keep myself busy."

Danielle sipped her drink, breaking off the eye contact. Glancing around, she shook her head in response. "Not bad, for a guy."

"I do have a housekeeper who picks up after me. And I swear, if I clean this place, then all she does is watch the soaps all day and maybe spritz a little Lysol. Anyway, getting back to your meeting with Mary. What exactly happened?"

For the next ten minutes, she detailed how she came to know and meet Mary Simes. And then, without her ever expecting to see or hear from the woman again, she got the phone message on her cell. She took a sip of wine, stealing an instantaneous glance at Alex's eyes in what appeared as an innocent confirmation of his interest in her story. She set her glass on the coffee table and continued, telling him about dropping to her hands and knees when she heard the popping sound, and minutes later, fleeing the IMAX theater. She related her pursuit of a medium-height individual with a slight limp who had pushed through the stable of patrons that were collected in the open corridor of the Smithsonian. Her efforts to catch the individual quickly faded when she caught a glimpse of him stepping into a cab.

"That's when you called me?"

"Not exactly. I jumped into a cab to follow him, but it got bogged down in traffic and the torrential rain. That's when I lost him and called you. Truthfully, I hope that the police won't consider me a person of interest. Because I didn't murder her."

Alex cupped the palm of his hand under his chin. "There must be some connection here that we're missing. Something Owen may have said or did."

"Nothing. I've gone over our voice messages at least a thousand times in my head." She kicked off her shoes and placed a pillow on her lap. Her attention suddenly shifted to her purse. Undoing the clasp, she retrieved her cell and opened it. With a half-smile, she said, "Low battery," as it chirped in her hand. She looked up, hearing the grandfather clock situated against the far wall chime quarter to midnight. "That incessant ticking." With a fixed stare at the, she said, "Time is running out. But on what?"

"I can't hear the ticking. I must be immune because I hear it all the time." Alex stared in silence at this attractive, apprehensive female. At first he didn't know if he could soothe the torn feelings she experienced. A chord, with a sour note, struck within him as he wondered whether her problems went far deeper. But surely Brooke jested when she expressed her own observations about Danielle's behavior. He looked askance, knowing that he possibly faced a mounting conundrum. He wanted to believe what she said. But what if he was wrong? Did she actually need help?

Alex reached out his hand. "I've got the same model cell. Give it to me, and I'll charge it for you." Danielle absently stared at the cell and hesitantly dropped it into the palm of his hand. Again, he noticed the same reluctance she had when Mark suggested that he keep the computer. After he plugged her phone to a charger, he returned to his seat, patted the chair's arm, and said, "Where did we leave off?" But his question to Danielle went unanswered. He was met with that glazed stare he had seen before.

"We've got to go," Danielle commanded, wide-eyed with a sense of desperation.

"Where?"

Danielle arched her eyebrows. "You don't understand. We've got to get that computer. There's not much time."

Alex finished his drink and set his empty glass on an end table. Then he rose and seated himself next to Danielle. "Don't concern yourself. Mark will be fine. The computer is in good hands." Her wrinkled brow and squint made him think that she was there, but her mind was somewhere else.

She abruptly twisted at her waist to face Alex. "Manipulate. Mary said they could manipulate. That's it." For a brief moment, she paused in thought before adding, "I'm the cause of Mary's death."

"Absolutely not," Alex replied, reaching for her hand and giving it a reassuring squeeze. "You're a victim as much as she was. Together, we will solve this puzzle." She seemed unfazed as his words filled the void.

The grandfather clock chimed the hour. "I've got to warn Brooke first." She jumped to her feet, leaving the grasp of his hand. "Let's go. Call it a sixth sense. Intuition. Let's go, now." She slipped on her shoes and bolted for the front door, leaving him sitting on the sofa.

*Hallucinations*, Alex thought. *They come and go as though she had somehow received a mental message from an unknown force.*

"Wait," Alex cried out. He caught her at the front door. "Think about what you're doing." He wanted to shake her, thinking it could make her come to her senses. He put his arm around her and hugged her warmly. He could feel her rapid breathing and the restlessness. Letting go, he looked into her icy brown eyes.

Danielle said emphatically, "I know I'm not losing it."

"Of course not." But Alex also considered the implications. Could it be symptomatic of schizophrenia? He hoped not, but he also recognized it could be his own denial. A fact he didn't want to face. These last few weeks her statements and actions appeared to border on the irrational at times, but he couldn't come to grips with the conclusion. "What do you want to do?"

Danielle looked at him distantly. Her expression was one of shock and fear. "Now, Alex, not later."

Minutes later, they were in Alex's vehicle and arrived on O Street. On a moonless night, Alex suggested they approach the townhouse with the utmost care, although he wasn't sure whether he was merely placating her or accepting her assessment. He glanced at Danielle, who sat bolt upright in the passenger seat. They slowly circled the block twice before Alex found a parking place. They sat in the abyss of darkness without saying anything. With their eyes trained on the townhouse, Alex played mind games and considered the stark possibility of what if what she had said were true. If that were the case, then her seeming madness was the product of manipulation. But how? He wasn't convinced one way or another, and he didn't know what would convince him.

"She's not there," Danielle blurted. "If she were, the upstairs light in the back would be lit. But I can't understand why she hasn't answered her cell, or for that matter, returned the messages I left."

"Let's get your things and get out of here. We'll stop at the hospital."

They strolled arm in arm to the house's stoop. The outside light of the townhouse was out and so was the nightlight in the front room. She keyed the door and they entered. Inside, she flipped on the light in the corridor and gingerly walked to the family room. There she switched on a jug lamp. Nothing appeared out of place; it still resembled a showcase for a home tour in *Better Homes and Gardens*.

"Doesn't look like Brooke has returned. That's good. I'll write her a short note in case she does." Her motions were almost robotic as she pulled out a sheet of paper. She scribbled a note and then threw her purse on the sofa. Stopping halfway up the staircase to the second floor, she said hurriedly, "It will take me a few minutes."

Alex responded, "I'll be here." While Danielle was gone, he undid the clasp and rummaged through her purse. He had to know whether she was on drugs. When he didn't find anything, he unraveled a note inside. The note read: access file, STAR. He folded and tucked it back into place.

He dismissed a creak overhead as Danielle walking upstairs. He bounded up from the chair and shambled to the kitchen where he flicked on the light. Opening the refrigerator door, he found a bottle of water. As he unscrewed the cap, he stepped to the kitchen table, took a swig of water, and found a note written to Danielle.

## WARNING!

Where have you been? Tried to reach you on your cell. No answer.

BE CAREFUL! Individual represented himself as FBI agent was here. Benjamin DeFore. He's looking for you. After he left, I checked him out. They have no agent working by that name in Washington or New York. Call my cell when you get this message. Brooke.

Fished-eyed, he finished reading. A shrill scream pierced the quiet. He dropped the water bottle and clambered up the staircase. He ran down the short hall and met Danielle in the doorway. She was shaking uncontrollably and threw herself into his arms.

At the door, Alex belted out. "What's the matter?"

Without saying a word, Danielle pointed to the floor next to the nightstand. He crouched down, thinking something was under the bed. He was greeted with empty space. That's when he saw a sheet of paper and flipped it over. His eyes examined the picture and then peered at Danielle. It was a picture of her stepping into a cab outside the Smithsonian. He stuffed it in his pocket and whirled around to find her with an overnight bag draped over her shoulder.

He recognized the timeliness of her uneasiness and the need to leave. "Anything else you need?"

"No," she said, masking her fear. "I pulled everything together and was about to leave when I found this picture under the phone."

He latched on to the bag with one hand and with the other grabbed her hand. "I think you'll feel a lot safer at my place. We've got one stop to make. The hospital." She nodded in agreement.

"Still with me?" Alex asked.

"Yeah," Danielle said, sweeping her wet hair back with one hand and holding a blow dryer in the other. "What do you think will happen?"

"I doubt if the police will do anything until morning. Between Brooke and Mark, they have a good description of him. While you were showering, I tried to reach Mark, but there's no answer. It's late, so I'll try to reach him tomorrow. I wonder who this Benjamin DeFore works for."

With a measured gaze, Danielle looked into Alex's eyes. "Thanks for being there with me." She knew that was not quite what she wanted to say. Her feelings had begun to run far deeper than she imagined. She hoped it was more than a whim or some irrational attraction.

"Oh, here's your cell; you should keep it charged." Alex stepped closer and set the cell on the countertop as his hand reached around her shoulder. He whispered, "I have waited a long time for you to come back into my life."

Karen's voice echoed in Danielle's heart. *You need to move on.*

Danielle leaned into his body and lifted her face to gently brush his lips with hers. Alex responded with a full, hard, wanting kiss as he pulled her tighter against him.

Danielle wrapped her arms around him. Her heart raced as he massaged the small of her back through her hooded robe. His firm but soft touch melted away any inhibitions. Washed away by a gentle stream of tenderness, her fears became a mirage and anxiety-filled moments drifted into obscurity.

Alex kissed her forehead and framed her face with his hands, caressing it like a soft breeze that touches a rose on a warm, sunny day. He said, "Close your eyes, and rest assured that I'm here for you.

We'll work together to unwind the haunting voices. But for now try to forget and relax."

She raised her hand and touched his lips. "All I need to know is that you believe me." She could feel the beat of his heart throbbing as her hand explored his taut, sculpted body. He undid the tie of her robe and ran his hands over the front of her satin pajamas. Then he unbuttoned her pajama top and removed the bottoms. His smooth fingertips gently explored her body. His short breaths were punctuated with meaningful, hard kisses on her lips, to which she responded with fervent kisses to his body. The rays of light in the room drew back and faded into the passionate and emotional moments of their bodies pressed against each other.

# 33

*College Park, Maryland*
*Monday, October15*
*8:15 a.m.*

After entering through the double doors, Danielle squeezed between a gaggle of attendees congregating at the rear of the spacious conference room. Rows of conference tables covered with a sun-colored cloth with seating for ten and arranged for two hundred or more faced a small center stage. At each seat, the usual collection of water glasses, complimentary tablets, and pens were laid out. She chose two seats at a table midway down the center aisle with an unobstructed view of the stage.

She strapped her purse over the padded back, pulled the chair from underneath the table, and seated herself. Although the conference was scheduled to start in forty-five minutes, she made a habit to arrive early at all conferences in order to clear registration and choose an ideal seat. She opened the three-ring binder, which was filled with course outlines and notes given to her at the registration table, and paged to the list of speakers.

Dr. James Greyson, the last scheduled lecturer for the morning, was slated to present on the subject of psychological manipulation. Her interest lay not only with the topic, but her fervent desire to corner him. With a half hour break allotted for questions and answers before lunch, she felt confident that she could pose several innocuous questions.

"Morning," Brooke yawned as she set her binder on the table. "What's the latest with DeFore ... the jackass? Wait, before you tell me, I need a shot of caffeine—can't get my blood moving until I grab a large cup of black coffee. Maybe two. And you'll need to fill me in about you and Alex last night." She craned her head over her shoulder toward the rear of the room. "I caught a scent of freshly brewed coffee in the back when I entered. Keeps me going at the ER on those graveyard shifts. How about you?"

"Coffee? Thanks anyway, but you know I'm not a coffee drinker. Coke's more my style."

"For breakfast! Yuk! But I guess we get our caffeine one way or another." Brooke yawned again and rubbed her eyes. "ER was hopping last night with the usual shootings, stabbings, and accidents. I tried to catch a few winks before this presentation. So if I fall asleep, give me a nudge. I'm usually catching a few more hours of sleep in the morning. That coffee smells awfully good. I'll be back in a few."

Danielle had actually slept quite well, although she had let down her guard. How could she allow her emotions to control her? It wasn't like she fell into bed with just any guy. What had she done? Even so, she could still feel his warm, gentle touch. His embrace melted any barriers. And it was Alex she dreamed about when she was younger. She took a deep breath as mixed feelings stirred within her. He was, well, the boy next door. He was everything she had imagined: kind, gentle, and understanding—a gentleman.

"Okay, now that I'm awake, let's talk." Brooke said, with a steaming cup of coffee in her hand as she seated herself. "When I saw Alex rushing into the hospital last night, I feared the worst. These last few weeks I've wondered whether you suffered from deep depression. You know, it can happen to anyone. Just because you're a professional doesn't make you immune. And then that FBI agent, Defore, throws a scare into me, showing up at the door like that and asking all those questions. It really makes you wonder what this world is coming to. What's true and what's false?"

"I know what you mean. After we left your place, Alex strongly suggested I file a report with the police, but what good is that going to do? It'll take days before they undertake an investigation. Nevertheless, I promised him I would stop there today. And I'll bet that they're as busy as you are in the ER."

"You're probably right." Brooke sipped her coffee. "Now this hits the spot. Okay, we agree that there's a crime scene at our townhouse— fill me in."

"Before I do, I'm returning to New York late tonight. Ann wants my help. There're only a few weeks before her wedding in November. You can reach me at my old apartment. And given the police are not going to post a guard outside, I strongly suggest that you don't stay at the townhouse until the police nab the guy."

"You're probably right. I don't understand how he entered, though. I'll call my parents and let them know I'm coming for dinner. They won't mind a houseguest."

Danielle replied, "Truly, I'm sorry I'm deserting you like this and laying these problems on you. But I'm concerned for *our* safety."

Brooke crossed her legs and then said, not questioning the advice, "You may change your mind about returning to Washington."

"Hardly. I'm not independently wealthy, and that new job now seems, more than ever, like a death sentence. I understand your reservations, and I've got them also. I'm not going back to HBR, but I'll land somewhere—the sooner the better," Danielle said with a sense of desperation as she thought about what she found in the personnel files at PERC and the confrontation at the Smithsonian.

"Let's look on the bright side. At least you and Alex hit it off."

That comment resurrected in Danielle thoughts about whether her feelings for Alex were rooted in her feelings as a teenager or, worse yet, a woman on the rebound. Too early and too soon, and yet, she did collapse last night. What was he thinking? Long time no see and then she falls for him. That's not the way she wanted it. She closed her eyes for an instant and remembered his kiss. She laughed inwardly at the thought that he seemed like some fairy-tale prince coming to save a damsel, but then it made her freeze up. She didn't want to be a damsel; she wasn't one. She opened her eyes.

"I won't ask," Brooke said. "I can see it written all over your face."

"It's not what you think … after yesterday I'm trying to regain my equilibrium. On my way here, I bought the *Post* and found an article on the investigation into the shooting. I'm still shaking. I was no more than ten feet away."

"Considering everything, the best thing for you to do is to leave town."

"True. The common denominator with both Owen and Mary Simes is me."

"I wouldn't go that far, but it makes for a troubling conversation. The facts are not in. Here I am telling you, a lawyer, what to think."

Danielle nodded. "I'm trying to reconcile their deaths. I'm at a loss." The conference's moderator asked for the attendees to take their seats.

"As a medical resident, I've seen more than I'd like to see. And when you know the person who was shot, it's even worse. Are we really civilized?"

Danielle bit her lower lip. "Last night, Alex and I met with Mark Rand—the guy who knows computers. He found a program on Owen's computer, but he didn't know what it meant." She murmured to herself, more as an afterthought, "Owen would send me affectionate cards."

Brooke touched Danielle's arm. "Danielle, that was then. Those cards kept the flames burning. They're not a replacement for his absence. And you called me and broke down on more than one occasion."

"But," Danielle protested, "he was protecting me. That's what Mary said."

"From what?"

Danielle shrugged her shoulders. "I'm not sure."

"Exactly! Please don't take this the wrong way. You and I have had these conversations over many guys. I know you loved him dearly, but did you ever stop to think," Brooke lowered her head and furrowed her brow, "that he was into something that neither you nor I want to know about?"

Danielle was somewhat stunned, though the thought had crossed her mind. If he was protecting her, then why didn't he say something? He could have warned her. And why did he permit her to accept the position as legal counsel? Why was she thinking this way? And if he was protecting her, why would he send the program to her? Did he think they wouldn't trace it?

The room grew quiet with the tapping on the microphone by an older, balding man standing at the podium. He glanced at the speakers on either side of him. "Ladies and gentlemen, if I could have your attention." For the next several minutes, he set out the morning's schedule of speakers, the fifteen-minute breaks, and location of bathrooms before the first of three speakers approached the podium.

At 10:55 a.m., the second speaker had concluded his presentation. Now the seminar was running behind schedule. The moderator announced, "To give Dr. James Greyson his full allotted time, we're going to limit the questions and answers in order to conclude the morning session on time."

Danielle looked at Brooke, who shrugged her shoulders and gave a disapproving smirk. At that point, she decided on only one question: Why did Owen seek out Greyson? She had an inkling that the answer might be more than what she wanted to know.

The moderator continued with his introduction, noting Greyson's undergraduate degree at Pitt and graduate degree at Cornell University. Without further delay, the moderator referred the conference participants to the extensive curriculum vitae, which mentioned the offices in Pittsburgh and Reston and the articles published in various professional journals.

After the moderator relinquished the podium, Dr. Greyson arranged his notes and adjusted the microphone before he spoke. "Thank you for the invitation to speak to this assembly on a subject with far-reaching consequences. Persuasion, like breathing, pervades everything we do. From the time we rise in the morning until we retire at night, we are bombarded with persuasive arguments. We may not see them as attempts to influence us because, to some extent, we have taken persuasion for granted."

Danielle began to review his curriculum vitae and circled a gap of time in his résumé where a footnote to the time frame was marked with an asterisk. He appeared to have worked for the government, a fact that Karen had previously reported.

"Take, for instance, your morning routine," Greyson began. "You choose a leaner, meaner breakfast, without the carbs, and with the nutrients needed for the day. And take the clothes you wear. For women, it's above or below the knee. Is it burgundy, black, beige, or the color in style? And for men, it's the two or more button sport coat and the wet or dry look for hair. Then out the door we go, driving a Lexus, BMW, Hyundai, Ford, or Chevy in order to make a statement. But all these choices and decisions were made based upon conscious decisions. And those decisions were rooted in part, like it or not, in persuasion."

Brooke nudged Danielle and leaned toward her, saying in a whisper, "Maybe we could team up and make a weekend trip to New York on a shopping spree. I need a new fall wardrobe."

"If my budget can afford it, I'm up for it."

Greyson turned a page at the lectern. "Persuasion in one form or another influences our actions and reactions to events. A doctor recommends a prescription for a treatment, or a lawyer faces a jury and sets forth his arguments in support of a proposition. These are direct and indirect forms of persuasion."

Brooke observed in a low voice, "You know, I never defined a script as persuasion. But he's got a point with the pharmaceutical companies pedaling their drugs at the hospitals and in doctor's offices. Anyway, judging from the way he handles himself, he doesn't come off as the sinister type."

"I'll give you that much. Then why would Owen have been so provoked to attack him?"

"Maybe he never did?"

She locked gazes with Brooke. Was it a convincing act by Denon? "What makes you think so?" she asked, eyeing an attendee who glared at them for talking during the presentation.

Brooke nodded her head sideways in the direction of the rear of the room, and the two of them stood and retreated to the rear. "We can listen to Greyson from here. You told me your boss said Owen attacked his shrink. But your visceral concerns outweighed the hard evidence. See, you believed your boss—the credibility factor—because of his position. You had suspicions, but those reservations were allayed by a person senior in rank within your firm. In a sense, he had, like Greyson contends, persuaded you. The persuasion took the form of planting a seed, and all he had to do was nurture it."

Danielle chilled at the thought Denon merely dropped the right ideas, and she took them as gospel.

"Advertising is a form of stimuli that affects our conscious and unconscious selves," lectured Greyson, who had poured himself a glass of ice water and taken a sip. "We illustrate this in the form of celebrity endorsements. If a star athlete endorses a form of running shoe, this affects us in several ways. One, we have the endorsement of an athlete we know and trust; second, we want to pattern ourselves after him or her, perhaps due to the knowledge that he or she is the best golfer, basketball player, gymnast, or baseball player; third, we want to equate to or identify with the star athlete. This makes us, in our minds, on equal footing with the celebrity; fourth ..."

In deference to Brooke, Danielle concluded that the obvious can blind you like a silent idea or concept. Surely, STAR was more than an advertisement. With the plethora of advertisements bombarding us from radio, television, billboards, and the Internet, how could his program be much different? But she could see celebrity endorsements, for which millions were paid, would make a new ad valuable.

"... shaping beliefs and attitudes." Greyson stopped for emphasis. "Look around you. Pick up a newspaper and you'll find all types of persuasion; for example, facial expressions, body movements, and selection of words. A hypnotic rift or music coupled to lyrics with an inflammatory bent both represent methods of persuasion."

Brooke nudged Danielle. "No wonder this psychiatrist is in Washington. The study of persuasion has an impact much further than what you'd think."

"Then there's persuasion as a weapon," continued Greyson. "Persuasion can mislead. Depending on which side of the fence you may align yourself, you could argue for or against global warming. You have scientists saying we've been under a global warming trend for years, and there's nothing we can do. On the other side, you have environmentalists pressing that the accumulation of carbon dioxide from pollution-choking autos, coal burning plants, and the expansion of our cities has caused a warming in our atmosphere that, in turn, causes intense storms. Each will use their compelling arguments of persuasion to convince you."

With that last comment, Danielle, transfixed by Greyson's analysis, thought back to the meeting with Mary Simes. As she stared at Greyson, his words on persuasion struck a chord within her. She remembered again one of Mary's last words: manipulation. Warily, she tried to understand how STAR lent itself to psychological persuasion. But she was bothered by Mary's observation. What was that supposed to mean? Mary didn't say *convince*. It was *manipulation*, a searing into a person's mind.

"Are you still with us?" Brooke asked as she poked Danielle on the shoulder. "I thought you may have fallen asleep standing up. We better take our seats; I don't think we'll get a question to ask."

"Yeah," Danielle said absently. "I was … just thinking about …" She paused. "Never mind. It wasn't important. What time is it?"

"Almost noon." Before they returned to their seats, Greyson relinquished control of the conference to the moderator, who announced the lunch break. "Fascinating," Brooke said. "I never stopped to realize we're shaped by so many forces. It's almost as though our choices were predetermined by some corporate hierarchy. What with technology the way it is, Internet, cell phones, televisions, and iPads, it's as though we're addicted. We've been systematically engineered. It brings me to the question: are we really in control of our thoughts?"

# 34

*Washington, DC*
*Monday, October 15*
*1:30 p.m.*

At Fifteenth Street NW, Danielle entered the lobby and strode across to the receptionist, who sat behind a massive, dark walnut desk. After she explained her business and signed the guest register book, she sat in a roomy armchair and extracted her laptop. Fingering the touchpad, she scrolled through her e-mail messages but stopped abruptly when she sensed her actions were being scrutinized. She slowly raised her eyes and found Alex standing over her.

"How was your seminar?" he asked, holding an ID guest badge in his hand.

"It was less than I expected." She shut off her computer and looked into his inquisitive, dark brown eyes. The masculine scent of his cologne resurrected thoughts of last evening.

"We can talk about it as we head to my office." Without asking, he deposited her laptop into its case and bent to tie his shoes. With a discrete glance toward the main entrance, he strapped the case over his shoulder. As they headed to the elevator, he commented, "I didn't hear you leave this morning." His examining look at her facial expression seemed like an attempt to uncover a hint to what she was thinking.

"Sorry, I wanted to get there early and … I didn't want to wake you," Danielle replied as she also strained one last look over her shoulder. That was not what she wanted to say and not what he wanted to hear. But her mind was a jumble of mixed emotions, and their relationship had been christened without much thought.

"If you're looking for someone in particular, I had Brooke double back before she dropped me off at the main door. We weren't being followed. Neither of us picked out anyone in particular."

"Under the circumstances, I think your decision was the right one. What time's your flight?"

"Eight. I figured I should be there at six thirty or thereabouts. I'm thankful I don't have any luggage. I left enough clothes in Ann's apartment to keep me for a little more than a week. But my only reservation is that Greg has moved in. My former bedroom is the spare; it's not the same." For a change, she was anxious to leave Washington. It would give her time to reflect on a job ... and Alex.

"I'll have you there in plenty of time. Got a few loose ends to clean up, and then I'm free for the remainder of the afternoon."

"You're sure? I don't want to impose."

"Nonsense. You'll need to wear this." He handed her a visitor's badge.

After she pinned it to her lapel, she related what had transpired at the conference, including the missed opportunity to approach Greyson and his stimulating presentation on psychological manipulation. As they shot up to the third floor in the elevator, she noticed that he appeared mesmerized by her. Exiting, they quickly strode down the narrow corridor past a number of ID-carrying employees.

Alex's office was small, with seating for two, and his desk was disproportionately large for the size of the room. Atop his desk were dual widescreen monitors, which took up a significant amount of space. The papers on his desk were neatly arranged in piles, and the room appeared antiseptically clean from dust and clutter. He set her laptop on the floor and motioned for her to take a seat while he dropped into his desk chair.

"What are you writing?" Danielle asked, craning her head slightly to the side to find him behind the monitors.

"While waiting for you, I started an article on disenfranchised voters. Do you recall the flap that occurred several years ago over hanging chads?"

Danielle nodded.

"Well, a number of states have stepped into the electronic age, replacing mechanical for electronic voting machines. But it seems the results are no better. A series of new problems confront election offices, especially the failure of equipment. Now they don't know which way to turn."

"I'm not surprised. Computers are not foolproof—junk in, junk out," she offered. Before graduating from college, she had worked as an intern during several congressional races to the point where she didn't know if it was sunrise or sunset, cooped up with attorneys and paralegals. She remembered the law firm stories: the army of attorneys working behind the scenes on hanging chads. Holes punched in a card. Who did the voter choose? It was no different than holes in a story.

"Be glad you haven't started your new job. Clarke has a daunting task to become senator. He dropped two points over the weekend, so that the point spread is now twenty-two. Rumor has it he's as stubborn as a jackass crossing an intersection at the height of rush hour. It'll take someone to hit him over the head with a two-by-four to knock some sense into him. Either your employer or Clarke have underestimated the battleground for the senatorial election."

She grinned at his suggestion. "Sometimes you'd wonder whether it would pound any sense into a politician."

"What grates me is that the special interest agenda takes precedent over the interest of the constituents. Politics." Alex shook his head in disgust.

"Before I left New York, Karen encouraged me to dig deeper into PERC. I have, and now I've categorically decided against it." She exchanged gazes with Alex, who had his elbows propped on his desk and his fingers steepled. "Any chance we could search the database?"

"Sure. But I don't think you'll find anything."

"Why's that?"

"Earlier, I searched for information on Mitchell and Wheeling and did another search on PERC. But I really didn't find anything out of the ordinary, at least from my standpoint. But if you have another angle, then—" Alex gestured with his index finger for her to step behind the desk. He closed two side desk drawers to make room for her.

She stood and squeezed between the wall and the side of the desk.

With his fingers on the keyboard, Alex said, "Give me your search criteria. On second thought, take my seat, and I'll guide you through the menus." After they exchanged places, she punched in the word *PERC* and limited her search to Maryland, Virginia, and the District of Columbia. One by one she scanned the headnotes, which were a series of announcements and commendations, and in fact, similar to Alex's conclusions, nothing piqued her interest.

Fifteen minutes later, he picked up a newspaper from his desk and assumed the seat she had vacated.

Oblivious to his leaving her side, she typed the search term "Anthony Cervasi." Again, she scanned the headnotes. One offered article snagged her attention: Candidacy and Cognitive Behavior Management. Diving into the news report from Puerto Rico, she discovered that Cervasi was part of a roundtable discussion on the influence of television and radio advertisements. Riveted to the article, she never saw Alex rise from his seat until his face blocked her reading the monitor. He stole a kiss from her lips. "I'll be right back." And with that, he stepped out of the office.

Another article featured an ocean cruise for audiologists from Florida to the Grand Bahamas. The convention was entitled "Audio Frequency and Hearing Deficiencies." She immediately recognized Cervasi in a photograph. He was pictured with none other than Henry Milsen, the keynote speaker from Arlington, Dr. David Bateman, who was identified as a noted psychiatrist in Washington, and William Parks.

With a narrowed focus, she honed in on the articles looking for a hint, a slip of the tongue, an innocuous comment, for an inkling of why Cervasi would be in attendance. He was quoted as saying, "We employ a number of psychiatrists and psychologists on a regular basis to assist in the analysis of voters and to develop methods that could affect voter preference." Scrolling down the newsprint, she stumbled on yet another article of an audiologist convention in San Francisco. Cervasi's picture appeared with a group of guests, including Drs. Milsen and Bateman. The convention was entitled "Audio Frequency and Hearing Deficiencies: The Impact of Audio in a Digital World."

Alex entered the office carrying two bottles of water and said, as he kicked the door shut, "Find anything?"

"Not exactly, but I figured you wouldn't mind me printing a few articles." Although she remembered Milsen in her perusal of the personnel files at PERC, she refused to reveal her surreptitious investigation to Alex, fearing he might reach the wrong impression.

"And on another note, I found a salon about a block away from here. Before I leave for New York, I'd certainly like to have my hair done. I called ahead and got an appointment. And it should take no more than two hours. How about I call you when I'm done?"

Alex's face was awash with a surprise. "Well," he paused, "I guess it's okay, but if you wait fifteen or twenty minutes, I'll go with you."

"I'll be fine. At least, it's broad daylight, and I'm not going far. Besides, you can have some extra time."

Alex handed her a bottled water.

"I'll leave my cell on." She grabbed the articles and scooted around the desk, reaching for her laptop case.

"Leave it here. I'll bring it with me when I leave."

"Thanks." Danielle then instinctively kissed him.

Alex opened the door and yelled, "Hey, Red." Seconds later, a young redhead with a freckled face appeared, rolling her eyes with an infectious grin. "She's my research assistant and a good friend. Kate Grohal."

"Everybody calls me Red, but that's fine. Some of the best actors and actresses and famous people were redheads. And I'm proud of it."

Danielle extended her hand and said, "If you don't mind, I think I'll call you Kate." After the brief introduction, she escorted Danielle to the main entrance.

Outside in the bright sunlight, the picture she had blown up on the computer revealed Cervasi, Milsen, and Bateman, but she also found Owen in the background. The more she delved into his life, the less she knew him. He was an unassuming person who maintained a low profile, and his role at PERC remained draped in mystery.

An hour later, Alex finished writing his news article and called Danielle's cell, but she didn't answer. He stuffed his keys in his pocket, strapped her laptop over his shoulder, and headed out of his office.

Catching up with Kate, he said, "If anyone should call, page me on my cell. I doubt I'll be back until late. I'm meeting Danielle at the salon around the corner."

"Sure thing. But she stepped out of the building and flagged a cab."

Alex returned to his office, dropped the laptop on the floor, and headed to his computer. But before he turned on his monitor, he spotted several pieces of copy paper in the garbage. Retrieving the paper, he examined one picture and then the other. He soon uncovered Danielle's interest.

"May I help you?" the receptionist asked. The twenty-five-year-old with shoulder-length, blonde hair raised her sleepy, afternoon eyes.

Danielle said, "I'm here for my appointment."

"Your name?"

"Danielle Madison."

"I'm sorry, but I don't have your appointment, and I can't find you even in our system."

"I'm positive," Danielle voiced. "I made a special trip. And my doctor made this appointment for me."

With pleading eyes, the receptionist said, "I'll be right back, if you'll have a seat." She retreated into the inner office and returned in less than a minute. "I'm sorry, but he has another appointment due here in the next twenty minutes. I can schedule you on another day. And who is the referring physician?"

"This will take five minutes, if that. Tell him I'll make another appointment when he has time, but for now, I want to discuss STAR. And I'm not leaving here until I see him." She didn't know what it meant. Reed once told her as an attorney, close all means of escape and press your opponent into a corner. Then you must press, press again, and keep on pressing. He used to say think of a grape press, squeezing until you can't get another drop.

The receptionist sighed. "Oh, but—"

"Just tell him," Danielle pressed.

A few minutes later, the receptionist returned and said, "Follow me." She ushered Danielle into a conference room. "Have a seat. Dr. Bateman will be with you shortly."

Danielle recognized the somber music selection from overhead speakers as "Nocturne" by Chopin. A collection of day and night photographs of the harbors in Boston and Annapolis and the beaches of Aruba and Bermuda were pictured in the low intensity pencil lights.

A man in his late fifties, bald-headed except for a curtain of black hair flecked with gray on the sides, sporting a full beard of similar color and wearing a pair of brown rim glasses, strode into the room and dropped into the chair. He wore a dark blue suit, pale blue dress shirt, and a red tie. With elbows planted at an acute angle to the conference table, Bateman said in a deep voice, "How can I help you, Miss Madison?"

She pulled out the convention picture and slid it across the table.

He snatched the picture, leaning his head onto the high-back chair. Then he peered over the top of the article with an unblinking stare. "What do you want?"

"The gentleman in the background is Owen Roberts. I'm sure you know him. He lost his life several weeks ago." The musical selection evolved from an andante to moderato tempo as if right on queue with the somber tone of their conversation.

Bateman continued to stare at her. "Go on."

"What do you know about STAR?" she asked with her best poker face. "Owen wrote the program, and I'm looking for answers. I was told you had them." She decided to play her cards, even though she was without any direct knowledge and desperately needed a lead.

Bateman lowered his head and pursed his lips before he looked up, his thick, black eyebrows knitted. "I don't know who sent you, sister. But you're not going to get anything from me. That picture means nothing. Now I'll ask you to leave my office." He stood with his arms crossed as he stared her out of her seat.

She bounded up from her seat and idly stepped to the door. She looked back at him. "It's more than a coincidence that two out of four people in that picture are dead."

"Milsen's death was a hunting accident. And Owen, well, he committed suicide. You're not getting anything from me—get out."

Alex wound down the window. "Are you going to get in?"

Danielle looked both ways before she stepped from the curb. "How did you know?"

"I found the discarded papers. On my way, I had Kate run the addresses on Drs. Bateman and Milsen, except Milsen died a few months back."

Danielle reflected for a moment. "What does a computer specialist, a political strategist, an audiologist, and a psychiatrist have in common besides two of the four dying in accidents?"

With a stone face, he replied, "Something they don't want you to know."

# 35

In his hotel room, John Candecki stood at the window facing the Capitol with a glass of scotch in his hand. From the twenty-fifth floor, the White House, bathed in a majestic coat of white light, was the quintessential hub of Washington's solar system. To him, the distant lighted monuments and memorials were planets captured in orbit, while vehicle headlights busily flickered like satellites equally caught by the gravitational pull. There, within the steady stream of light in the halls of government, he imagined stood the desires of two candidates who would make political deals in the interest of becoming Virginia's next senator.

As he turned away, the regional news was being televised. With a remote control, he notched up the volume and seated himself in a cozy chair a short distance away from the computer that silently sat on a writing table. If he was to believe Matalino, the program was worth millions, and surely he should be entitled to more compensation for his efforts. After all, he risked his life facing a vile animal and then rubbing out one of Matalino's men. That alone should entitle him to more than what he had bargained for.

In fact, when Matalino discovered the loss, Candecki would have a price on his head. That meant he'd need to disappear, and fast. The expense of hiding, maybe in the Bahamas, would cost plenty. He wasn't sure how many months he would have to lie low, but it was more than what he wanted to think. Matalino wasn't going to take the loss of his men sitting down, and then the loss of the computer would only add fuel to a raging fire. No, within hours, Matalino would send feelers throughout the city.

To pop a man cost twenty-five grand, and that wasn't too bad for a night's work. Yet the computer seemed to increase in value with each day, making this job, from his standpoint, easily a seven-figure payoff.

For a moment, Candecki played with the idea of keeping the computer for himself and possibly making lucrative deals like Matalino did. He decided to nix the idea, not wanting to deal with computer engineers and the like or having someone competing with him. No, the answer was to collect his commission and return the equipment.

After his work over the last few days, with little sleep, he conducted an auction in his mind. How much? He took another swallow from his drink. As his eyes skated around the room, he settled on the television station: fifteen. Then he decided on $1.5 million. If he had to share, why shouldn't he ask for more?

He lifted his shifting eyes to the television only to find Clarke at a political fund-raiser in McLean, hobnobbing with the social elite to raise money and rally supporters. And how was Clarke going to sway voters in a love-hate relationship with the former congressman? At twenty points behind in the latest poll, Clarke hadn't moved any closer since the inception of his campaign. Candecki merely smirked at the assessment. It was imperative that he close the deal before Clarke became a singed bush on the political landscape. With that, he drained the remainder of his drink.

After she and Alex said their good-byes, Danielle passed a bountiful number of purveyors that included eateries, bars, and specialty stores. As she entered the busy concourse with travelers briskly stepping between boarding gates, a musical rift from an overhead speaker reminded her of the song "Private Eyes" by Hall and Oates. Could they know her every move? She was like a fish in a bowl, being examined and observed.

At the boarding gate for her flight, she settled down into a stiff chair at row's end and called Karen, who answered on the first ring.

"*Karen*," Danielle said as her eyes wandered and settled on men with long hair, unshaven, shabbily dressed, portly, and clean cut.

Young. Old. What were the characteristics of the person behind those private eyes? It could be anyone. That was the problem.

"Dear, where have you been? I've wanted so many times to pick up the phone and call you. But I knew you were going to be busy searching for an apartment, settling in with your friend, and trying to establish yourself. So I decided to wait until you surfaced."

Danielle remembered that she and Karen were intense when they worked late into the night. And her search for a tail was equally as intense. "I'm about to board a flight to New York."

"Welcome back. I was anxious to hear from you. When we last spoke, I didn't know what to think. And you not calling heightened my concerns, especially if Denon is involved. In fact, I started to nose around, discreetly of course, and it became apparent that I've got more questions than answers."

"Oh?" Danielle stiffened, waiting for a further explanation, but when none was forthcoming, she concluded Karen had her reasons. "And I'm anxious to return. I'm looking forward to getting together. I have a fitting this Friday, and Ann wanted my opinion on a few matters for the wedding. Believe me, my getting out of town is a welcome relief."

"Greg's been busy with a trial all week; he's been here until the wee hours of the morning, preparing trial briefs, motions, and closing arguments. I don't think he's been home in days. I don't know how he does it."

Danielle said in a quieter voice, "At least Ann and I will have some time to prepare for the wedding. I never told her about my change in plans. I still have my key to the apartment, so I'll be staying there. But for now, I have a small favor to ask."

"Go ahead. I'll do my best."

Danielle realized that what she wanted was beyond a reasonable request and, in fact, placed Karen in an untenable position. It compromised Karen and HBR, but the significance of what she might find was too great. "Could you search our files for, oh, say, the last eight years for agreements, notes, memos, or anything that might mention PERC, Anthony Cervasi, Dr. David Bateman, or Dr. Henry Milsen?" There was silence on the phone. She awaited Karen's justifiable epiphany on the merits of working for PERC.

Instead, Karen said conspiratorially, "What am I looking for? And besides, I could pull up thousands of memos, e-mails, documents, and the like."

"If you could provide me with dated file names, documents, e-mails to and from these individuals, it might prove helpful."

"How soon?"

"A couple of days?"

"Consider it done. I presume you need this in your capacity as a consultant and a future assistant at PERC. Right?"

Danielle recognized Karen's rational justification for the request. "Right. And thanks. I've got to run—they're boarding. Talk to you soon."

Danielle slipped her cell into her purse and slung the strap of the laptop case over her arm when she stopped. Her mind hung on the words "access file" like rippling tides breaking against a beachfront. Walking down the brightly lit boarding ramp onto the plane, she pictured the outside panel of the computer being removed by Mark Rand. It was as though she was consciously locked to the computer's contents. Shaking off the image, she coursed down the center aisle of the plane. A cold feeling swept through her. *Where would it end?* she wondered as she tossed the laptop in the overhead compartment. Were they lost thoughts of Owen, or was STAR seared into her mind? If Owen hadn't written anything in the treatise, perhaps he left it where she would least expect it.

"Did you receive my message?" Candecki questioned.

With the venom of a snake about to attack its prey, Clarke said, "Are you out of your mind? First it was my house, and now you risk my candidacy by showing up here. What if someone recognized you? You know the press would eat me alive. They're always one step ahead and looking for a story." Rubbing his fingers feverishly across his forehead, he could feel beads of sweat forming on the back of his neck.

"Senator, you don't have to worry. I told your staff I was assigned by the FBI to ensure your safety for the next few days. I flashed my credentials, and they didn't seem to be worried," Candecki said with an impertinent smile.

"Don't patronize me." Clarke paced the floor. "You've got to get out of here. I hired you to do a job, and now you keep coming back like a bee to a hive."

"You'll blow a gasket, Senator. Then what? I heard you were working to raise more than a half million at tonight's event. Had I known you had the money in hand, we could've finalized our deal. But I figured you needed time. Wouldn't it look odd, though, if I showed up with the computer? I can see the headlines: 'FBI carries a computer into meeting with Clarke.' There would be a lot of questions. But that's why I'm here. I've got the package, and I want assurances that I'll receive my money. But a suitcase of money won't do. Too clumsy. Rather, I have this Swiss bank account."

"Anything for you to get the hell out of here. Get me the routing numbers." Clarke growled.

"Good. Now that we understand each other, there's just one more thing. I decided to rewrite our deal. This is not too dissimilar to those professional football and baseball players always holding out for more. So that's nothing new," Candecki intoned in a matter of fact way.

Clarke stopped in his tracks. "You have it?"

"Let's say it's in a safe place." Candecki knew this magic lamp of a computer had some powers. But he wavered on whether to hand it over.

Clarke gave him a vacuous look. "What do you want? I've already made a down payment."

Candecki pressed his fingertips together like a prayerful altar boy. "Simply one and a half million dollars."

"Million?"

"That's right. One and a half million. You can hold more fund-raisers."

"I … I can't get my hands on that kind of money. Besides, it's only a computer with some type of program on it that Tony needs for my campaign." Clarke raised his hands palms up to emphasize his point.

Candecki quickly retorted, "That's not exactly correct. That's what Tony wants you to believe. Between you and Tony, I'll get my money. And Senator," he paused, noticing the egotistical acceptance of the designation *senator* by Clarke, "the price might keep going up.

I suggest you make delivery tonight because tomorrow I may be out of town, or I might change my mind."

"You know," Clarke's face turned crimson, "*your parents* were good people, unlike you."

Candecki's parents were respectful, that much was true. But he also knew that good people finished last. "My parents thank you. I'll ignore your distasteful comments. This is a business deal, nothing personal, Senator." He noticed the panic on Clarke's face. "Senator Clarke. Now that has a nice ring to it, although the newspapers say you're a little behind in the race. Is that twenty points? That concerns me. With only a few weeks left, I would think that you would move a little faster."

"Why, why you *blackmailing* son-of-a—"

"Son-of-a what, Senator? A person of your stature could ... let's say ... arrange for delivery. This is your chance. And I wouldn't blow it. Save your sparring for Thomas McClay."

Clarke glowered. "Have it your way, but there will come a time—I promise you. I'll place a call to Tony. If he agrees, where do we meet?"

Walking toward the door, Candecki turned to address Clarke, who now appeared like a waxen figure. "I'll call you in two hours with wiring instructions. Once the money is deposited and confirmed, I'll call with complete instructions on where you can find it. I'm a man of my word." With one hand on the door knob, he said, "Don't worry, Senator. Between you and Tony, I'm sure you'll figure a way. Oh, one more thing. Don't forget to ask for program instructions. You should know what you're buying."

Tony Cervasi removed his black tie and threw his tux coat over a chair. He settled down at his desk at the corporate headquarters. It was late. The little light from the moon that reflected off the pond created as the illusion of a shimmering oasis.

It was a profitable evening for Clarke, but the race was closing in on them. Yesterday, the veterans and the teacher's union endorsed Thomas McClay. The question continued to float among the political advisors and analysts whether anyone could trust Philip Clarke. Even interviews with reporters and television anchors had failed to change the electorate's minds. It was what Halstren and Hart had warned.

Clarke was a worn-out tire flapping away with no traction as the race kicked into in a high gear. Clarke's personal ethics were a matter of investigation, but that was politics, and Washington had more pressing matters like terrorists, war, international politics, and global warming. Millions of dollars' worth of commercials across the state failed to make any impact.

Survey after survey showed Clarke was on the wrong side of the fence with same-sex marriage and civil unions, taxes, and ethics in government. The latter was his real Achilles heel. Although Clarke's terrorism campaign seemed to have softened the blow, the momentum was squarely with McClay. Cervasi sensed an erosion of voter confidence would continue unabated, only to intensify in the days ahead.

A rap at the door pulled Tony from the depths of his frustration. Carl Matalino slowly entered the room.

Matalino grunted, "The authorities have written it off as a drug deal that went bad. Rocco and Lanny were both good men." He made the sign of the cross with his thick fingers and then kissed the gold cross dangling from a gold chain around his neck.

Cervasi said, "I've got confirmation." He arched back in his chair. "Our candidate, Philip Clarke, in a panic befitting a wild animal, was quite clear it was Candecki. He is the culprit. And he has the merchandise. But he won't hand it over unless one and a half million dollars is wired to his Swiss account tonight. That means we have little time."

"There's no doubt we could get the money. If we wire it, I don't know whether I can have people in place that fast. He'll close and open accounts in an attempt to cover his trail. Once he leaves Washington, it will take some time to find him."

"I suspected as much," Cervasi said. "Richie Davis is chomping at the bit to get the computer back. The number of uses on the beta version of the program are counting down. And it's had a limited effect. Maybe it's holding voters in place rather than bolting to McClay. We have no choice but to pay the ransom. We've got a huge investment wrapped up in an upcoming television campaign. And it's about to begin. If we wait much longer …" he shook his head in disgust.

"Yes." Matalino nodded in agreement and rested his chin on his chest.

"Get the money wired. Once we know we've got the merchandise, we'll find Candecki. But for now we've got work to do on Clarke's campaign," Cervasi said angered and frustrated by the events that had unfolded. "If this program works, then it was worth it. I won't forget about Candecki. He'll have my money, and I want a full refund."

Matalino slowly rubbed his hands together. "I understand. We haven't missed getting who we want in the end. They poured the foundation today. We won't be hearing from Parks."

Cervasi raised his eyes to meet Matalino's gaze.

At 10:30 p.m., Danielle opened the apartment door, flipped on the hall light, and dropped her suitcase at the door. From the looks of it, the apartment hadn't changed during the last several weeks. Locking the door behind her, she headed for her old bedroom, which, from what she recalled, Ann intended to change into the guest bedroom. With building anxiety, she burst through the doorway and switched on the lamp. Much to her relief, the bookcase and books were right where she left them.

# 36

*Washington, DC*
*Friday, October 19*
*12:30 p.m.*

Fifteen points," Tony Cervasi exclaimed, holding a vodka and tonic at an old-fashioned noontime political rally at the Hyatt in Reston. Although Clarke had not caught McClay, polls showed a demonstrative shift, which Cervasi believed was good news. His only misgiving, with three weeks to the election, was whether it was too late. As he looked around the room, he caught a glimpse of Alex Preston seated at the press table a short distance away. Cervasi knew how to handle the media, and for him, a quid pro quo exchange was not enough. The name of the game was persuasion, and he demanded more print and video coverage footprints for Clarke as he clawed for votes.

Cervasi swaggered over to the table. Gloating, he raised his glass and looked directly at Alex. "Do you want to retract that article you wrote?" He grinned and took a hearty gulp of his drink, alluding to Alex's analogy of David versus Goliath penned in a satirical depiction of McClay versus Clarke. There had also been a cartoon embedded in the article that depicted Clarke, wide-eyed, opening a war chest of money as a rally supporter and a special interest group dumped money into it. Cervasi chose to ignore the fact that he, along with the other key architects at PERC, had been in a quandary just a week ago. Leaked reports from an insider showed that McClay's performance was rock solid, and overcoming his substantial lead was virtually impossible. Cervasi knew it quite well.

Alex responded, arching his eyebrows, "Congratulations. But the polls continue to show McClay leading by a comfortable distance, and the sands of time are running out."

Cervasi recognized that Alex, like his fellow reporters, pondered the unexpected sharp rise and probably dismissed the poll as an anomaly, a fluke in the pollster's sample. Inwardly, his smile turned to a scowl. Then he broke into a deep laugh. "You know, I like you. Maybe I'll hire you to write press releases."

"Your staff seems to be doing just fine without me," Alex retorted. As part of the new advertising blitz kicked off by Clarke, newspaper and television reporters had been invited to the luncheon.

Not to be outdone, Cervasi responded, "Mr. Preston, there's plenty of time. We're entering the fourth quarter, when the winner takes all. You might learn a thing or two from us. I'm sure you've read history." He leaned forward and added, "Don't get caught up penning Clarke's obituary before Election Day. Someone forgot to tell the news reporters that Dewey lost the election." He wheeled around and proceeded to pump hands like a seasoned politician.

"When are you running, Tony?" yelled someone among the throng of supporters, contributors, and the news media.

Confidently, Cervasi merely gave a thumbs-up as he beamed with the knowledge that PERC had a commanding lead on numerous races throughout the country and was about to make the race for Senate a dead heat before pulling ahead at the end.

As he sauntered to the other side of the room, he was struck by the silverware and fine china, which replaced the plastic cups and utensils from his earlier days on the campaign trail. Today was a far cry from the rubber chicken banquets. The game of politics had also changed dramatically. Campaigns required cutting edge technology, good security, and better ideas to counter an opponent's moves. It was a chess match and not for the faint of heart.

He raised his eyes to find Philip Clarke entering through the outer doors. Two years ago, having dinner with Congressman Clarke in the same hotel ballroom, Cervasi recollected Senator George Montgomery, the robust, folksy-style politician whose interests ranged from charities to education, had hosted the charity ball. That was the beginning of the association with Clarke, and in retrospect, a decision he had made out of sheer exuberance.

Cervasi had put his hand out first, clasping Clarke's hand in a firm grip. "Congressman Clarke, it's a pleasure. I believe you're seated next to me for this evening's affair." He recalled their handgrips were like the opposite ends of a vice butting against each other.

And it wasn't until Senator Montgomery announced in his closing remarks, "This will be my last term in public office," that Cervasi decided to seize the moment.

"Now that's earth-shattering news. Don't you think, Senator Clarke?" Cervasi recalled saying. What he didn't know was that Clarke's portrayal of the consummate politician to all constituents was actually a façade built on wayward activities and lack of ethics and pumped up by the coffers of special interest groups. And that quagmire, developed, funded, and supported by Clarke and his cohorts, was brought to the forefront in this present race. Cervasi knew he had chosen the wrong horse, but he was unwilling to concede or admit his misjudgment.

A broad smile swept across the congressman's face as he picked up Cervasi's business card. Clarke opened his wallet and stuffed it inside.

Cervasi traced the movement of Clarke through the crowd until the full face and furrowed brow of Carl Matalino came into view. He blinked twice, returning to the present and the realization that his thoughts of yesterday were but a dream. The senatorial election loomed ever closer, and he felt unsettled at the thought that Clarke might lose.

Matalino said in a calm and collected voice, "Richie Davis assures me that he should have full implementation of the network within the next several days. There are limitations, of course, but he believes the program pulled from Owen's computer will breathe new life into the campaign."

Cervasi had heard this before. Without opening the source code and removing the number of uses for STAR, the program would expire. It was no different than those prepaid telephone cards. After you used the allotted minutes, you could either replenish it or throw the card away. Now that they had STAR, all they needed was the access file, which was the key to opening the source code and removing the limitations.

Cervasi said in a biting tone with knitted eyebrows, "Find Madison. She's got to have the access file."

"She's in New York. I had it confirmed through Denon. She hasn't answered his phone calls, but he spoke to someone in his office."

Cervasi nervously twisted his gold ring. "Who do we have in New York?"

"Carmen. And I've called him with all the details."

A broad grin replaced the sickening feeling he had in his stomach. Cervasi knew that if the source code for STAR could be opened, Richie could make the changes he needed to the program in order to canvass the entire state of Virginia. "And the money? I'm not going to let John Candecki get away. I want it back."

Matalino replied, unlatching his antacid pill case, "We're following the money. I've made a few phone calls. I believe we'll see it again. We've got the routing and account numbers." Then he launched into a raucous laugh.

Cervasi didn't join in. He remained dubious until he pictured himself at the political rally as he celebrated a Clarke win.

"Mr. Preston." Les Baker extended his hand with cold staring eyes.

Alex glanced over his shoulder and shook the stranger's hand. "Sorry, I don't believe we've met before."

"No, we've not had the pleasure. Les Baker—I work with Tony Cervasi."

Alex recoiled imperceptibly. It was Baker who had confronted Danielle, sending her into a state of fear only a block away from the hotel. A myriad of thoughts collided in his mind, but seeing the middle-aged man dressed cleanly and seated in a wheelchair failed to raise any suspicions in Alex. Baker had an insouciant smile, and his demeanor appeared contrary to insidious. He was far different than how Danielle described him.

Baker continued above the growing din in the crowded ballroom. "From a distance, I noticed indignation while you were speaking to Tony. For PERC, the Clarke-McClay election presents a challenging race. I've been in the political campaign business for too many years. And this does seem like a David and Goliath race, as you so stated in your recent observations. But quite truthfully, I've seen Tony pull a candidate from the jaws of defeat in the nick of time. I know that he intends to do it again."

At first, Alex didn't know how to answer. "I've read and heard about his exploits. And it appears PERC, according to my research assistant, has had an unblemished record." As he returned Baker's stare, Alex remained uncertain why Baker had sought him out.

"Perhaps we could do some horse trading," Baker suggested.

Confused by Baker's choice of words, Alex had to ask himself where the conversation was headed. "I guess that would depend on what you have in mind." He merely reported the news and worked on investigatory reports. He had nothing to trade.

Baker handed Alex a business card and said with a stone cold expression. "Call me, and we'll meet." With one touch of the control lever, the wheelchair whirled around and Baker headed into the throng.

At the Aureole restaurant, Danielle arrived early and was seated at a corner table covered with a white, linen tablecloth. The luminance of the restaurant, coupled with walnut and oak appointments, created a bright, cheerful, and warm ambiance as though she was seated in an outdoor garden.

Danielle drank from a goblet of water, which the waiter, dressed in a clean, white shirt and black tie, had poured for her while she waited. As she flipped through a book on persuasion purchased from a bookstore, the waiter brought her an order of flatbread with a creamy, smoked bluefish pâté and a glass of the house chardonnay.

At the sight of Karen, Danielle swept the cloth napkin from her lap and bounded from her seat to give her a hug. Karen's outward appearance—the plain skirt, blouse, and limp hair—and her demeanor—the crooked smile on a soft face—hadn't changed in the weeks Danielle had been gone.

Karen said as her eyes roamed the restaurant, "You didn't need to be so extravagant. We could have grabbed a bite at a diner. It would feel more like home."

Danielle chided, "Nonsense. You've got to indulge sometimes. And that's why I invited you to lunch. I had hoped to see you before this, but I needed my bridesmaid gown altered and I had to make arrangements for the bridal shower, not to mention last-minute shopping."

"But how do you feel, dear?" Karen questioned in her analytical way. "I think about everything you've gone through. Well, it's enough to make someone run off and hide."

Danielle spread a spoonful of pâté on a piece of the flatbread, not wanting to confess the other encounters that had befallen her. "You're right, I do feel a deep emptiness. I think what keeps me going is the determination to find what's around the next corner. It's engrained in me, like turning fear inside out. Fear feeds my determination."

"You can't hide what you're thinking from me. So let's start from the beginning, and we'll go from there."

For the next half hour, Danielle detailed the meeting with Denon; the incident at the Smithsonian; the conference with Mark Rand; and lastly, how Alex Preston walked into her life.

Karen had gone from being wide-eyed to her jaw dropping, but now she had a worried look on her face. "Obviously, you've raised someone's ire. Now we've got to figure out why and who. But I'm glad you've hooked up with a friend—Alex."

Danielle smiled. "I know what you're thinking ... he's a friend. Let's not think ahead." She knew that wasn't exactly accurate.

"You know my feelings." Karen paused for a short moment as though collecting her thoughts. "Now here's the skinny on Greg and Denon." She leaned forward closer to Danielle in order not to be overheard. "You may be right. After Greg finished that criminal case, the one he started just before you left town, he's been flying back and forth to California like he's getting on a crosstown bus. And Denon has had your replacement setting up offshore corporations. This week, things really got heated. At one point, Greg flew out of his office and didn't say where he was headed."

Danielle didn't recall in her conversation with Ann hearing about any unusual behavior from Greg. If anything, it seemed Ann was content with him being busy so that he wasn't a distraction.

Karen reached into the deep pocket of her purse, keeping her eyes glued to Danielle. She pulled out a DVD in a jewel case and passed it across the table. "This is what, I believe, the doctor ordered. I even managed to find preliminary documentation on the new corporations."

Danielle's attention was briefly attracted to a gentleman seated several tables away before she said, "You never cease to amaze me."

Karen smiled knowingly. "And they're indexed. You know some had embedded passwords, but that didn't make sense. Well, at least for me, since I know where Greg and Denon keep their passwords. Kind of defeats the purpose?"

Danielle leaned slightly to the right, using Karen as interference to steal a peek at a man. His high cheekbones, dark eyebrows, and swept back black hair struck her as familiar. Then she swayed back to her original seated position as mental pictures ran through her head in an attempt to match a name to the face. "And did you find anything?" she asked as she leaned to the side and stole another glance.

Karen picked up the menu and continued in a conversational tone. "Representation contracts with political candidates … contracts with advertising companies, you know, the kind that produce the negative spot political ads … employment contracts with those two individuals, Bateman and Milsen. And transportation contracts, publicists, and so forth."

Danielle could feel her shoulders drop when Karen didn't uncover anything of significance.

A knowing smile crossed Karen's face, as though she had saved the best for last. "But, then there was an investment in a telecommunications company, Shannon Telecom. The stock passed through a number of companies and holding companies. I had to trace it back through the companies to determine how Anthony Cervasi became the owner. What do you make of that?"

Danielle shook her head, thinking about the implications of offshore corporations.

"Oh, one more thing." Karen grinned. "You mentioned a Dr. Milsen." She spooned pâté on flatbread before she met Danielle's eyes. "Greyson, Owen, and Milsen worked together … at the CIA."

Danielle dropped her eyes to the table and took a deep breath. "And?"

"That's all I've managed. But I haven't found any connection with Dr. Bateman and the three of them."

Danielle settled back in her chair and remembered the picture where Owen was in the background with Milsen, Bateman, and Cervasi. She craned her head around the menu held by Karen.

"Answer me this," Karen said, "the way you're swaying back and forth makes me wonder whether we're on a cruise ship on the high seas."

Danielle said with a quick, impish smile, "There's a man whose seated behind you, and I know him, but I don't know from where. I can't remember whether he was seated when I arrived, or if he came in after me." Danielle leaned again to the side, but he was gone. She settled back into her seat, somewhat relaxed. "It doesn't matter; maybe it will come to me later."

As the waiter passed their table, Karen gestured for him. Pointing to Danielle's drink, she said, "I'll have the same, and I want another drink for my friend."

As she placed the CD in her purse, Danielle pulled out a paperback book that she had recovered from the shelf at Ann's apartment. "I think I found it." She opened the book and retrieved a thumb drive embedded. "This, I believe, is the answer. I just know it," she said, holding the drive between her thumb and index finger.

"What makes you think so?" Karen perched her glasses on her head.

"The date October 1, 1969, is written on its side. That's the date we used to unlock the program. And I wonder if it opens the source code behind the computer program." Danielle explained what she learned from Mark Rand. Computer programmers write the program and encode it with an access code. It could be a file. Once the program is written, the program is compiled into machine language, 1s and 0s, so that a computer can read it. If you want to change the program, you need a key to unlock it.

A moment later, Danielle found herself on the floor with the waiter sprawled over her. The aroma of tropical fruit, apples, and citrus filled her nostrils. With one hand, she wiped the wine from her face.

The waiter sounded like a broken record. "I'm so sorry, I'm so sorry." As he stood, he reached down to help her up.

Danielle could feel a rush of blood to her face and realized all eyes were on her. The maître d' shouted orders to waiters and waitresses as he cut through the few patrons standing nearby.

As she handed another napkin to Danielle, Karen attempted to calm the maître d' who apologized profusely to Danielle and blamed the waiter. "But it wasn't his fault … it was—"

But the maître d' hit his forehead with the palm of his hand and demanded the attention of a waiter for a new tablecloth.

Sitting down, Karen muttered, "It was more of a tackle than a brush. I never saw the guy that hit the waiter."

Danielle said, "The thumb drive, where is it?"

Karen's eyes dropped to the table top, the seats, and then underneath the table. "It's got to be here."

Danielle knew otherwise.

# 37

With the phone cradled to his ear, Alex drummed his fingers on his desk while he waited for an answer. His eyes narrowed as he studied the monitor. Suddenly, he began to consider the unthinkable. Philip Clarke was behind twenty points at the beginning of the week, fifteen yesterday, and then thirteen according to a recent poll conducted overnight. He closed his eyes and then opened them, looking at the poll again as though he misread the results.

Finally, on the fifth ring, Danielle answered, much to his relief. He entreated, "Where have you been? I've tried to reach you for the last several days. Left messages on your cell, at the law firm, and even sent a series of e-mail messages." Unsettled, he rose and commenced a slow and deliberate pace within his office.

Danielle answered wearily, "I simply tried to hibernate and think. But I wasn't trying to ignore you. Ann returned last night from her West Coast trip. So to make up for lost time, we got an early start and returned late this afternoon. Oh, and more importantly, I found the book … the book that Owen sent me. And that's *not all*. Embedded within it was a thumb drive. But—" Danielle paused.

"But what?" Alex walked around his desk and dropped into his chair.

"*I lost it*," Danielle sighed. "Actually, it was taken out my hand." Then she related how the mass confusion at the restaurant had led to the loss. "And to think, I had in my hand, maybe the key to what they're doing." For the next few minutes, she explained the where, the when, and the how. "And, I didn't recognize him at first, but I think it was Carmen Vittorio, the guy I met in the restaurant with Leonard Wheeling."

"Intriguing." Silence filled the air before Alex said, "And Mark was mugged. He's okay, but he'll spend a couple days in the hospital. The computer is gone."

Danielle was stunned. "Oh no. *Now what?*"

"And Clarke is closing the gap. He went from twenty points to thirteen within a week. A candidacy turning around so fast? Go figure."

Danielle chimed, albeit in a subdued way, "There's been some type of sudden shift. Could it be that he's the better of the two candidates?"

"What can anyone say? Politics, I guess."

"No," Danielle said, "there's something else afoot. And we're going to find out."

"We will. When are you returning?"

"Soon, but I've got to run. I'm having dinner with Ann and Greg. Talk to you soon."

Alex slowly dropped the receiver into its cradle. With his elbows planted on the chair's arms, he stared at Clarke's results. He raised his eyebrows, thinking that elections in the past had never turned that fast without a root cause. But he couldn't assign a single fact, and he had covered the race from the day when Thomas McClay had first announced his candidacy. The well-educated, respected legislator bolted out of the gates. He had led the entire time and needn't look back as he headed to the finish line. McClay should win, from all indications, but now Alex wasn't so sure.

Alex admitted that the negative campaign ads, which started in earnest in late September, may have had the intended effect. The ads had resurrected anecdotes of actions McClay took in college, law school, and then as a lawyer. He had defended companies on defective and warranty claims. In some instances, the ads depicted him all smiles descending the courthouse steps as headlines flashed another win for business and a loss for maimed individuals. Negative ads were effective, otherwise they wouldn't show them. McClay, on the other hand, ran a clean race without resorting to Clarke's problems while he served in Congress.

Alex shifted his attention to Vittorio. If it was Vittorio, it may have been a mere coincidence. One statement, though, rang in Alex's mind. Vittorio had said, "If you want to know about PERC, ask Denon."

Danielle admired the warmth and beauty of the country club with its wide hallways of oak plank flooring and rich green carpet. Electric candles mounted on brass sconces illuminated the cavernous corridor. Rich, dark, cherry wood climbed halfway up the wall. Framed in gold leaf were several paintings of the club's more famous golf holes.

In the main dining hall, she spotted them seated at a candlelit table overlooking the lush, velvet, eighteenth fairway tinged by a golden bronze sunset. Upon seeing her, the waiter scurried over to pull out a chair at the table and suggested a cocktail. She settled on an Australian cabernet similar to what her friends were drinking as the lights dimmed. A pianist played Debussy at center stage.

"Congratulations. I understand you won the case," Danielle said.

Greg raised his eyebrows and nodded. "At least, it's over. He'll be in a mental institution for a while." He swirled the remaining wine in his glass, and with unseeing eyes, said, "I know what you're going to say: the guy was a murderer. His actions spoke untold volumes. He knew what he was doing. Premeditated murder. How could I get him off, so to speak? Well, truthfully, I remained skeptical of his capacity to understand the nature of his acts, so I decided to argue his actions were the result of diminished capacity."

Greg drank the remainder of the wine and set the glass on the table. "In my opinion, the guy was brainwashed. The jury bought the idea that he suffered from diminished capacity. That's better than being found guilty of murder."

"You know," Danielle said, "I recall reading about Patty Hearst and the Symbionese Liberation Army. She was about nineteen, I think. The gist of the case related to her kidnapping and then her subsequent participation in a series of armed robberies. Her attorney argued that she was brainwashed."

"You're right, but I would think it's more like a personality transformation. Do you remember Charles Manson? Jonestown? A group of followers with fanatical loyalty associated with a cause. Brainwashed. Altered capacity. It's all the same."

The waiter brought Danielle her glass of wine. As she swirled the wine in the glass, Danielle said, "So you believe a personality transformation equates to brainwashing? If so, what about subtle changes that sometimes affect our judgment? The loss of a relative or a friend? Or an event that instinctively changes the way we perceive matters? Is that brainwashing?"

Ann exchanged glances with both of them. "Don't mind me. I would have held the announcement of the case's outcome until after dinner. But you two go ahead while I find an appetizer."

Seemingly ignoring Ann, Greg frowned as he shifted in his chair. He glanced away before he exchanged looks with Danielle. "Don't get me wrong ... not all personality changes represent brainwashing."

Danielle knew a lawyer's job was to defend a client, but she had a sense of morality that made it difficult to represent known felons. "I would think a person must be under extreme pressure or indoctrinated to be brainwashed. And only then should we consider a person truly under diminished capacity or brainwashed. And Greg, your client, from what I recall of the case, was under neither. You know it, and I know it."

Ann interrupted, tapping her spoon on a water glass. "End of round one. We will now have a minute delay while we order an appetizer. And we don't need to talk shop all night. Besides, we need to talk about the wedding," she said, giving Greg a long glare.

After they settled on an appetizer, Greg started up again. "A few more points before we end. To your last point, I think brainwashing may be more than a molding of a person under extremes. What if he exhibits the symptoms but never had been the subject of physical abuse or mental deprivation? And before you answer, the court of public opinion would judge him brainwashed."

Danielle countered, not to be outdone, "But we have a free will— we can choose good or bad. Why should a person hide behind the curtain of unaccountability? If a person knows the substance of his acts, then how can he be brainwashed?" The flame of the candle on the table flickered when she shook her napkin as if to punctuate her point.

"Time out." Ann formed a letter T with her hands. "Let me add something to this brouhaha." The diamond on Ann's finger caught the glow of the flickering candle. "I would suggest that our perspectives, and perhaps our personalities, change on a daily basis. Take, for example, television advertising. We parade the attributes of a particular product before viewers. It could be a cologne, shaving cream or, for that matter, a new mop. But we do not call a change in our normal shopping behavior brainwashing."

With a sly smile, Greg welcomed Ann to the discussion. "Let me add this—if a person is subjected to punishment, torture, or inhuman conditions resulting in the adoption of a different ideology, I'd call that brainwashing, but I think you could stretch it to mean more. The real problem lies with the methods used to mold the person's beliefs."

The waiter brought the appetizers and warm bread and asked whether they were ready to order their meals. But Greg waved him off.

Ann said, increasingly annoyed, "You two have gone back and forth over the idea of brainwashing. And I do admit, in this day and age with cults, extremists, and terrorists, it makes you wonder."

Danielle noticed Greg was not about to end the debate. Although she and Greg were good friends, she had to consider Karen's comment that Greg had changed, making her wonder whether he covered up the break-in. One day he was decidedly for her, and then the next? She didn't know what to expect, but she dared not share her reservations with Ann. Greg was aggressive and sometimes demeaning. She decided to end the debate. "I don't know if we can actually define brainwashing, but it seems to me it's common to action and inaction. And it happens on different levels. I think it will evolve over time. But turning to a brighter subject, I think that Ann's wedding dress is absolutely stunning."

Ann disregarded the hint of Danielle raising the flag of surrender. "Our brains, for whatever reason, do not process everything we see and hear right away. For example, when we advertise cologne, it's our intention that you purchase the item. To ensure that you don't forget about the product, we advertise it every hour. We are, in effect, trying to influence your behavior. That's advertising, and we accept it as normal. And although people have been influenced, they are free to make choices. Brainwashing reflects, I think, abnormal or uncharacteristic behavior that the person might not otherwise choose."

Greg exhaled strongly as though to say the subject was more than advertising. "So you're asserting that brainwashing results from an out-of-the-ordinary behavior that does not fit the norm of that person or, perhaps, of a civilized society. You could change your behavior completely and not cause any problem to society, which would indicate that you have been influenced but not brainwashed."

"Certainly," Ann replied, "advertising attempts to change the way you think with its repetitive messages. Companies vie to have their products represented in a movie for the same reason, whether it's a car or a piece of furniture sitting in the background. Corporate logos reflecting off the walkways in airports serve the same purpose."

"These create subliminal impressions that influence our behavior," Greg asserted. "The messages could be positive or negative. And while they may manipulate us, I don't consider it brainwashing."

Not skipping a beat, Ann continued, "The Federal Trade Commission Act prohibits deceptive or unfair advertising; however, it hasn't stopped subliminal advertising, which could be interpreted as an attempt to affect our subconscious. That's a form of brainwashing in my book. We are creatures of our conscious and subconscious thoughts. At what point do we stop acting independently?"

Danielle divorced herself from the conversation and stared absently at the flickering candle with its mesmerizing motion. She was drawn back to the day that she saw Greg talking to Harry Mitchell outside the office building. In most contexts, she would have ignored it, except that Mitchell raised suspicions within her. Was Mitchell's warning due to his having drank too much, or was there something no one wanted to discuss?

Danielle searched for an answer, but she had none. She picked up her white napkin and waved it. Both Greg and Ann got the message and grinned.

Greg exchanged glances with Danielle before he turned to Ann. "You should've been a lawyer."

Ann quickly retorted, "One attorney in the family is enough. We'd get nothing done if there were two, especially if we had different viewpoints."

As he rose from his chair, he imitated Danielle's towel-waving surrender with a cell in his hand. "You two enjoy yourselves while I take this call,"

After Greg stepped away, Ann said apologetically, "He gets like that sometimes. We had this conversation only a few days ago. I don't know why he's so touchy. Imagine if someone could brainwash us; we would be a bunch of mindless individuals."

It was rather early when they returned home. As they entered, Greg said, "I've got a few things to clear up at the office. You'll excuse me."

Danielle was perplexed. "Before you go, I have a question. It completely slipped my mind until now. Do you know a Carmen Vittorio?"

Greg's eyes froze in fear. He replied dryly, shaking his head, "No." He quickly kissed Ann on her cheek and was gone in a heartbeat.

Danielle thought, *Greg misspoke. Why? And why is he going to work so late on a Saturday night?*

Ann dropped her purse on the chair and tilted her head to remove her diamond-studded earrings. "I'm beat from a long day. I think I'll retire, if you don't mind."

Danielle agreed with a nod, "I'm with you."

In her old room, Danielle pulled on her nightshirt and slipped into bed. She stared at the wallpaper, the patterns of gold and green stripes, and then her eyes wandered over to her laptop. With the dinner conversation still swimming in her head, she snatched the laptop and pulled the DVD from her purse. After she inserted the disk, she immediately headed for the Shannon Telecom agreement. The document was too long for her to read at this time of night. The consideration for the sale of Shannon to Cervasi was an eye-opener: one hundred million dollars.

Catching a second wind, Danielle flipped on the television with a remote for noise background as she perused the contract. At one thirty in the morning, she turned to the agreements of Drs. Milsen and Bateman. Both agreements evidenced no unusual or extraordinary terms.

With heavy eyelids, she grabbed the remote and pointed to the TV when she caught sight of the droopy, glazed eyes, muffed hair, and red-nosed person reaching into the medicine chest in the commercial. The announcer said, "Sneezing, runny nose, watery eyes, and ringing in your ears. You'll need—" Half-asleep, heard the ad's warning, "If the frequency persists, see your doctor."

She succumbed to her eyelids being pulled by gravity and dozed off. But a minute later they shot open to focus on Bateman's résumé on her monitor. Almost in a daze, she read: "Thresholds: Frequency and Physics of Sound—A suggestive response due to auditory stimuli," by Dr. David Bateman. Her eyelids fluttered in an attempt to stave off sleep. In slow motion, she slid the laptop to the floor, turned out the light, and fluffed the pillow under her head. With soft, rhythmic breathing, she ushered herself through the corridors of drowsiness, and past the doors of consciousness. Right before she reached shut down, she whispered, "subliminal impression."

# 38

With his legs stretched out and his feet leisurely mounted on the desktop, Alex stared at the white ceiling as he collected his thoughts in a desperate attempt to explain what had occurred in the Clarke-McClay race. He winced for a second and then pressed the call button for Kate. He had always known her not as a fiery person, but as a conscientious researcher admired for her dogged tenacity in finding an answer to the toughest of questions.

Alex furrowed his brow. "What do you make of it? Here we are less than two weeks away, and Clarke mounts a last-minute charge as he tightens the race with another point. He reminds me of a runaway train bearing down on an unsuspecting city. What's fueling this unexpected turnaround?" He had studied the issues and strategies of each candidate, and yet, with all his years of covering election races, this one remained an enigma.

Kate set her cup of coffee down and shrugged her shoulders. "Yep. This one defies a reasonable explanation. I mean, anything could cause a change in the results. But a race that changes virtually overnight ..." As one might study a tip sheet handicapping horses, she studied the newspaper's political races.

Alex caught a bead of the article she was reading. "If I recall correctly, the race between Bush and Gore was in a virtual dead heat in the closing weeks. And historically, other races have run neck and neck, but generally, a gut feeling prevailed over who would win. No—" He shook his head. "This race is just peculiar. Something happened within the last few weeks, but for the life of me I can't figure out what." Reading the headlines again, he said, "Clarke Notches another Point. Has a certain ring to it, like a gunslinger. At this rate, he'll meet or pass McClay a day before the election." His desktop was crowded with a half-eaten lunch, a can of Coke, newspapers, reports, and marking pens in a rainbow of colors.

Kate rested her head against the high-back chair. "There's no denying that Clarke's got momentum and money behind him. How far it will carry him remains to be seen. But it's interesting news copy anyway, and when you consider his populist positions on traditional marriage, education, and stem cell research, he's making some points. And, of course, we won't get into the negative advertising and special interests that have kicked in. It's not a boring race." She grasped her coffee cup and took a sip. "This coffee is wicked. Yuck! Hey, when's Danielle due back?"

"Tomorrow. I'm not sure what's delayed her other than she's been running down those—" He stopped in midsentence and said unconvincingly in a whisper to himself, "leads." When she left for New York, he had hoped that the time with her old roommate would distract her from Washington and those auditory hallucinations. "That reminds me. Tonight I'm headed out to Falls Church for a barnstorming kickoff McClay is having. We'll see how far I get before I call it a night." With desultory thoughts, Alex finally pulled out a tablet and scratched out several past events. "For some reason, I can't get this election off my mind. Here's what I want you to research."

As Kate scanned the page, Alex narrated his mental notes, "Find a chronology of important events, say news events or anything of major importance for the last eight or ten weeks. I want you to superimpose those events over a graph of the tracking polls for Clarke and McClay. We know there's a sharp upward tick in popularity. Maybe we can find a triggering event."

Kate questioned, "That's a little much? There are only so many hours in a day, and you've read everything there is about the two candidates. Heck, you know what they're going to say before they say it. To go back and do a time line will require days."

Alex frowned, figuring inconsistent positions and inarticulate comments had to be a factor. He knew Clarke's voting record, which was less than superb and was actually against the populist, was capitalized on by McClay. Clarke's checkered past carried a lot of baggage from political favors in past campaigns. "His popularity grew too fast for some inexplicable reason."

Kate shrugged her shoulders. "If that's what you want, it's fine with me. But considering Clarke remains a distance behind even at this late date, I don't understand the purpose."

Alex replied, "If Clarke's candidacy is for real, we'll have the research ready for an in depth article when he wins. It's merely a hunch, anyway ... so don't put an extraordinary amount of time into this project." He knew his limitations would go unheeded by Kate because she was thorough. "We've got all sorts of information in our databases and, before I forget, find someone in the MIS department to compile your findings in a chart or graph. You know, so that we can see the big picture. No pun intended," he said, trying to lighten the mood as she gawked at him in disbelief. "Let's plan to view the results in a few days."

Kate glared at Alex. "And what about the other news deadlines?"

"I have confidence in you," Alex said jovially. "Call me if you find something. It doesn't matter how late it is."

"Time's wasting," she snapped. "If you have any other bright ideas, *don't call me*. You knew I was going home for some much needed R and R."

As she made her way to the door, Alex called out, "If you get this done, I owe you dinner at the restaurant of your choice."

She turned abruptly, with her hand on the doorknob. "That's the least you can do. But you owe me a dinner for two. And get your wallet out; this is going to be expensive."

"You're on," Alex retorted. He pictured the headlines the day after the election. "Clarke Overcomes All Odds to Win Senate."

From all indications, Clarke's election track was greased for a lighting finish, and Alex had to admit that if Tony Cervasi pulled it off, it would be a masterful job. As he stood in the doorway to his office, he looked at the buzz of activity with news assistants, staff writers, interns, and staff all working hard to get the paper out. These same people were going to vote in their respective jurisdictions for local representatives, congressmen, and state legislators within the days ahead. Even though they worked at a newspaper, he wondered how many actually sat down and studied the political issues.

On his way out of the office building, he pulled his cell from his jacket pocket, and with it came the copy of the clipping from the Florida audiologist convention, which had escaped him. With renewed intrigue, he stopped, programmed his phone to forward his calls to his cell, and unfolded the article to read.

Almost sandwiched by the revolving doors in the lobby, he strode onto the crowded sidewalk. Four people were in the photo, now two were left. And Dr. Bateman's reaction to Danielle's inquiry about the article and PERC suggested, perhaps, some impropriety in his relationship with the company. Coincidence? Maybe, maybe not. He refolded the article and stuffed it back in his pocket.

The sign mounted to the traffic signal flashed "Walk" in white letters. He and a group of pedestrians edged out from the sidewalk and crossed Pennsylvania Avenue. Side-stepping pedestrians coming from the opposite direction, he noticed about halfway across that the signal began to flash intermittently. He wondered whether the person who set the timer was a runner. He shook his head. When he reached the other side, he looked back. The pedestrian signal flashed, Don't Walk.

He stood at the street corner for a moment and watched pedestrians, thinking that they behaved as though preprogrammed like birds migrating to the cues of nature. He again pulled out the article and looked at the photo underneath the streetlight. Birds flew overhead and squawked as he stared at the picture. Why would Cervasi and Owen be interested in attending an audiology convention? He could not imagine even the remotest connection between the study of sound and the study of political strategy. With an increased curiosity, he called Kate. "I'll throw in a night on the town, within reason, that is, but I need all you can find out about Henry Milsen and David Bateman."

Silence. He could feel Kate's steam; luckily, he was not in the office.

"We'll see. No promises. And the price keeps going up."

"That's my girl," Alex said with a cunning smile.

Cervasi reviewed the results of recent surveys from various campaigns undertaken by PERC. There were 145, but none would garner the political promise, prestige, and future business as the senatorial race. He sat behind the helm, steered the candidates, and oversaw the political organization similar to a chess match.

Gratified by the latest poll results, he sensed STAR was working without any glitches. In future elections, Cervasi could virtually guarantee a win. By introducing the psychological programming into the campaign earlier, the company could jump-start a politician's campaign. Once the candidate had an edge, the momentum from public favor could carry the race to the finish. Cervasi pictured going before the board of directors with a win for Senator Clarke. *They would eat their words at the post-election review*, so he thought. And future funds from political candidates would be readily assured. The intercom on the phone interrupted his thoughts. "Yes?" Cervasi asked.

"Mr. Matalino is here to see you," the secretary said. "And is it possible that I could leave? I've finished the reports you wanted copied, and it's now seven o'clock."

"Send him in. And you can leave."

With his white shirt opened and his red-striped tie pulled to the side, Matalino strode into the office. He took a seat across from Cervasi, gave a deep nod of respect, and stared blankly.

Cervasi started, "Now that we have the computer, I want a copy of the program, the access key, and source code transferred to our computer system and another backup copy for the safe." Pausing, he twirled the gold ring around his finger and grinned. "We should win by a wide margin."

"You've seen the latest polls, I take it?" Matalino asked.

Cervasi beamed. "Yeah. If it wasn't for Vittorio, we would be in deep shit. On the heels of his handing us the access file, I sent Denon to Shannon to negotiate a possible contract. After these elections come to a close, Richie and I will map out a strategy for a licensing contract. But I think we'll use the newly established offshore companies for our sales. We can then use the money from the licensing to pay down our debt for the purchase of the telecom company. We're in the driver's seat." Cervasi stared at Matalino's unblinking eyes and drawn facial features. "Something wrong?"

Matalino screwed up his face before he said, "Despite my efforts, I have no clue who knocked off Mary Simes."

"Candecki?"

"No. I don't think so. What reason would he have?" Matalino questioned with knitted eyebrows as he stared distantly in thought.

"Carl," Cervasi said, "her death creates additional problems for us. What if the police tie together the death of Roberts, Milsen, and now Simes? Sanitize our records, if necessary. On second thought, we've got a lot of friends in the right places. But just in case …"

Matalino nodded his understanding as he poured himself a glass of red wine.

Cervasi merely shook his head. "I'll be glad when I see Clarke ahead. This whole election season has been like Pandora's box."

Matalino peered out the window at a shadow crossing the courtyard. He pointed with his raised glass. "That Baker he's up to no good."

Cervasi joined him. "He knows too much. We have no choice but to wait. We'll deal with him another day."

# 39

*Lexington, Virginia*
*Friday, October 26*
*4:35 p.m.*

On a windy two-lane road cut deep into the Virginia mountains, twenty-five miles off the interstate and one hundred twenty miles from Washington, Danielle slowly rounded the hairpin turn marked by a series of yellow road signs and white pavement markings. After she landed at National, she had labored over the inescapable decision that she had made during the flight: Shannon Telecom, with its circuitous record of ownership, must be tied to the merry-go-round of mind-numbing incidents of these last six weeks. She was reminded to follow the money, and it took plenty to buy the company.

There was a mist of rain as well as ice pellets and patches of fog in the higher elevations, and Danielle shivered from the temperature drop displayed on her lighted instrument panel. The rented car's wipers swept the windshield free of the mixture of rain and ice, but as the vehicle snaked up the mountain, the blades stuttered against the windshield. Now and then the wind edged her closer to the centerline and kicked up leaves, splattering them against the vehicle and making her wince as she white-knuckled the steering wheel. She hadn't passed another car in ten minutes, and the last service station was fifteen miles behind her.

That's when she decided to call Alex about her plans. Despite his protests, words of wisdom didn't affect her in the least bit. Thoughts of turning around crossed her mind, but she decided to press on. She could hear him saying, "Danielle, you can't do that. What if you're caught? Then what's going to happen?" What was she supposed to do? She couldn't merely play dead.

The turnoff, she knew—after another glance at the GPS—wasn't far. With the weather on the ugly side, she also made a conscious decision to make it a short visit, not wanting to strand herself in mountainous country.

A clearing cut into a swath of trees revealed itself in the crosshairs of the headlights against diminishing daylight. She slammed on her brakes, flinging her cell to the floor on the passenger side. With the vehicle idling, she took note of two arching brick walls that separated the wide driveway that marked the entrance to Shannon. As she made a left-hand turn, she noticed in smaller block letters underneath the main sign: Communication Software. Through the partially fog-shrouded roadway, blankets of leaves edged the road that parted a thickly wooded forest. A large communication tower with dish and candle antennas from top to bottom and topped by several red beacon lights and a strobe was planted on a knoll above the pines.

Inching deeper, she saw a canopy of tree limbs hanging over the twisted driveway until it opened into a large parking lot several hundred yards from the main road. She cut her headlights, driving no faster than a walking pace. She circled the lot until she found an empty space and coasted to a stop. Cutting the engine, she shivered slightly as the wind kicked bits of ice against the hood.

Two separate buildings, an older, brown brick with its squared-off, paneled windows, and a newer glass façade, each with lights lit on every floor, were in distinct contrast—the older, a foreboding, two-story structure and the newer, a bright, five-story beacon.

In her gray, quilted pantsuit and new, black high heels, Danielle was mindful of her professional appearance, but now, with the cold weather, her dress seemed out of place. And her warmer clothes were packed away in a suitcase in the trunk.

She turned off the dome light and then emerged into the penumbra cast by a light high atop a lamp pole. She retrieved a camel-colored toggle coat from the backseat and put it on, pulling up the collar and striding quickly toward the entrance. Stamping her feet as she entered the older building, she reached in her purse and pulled out a business card from Higgins, Biggs, and Reed. She took a deep breath and stepped to a counter where a receptionist sat listening to an Internet radio station.

The young woman, with stylish brown glasses and brown hair swept back in a clip, peered over her monitor and asked, "Can I help you?" She was chewing gum and glanced at the wall clock, which read 4:54 p.m., before she returned her questioning gaze to Danielle.

"Yes, I was looking for Mr. Stewart; that is, Howard Stewart." Danielle recalled he signed the sales agreement that ultimately vested the ownership of stock in the hands of Tony Cervasi. And Stewart was listed as the former CEO of the company according to the records found by Karen.

With her elbows on the desk and holding the card a few inches away from her nose, the receptionist peered over it and said rapidly, "Sorry, he's not here. He left earlier this afternoon, and I don't expect him back today." She laid the card on her desk and pushed an on-off button on her monitor. It appeared that she was about to call it a day.

"I drove up from Washington hoping to ask him a few questions," Danielle replied plaintively. Actually, she didn't know what, if anything, to expect from her visit in the first place, but she remained steadfast.

The receptionist stood and stepped a short distance away. Without saying anything, she retrieved a coat from a closet and shook her head as she put an arm in the right sleeve. "Our quitting time is five o'clock. If you want to talk to Mr. Brad Stewart," she said impatiently, putting her other arm into her coat. "I'll check to see if he's still here." She punched in a telephone extension. Seconds passed as she tapped her foot and waved to a few exiting employees. "I've got an attorney from Higgins," she started as she wrapped her scarf around her neck. "Uh-huh. Okay." She replaced the phone in its cradle. "He'll be here in a minute. Have a seat." She pointed to a darkened reception area with drab-colored walls where cracked brown leather chairs and a sofa were situated. A scratched and chipped mahogany coffee table served as its centerpiece, with the face of a lion underneath the table's glass top.

Danielle replied, "Thanks, but I think I'll stand."

The receptionist gave a faint smile and checked the clock, again. It now read 4:58 p.m. as a number of employees herded through the lobby past Danielle and exited through the front doors.

Shortly thereafter, a gentleman in his midthirties with a tan complexion, dressed in a designer suit with a razor sharp crease in his pants and gleaming white teeth, swaggered into the foyer. The receptionist handed him Danielle's card and then, with a brief, unforgiving smile, said, "Good night."

After exchanging glances with her, he said, "Brad Stewart, vice president. Glad to meet you." He cupped her hand with a firm grip before she pulled her hand away. "Did you have trouble finding the place?"

"No," Danielle answered, half wondering whether he was mistaken or whether he knew she was coming. "It's a little out of the way." His dreamy, examining look told her that she could have answered anything, and he would have accepted it. She took note of the initials on his shirt cuff and the black onyx ring on his finger.

"We like it that way, but you can always find us with the blinking strobe mounted to the top of the tower," Stewart said, beaming with glistening eyes. "You're probably wondering why we're located out here. We pull many of our employees from West Virginia. Plus, we're close enough to Maryland that we can pull from there if we need them."

Danielle hadn't seen a business establishment except for the service station located at the exit off the interstate. To her, it was a desolate area.

"I should be more hospitable." Stewart glanced at his watch. "We've got time. I'll give you a quick tour before the meeting." He extended his hand. "Let me take your coat. We'll put it in the closet."

She removed her coat, her mouth dry and her hands slightly clammy. Tense but determined to carry out her plan, she cleared her throat and asked, "Meeting? I didn't want to hold you back after five o'clock."

Stewart furrowed his brow as though he misunderstood. "Oh, Howard couldn't make the meeting. He left earlier for Washington, you know, with the election heating up. So I'm here in his place. You'd think that they would wait until after the election to look for new business, but no, this was an urgent matter, and they couldn't wait." He gave her a wink and said, "I'm rather glad Howard had other business."

Stewart was obviously under the mistaken impression that she had a meeting with Howard, which was more than fortuitous. Danielle relaxed, knowing her surreptitious presence was errantly approved. "I must say, you're quite the gentleman," she said with a faint smile and a slight rise of her eyebrows. "I merely have a few questions about the operations."

Stewart said, with a grateful smile, "I'll be more than glad to answer them." He gave a fleeting glance at the clock on the wall and winked at her. "I hope you don't take this the wrong way, but you're too beautiful to be an attorney. And I can read people, and you're simply ... quite charming compared to your male counterparts with their abrasive and adversarial traits. And if you are an attorney ... you'd certainly fool me. I'd probably agree to anything you'd say."

Danielle answered, "In that case, lead the way." If she got into trouble, the thought of feigning a stomach virus might prove helpful. Stewart's slicked-back hairdo resembled that of a model from a men's fashion magazine, and his ego appeared as big as Manhattan.

Stewart led her through a glass door and down a low-lit hallway. He explained that his family founded the telephone company, which serviced a small community during the early thirties. As time passed, the community grew, and then the Bell companies gobbled up the smaller companies, but his family resisted. Then the Internet rage was upon them and required a large investment by the struggling company, costing more than what they had expected. Next was the establishment of cell phones that, at first, due to their cost, had no impact on their business model. But the price of a cell phone dropped, and so did the cost of minutes, which in turn made cells ubiquitous throughout the world. Without much of a push, their customers slowly began to drop their landlines.

As they proceeded through the older building, he pointed out where the telephone operators had initially connected lines in order for one party to talk to another. Danielle recalled pictures of operators seated in front of a switchboard with a headset, a plug in hand, and a board filled with sockets. *Today,* she thought, *you are lucky if you speak to an operator, and if you do get a person on the line, they might only speak broken English.*

The painted, spider-webbed, plaster walls, the oak doors, and the high baseboards had darkened with age. Stewart pointed out that the second floor temporarily housed business offices, and the basement had a collection of past artifacts, including the spiked shoes from service technicians who climbed telephone poles, the old switchboards, ceramic connectors, dial telephone sets, and telephone cables and wiring.

As they stepped through an enclosed corridor from the older building to the newer structure, Stewart informed her that the older building would be razed early next year.

They strolled down a brightly lit, granite corridor, passing a number of darkened offices marked with nameplates for accounting, engineering, and technicians. At a bank of elevators, she noticed the hall opened to a larger lobby area not readily noticeable from the outside.

Stewart continued with his building tour. "Many of the staff is gone, but you'll find a group of computer engineers still at work upstairs." He checked his watch. "Our timing is good. I'll show you the observatory."

As they waited for an elevator car, Danielle pondered his mini-epiphany and framed her question, "With cell phones, how did the company grow?"

Stewart grinned as though he thought she was kidding, "Why, of course, software writing and distribution for the major cell companies. You legal types dismiss code writing as mere bytes of information with no substance like those dot-com companies. But hey, how do you think those programs work? Without computer software engineers, all those computers and cells come to a screeching halt. Remember, what we write in those programs affect each and every one of us."

As Stewart held the doors open to the car, Danielle commented, "I presume you're also a software or computer engineer."

"Me? I don't have the time. That's why we hire those geeks. Richie Davis directs what we do around here. He might be here tonight. They've been working out a glitch in programming for, oh, maybe the last few months. Then, out of the clear blue like a shooting star, they had a breakthrough within the last two weeks. Now they're reprogramming day and night."

As the car climbed to the fourth floor, she became increasingly uneasy since Stewart mentioned Davis. That's one person she had met with Owen. The question was whether Davis would remember her. A knot formed in her stomach. She was hesitant to press her luck, and what she had heard so far had raised nothing unusual until Stewart mentioned STAR.

Emerging from the elevator into the foyer, she noticed a set of staircases to her immediate left and right that arched to an upper floor. Stewart pointed out, "Overhead, from the fifth floor walkway, there's an unparalleled view of the forest and the valley. On a clear day, you probably could see maybe seventy miles. We'll do a quick walk around this floor, and at the other end, we'll take the staircase to the top. I doubt whether we'll see much due to the weather, but if we get a clearing, you'll see what I mean."

Her attention was distracted by a number of people flying in and out of what appeared to be a glass-enclosed room located in the center of the floor. She could see an array of large computers blinking red, green, and yellow lights assembled in rows and a host of unmanned monitors that reminded her of the control room of a shuttle launch.

"This here is the vortex of our communications system. We provide the software programming and engineering for those towers dotting the countryside on a contract basis. Communication programs between the cell towers and phones require constant updates. Signal technologies improve, tower leases expire, and new towers are constructed all the time. Our programs feed cell phone protocols for a communication link between phone and tower. We're under contract, you know, with the major carriers to write and maintain those programs."

"Like STAR?"

Stewart's eyes narrowed and his stare told her the reference to the program name touched a chord of suspicion.

Danielle quickly made amends. "Shooting star. I'll bet you'd get a clear view from up here in the mountains."

"Yeah … sure."

"You know, I upgrade my cell on a regular basis due to all the traveling I do. That's what my carrier said I should do."

For a moment, Stewart studied her. The glint in his eyes told her that he was weighing her explanation. But then it seemed his suspicion faded. "Follow me." At the end of the corridor, as they climbed a carpeted staircase, Stewart said with obvious satisfaction, "That three-digit code directed your cell to our service center; it's all done by computers without human intervention. And we've instituted a new program that upgrades your phone without you knowing it. Our contracts provide us the necessary codes to gain access to the operating system installed on your phone."

Danielle shot a side-to-side glance with the hope that they wouldn't meet Davis. Then she ran through the excuses in her mind, which all seemed lame, to scoot out of the building before the meeting started.

"Our main conference room is on this floor. We're headed there next for the meeting, after I show you the observation deck." Stewart directed her down the open corridor past a number of private offices. "You know, the leaves from this vantage point are quite colorful. It's a rainbow of colors during the day, but it's more than that. It's like opening a box of crayons with all the variant colors."

As she grew ever mindful of the upcoming meeting, Danielle's heart fluttered and her knees weakened. The inner message was loud and clear: she needed to excuse herself and make it back to her car. "Meeting?" she asked dryly. It was then that she recognized the person disgorged from the elevator. Denon Pierce. And he had one foot on the first step of the staircase when he turned and greeted Leonard Wheeling. She closed her eyes and froze. Her hand quivered.

"Are you all right?" Stewart asked.

"Yes. It's the height up here. Vertigo. But I'll be fine. I just need to catch … my breath." She pressed herself back against the wall, knowing if Denon looked in her direction she'd be dead. She couldn't think fast enough of an excuse for what she was doing there.

"You don't look very well. In fact, you look exceedingly pale. Do want a glass of water?"

Danielle swallowed. "Ah, yes, that would be fine."

As Stewart hurriedly retreated across a catwalk connected to the other side of the open room, Danielle's heart pounded in her chest. She could feel a rush of blood to her face. Trapped. It would be a matter of minutes before she was discovered. With her hand shielding her face, she rushed down the corridor quickly and deliberately, hugging the inside wall but in plain view. Once she reached the staircase at the opposite end, she heard the clamor—shouts and footfalls. This was not a fire drill. She found the fire escape and frantically stumbled down the stairwell.

As she rounded the second floor, she heard the frenzied rush of someone descending at a rapid pace. That's when the heel of her shoe broke. Damn heels weren't made for mad dashes. She removed her shoes and threw open the fire escape door. Breathing hard, at a near pant, she sprinted down a dimly lit corridor until she was swallowed in the darkness.

Her pursuer opened the fire escape door and froze, waiting for a noise to tell him which way she went. He yelled out in an almost teasing way. "Danielle. We know you're here, you can't get out." Then he headed in the opposite direction.

She emerged and gingerly, in her stockinged feet, headed in the direction of the lobby. Her only chance was if she acted fast. It wouldn't take long before they sealed off the entire building and did a thorough search. She could see the corridor that led to the old building, but it was blocked.

With a hard pitch, she fired the broken heel and shoe down a darkened side corridor. As the individual stationed in the hallway took the bait, she dashed into the old building only to hear the outcry of a person shouting orders around the corner. Blocked, she picked a door to her immediate right. With a heave, the swollen door swung open, and she stepped into the depths of the basement. She caught the second step and immediately pulled the door closed. As she fumbled for a light switch, she prayed that she had time to hide as footsteps grew louder and closer.

She flipped the light switch up and down, but only darkness greeted her. Feeling the wall as she descended one step at a time and panting in short breaths, she reached the bottom of the stairs. With the hair bristling at the nape of her neck and sweat rolling down her back, she heard the sound of dripping water. The basement reeked with a musty smell, and she imagined what lay deep within the belly of this pitch-black cave. She wondered when someone was last down here. It was cold as she touched the floor and wall for some type of guidance.

Another odor played havoc with her. Coal. They must have had a coal furnace to heat the building at one time. And with a coal furnace there had to be a coal shoot where the coal was fed and maybe a door leading to the outside.

Momentarily she was distracted as the sounds of steps overhead reminded her of mice in the attic when she was a kid. One minute she'd hear a gaggle of footsteps and then silence. But no one switched on the light for the basement, and no one ventured down into its bowels.

Finally, the faint smell of coal grew stronger as she stepped gingerly along the floor. When she reached the furnace room, she considered whether this might be her grave. She closed her eyes and tried to wish away what had occurred like a bad dream, but she was left in the putrid darkness. With her back pressed to the wall, she slid to the floor and folded her knees.

Water dripped incessantly as she wondered what they would do when they found her. She remembered being accidentally locked in the basement of her grandmother's house while playing hide and seek. After that, she never liked being in the dark.

Checking her watch, she had been entombed for more than an hour. There was a backlight, but the watch emitted little light. The watch, with its alarms and USB connection port, was pinpoint accurate, just like Owen, who had a habit of working on cutting edge projects and acquiring gadgets in the same vein. Time passed slowly as she waited. She wished she could call Alex, but that was out of the question. Her cell, she remembered, was on the floor in her car.

She illuminated the watch dial. Ten forty-five. And she had no idea how to find her way out. She stiffened and began to hyperventilate. The room was cold, and her toes felt numb. Was she delirious? Her thoughts turned to hypothermia. She rubbed her arms and toes to generate heat. Her teeth chattered. She had read hypothermia could occur at forty degrees, but she had no idea what the temperature was. She took a deep long breath and stood.

She flicked the watch on and off as she moved along the wall, hoping she wouldn't find any creature dead or alive. And then she finally found it. She turned the door handle and pulled. The door was swollen shut. *Hopeless*, she thought, until she found the obstacle: the latch. She pressed her weight against the door as she worked at the rusted latch. Her fingers ached and her feet were cold. She brushed a tear away and took a deep breath as she hit the latch with her shoe. It released, giving her a sense of achievement.

The door and the hinges groaned as thick, moist air from the outside wafted in. But she was greeted by dank leaves with an overriding stench that made her pause. She remembered her father had said, "Danny, you'll enjoy being a Cub Scout." What he really meant was a Brownie, but he never treated her as a girl, and her mother was indifferent. Her heart beat both out of triumph and fear of what lay ahead.

A draft of wet air reached her from above as she stepped into a bed of leaves knee deep. Her bare foot found a step, and then another. She bent over and pulled the door shut. Latching onto a side railing, she pulled herself from the wet leaves. But before she did, the rusted railing broke in her hand, sending her backward.

Crawling to the top of the stairwell, she found the parking lot steeped in a thick fog; with the exception of a few overhead lights, visibility was zero. Her feet cried for warmth as she slowly slipped across the parking lot until she found her car. She opened the trunk and ripped through her belongings. Finding a sweatshirt and a pair of sweatpants, which she hurriedly donned, she crawled into the trunk and pulled the lid closed. Even if she tried to leave, she wouldn't find the road. She'd have to wait until morning.

# 40

*Reston, Virginia*
*Saturday, October 27*
*1:45 p.m.*

Tony Cervasi stopped his pacing and turned abruptly toward Denon Pierce as the quarterback heaved an out of bounds pass to avoid a sack on the large-screen television. "What was she doing there? You know that was no coincidence."

Seated in Cervasi's office, Pierce, seemingly unflappable, said, "Her presence there does have me worried. I'd like to know how she connected PERC and Shannon."

"There's no doubt that she's putting two and two together. But she's doing it with the help of others."

"Right. Besides, what I wondered is how she scrambled out of the building and disappeared into the night. It was like she was swallowed up. Houdini."

Moving his gold ring up and down his finger, Cervasi said in a harsh tone, "That's where she's going to end up." For him, Danielle's interference could cause the collapse of the campaign; that is, unless she was silenced.

Denon crossed his legs and smiled when the Redskins scored before he turned his attention to the discussion at hand. "Admittedly, we're going to have to deal with her. And it's not going to be easy. She's analytical, methodical, and deliberate on how she dissects a case. Questions. She'll have many, but I fear she already has answers. You can't underestimate her."

"Yeah. Questions. You lawyers all think alike. Ask questions. Find answers. Well, we don't have time to find answers. What's troubling

319

is that she wandered through our offices unstopped, and now she's found her way to Shannon. For all we know, she could be listening to our conversation. *Denon, she broke into human resources.* You said: 'I'll take care of her.' Then she ends up with the access key. What proof do you want? I can't shut down the campaign at this stage. And that means we have very little time to find her and then—"

With his hands on his hips and shaking his head in disgust, he drew a bead on Baker as the invalid crossed the courtyard from the far building. "There he goes, *again*. Strange bird. Keeps to himself. I swear he covers more ground than most long-distance runners do in a day." But he wondered inwardly whether Baker had another agenda.

Denon shifted in his seat. "Forget him. Danielle is a bigger concern. She ran when she saw me and now—"

Cervasi threw up his hands. "What did you expect her to do? Smile and ask how your day was going? The whole thing reeks. We've had nothing but screw ups. That's all. Her interest is piqued. And with Candecki circling like a hawk waiting to snatch his prey during these last few weeks ... we've taken it on the chin."

Denon stared distantly.

Cervasi asked in a huff, "Now what about my brother, Leonard?"

"After what happened to the two of you in California, he's expressed some reservations. You can't blame him. But I convinced him that this deal is worth it. Of course, he wanted to know how the system works. I told him no deal. He balked at the initial investment and the residuals, but I think he'll come around." Denon stole a glance at the football game before he continued, "As I was saying, if we close this deal, you're in the money. I told him you were interested in licensing, not selling. I have my doubts whether he wants to deal with you."

Cervasi ranted, "I'm in the driver's seat. I name the price and conditions." He began to pace, turning his head side to side.

"I know. But if I didn't intercede, you couldn't name a price. It's lucky Wheeling contacted Vittorio. He actually did you a favor."

Cervasi stopped and shook his head. "I won't hear any of it. That was a favor for which I owe my brother nothing! If it wasn't for me, he'd be behind bars where he belongs. I paid you to represent him, and then I paid off the judge. Now he wants more. Well, he's not going to get it! And I don't even know why you called him. I didn't ask you. Carl has contacts in New York."

"Tony, we don't want henchmen. All Leonard wants is a part of the action. He's willing to pay."

"No. Absolutely not. It was your fault he got involved in the first place."

"Fine," Denon said. He cleared his throat. "You're his lost brother, and he'd rather keep it that way."

"Business comes first even between relatives." Cervasi hadn't seen or spoken to his brother in a number of years. "Secrecy, to me, is paramount. Too many people are going to know. Tell my brother no deal. And tell him Carmen snatched the wrong item. He won't know you're lying."

The door leading into the office swung open. Matalino, looking perplexed, lumbered into the room. With a single nod to Denon, Matalino dropped his heavy frame onto a sofa.

"I see you got the message," Cervasi said irritably after exchanging glances with Matalino. With days left in the Senate race and Clarke about to overtake McClay, he was not going to let Madison or anyone else stand in his way. "That's a security breach that we didn't count on."

With a deep nod, Matalino crossed his arms over his broad chest. "Shannon will have security when we open the new building. But for now we have to count on our employees and the leased security detail. I know Stewart did compromise our operations, but what other choices do we have? I doubt Madison will make another trip there. We are on the lookout for her."

Cervasi knew he could count on Matalino but, on occasion, he made mistakes, and this was one of them. "I'm telling you she's hooked up with that reporter, Preston ... Alex Preston. He was asking too many questions the other day. And then we have Stewart, who has a wandering eye when it comes to women. He has no concept of secrecy. She smiled and he almost spilled the beans. His interest lies solely in a pretty face."

Denon exchanged glances with Matalino and Cervasi, "As part of his mini-tour for Danielle, I understand he divulged that Shannon develops and maintains communication software. This girl is tenacious. She's going to connect the dots, and that means—"

"That's right. And that's why we need that bitch off our trail," Cervasi said, slamming his hands down on his desk to make a point.

Denon, perched on his seat, pulled a piece of lint from his suit. "I agree. One thing's for sure, and I hate to say it, but until she's satisfied that there's nothing afoot, she won't stop. There's no doubt she wants to find out if Owen was murdered."

Matalino jacked himself up, wandered over to the bar, and poured himself a glass of wine. He stared at Denon as though he had more to say but didn't.

Cervasi ran his fingers through his hair. "She won't find anything. We've got that tied up. But if she uncovers STAR …" He paused and then added, "Her presence must be treated as a major breach. Granted, we can deal with her later, but we don't want her interference with the senatorial campaign. Do you realize that we'll have a host of problems if she costs us this election?"

Matalino took a swallow and wiped his mouth with the back of his hand. "We've got no choice, the way I see it. She needs to be whacked."

Denon rolled his eyes. "I know you must come to terms with her. But, Tony, I must warn you that Carl's methods can't be tolerated. They only serve to focus attention on PERC. And yesterday, ReAnne informed me that a detective stopped to ask questions about Simes. The implications are quite disconcerting."

Matalino tasted his wine before he added his defensive comments to the clash. "Window dressing. That's all. And anyway, we had nothing to do with her being knocked off."

"Madison is a nuisance. And you have to deal with her," Denon offered." But if the trail leads even near here, you can forget about running any presidential campaign."

Cervasi rubbed his brow with his fingertips. Denon was right. Madison was a roadblock to their success. What else could he do but orchestrate dispatching her? As for Parks, well, he had it coming. And no one would be the wiser. Even his sister would agree. As long as she received his payroll check, she wouldn't care. Their rocky marriage and loss of his investment could explain his disappearance. A smile spread slowly across his face.

Matalino commented, "I told you what to do with Madison."

"Taking her out is not the answer—at least not yet," Cervasi fired back.

Pierce roiled in his chair. He undid his tie and unbuttoned the top button of his shirt. "Her demise is between you two. Count me out."

He turned toward Matalino and said, "As for Tony and the company, they never authorized or condoned the killing of anyone." He paused and locked eyes with Matalino. "We're not living like they did fifty years ago. Business is business. That's why we have courts."

"Denon," Cervasi interrupted, "Carl gave his word that he didn't have anything to do with Simes. Our pressing problem is Madison. Wake up to the reality that she's not going to get away with it."

The room grew silent except for the football announcer's voice.

Cervasi broke into the thoughts of Denon and Matalino. "An accident. It's got to be an accident with a message." To him, the idea seemed perfectly logical.

"Wait a minute," Denon said. "I'm not sanctioning these actions. Granted, something must be done. But you're not going to involve me." He quickly strode across the room and opened the door. "Call me," he told Cervasi and then glared at Matalino.

"What made him so self-righteous?" Matalino asked with disdain.

With his eyes glued to the door, Cervasi pursed his lips and slowly turned his head to meet the stare of Matalino. "What I'd like to know is who rubbed out Simes? Let's make some discrete inquiries. We've got a few detectives on the take. Surely someone must know where it leads. As for Miss Madison, we'll need that accident soon. I don't care who she is; she's going to run out of rabbits to pull out of her hat sometime. And ask Richie to see me. I want a message sent to her."

"I'll see to it," Matalino replied as he set the empty glass on the table.

"Oh, and one more thing." Cervasi nodded tightening his lips. "Did you notice that Denon has changed? He's a little edgy. Maybe too edgy. Denon agreed that if Madison puts this all together it could mean trouble. But for whom? Now we need to contend with Simes's death." Before Matalino answered, Cervasi continued, "And we do know someone broke into Madison's office in New York, but we never found out who did it. Odd. I don't know, Carl, but I think it's too many coincidences." He raised his eyebrows.

Matalino tilted his head. "Yeah, and he even suggested that Wheeling be cut in on the deal."

"You're absolutely right. My brother didn't call me. He called Denon. Maybe Denon's not telling us something about whose side he's on."

"Whoa. If you don't mind me saying, you look like you finished the Marine Corp marathon," Alex expressed, finding Danielle at the door. Without makeup, her normal arresting facial features were taut and drawn. Her starlet eyes appeared tired. Her normally full-bodied hair was stringy. Her clothes were rumpled, and she was wearing a pair of running shoes, but she looked ravishing nonetheless.

"I feel like it. I've had little sleep. And when it comes to anxiety, I'm on overload. I haven't thought straight for hours. Now that you know how I feel, I could use a hot shower."

Alex opened the door wider as Danielle angled through. "You didn't. Did you?"

Danielle surrendered. "I had to. I can't go back to PERC. If I'd go there, I may as well sign my own death warrant."

"Then you were at Shannon?"

Danielle gave a tired nod. "What's worse? They know. And it all fits together. The way I see it, they've got Owen's computer and the access file." She headed for the staircase and began to climb. As she took the next step, she turned and said, "I'm still confused what this all means." With a distraught look, she said, "My luggage is strewn throughout the trunk; I had to stay warm. I'll fill in the remainder later. But for now, if you don't mind, I need my things," and handed him the keys.

"Sure thing."

Danielle managed a faint smile before she turned and disappeared upstairs. Once he heard the water running, he ran outside to retrieve her luggage. She never mentioned the haunting voices that echoed through her mind. Except for the trip to Shannon, maybe the New York trip, away from the Washington scene, had done her some good. With a grip on her bag, he knocked on the bathroom door and told her that he'd drop it in the guest bedroom. He retreated downstairs and made her a cup of onion soup with melted, crusty cheese and a club sandwich.

When she finally appeared, she was dressed in a pair of jeans and sweatshirt and was towel-drying her hair. With a bright smile, she seated herself at the kitchen table. "Alex, I know what you're going to say, but at the last moment, I had to make the side trip to Shannon."

For the next ten minutes, she detailed the private tour, the control room with its high level of activity, and her enlightening conversation with Brad Stewart, especially as it related to STAR. Next she filled him in on her escape.

Leaning against the kitchen cabinet and gripping a cup of black coffee, Alex swallowed hard and could feel the chill of the dark, dank basement running through his veins. Words were difficult to form when he asked, "How did you manage to get out of there?"

She closed her eyes as though it was a tale she didn't relish. "When I got out of the basement, a veil of fog had draped the parking lot. Visibility was car length, leaving me with little choice but to take refuge. So I slid into the trunk of my car and wrapped myself in my clothes. I waited until morning before I made my move through the backseat. After the battery died on my watch during the night, I was awakened by the closing of car doors in the morning, which I figured were employees returning to work. But rather than making my move, I waited for an hour, maybe two. I waffled a bit before I finally crawled out. Believe me, my heart was in my throat when I pulled on the tab to fold over the backseat. What was left of the fog had thinned out, leaving a cold, damp mist that settled on the windshield. After I started the engine and the wipers cleaned the windshield, I was surprised not to see someone standing there."

"Don't you think they would have spotted your car?"

Her eyes reached for the ceiling as though thinking of an answer. "The only thing I could figure was I had Virginia plates, and I was parked in the employee lot."

"Danielle, your luck is bound to run out."

"During the night, I dozed off and on, but one thing came to mind. I tried to remember what Owen said. Then it dawned on me."

"The books?"

"It has to be the Jefferson treatise. Could I have missed something? That letter was stuck in the middle of Volume 15. Why? Why did he stick it there? Why not underneath the cover? And why not Volume 1?" She sipped her soup. "There had to be a reason." She looked up as though it was imperative they get moving now. "Give me fifteen minutes; I need to put on my makeup." She darted out of the room and yelled, "And wrap that sandwich for me; I'll eat it on the way."

"Where are we going?"

"McKeldin Library."

325

A half hour later they had arrived at McKeldin and discovered the treatise had remained in their original boxes. After they found Volume 15, she leafed through each page as though it might hold a clue.

"I don't remember the page where I pulled out that letter." For the next half hour, she scanned each page looking for a stray mark, but there was none.

As she thumbed through the pages, she came across the quote at the beginning of a chapter. There she stopped and read aloud. "I have sworn upon the altar of God eternal hostility against every form of tyranny over the mind of man." She looked up into Alex's eyes and exclaimed, "This is it."

"What's that supposed to mean?" Alex asked, puzzled by the quote.

Her mind swirled with thoughts. "But I lost the access file."

# 41

*Reston, Virginia*
*Saturday, October 27*
*5:15 p.m.*

How did she miss it? That was the question that ran through her mind as she and Alex sped around the Capital Beltway. She should have known better when she removed the letter that led them to Owen's computer. Now, she wasn't exactly sure from where she had pulled it in the treatise. Was it a pure coincidence, or did Owen select that particular chapter for a purpose? She ran the quote through her mind again. "I have sworn upon the altar of God eternal hostility against every form of tyranny over the mind of man." *The mind,* she thought.

Attuned to the missed exit off the Beltway, Danielle asked, "By the way, where are you going?" At their speed, headlights that passed in the opposite direction seemed to dizzily blink on and off.

"While you were in New York, I played a hunch. There's more to Owen and Greyson that you don't know."

Danielle raised an eyebrow not so much in disbelief as in dawning realization. "They're tied together. Except, according to Karen, Milsen is another missing piece."

"And add one more: Dr. David Bateman. That picture you cut from the newspaper piqued my interest. The common denominator is the CIA. Now all we need to do is figure out what they did there." He glanced at her with a knowing smile.

"You know, now that you bring up Greyson, I always wondered about the medical statement he filed with the police. I never bought it. Owen wasn't delusional. Now I sound like a parent. Owen seeing a psychiatrist? Hardly. It couldn't be true then or now." Danielle's cell phone rang five times. Her eyes drifted from Alex to the phone. She didn't reach for it. Within her, an unsettling feeling surfaced.

"Aren't you going to answer it?"

Hesitating, Danielle said, "Sure." She paused for a moment, and the cell stopped ringing. A sharp, shrill beep rang out, indicating a waiting voicemail. She punched in her security code and heard Brooke's voice. "Danielle, got your message. Glad to hear you're back. Meet you at nine o'clock at home."

"Who was it?"

She heard Alex, but she searched the recesses of her mind. Was there a reason why Brooke wanted to meet? Finally, she answered, "Brooke. I'm to meet her at home."

"That's all?"

"*Odd.* I never called her. And a *message*? I never left her a message."

"Call her cell."

For the next ten minutes, Danielle alternated calling the landline, Brooke's cell, and the hospital, but she had to leave messages.

"Tell you what. You and I will keep trying. But we have another appointment to make first, and it shouldn't take long. And if we haven't heard from her," Alex took a deep breath, "we'll head back to the apartment."

The office foyer was small but well-appointed with two chairs, a love seat, and end tables. Blended into the décor was a plush, dark plum-colored carpet that sank beneath each footstep. Classical music played through the overhead speakers. And the solid oak door that separated the waiting room from the inner offices was ajar.

Alex drew the door open and called out, "Hello, is anyone here?"

They didn't wait long before hearing footsteps round the corner and head in their direction. Upon recognizing Danielle, Greyson's grin turned sour.

"*You again,*" Greyson said with deep-seated eyes and a furrowed brow. His gaze shifted from Danielle to Alex for an answer.

"She's with me. But I assure you," Alex replied, "she's not here to ask you any questions."

Greyson's eyes darted between the two of them until he finally settled on Danielle. "I know I'll regret this." He stepped around them and across the waiting room to the outer door. Locking it, he returned and flipped the light off. After they entered the corridor, he proceeded to throw the lock on the inner door. "Follow me."

It was rather obvious that the precautions he took were intended to ensure their privacy. If anyone showed up, they were intruders.

Greyson escorted them into his office, which was a mixture of old and modern décor. Behind a large computer monitor atop an old cherry desk stricken by a rash of scratches, he seated himself in an olive green leather chair. The remainder of his office was filled with plaques and posters that evidenced he had a rich past in his profession. With his elbows firmly planted on the arms of the chair and his fingers intertwined, he smacked his lips together. "Sorry," he said, eyeing them, "but there are matters that are of concern to me that I won't get into. But her presence here," nodding toward Danielle, "may complicate matters that have remained undefined."

Alex assured Greyson that no one in his office had known of their appointment, and if Greyson wanted to maintain his anonymity, his name need not be mentioned in the news piece.

Drawing his chair closer to the desk, Greyson's expression darkened. "Seeing Miss Madison with you makes me believe that you're here for another purpose."

Alex paused for a moment and then declared, "I understand you're an expert on a variety of psychiatric abnormalities, which is what brings us," clearing his throat, "to seek your help."

Greyson took his cue from Alex. "Yes, I've worked with a number of patients." His eyes shifted between them. "That is, the mentally challenged. Many problems are perceived as a possible mental illness when, in fact, a disease is attributable to the physical condition, either permanent or temporary.

Alex gave an almost imperceptible nod. "I thought, if you don't mind, you might answer a few questions off the record, so to speak."

"That would depend on the nature of your questions."

"Naturally," Alex replied. "You can stop me anytime you want."

Greyson said, with the look of a poker player, "And I will. But I'll warn you like I did Miss Madison." His eyes bore into Danielle.

"It's best that you leave matters beyond your control alone. Let the past remain in the past. You or I can't change what has happened."

Danielle piped in, "Or going to happen?"

Without answering, Greyson turned his attention to Alex.

"According to your recently published article in the *Journal of Clinical Psychology*," Alex continued, "which I must say was well written, psychological persuasion can take many forms. You mentioned advertising that we have grown to accept in society as a subtle form of persuasion."

Greyson struck a thin smile. "Why, thank you. Your point?"

"Mind manipulation."

Greyson snorted as though annoyed by the conclusion. "Mind manipulation, or better yet, brainwashing, a word coined in the fifties, I might add, remains a controversial subject. Even Miss Madison, who is an attorney, from what I learned, will enlighten you that insanity-by-brainwashing is a questionable defense. Brainwashing is similar to a dissociative disorder. And you found undoubtedly that a dissociative disorder can take many forms, including amnesia and identity and behavioral disorders."

Danielle submitted, "Was Owen suffering from a disorder?"

With knitted eyebrows and taut facial muscles, Greyson said, "Again, I thought we were not going to discuss patients."

She pressed on, "Your medical opinion given to the Pittsburgh police was that Owen suffered from a delusion, an oversimplification or an analysis you made based upon careful and lengthy observation. But he had no mental problem—you know it, and so do I."

"Let me make this clear: I didn't write any medical report," Greyson said adamantly.

Alex turned his head toward Danielle and waved her off. "I think I can ask this."

"But—" Danielle submitted.

"Dr. Greyson," Alex interjected, "Owen, Dr. Bateman, Dr. Milsen, and, of course, you worked together for the CIA. And Owen and Milsen met with their deaths. Are you next? What did you hide from the police? We know that Owen was here for a meeting. And he wasn't your patient."

With his arms resting on the desktop, Greyson said, "Okay, I see where this is going. And I understand that you want answers, Mr.

Preston, and certainly, Miss Madison, who has hounded me for what seems like forever. Yes, I worked for the CIA, but that was years ago, so whatever I know stayed with the agency."

"Manipulation?" Alex asked rhetorically.

Greyson replied in kind, "You can call it what you like, but you never got that from me." Then he turned to Danielle. *"And for the final time. I didn't opine on—"*

"But you signed a medical report that claimed Owen's delusions were brought about by a drug-induced state," said Danielle. "And, based ... never mind ... he was doctoring with Dr. Milsen, who had reached the same diagnosis."

"Really?" Greyson answered in astonishment. He furrowed his brow. "Wherever you got your information, you're badly mistaken."

"But I read it, and it was signed by you," Danielle stammered.

Greyson shook his head. "I *never* wrote that report."

Alex asked, "If you didn't write it, who did?"

Greyson looked toward the ceiling before his eyes landed on Alex. *"I don't know."*

"Can't we level with each other?" Danielle suggested. "You called me once, but then you refused to talk to me when I showed up at your office days ago."

Greyson seemed to ponder her statement. His eyes drilled into her. "There were two men who paid me a visit shortly after Owen's death. It was several days after the police interviewed me. But I assure you, I don't think they would ... well, change the investigative report."

Alex turned and met Danielle's perplexed glance before he posed the question, "And who might that be?"

Greyson said in a nonchalant tone, "The Agency, of course. They had an obvious interest. Owen had worked there with the appropriate clearances. I'll say this much, they weren't volunteering why they were interested in Owen, or why they decided to interview me. All they wanted was information. And I didn't want to be bothered."

"What type of information?" Danielle inquired.

"You know: what he wanted, what he said, what happened—the usual. But I'll tell you this, the guy who did the talking looked like he stepped out of a gangster movie. You know the type—wavy, black hair, dark complexion, Rolex watch. Don't remember the names, but I did see their badges." Greyson looked as though he expected dispensation. "I worked with Owen when he first graduated college. Along the way, we became friends. Sometimes when I saw him at lunch we'd discuss the news, like headline news, sports, whatever was on our minds. Then I resigned. The next time I saw him was in my office."

"And?" Alex inquired.

"And nothing. You came here to discuss my topic at the conference, but I consider the appointment made under false pretenses. End of interview. So if you'll excuse me, I'll end this meeting on the same note. You're wasting your time. Now either leave peacefully, or I'll call the police."

After Danielle and Alex left the office through the back door, Greyson pulled a FedEx box from the bottom drawer of his desk. Setting it on his desk, he opened it and pulled out ten thousand dollars. He tapped his fingers on his desk and then picked up the phone. When the person answered on the other end, Greyson said, "We need to talk."

*9:30 p.m.*

Alex and Danielle turned from Wisconsin onto O Street. It wasn't long before they spotted the flashing lights of an ambulance and a police car parked outside the townhouse. Traffic was being rerouted around that section of the street.

Danielle jumped out and jogged down the sidewalk until she came face-to-face with a police officer, who stopped her. "That's my house," she snapped in a state of panic. "Is she all right? Brooke, is she all right? Tell me!"

"Sorry, ma'am, but I can't let you go beyond this point," the officer said in an authoritative voice.

"But that's my friend."

"We'll get to the bottom of this." The officer tilted his head and spoke into a mic mounted on the upper part of his shirt. He turned away and mumbled something unintelligible.

A moment later another officer, stern in appearance and heavyset, pulled her aside. After he satisfied himself with her connection, he drew in a heavy breath and said, "Your friend was roughed up a bit, but she's fine. She'll need some medical attention. Overall, though, she'll be okay. And from what we've found, she put up a hell of a fight. As for the intruder, well, he'll probably show up at a hospital somewhere with a knife wound."

Danielle let out a sigh of relief. Anxiously, she asked, "Can I see her?" Closing her eyes, thoughts streamed through her mind like a gale force storm. She never thought it would come to this. Brooke could have been killed. No … no, this couldn't be happening. They were ruthless.

"Miss," said the officer. Danielle blinked and stared into the officer's steely eyes. "If you follow me, I'll take you to her."

Now there was only one thought in her mind: *it's only a matter of time before they pay.*

# 42

Cervasi read the newspaper headline, "Clarke Surges to Close Gap: Four Points Behind in Latest Poll." An instant smile crossed his face. None of the political races had fulfilled the pinnacle of success that he now believed was within his grasp. He savored the moment. Within days, he could claim, with any luck, his rightful position as a political icon.

But his wide smile turned to a frown when he thought of Danielle Madison. She was probably dealing with her friend, and for now, she had remained relatively quiet. But that could change in short order as he had previously learned. In days, the general election would be over, and then he and Matalino could explore the appropriate resolutions to their pressing problems. For him, Madison was number one.

Then there was Denon with his growing ego. Who knew what he was capable of? He was intelligent, no denying that, and his knowledge of company affairs was extensive. That made him an asset and liability at the same time. In Cervasi's mind, Denon was expendable due to the current flap with Madison.

With a single, hard knock at the door, Matalino trudged into the office carrying a white bag. He gave a deep nod of respect and seated himself in a wing chair in the lounge area of the room. As he opened the bag and pulled out biscotti that he bought from an Italian bakery, he said with a cold smile, "We've intercepted the Swiss money. The money will be wired in the morning to your private account."

Cervasi beamed anew. "That's the news I wanted to hear. Our investments are going to return a fistful of gold. We're going to need it once we win this senatorial race in preparation for a presidentiot campaign. On another note, I've decided to keep this company private. No investors. No accountability."

Matalino brushed the crumbs from his large frame. "And what about Baker?" he asked as he chomped down on the cookie.

Cervasi leveraged his hands on the armrests and pushed downward to stand. As he scanned out the window in the vicinity of the courtyard where Baker wore out his chariot, he commented, "Baker, huh. We owe him no loyalty. What's he done lately? We took all the chances. Thinks he owns the place. Sure, he helped wrestle your brother-in-law's money free, but he's been paid handsomely for that. I know I promised him a piece of the action after he helped us. But I've changed my mind. There's no room in this organization for two bosses. I like it just the way it is." And in this case, Baker, being shrewd, cunning, and intelligent, was a lethal cocktail, one who he needed to keep in front of him. He'd knife Cervasi in the back. That was obvious by the way he had handled Parks. Baker must be stopped, and it was about time he that became a permanent part of a freeway.

Matalino stumbled to his feet. "Got a meeting tonight at the construction site. Have to make a delivery and a pickup. And may have a lead on the whereabouts of Candecki."

Cervasi spun around, knowing the irritant was a professional with a gun. "You better get to him before he gets to us. Once he discovers his money is gone, he's going to come looking." Cervasi knew that was music to Matalino's ears.

"And what's the latest with our new attorney?"

"I doubt whether she'll leave the side of her friend anytime soon," Matalino answered. He crumpled the bag and nodded.

"At this late date," Cervasi said, shifting in his chair, "I don't want any surprises like we had the other night when our compatriot unexpectedly ran into trouble. We can't afford any more screw-ups. He's lucky that he was only nicked by Madison's knife-wielding roommate." Cervasi tugged at the gold bracelet around his wrist. "I want that noose closed around Madison's neck. And that means that both she and Candecki must meet their ends—and soon. Got it?"

"Yes. I'll take care of it. This is what I do best, and thank you," Matalino said with a simple smile. "Oh, and I attempted to reach

Denon, but he hasn't answered. He was scheduled to meet with your brother, Leonard, once more."

Cervasi added, letting go of his bracelet, "As soon you get in touch with him, call me." He slapped the desk. "I've got a feeling that we're going to lead in the polls by tomorrow night. Clarke will thank me profusely. And I'll make sure he's in my pocket for good. Shannon will have its hands full gearing up for other elections. Oh, and we won't need those fake pictures of McClay. This election is in the bag."

Inside the conference room, Kate loaded the diskette in a laptop computer and connected the LCD projector. With the lights dimmed, Alex read along the bottom of the graph the months of the year, beginning with January and ending with October. Running along the vertical side were the numbers one to one hundred. A solid line marked the progress of Clarke and a broken line marked McClay.

With a red highlighter, Kate pointed to the chart and said, "With the data we collected from the various election polls, we charted points on the graph. It's clear that the first nine months of the year showed a marked difference between Clarke and McClay. You'll notice the rise and fall between their respective campaigns. But Clarke clearly never came close to McClay during that period of time. In fact, the point difference varied between twenty and forty, leaving no doubt that McClay was the leader."

Alex studied the graph and noted with each new endorsement or piece of negative news on Clarke, the result was a predictable gravitational pull. For weeks, the graph showed no change, and then his candidacy began a steady decline, with no upward trend lasting more than a week.

"You'll notice the trend carried into September, but then a peculiar spike occurred in October. And Clarke never retraced south. His popularity increased in every poll. Now," Kate paused as she moved to the next slide, "every poll showed an improvement. You'll see the same results no matter how we decided to measure the responses. Although the number of stories favoring McClay increased, the articles never translated into a positive response. But more perplexing was the lack of endorsements for Clarke. There was no outright endorsement for him."

The graph confirmed what Alex had always known: Clarke had no chance of winning the election. "Were you able to find anything to explain the rise and fall between the candidates?"

"Yes, we tracked the ups and downs to endorsements, news articles, and advertisements. When Clarke received an endorsement, although there weren't many, we found his poll results spiked, but he never approached McClay. There was a constant difference between the candidates. And, although not presented here, we found these results held true across blue- and white-collar workers, per capita, age differentiation, social groups, race, the number of ads in the news media, and the number of news stories regardless of the medium. Oh, and when it comes to endorsements, McClay received the most and special interest groups had a significant impact."

Alex suspected as much from having written articles on the subject, but he had no idea the breadth of endorsements, positive articles, and cross section of socioeconomic strata that had favored McClay. But that trend was now in reverse, and it appeared the backpedaling was out of control. And like Danielle's actions, an inexplicable reason had gone unnoticed. It was true that the political pundits had given garden-variety reasons, including dissent within the ranks, lack of money, and the alienation of voters on a variety of issues by McClay. But to Alex, after Kate canvassed the records, those seemed more like lame excuses rather than demonstrative evidence why McClay's campaign had gone awry.

She illustrated the last graph. "We rated news articles whether favorable or unfavorable on a one to five scale, with five being favorable and one being unfavorable. Due to your time frame, we did some arm-twisting and managed to quickly scan newspaper archives. You must remember, the data for this graph becomes suspect due to the limited time we had to assemble it by someone we all know and, ah … hmm, love. Those marked by a small star on the graph indicate a matter of significance."

Alex now stood with his hands planted firmly on his hips. The final analysis again proved what was already known; that is, the acute upward trend in Clarke's favor. Alex ran his hand through his hair and ended at the nape of his neck, where he began to massage. The chart showed one problem that at first he could not reconcile, which was that decided bias for McClay existed in the strata of voters fifty-five and older.

"You'll notice," Alex said, "the acute increase in popularity for Clarke occurred in each category of ages except for one: those fifty-five or older. And the point difference between them increased even more acutely for the twenties and thirties. Why?"

Kate looked equally perplexed by what the graph showed. "Perhaps they haven't paid much attention to the election or don't read the news. We initially dismissed them as being a fluke in our data."

Alex reached for a laser pen and pinpointed a day a few weeks ago. "Here," he said hesitantly. "On this day, I must mark an additional point on your graph. No endorsement, no announcement, no story, but nonetheless a significant date to both candidates. I believe this date set in motion the outcome to this election, an unwritten story. The answer lies with a murder a little more than eight weeks ago in Pittsburgh."

With Alex and Mark standing behind her, Danielle flipped through the analysis page by page as Alex narrated Clarke's candidacy. It was as though another piece of the puzzle was staring at them.

Alex walked away ankle deep in papers set in a pattern around the desk and equally deep in thought. He seated himself on the arm of a sofa situated in the family room, which was connected to the study, a converted dining room. With his eyes riveted on Danielle, he said, "I thought you'd find that research of interest. Both Mark and I think it holds some significance. And again, I'm brought back to Owen and those psychiatrists working together at the CIA."

Danielle rose and relinquished the desk chair to Mark, who settled behind the monitor. She muttered, "The mind of man." Was that supposed to mean something? She glanced at Mark, who was busily typing on the computer, while Alex's gaze was glued to her. "What are you suggesting?"

Alex replied, "It had to be an experiment of some sort."

"Maybe, but how are we going to find out? Greyson won't say, and I'm sure the CIA won't divulge any information." Danielle stared distantly again, trying to sift through the pieces.

"Sorry, but I'm so wrapped up with this matter that I regretfully failed to ask about your friend Brooke."

Danielle turned to face him. "A few bumps and bruises. She's taking a few days off to recover. She'll be fine. Whoever it was didn't know she would put a fight. And from what I understand, she grabbed a knife and got him at least once. I'm sure her attacker is not looking for another encounter with her," Danielle replied.

Mark spoke into his twentysomething-sized monitor, "That's good news. You know, the night I was mugged, I made a backup before I saw you," as though apologizing for what had happened. "You never think someone is going to outright steal your computer. When I think of a backup, I think of fire or other catastrophes. Maybe I should take a few lessons on self-defense from Brooke. Sounds like she means business." They were silent for a while as they stared at the computer screen and the blinking monitor that requested a password in order to access STAR. "There's no doubt, with what happened to Brooke and me, that someone believes you have something of value."

Danielle, with her arms crossed, muttered, "If I only had held on to that access file, we probably would have examined the program by now."

Swiveling around in his chair, Mark observed, "You know it can be a simple group of letters and numbers or merely letters or numbers alone. Usually it's something that the developer wouldn't readily forget. And when it comes to ciphers, breaking them can be accomplished, but it can be time-consuming."

For the next hour, Danielle ran through a series of obvious passwords that included Owen's mother and father's names, street address, and city and state, but Mark shook his head with each one. Then it dawned on her that the password might be as simple as 3 Jefferson 1801, which was written on the spine of each book in the treatise.

With that, Mark spun around in his chair and said, "Bingo." With a wide smile, he asked, "How did you know?"

"I didn't."

For the next half hour, she and Alex watched Mark's examination of the lines of computer code. Mark's eyes were glued to every line. As he typed furiously, he occasionally talked to himself about loops, pointers, and arguments in the program. Sometimes he would jot down a note or two. He squinted several times, rubbing his eyes. He grabbed his bottle of water and took a swig. Like an archeologist who had found the hidden alphabet of a code written in an ancient cave, his face showed his emotions, which ranged from stark lines of determination, to dropped shoulders of lost elation, and lastly, to a smile and bright eyes of jubilation.

Mark stood and stretched. "A virus."

Alex shook his head in disbelief. "They're after a virus?"

"Not quite," Mark answered. "There's more to it. STAR is the main program, but it looks as though it connects to another agent, so to speak, to send the message. It's like having the components of a car, but you need a key to start the engine. That's what we've got here. In this case, the program transforms, regulates, and imprints digital sound waves." He glanced at both of them as though waiting for their rhetorical response.

"But you said it was a virus," Danielle said dismissively.

"Yes, but not the ordinary kind that you would normally expect. This is a virus designed for a cell phone. It's implanted into the cell like a Trojan horse, and it's being directed by an outside source. Apparently, it separates code into messages of a sort. At least that's what the telltale signs seem to indicate."

Alex shut his eyes for a moment and shot out, "Wait a minute. There's got to be virus protection similar to a computer."

"You're right. But what's different is that it acts like part of the operating system. It actually masks its true identity," Mark cautioned.

"Then what?" Alex asked.

Mark continued with his explanation. "Computers control and maintain signals between your cells, the towers, and telephone landlines."

Danielle nearly jumped from her seat. "That's it, Mark. Brad Stewart, that's the guy at Shannon, said they were installing a new program." She picked up the political chart they were studying earlier. "There's our confirmation, pointing to a date on the chart. Twenty-four to forty-eight hours after they stole Owen's computer, it started."

Mark arched his eyebrows as he glanced at Alex. "Started what?"

Danielle's cell chirped. She glanced at caller ID on the fourth ring: Karen. On the ninth ring, she merely raised her eyes to meet the pointed stares of Alex and Mark. On the eleventh ring, the cell went silent. She combed her hair behind her ears with both hands and switched the ringer mode to vibrate. "I should have known. I've been thinking it was me. And it wasn't. What Mark said makes perfect sense, and even the political polls support it."

Alex said dryly, "Care to cut us in on what you're thinking?"

"Sorry, I got ahead of myself." She took a deep breath. "Here goes."

What churned in her mind was Denon Pierce. Surely he knew and led her into this morass. But she was unsure why and what he intended to accomplish. To think that he had recommended her for a position with PERC. And now she had stumbled onto a theory capable of changing the landscape of electioneering. But more importantly, it also had the effect of changing how people reacted. And it was no different than the impact of the discovery of psychological persuasion on how people behave when subjected to various stimuli. This went beyond reason.

# 43

*Reston, Virginia*
*Sunday, November 4*
*7:15 p.m.*

"Okay, Counselor," Mark said, holding a scotch in his hand, "you've got the floor. The jury awaits your closing."

Danielle didn't know whether his comment was patronizing or an earnest attempt to dismiss her before she had an opportunity to put forth her rationale for what had transpired over the last several weeks.

Undaunted, she launched into her argument. "What I'm about to propose resulted from a meeting I had in New York." Gingerly, she tiptoed around the stacks of paper on the floor, which seemed to follow the professor from his office to his home, and grabbed a printed copy of Alex's analysis for emphasis. "It dawned on me while we were looking at the results that maybe, just maybe, the election results point directly to STAR." The blank stares on the faces of Mark and Alex told her that it might be a tough sale. "Okay. Two days after Mark was assaulted, we saw a difference in the polls. Granted, the differences are small at first. It's a stretch to connect the two incidents. But think about it."

Mark straightened up and chimed in, "And how would they do it? I mean, well, I frankly don't see any correlation between STAR and the election. By its nature, politics embraces the voters in uncertain ways and at inopportune times. And Clarke's surge may simply be a product of polls without substance. They're only polls, not the actual vote."

Before Danielle could answer, Alex suggested his own interpretation. "I wholeheartedly agree but for one fact. STAR. And

I'm in the dark as much as you, Mark, I must admit, and I agree with Danielle it may be a stretch, but it causes me to wonder how Clarke moved up the charts virtually overnight. It just doesn't make sense when you consider his history."

Danielle, undaunted by the skepticism, offered further proof for her theory. "Unless I misread Stewart when I mentioned STAR, he became conspicuously rattled. And with all that activity on the fourth floor, they were working on something significant." She exchanged glances with Mark, who had his arms crossed and impatiently tapped the heel of his foot against the carpeted floor.

"Sorry to disappoint you but, again, I don't see any connection. Their computer engineers may have been working on a special project. I mean," Mark shrugged his shoulders, "they could have been doing normal programming under a stressful situation. And I haven't heard anything yet to change my mind." He reached out and snatched his drink from a side table, tipping it slightly toward her, which she understood as a nod for her to continue.

Danielle reflected on Mark's observations. It was true that she had no idea. But the sight of Denon and the mention of Richie Davis did make her intuitively believe that their presence at Shannon was not coincidental. And in her mind, there was no mistaking the pandemonium that broke after her true identity was discovered. No, there was more to it. "Mark, all I'm asking is for you to consider my proposition. Nothing else."

"Done," Mark replied with an obvious tone of disbelief.

Picking up on Alex's confident nod, Danielle continued, "Let's suppose Shannon sends this virus to your cell and … it's embedded there." She paced the floor, and then she turned and pointed her finger at Mark. "And it sends out a signal that we interpret as a command."

Mark turned his head toward Alex for confirmation on the last point. "Did you get that one?" said he asked, again with a dismissive demeanor. "I think what she's going to say is that the electorate are programmed. That's imaginative, but highly unlikely. And I wouldn't hold the presses on a news story about people walking around like zombies."

"No, but I really think that she may have a point." Alex, who had heard her argument and seemed receptive to the idea, rested his elbows on the arms of the chair and intertwined his fingers.

"A signal. That could be it." He perched himself on the edge of his seat. "The other day I was fascinated by how many people glanced at a pedestrian signal: Walk and Don't Walk. A few glanced to see whether traffic had stopped, but most crossed the street unthinking. It was as though they were programmed. They had accepted the signal without questioning it."

"Exactly," Danielle said feverishly, as though Alex may understand where she was headed. "Mark, you said the program was similar to a virus. But it was designed for a cell. And that's what makes it unique."

With building impatience, Mark replied, "Now, don't get me wrong, that was my preliminary report. It's a program that needs studied, especially with all those lines of code. And believe me, I haven't diminished the importance of Owen's program. But this, quite frankly, Danielle, is a little far-fetched."

"Mind control is not preposterous," Danielle suggested, looking at Mark, who fidgeted in his seat.

Alex said almost reflexively, "She may have uncovered a new intrusion. We may be victims of mind control or some sort of behavioral modification. The CIA was working on mind control experiments. The implications are becoming evident. With that caveat, I don't think this is a CIA project."

Danielle continued, knowing she may never convince Mark. She even had her own doubts. It was like thinking the unthinkable. "Mark, I don't want to diminish what you're saying. But let's look at the possibilities to explain the latest polls. Hypnotism. No. Implanted devices. No. Someone would have noticed. Behavioral control through physical means. Transmitters. Nope. No evidence. But I think we're getting closer. Sound waves."

Mark raised a skeptical eyebrow and shook his head as soon as he heard the theory. "Frankly, that's harder to believe. And you're going to have a hard sale. So I'll ask the same question. How? How could someone accomplish what you're proposing?"

"Simple," Danielle replied. "A cell phone. Its place in society is documented by the number of people carrying them. Some have more than one. It's ubiquitous."

Mark shook his head. "No, that's not possible. There are too many other competing theories to explain Clarke's election. But I'll grant you this, I'm beginning to understand what you're proposing."

Mark sipped his scotch, appearing genuinely interested in Danielle's proposal. "Sound waves are admittedly interesting. Yeah, sure, the government has studied them in warfare. And medicine has resorted to sound waves for crushing kidney stones and body scans. Anything is possible. Yet, I'm back to how."

Danielle's cell, which was set to vibrate, began a slow dance and then erupted into a temper tantrum on the table. But she was not answering. She wrestled with an unmistakable feeling of uneasiness from an earlier phone call. But she didn't know why. It was a visceral demand, and she didn't want to hear it again.

Mark observed, "That was the second time your phone rang, and you didn't make any effort to answer."

"I'm in the middle of my closing argument," Danielle said unconvincingly. But she knew the reason. Her mind threaded through the dropped calls, the clicking and fuzzy calls, and then there was the telecommunications company. It was now becoming clearer. The phone was the problem, a viral infection of sorts. What kind of infection, she didn't know and really didn't want to know. Her response appeared unconvincing as she shot a glance at Alex and Mark.

Alex scratched the side of his head. "But don't you think, Danielle, someone would've heard the instruction ... the one that you're suggesting ... whatever that might be?" His eyes darted toward her phone.

Mark pitched in, "That gets us into the conscious and subconscious mind. And there are a plethora of individuals out there who suggest ways to convince our inner selves that we don't need to smoke, that we can improve our self-images, and a whole host of self-improvements. From what I understand, it's mostly gimmickry."

"And they rely on the spoken word or some form of self-hypnosis," Alex offered. "But what Danielle is suggesting is more than the spoken word; it's the unspoken word. It's like seeing the unseen and hearing the unheard."

"I don't proclaim to know how they did it. But the only means to deliver their message is a cell phone." Danielle tucked her chestnut hair behind her ear with obvious nervousness.

Mark massaged his forehead with the tips of his fingers. "Devil's advocate here—what about radio and television ads? Wouldn't they have the same impact?"

"That's the unknown, Mark," Alex said. "Clarke's ads haven't changed. Yes, they're negative toward McClay, but that can't explain it all. And my inclination at times, especially as the races heat up, is that the ads increase and so does the negativity to the point that when I hear the first few words, I switch stations."

"Go on with your theory," Mark requested as though he was receptive but not convinced.

Danielle crossed her arms and stood in the center of the room. "We haven't, to the best of my knowledge, measured the impact on our subconscious minds. That's virgin territory. In fact, I've read our minds pick up not only the spoken word, but our subconscious minds are also interpreting the body language and the vocalization of the speaker. In a sense our subconscious helps us interpret what the speaker is saying. It's like our subconscious helps decide whether the speaker is telling the truth."

Mark arched his eyebrows, and his flippancy returned. "Hmm. Unspoken words within our cell phone conversations, playing silently but purposely beneath our threshold of hearing. Okay."

Alex leaned forward. "You know, I recently read about an ultrasonic tone that resembled the buzz of a mosquito. A high-pitched sound created by a device that could only be heard by young adults and teenagers. It was designed to deter crime. What was interesting was that older adults couldn't hear it."

"Yes," Mark said, "and what we hear falls within a range. The younger we are the better we hear, and as we grow older, the less we hear. That's my point. We lose certain pitches."

Danielle let out an exhaustive sigh. "That would explain the rise in younger voters, but no change in older voters in your chart, Alex. All I'm suggesting is a nudge, a subliminal impression that pushes us in one direction or another. The message lies underneath the spoken word. And it plays to our subconscious mind like a broken record, over and over." She waited for a response but none came.

Mark took a deep breath and forcibly exhaled. Then he swallowed the remainder of his drink and rose. "I'll look at the program's code but ... subconscious? Ah, I don't know. You lawyers sure can dig up some bizarre arguments to support a position."

Danielle's face reddened, but she knew pushing the envelope might prove counterproductive.

With arched eyebrows, Alex muttered to Danielle, "Anything else?"

Alex, thought Danielle, seemed more receptive and willing to explore ideas outside the box. She raised her head with confidence. "Ultrasonic commands can be embedded in the background of our conversations or the white noise we commonly hear. Those words are merely subliminal impressions or commands that continually play for minutes or hours as long as you're using a cell phone. It's like a … celiminal message."

Alex, somewhat surprised, said, "Celiminal … hmm."

"Yes," Danielle reiterated. "A subliminal message delivered by cell. Celiminal."

"Anyone care for a drink?" Mark asked, but he had no takers. "This has been an enlightening evening. Frankly, I don't think the police would buy into this theory. And even if they did, where's the proof? You'll find skeptics abound. Proof. That's what they'd say. And you can't blame them."

Somewhat deflated, Danielle felt a sense of resignation, knowing it sounded beyond belief.

Alex put his arm around Danielle. "We'll let Mark examine the program before we pursue this idea."

Danielle's phone rocked on the table. But she made no effort to reach for it or even to know who it was.

With his free hand, Mark pointed to the phone. He gestured as though he would answer it. "Do you mind?"

Danielle shook her head.

Mark clicked on the phone and greeted the person on the other end of the line. "No, she stepped down the hall. Who is this? Karen Spiel."

Danielle could feel his gaze drilling into her.

"And it's urgent," Mark repeated.

With her palm up, Danielle reached out for the phone. The weight of the phone felt like it was a dumbbell. And she sensed their eyes riveted on her. Before she answered, she was being sentenced similar to the Stepford wives. She squinted, and then taking a short breath, she cradled the phone to her ear.

"Karen. It's Danielle."

Karen blurted, "Sorry to bother you, but I thought you should know Denon's back in town. He's here in the office. He's almost a raving lunatic. Get this—he's been purging files from the computer and shredding papers."

Danielle's heart raced. "Why?"

"I don't have a clue. I was ready to call it a day when he flew into the office. I asked whether I could help him, thinking I would know what he's up to. He asked me to leave the office and said he would handle matters his way."

"I've got a few ideas, but I'll need to call you back later," Danielle voiced.

"Can't talk?"

"Nope. Talk to you later." With that, Danielle pressed end, not knowing why she didn't want to share anything with Alex or Mark listening in. Besides, she had a nagging feeling that she should return to PERC. She suspected her presence at Shannon had caused a raft of problems for Denon.

"Problems?" asked Alex.

"No. I'll need to call her later." Danielle brushed off the question.

Mark said pointedly, "I didn't hear anything in the background when I was talking to your friend."

"I didn't think you would." For a moment, Danielle wondered whether he had known all along what STAR revealed, but he wasn't saying. And she had no idea why she thought that way. Then again, skeptics sometime merely probe to determine how committed you are to a position.

# 44

With one hand on an election poll conducted the previous night and the other thrust to his waist, Alex cocked his head and turned over in his mind Danielle's pseudo closing statement. He had already prepared an in-depth article on McClay. But now the latest poll was inconclusive, leaving the election too close to call. In little less than three weeks, Cervasi had managed to engineer a potential win, but like Danielle, Alex considered the implications of an underhanded stimulus.

No longer was a Clarke win improbable. The candidate was knocking at the door, and the momentum swing was ready to breach the collected wisdom that had called McClay the winner. He dropped the results on his desk and stared fixedly at his computer adorned with red, green, and yellow post-it notes. As he pored through his messages, he found a call from Mark Rand and ripped off the note, wondering whether he had finished the analysis. Reflexively, Alex keyed in the number and got him on the fifth ring.

"Did you find anything?" Alex asked with guarded anticipation that Mark had unearthed a fragment, an answer, a purpose, for STAR, and what, if any, connection existed between the program and the senatorial election.

"I've got your answer. Well, sort of. After our meeting last night, I got to thinking about what Danielle was saying. And, truthfully, I'm impressed with her unyielding position over my rather sincere attempt

349

to discredit the idea. I thought it was downright absurd. Me—a professor who should know better than to squelch an intriguing concept. I hope I wasn't too hard on her."

"She's an attorney, thick-skinned and unwilling to back down from a position. So I would have to think that she's been down that road before." After they had left Mark's apartment, Danielle remained unusually quiet, which he attributed to her being tired, as he drove to the home of Brooke's parents, where she had spent the night. "And she didn't express any displeasure this morning. In fact, she was upbeat and seemed perfectly fine. She and my assistant, Kate, are doing further research into the proposition." Looking at his watch, he realized that he was short on time, having promised Kate and Danielle a lunch.

"Alex, before I let you go, let me quickly outline this for you. I was roused out of bed by the thought that if she were right, then I could easily test her theory. And that's what I did. Earlier today I met with a buddy of mine who lives in Virginia to examine his cell phone. I won't bore you with the scientific complexities of frequency and amplification, not to mention decibels and the ranges for human hearing. But we managed to replicate the sound and replay it on a computer using different modulations. Sure enough … she might … it's a stretch, but … *she might have a point.*"

Wide-eyed, Alex froze while the revelation filtered through his being. He wanted to bolt out the door, but he needed to hear more. His thoughts raced to the cell phone calls laced with messages. The voices Danielle had heard. Is that possible? And then there was Shannon Telecom. His mind whirled as he tried to make sense of what it all meant. What impact had the subliminal message—*celiminal* message, as Danielle had termed it—had on her? On the election? "I should have listened to what she was saying weeks ago." He slapped the desk. "I'm too late."

Mark interjected, "Whoa. What we suspected could be pure noise, and even so, what impact could a subliminal message have. Why—"

"What was the subliminal message?" Alex looked at his watch—2:15 p.m.—as he drummed his fingers on his desk.

"'*Clarke. Vote Clarke.*' Something like that. But, again, it could have been noise. That's all. But I do admit, there was something there, and it was repetitive."

"Mark, I've got to run. Where can I catch you?"

"My cell."

"Right. Later." Alex examined his cell and then signed off. He bounded out of his chair, grabbed his overcoat, and flew out of his office and down the corridor.

As he stepped into Kate's office, she turned suddenly to meet him. "Where's Danielle?"

Kate removed the strap of her purse from her shoulder and set it on her desk. With a frown, she tapped her index finger on her watch. "You were to be here by one fifteen. When you didn't show, we grabbed a bite down the street." She raised her eyebrows to meet his desperation. "Oh, Danielle. I don't know where she was headed. She told me to tell you that she'd meet up with you later, and then she added, 'I have someone to see.'"

Alex pulled out his cell and speed dialed Danielle, but she didn't answer. He switched the phone to sleep mode and pocketed it. As he spun around to leave, Kate called out, "By the way, she pointed me in a different direction on the analysis. And get out your charge card, I've decided to have dinner at Citronelle. One more thing, she did say to let you know that Drs. Greyson and Bateman are related to each other—they're half-brothers."


When she stepped across the threshold into an empty waiting room, Danielle hesitated, knowing the last encounter had been less than receptive. And this one could be more than contentious, that's if he agreed to meet her.

"Can I help you?" the receptionist asked in an acerbic tone. Her facial expression revealed that Danielle was not welcome.

Danielle recognized the blonde seated behind the desk and answered curtly, "Yes. Tell him I'm back. The CIA sent me."

The receptionist reeled back in her chair and jumped to her feet, disappearing into the back office. A minute later the connecting door between the inner rooms swung open. Dr. Bateman appeared with narrow eyes and a scowl.

Bateman growled, "Listen, I don't know your game, but I told you the last time what would happen if you returned."

"No, Doctor, you told me not to look into matters that I don't understand," she countered with tight lips. "Now I do know. And I was on the right track when I visited you last. Now the difference is that I'm further down that track, and I'm approaching the station. I figured out STAR. It's only a matter of time before you and PERC crumble under the pressure when the story hits the news."

Bateman drew back and his dark expression changed to one of alarm. His nostrils flared, but he controlled lashing back at her. "There's nothing I need to say."

"The dead do talk. Owen died and left me the answer, but I only discovered it recently. He encoded the access in a book. And the quote told me everything. Owen was murdered over what he perceived an injustice: a tyranny over the mind."

"Delusional. That's how I would describe you."

Danielle grinned, knowing she had the upper hand. "I'm afraid it won't work a second time. You wrote the medical report and signed your brother's name. Owen was never delusional, and neither am I."

"What are you talking about?"

"Money. You're not working for PERC anymore, but that doesn't mean you weren't paid off. You see, those pictures on your wall are not mere vacation spots. You made a mistake. You should have never put the nameplates underneath them. Undeniably, legal records point to your ownership of properties in those cities and resorts—a dead giveaway."

With narrowing eyes and his frown lines deepening, he barked, "You are a problem." Then he released his tension and a cruel smile formed on his face. "Mere accusations from a small mind. Why, I've made more money than you'll ever make. You have no proof. It's all trumped up. Sensationalism."

"Dr. Bateman, the words you wrote will hang you."

"Good-bye, Ms. Madison." He abruptly spun around and strode away quickly.

*No*, she thought. But she sensed the game was in the first quarter, and she had scored a touchdown. She knew it was a matter of time before they'd find her, but not before she wrestled away the proof she needed.

As she entered the sharp curve, her vehicle slid across the center line on the wet pavement before she innately downshifted into neutral, tapped the brake, and slowed down. Once she regained control, she upshifted to drive and resumed her venture into the evening through the vehicle-barren mountain passes. Driven, in part, by the knowledge that Shannon was a large piece of the puzzle, her tight grip on the steering wheel caused her to wonder whether the trip was embedded in her subconscious.

With a dose of adrenaline rushing through her veins from her encounter with Bateman, she slowed and sought reassurance. She didn't want to use her cell, but she reluctantly yielded to the desire. Her mind had been churning as she drove the last few hours as the political pundits, supporters, and dignitaries were headed to their respective parties. She suspected Denon had left New York.

She powered up her cell and placed a call to Karen, who answered on the second ring. "Sorry I didn't call you earlier, but here I am. Now what's this with Denon?"

"I thought you would surface sometime. Where are you?"

"Right now, I'm trying to relax after driving through a torrential downpour on an unlit road. Hydroplaned on a slick spot. And it's all in search of an answer." Danielle shook her head, not understanding why she was experiencing the sudden urge to continue.

"It's not like you need to venture out into bad weather."

"Things have changed. Denon was in on it from the beginning— he had to be. Bait, that's what I am. Where's Denon?"

"He spun through this office like a tornado. Drawers ripped open, papers flying, and, get this, mumbling to himself. That was a sight. I asked whether he needed any help. But he only stared at me. He was demented. An hour later he flew out of here."

Danielle slowed her descent over the crest of a slight grade in the road. "Something must have gone wrong. This is his time for wining, dining, and hobnobbing, as he liked to say, when the stakes were high and the payoff great. He wouldn't miss the Washington scene."

"By now he could've returned to Washington. But his presence here was certainly bizarre. After he left, I couldn't help myself. I filed the papers littered over his desk and floor. And then I checked his computer. The files he accessed were all related to PERC."

Danielle considered the employment contracts, the Shannon sales agreement, and the interconnecting and offshore companies that hid the true connection between Cervasi and the telecom company. She flicked on the high beams as she approached the turn off from the main road. "Evidence. And there's only one place I can find it. No one is going to believe me, not you, not Alex or Mark. I have no proof. It's all supposition."

Karen fired back, "What kind of proof are you looking for?"

"Funny you should say that ..." The cell fell silent for what seemed a minute. Danielle asked, "Karen, you still there?"

"Yep. Just thinking ..."

"I'll let you know what they're up to."

"And the program? Did you ever find it?"

"Yes, sort of. Mark had made an extra copy as a backup. He's trying to analyze it as we speak. But who knows how long it will take. And even if he found something, it doesn't make it any easier to prove Owen was murdered, or what they're doing with it."

"I thought you needed a cipher to gain access."

"You do, and I've got it."

"Fill me in," Karen rejoined.

Danielle flipped on the radio and began to thumb through the radio stations. That's when she noticed she was running low on fuel. "Call you back. I've got to stop for gas. Give me a few." She hung up and pulled into the desolate station. Its four gas pumps were partially lit. A sign clanged overhead from a forceful wind. The lone, unrecognizable face that peered through the window made her shiver. Minutes later, she was behind the steering wheel with the doors locked. Rubbing her hands for warmth, she started the engine and crept back onto the two-lane road for the last leg of the journey.

A half hour later, she spotted the strobe on the cell tower. Eerily, it lit up what seemed snowcapped trees as she approached. A sudden realization occurred to her: how was she going to enter the building? She couldn't leisurely walk through the front door. And for that matter, if what Stewart told her was correct, the answer to the puzzle lay on the fourth floor.

Before she entered the main parking lot, she cut the headlights and inched forward through a howling wind that swept across the vehicle, rocking it back and forth. The lot appeared empty. That came as a surprise, but then again, it was Election Day. In another hour, the polls would be closed. *The election mayhem from STAR*, she thought, *will run its course.*

The radio announcer reported from Clarke's election headquarters that the ballroom was beginning to fill in anticipation of an election night win, while McClay's headquarters was rather somber.

In the distance, she spotted a narrow beam of light flickering across the pavement headed in her direction. She swallowed hard and cut the engine. About a hundred yards away, the light burned out and an interior car light came to life. She waited with her hand on keyless ignition. The exterior car lights powered up, and the vehicle lurched forward and around the side of the building out of sight.

She found the new building was curtained in darkness, with faint lights emanating from what appeared to be the fourth floor. An icy chill coursed through her. Moisture began to fog the windows as she waited to gain enough courage to carry out her plan.

Cervasi peered from the window when the vehicle came into view. A grin formed on his face, knowing that he had gained the upper hand. It was just a matter of time.

"Mr. Cervasi," said a voice from behind.

Cervasi craned over his shoulder to find Matalino. His necktie barely reached the top of his belt buckle. And his irritated expression signaled a matter of utmost importance.

"Problems?" asked Cervasi as he watched Clarke exit the limo underneath the alcove of the Hyatt Regency. He had never understood Clarke's shenanigans, and this was another example, being late for their meeting.

Matalino gave a guarded look around him to ensure the utmost confidentiality. Then he stepped closer for a whispered conversation. "Baker called and informed me that Madison was in Bateman's office. She was asking questions. And when he spoke to Bateman, Baker said the guy was a blithering idiot over the phone. He didn't know what Bateman revealed to her."

Underneath his breath, Cervasi ran off a series of swear words before he pointed with his finger. "Call Bateman and tell him to meet me at our offices in an hour. Tell him I want to catch up on our financial transactions."

"Do you think he'll show?"

With multiple head nods, Cervasi admitted reluctantly, "Where there's money, he's going to be there. What I don't get is why did Bateman call Baker?"

Matalino shrugged his shoulders.

Cervasi cocked his head and then returned Matalino's gaze. "Clarke's limo arrived a few minutes ago. Give me ten minutes. I'm going up to meet our egotistical candidate and listen to the asshole whine about how he won the election without our help. Get the car, and I'll meet you out front."

Matalino nodded and walked off.

Cervasi murmured to himself, "The meeting with Bateman won't take long." Cervasi threw back his head and slugged his drink. He had one message for Clarke, and it was that any announcement of an election win had to wait until he returned. No exceptions. And there would be a price to pay if he didn't cooperate.

# 45

*Reston, Virginia*
*Tuesday, November 6*
*Election Day*
*7:00 p.m.*

Days ago, it was the thick fog that made it impossible for Danielle to find her way in the parking lot. Now in a driving wind, Danielle pulled her hood over her head as she skirted the perimeter where tree branches whipped back and forth. Lamp posts flickered on and off, buffeted by strong bursts of wind. It took longer than she had expected to find the location of the basement door.

Once she did, a flash of lighting nearly sent her flying out of her shoes. Her thoughts ramped up to her father's admonition that she had nothing to fear.

Skimming across the pavement between flashes of light, she stepped down toward the belly of the building. She rooted herself and fished out a penlight. In the narrow beam of light, she traced the stairwell. When she reached the corner next to the basement door, two unflinching, beady eyes were caught in the reflection. Reeling back with a pounding heart, her stomach did somersaults.

The raccoon was unwilling to retreat from its position. Her only hope was to scare it off. Running through ideas, she decided her only choice was to throw rocks. She found her weapons in the river rock abutting the sidewalk.

Wielding the rocks, she heaved them into the pit of the stairwell, not knowing where they landed or waiting around to find out between rounds whether she had scored a hit or scared it off. Minutes later she inched her way to top of the stairs with her penlight. The beady-eyed animal appeared to be gone; at least, she hoped it hadn't taken refuge in an unseen cavity waiting to strike.

With her hair standing on end at the nape of her neck, she descended. Bracing herself, she reached out for the concrete wall for balance until she reached the door. Someone had cleared the leaves since the last time she was there. She reached for the door and leaned into it with her shoulder. And again, it refused to open. She tried a second time with no luck.

There was no lock to pick. She angled herself and pressed against the bottom of the door, remembering it refused to budge once before. It didn't take long before the rotted, swollen door broke free.

Taking a deep breath in the pitch black, a chill ran through her. Besides stepping into an inhospitable room where imaginable creatures lived and died, she had to deal with other unknowns in this foray. What if she was wrong? What if she didn't find anything? And what if she was caught? She'd be charged with breaking and entering, and her license to practice law would be yanked or worse, she could be killed, and in these wooded lands, her body would never be found. She heard a steady drip hitting a puddle of water in the distance.

She crossed the basement with penlight in hand and found the steps to the main floor in seconds. Putting one foot on the first step and then the next, slowly and deliberately, she ascended on the complaining wood steps that smelled of mold and mildew until she reached the top. With her hand on the doorknob, she thought perhaps she should retreat. But she wasn't going back. She had to move forward regardless of the consequences.

The door swung open into an uninviting, dark corridor made slightly visible by the light from the lobby. She gingerly tiptoed down the hall through the empty lobby to the steps where she had exited during her escape. The stairwell was lit, making her passage to the fourth floor easy. Once there, she opened the door and angled herself into the cavernous room where only red emergency lighting cast an eerie glow.

With no hesitation, she dashed for the control room, which Stewart had identified during the tour. She found it divided into a maze of partitions. Stewart never pointed out the importance of any one person. And, consequently, she had no idea what to do when she found the right cubicle.

Her penlight grew dim, leaving her little time to search each cubicle. Instead, she chose one where papers were strewn on the floor and flowed over the desk. It reminded her of Mark with his paper tower of terror. She decided it was someone who held a position of importance.

She settled into a vinyl chair behind the desk and caught herself before she fell off. Whoever was seated there had consistently leaned to one side and worn out a stabilizing bolt in the chair. Doing a balance act, she reached over and turned on the monitor. An array of programs stared back at her. The stark reality of not knowing the right computer program made her wince; it could take hours, and time was of the essence.

Flipping open her cell, she punched in the speed dial number and waited impatiently. "Mark," she whispered, "it's Danielle."

"Where are you? Alex called here asking whether I had heard from you."

"Never mind. I'm going to send you a picture. I need your help." Danielle aimed her cell at the monitor and snapped away.

"But—"

Danielle cut him off. "There's no time. You've got to read this now!"

"Fine." Seconds later, Mark said, "I've got it." There was a pause before he said, "Tell me you're not at Shannon."

"We need the evidence, and I'm here to get it."

"Danielle, you've got to get out of there! Do you hear?"

"Don't worry."

"No. You can't. I *believe* you. I think I've got what we need."

Danielle ignored him. "Either you're going to help or not." She heard silence for a moment.

Mark said with resignation, "Go ahead."

For the next ten minutes, while she listened to Mark's instructions, she drilled down into the programs in a vain attempt to unearth some connection. But the programs they examined had yielded nothing in terms of proof of any nefarious actions. Growing tired of Mark's frustration and unyielding exhortations to leave, she simply clicked the phone off.

"Never mind. I'll call you back if I need you," Danielle said to herself in despair. She didn't have the luxury to discuss programs, troubleshoot accessibility problems, or for that matter, deal with his disapproval over her actions.

Leaving the control room, she swung down the corridor and read the nameplates affixed to the office doors. She stopped abruptly and read: Richie Davis. The door was locked, which she had expected. Further down the hallway, she opened the door to a small conference room with seating for six around an oval table. Inside, with the faltering penlight, she found a connecting door, which she believed led to Davis's office. As she tried to gain access, her efforts were stopped suddenly by the florescent lights coming to life.

She spun around. "Denon?" Danielle said, with her mouth agape. She dropped her penlight to the floor and felt the rush of blood to her head.

Denon quickly chastised her, "I don't think you're authorized to be in this office, and needless to say, this building. Mr. Cervasi is not going to like this one bit."

Before she could answer, another man with wiry hair, medium build, and a squared jawed entered. He had a self-assured smile on his face; she didn't recognize him at first.

"Good evening, Miss Madison. Or should I say, we were expecting you to come through the front door. But it really doesn't matter. There's no way out." Baker grinned.

"But—" Danielle looked at him head to toe.

"That's right. It's not a miracle … I threw away my crutches. You see, I could always walk." He pulled out a chair and seated himself as he gestured for her to sit down.

Danielle shook her head.

"It doesn't matter," Baker chuckled in amusement. "That wheelchair has served me well. You're probably wondering. So I'll tell you. I was injured in an auto accident years ago. At the time, call it fortuitous if you like, Tony Cervasi needed help with his fledgling company. He thought I was crippled. I used it to my advantage. And he thinks that to this day. I wouldn't want to disappoint him."

Reflections of a man limping from the Smithsonian penetrated her mind. "It was you at the Smithsonian."

"How'd you recognize me?"

"I didn't, until now." Danielle pondered the moment, and it dawned on her. "You killed Mary."

Baker frowned. "She called me shortly before she met you. Naturally, I was afraid she might say too much. I didn't have a choice. With Carl Matalino and his cohorts bearing down on you, I needed to act fast."

"And Owen? Was he expendable also?" Danielle asked.

With a poker face, Baker replied, "Owen became increasingly difficult. That's how you entered the picture. Denon figured we could use you to control Owen. So he suggested you as the company's in-house counsel. And luckily, Tony bought into the idea. But sadly, it was too late. Time was running out, and Owen, well," his voice trailed off, "what can I say."

Danielle shuddered to think that she had been used a pawn. There, across from her, was Denon brushing the lint from his suit coat. "How could you?" She could feel the tears welling in her eyes.

Denon said, with furrowed brows in sincere honesty, "What does a silent partner do?"

"Silent partner?" Danielle asked.

Baker patted the conference table. "And he's got the political, judicial, and foreign contacts all under a legitimate law firm. That's why he's going to continue to work at HBR. If it not for him, I could never have pulled off the sting against the esteemed William Parks." His mood became increasingly dark and grave as though the incident with Parks was a source of repugnance. "What I accomplished for Tony put his company on solid footing. But Tony reneged on making me a partner after all I did for him. That's when I figured I should cash in my chips. I was the brains behind the purchase of Shannon, and I'm not going to let Tony walk off with my idea."

Danielle turned a glaring gaze on Denon. "You had everything. Managing partner and money. Why?"

He responded, unaffected by Baker's confession, "Oh, I'll make managing partner at HBR." He shrugged, "It's the money I could never make otherwise. And I'll reap the dividends by being only a silent partner."

Danielle recognized Denon failed to mention one other motivation: power, a black hole of ego. And it had to figure widely in any decision he had made.

"You know," said Baker, as he bobbed his head and glanced at Denon, "I thought you might have recognized me when I was in New York. I guess we missed each other at the Four Seasons."

For a brief moment, she recollected the incident—the person with a limp who left the bar. "You?"

Baker appeared to relish her realization. "Very good. When you almost ran into me that rainy night, well, I thought my identity had been exposed. Thankfully, Denon gave me the code to the office, and my failure to find anything, or should I say Owen's failure to cooperate with us, led to his undoing. Unfortunately, it now leads to your undoing. Denon was right, you are tenacious and resourceful. But you're resourcefulness has snagged you into a fatal web. A promising lawyer snuffed out ..." he exhaled a long breath, "too bad."

Danielle remembered the black and white umbrella. The closer she examined his facial features, it became increasingly clear.

With his arms crossed, Denon shook his head as though he admitted the situation was regrettable. "When we lost STAR and Owen's computer, I needed Greg to help our new business partner, Leonard Wheeling. But as you know, it was nearly impossible to wrestle that computer program from you."

Baker intertwined his fingers. "That brings us to your involvement. You're very good, and that's why you came highly recommended, I guess. You went too far though in your investigation. Who would have thought you would be tireless in your pursuit? Now, with the access file you managed to find, STAR works better than we initially thought. Sorry, but we don't need any new partners."

Danielle broke into a confident smile, wanting to hide her fear. "You're going to let me go. See, there are others who know what you've done and where I am. It won't take long before they piece it together."

Baker leaned forward. "That's where you're wrong. The polls will close in a half hour. The viral program will shrivel up and change its appearance similar to a rogue gene. A chameleon. No one will spot it. And so it goes for the Subliminal Telephonic Auto Response program, or STAR, as you've come to know it." He beamed with confidence. "No mess, no proof, no nothing. And that's what is going to happen to you. You wouldn't have come here alone if they were involved."

Danielle's heart sank. If she couldn't get to the program within the system, her only hope was for Mark to show the authorities the access code.

Denon checked his watch. "If we're going to make the festivities in Washington, we need to get a move on."

Baker added sarcastically, standing over the table, "Yes, we've arranged to hand you over to an FBI agent, Benjamin DeFore. He's anxious to meet up with you, from what I hear. Oh, and I voted earlier, so we won't be stopping at a polling station."

Cervasi emerged from the Cadillac and slammed the door. This was not how he planned to spend election night. In years past, he had spent time in the war room where he managed campaigns for days and nights prior to the big day. But this year, he had handed the state and local elections to Paul Hart. It was Cervasi's responsibility to focus on all federal elections and primarily the senatorial election.

"I couldn't wait for you to arrive," a heavy voice announced from the darkness.

Cervasi barked, "Who is it?"

"My money. Did you really think that I would stand still? After all, I earned the money," Candecki said as he stepped from the darkness.

"You got your share."

"No. You and Carl withdrew money from my account. I don't know how you did it. but I'm back to collect with interest."

Cervasi saw the nose of a gun barrel protruding through Candecki's overcoat.

Candecki pointed the gun toward the entrance. "Let's get inside. I don't have a lot of time."

They stepped into the atrium where the receptionist waved. After they boarded the elevator, Cervasi said, "I know we've had our differences. But we could use someone in our organization like you."

"Forget it," shot back Candecki. "You had your chance before, and you blew it. And now you owe me." The elevator doors opened, and they turned in the direction of Cervasi's office.

Once inside, Candecki snapped in a loud, demeaning voice, "The safe. Let's get my money before you spend it."

"You're mistaken. I don't keep that much on the premises."

"My sources say you've got the money here." He pointed with his gun toward the connecting door to the back room. "Let's finalize this financial matter. I've got other arrangements for the evening."

Cervasi strode across the room with Candecki in step immediately behind. He watched with interest as Cervasi dialed the combination. The safe swung open.

Upon seeing the stacks of money in the safe, Candecki pointed out, "I'm not going to wait for you to count it. Put it all in a bag. And we'll call it even for all the trouble you put me through. Oh, and one more thing, you'll have to hand over the program and the access file—and if you want to see tomorrow, you'll do it. You see, Tony, your greed only makes this easier." After Cervasi placed the money and storage disk in the bag, Candecki beamed with satisfaction. "Now I need an escort. That's just in case you notified your henchmen about me being here. Let's go."

Cervasi questioned, "I can't change your mind? We could use an ally like you. Our business is expanding."

"Not a chance."

"At least the program. You have no use for it."

Candecki said, "That's what you think."

Outside Cervasi's office, Matalino rounded the corner and stopped in his tracks when he saw them.

"Carl, our friend has come here to collect. Wait for me in my office. I'll be back."

Candecki added, "Yeah, you just do that. And the next time we meet, we'll see who the professional is." He chuckled as the elevator doors closed. Before he walked out of the building into the night, he said, "It was nice doing business with you. Maybe I'll see you again."

When Cervasi returned to his office, he found Matalino standing at the window. "We can catch up with him later. We've got bigger problems." He flew to the back room with Matalino in tow. He stepped into the safe and pointed to the drawer. "Candecki has a bag full of counterfeit money and a disk full of music." But his attention had been drawn to the missing duplicate program and access file. He turned abruptly, saying, "And there's only one person who could've taken it—*Baker*. It has to be him! *Find him.*"

"What about Bateman? He should have been here over an hour ago."

"We can deal with him later. Right now, I want Baker." Cervasi twisted the gold ring around his finger. "On second thought, I know where we can find him."

# 46

After the van pulled into the parking lot, Denon dropped out of the driver's seat while Baker removed their passenger from her restraints in the backseat. Baker unlocked a service door at the rear of the building. A faint light at the end of a long, darkened corridor suggested that the building was vacant. Less than halfway down the hallway, Baker came to a sudden stop and opened a door.

As he flipped the light switch, Baker quipped, "When the dot-com company owned this tract of land and buildings, they dedicated a soundproof room for their employees who wanted to play an instrument. So it's fitting for you to be in it. Because, you see, no one will hear you." He snickered, "And don't think a night guard will find you. This building is unoccupied. So you can scream all you want." He tightened his grip around her upper arm and shoved her into the room.

Denon, unruffled by her plight, was expressionless. His demeanor was the cool, calculating attorney that he was in a courtroom.

Baker announced with a hint of sarcasm. "We've got a prior engagement hosted by the next senator of Virginia. So make yourself at home. Oh, one more thing, I need your cell." He appeared amused by the request. "And if you don't hand it over, I'll be forced to search you." His gaze told her that he would welcome her resistance.

Without hesitation, Danielle reached in her pocket and handed him the cell.

Removing the battery, Baker pocketed the phone and patted his pocket. "I promise you it will have a good home in my display case. We embedded your cell with a little message sent via STAR. That's why we expected you. Of course, it's not foolproof, and we're still learning, but you proved it works well enough."

Denon managed to utter, "Danielle, sometimes bad things happen to good lawyers. I really didn't want to see you go down this way." He pivoted and headed toward the open door.

Baker looked back as he stood at the door. "This won't take long ... until then." His look was one of disdain as he pulled and locked the door.

With her eyes glued to the door, Danielle immediately noticed there wasn't a door handle. She was in a virtual tomb, sealed in and with no windows. The white walls reminded her of a snow cave. The veins in her throat constricted, making her breathe in short bursts. She closed her eyes, pressing her middle and index finger tips against her forehead. *Breathe deeply,* she thought, *there must be a way out.*

She wasn't into playing an instrument, but she presumed a number of dot-commers who previously occupied the campus were accomplished musicians by the looks of the odd-shaped sound diffusers mounted to the walls. She surveyed the carpeted, conference-sized room before she stepped to the far wall. *Behind a panel,* she thought, *might be a hook or a bolt that might come in handy as a weapon.* With the tips of her fingers, she tried to pry off a diffuser, but it wouldn't budge.

"Hey, can anyone hear me?" Her voice, rather hollow and without vibrancy, diminished in an instant. She curled a strand of hair behind her ear and then began to twirl it. Turning her head to the side, her eyes caught a faint line running from the ceiling to the floor. She jetted forward and ran her fingers along the seam looking for a hidden latch or handle. Then she examined the floor and noticed the markings on the thick plush carpet. She leaned into the panel with her shoulder; it didn't budge. But it appeared to be a panel held in place by a latch. Her hand ran alongside a nearby sound panel where she found a small lever that she pulled. Relieved by the find, her fingers curled around the edge of the panel door and pried it open. As she did, her shrill scream was muffled by what fell and pinned her to the floor.

She was flat on her back. Her heart fired rapidly. The shock and despair had little time to grab hold of her. His dark brown, fixed eyes were wide with fear. She wiggled back and forth, working up a sweat. She grimaced and gagged, not wanting to face him. His weight crushed her lungs and felt like concrete blocks pressed against her chest. With a wellspring of determination and exertion, she leveraged her hand underneath his shoulder and shoved. She maneuvered him enough to gulp a small amount of air. Straining, she heaved the dead man to the side.

Her head hung as she turned to find Bateman splayed out on the floor with a bullet through his forehead. She looked away with a putrid feeling in her stomach. Maddening. The whole series of events reeked with men pursuing power, glory, and money.

She forced another glance. His sport coat spread open revealed a cell holstered to his belt. Bending over she detached the phone and powered it up. No reception.

Unstable, she rose and stepped into what she thought may have been a closet for musical instruments. She flicked on the light to find a small room filled with electronic gear, monitors, and recorders. "Exactly," she whispered to herself, "eavesdropping. That's how he knew what was going on behind closed doors." She threw a couple of switches, but the system was dead.

As she fled from the room, she dropped to her knees, unbuckled Bateman's belt, leveraged her feet against him, and yanked.

At the outer door, she used the buckle to rip the carpet from the tack strip. She tugged at it until it gave her room to work. Breathless, she reached for the cell she had dropped. With a sense of satisfaction, she frantically typed a text message. On her knees, she held the cell between her thumb and forefinger and was about to shove it underneath the clearance she had made when the door swung open, knocking her backward. She landed a few feet away with the cell phone in her hand.

The door opened wide. Standing there was Carl Matalino, who grabbed her arm and pulled her up. She kicked him in the groin and darted out of the room, pressing send before Cervasi slapped her hand and sent the phone skidding down the corridor.

Matalino, partially doubled over, stumbled out of the room.

"The cell," Cervasi commanded Matalino, who smashed the cell with the heel of his shoe before he picked up the pieces. "Where's Baker?" he demanded.

Matalino locked his hand over her shoulder and squeezed. "I should—"

Danielle grimaced in pain. "I think they went to Clarke's campaign headquarters."

"We'll take her with us. Bind her up and throw her in the trunk."

Alex quickly emerged from the building's elevator and ran down the corridor. Without hesitation, he tried the doorknob before he banged on the door. The door opened as wide as the security latch would allow.

"Where is she?" he demanded.

Startled, Greyson said, "I'm sorry. Who are you looking for?"

"You know who. Danielle Madison." But before Greyson replied, Alex's cell chattered. Slapping the phone to his ear, he heard a familiar voice.

"Alex," Karen said, "I just received a text message from Danielle. She's being held in a vacant building at PERC … something about a *music room*?" Without saying anything, he clicked off the phone, turned toward Greyson, and shook his head.

"Wait," Greyson said, "there's a gentleman here from the FBI. He's asking questions about PERC."

Without an introduction, the smartly dressed, tanned individual whipped out his identification and said, "I'm coming with you." Turning toward Greyson, he said in a demanding voice, "You're coming with us."

Fifteen minutes later, with Alex behind the wheel, they barreled down Route 7 as he related what had happened and how Danielle was determined to find answers. Alex hung a right off the main artery and then a sharp left onto PERC's campus before he skidded to a stop at the entrance.

Before Alex got out, Greyson pointed to a car in the distance. "Do you see that? There."

"What?"

"I'm positive it's Cervasi."

Alex stomped on the gas pedal.

In a deep voice, the FBI agent, who had remained inquisitive but offered little help, asked, "Do you think you can catch them?"

Alex heard the question but never answered. Tearing through the dirt and chips on the rear lot, they shot forward.

Greyson confessed, "My brother, who I disowned years ago, told me they were working on subliminal impressions. But he refused to admit that he was part of a conspiracy. He insisted that he was threatened." As Alex stomped on the accelerator, sucking in air and gas, the vehicle dipped back and to the right. Greyson braced himself for a collision with the car in front of them.

Alex swerved at the last instant, cutting between cars.

Greyson turned his head toward Alex. "What I was about to say was I received ten thousand dollars with a copy of my original medical report a few days ago. After you and Danielle were in my office, I realized I had better make a few calls."

With his eyes glued to the taillights of Cervasi's car, Alex called out, "Hey, you might call for reinforcements. I'm losing them."

"Like I was saying," Greyson said, "I gave a statement to the police, and then Mr. Defore," Greyson nodded to the person in the backseat, "showed up, just in time. Opportunistic. When I received that package of money, I figured it was a bribe to keep my mouth shut."

Alex's eyes glazed over. He left off the accelerator and grabbed his cell, catching a glance of Greyson and wondering whether he was part of the cabal. Alex's adrenaline kicked into high gear. It was them or him. With one hand on the wheel, he depressed a speed dial button on his cell with his thumb. Hearing Kate's voice, he said, "I'm on my way, I think, to Clarke's campaign headquarters at the Hyatt. I'm tied up. Later." Closing the cell, he hoped that she understood the message as he glimpsed in the rearview mirror. But he was too late—a cold, metal barrel was pressed to his neck.

"That phone call was cute … tied up." Candecki pushed the gun deeper into Alex's neck. "You wanted reinforcements, so here they are. You keep driving, and don't lose sight of that Caddy. Hand me your cell."

Candecki clutched the cell and pitched it out his open window. Alex turned slightly and exchanged glances with Greyson, who appeared paralyzed. For the next few minutes, they rode in silence until Alex asked, "Who are you working for?"

Candecki growled, "Myself. I like it that way. And don't get any bright ideas. Your brains might end up splattered against your window."

Alex responded, "You don't have to worry."

"Good. Don't flash your high beams or try anything funny. Just keep a bead on that Caddy. Got it?"

"Right."

"I've got a score to settle, and it's not with either of you."

As they approached the hotel, Alex, at the direction of Candecki, stayed a short distance away. Cervasi emerged from the passenger side and walked to the rear of the Caddy. He seemed rattled as he surveyed the surrounding area. Tapping on the trunk lid a few times, he bent over and appeared to be talking to the trunk. Then he straightened out his suit and walked into the hotel.

Candecki pressed the gun, now with a silencer, against the side of Alex's head. "Now we know what's in that trunk. If you want to keep her alive, you'll do what I say. Do you understand?"

Alex nodded slightly.

"Good, now if you notify the police, I'll kill her. She's my ransom. I'll call you, Mr. Preston, at the newspaper and tell you where you can find her. Dead or alive. Now hand me the keys."

Alex replied as he handed over the keys, "If anything happens to her, I'll hunt you down myself."

"You do that, and you'll be rewarded with a bullet in your head." Candecki jumped out and caught the Caddy before it pulled into traffic. He opened the door and jumped in.

Alex turned to Greyson and said, "For your sake, I hope you're not involved." With that, Alex dashed out and approached a cab parked at the curb of the hotel. The driver emerged from the vehicle to open the rear door for a woman dressed in an evening gown. Wasting no time, Alex slid into the driver's seat. With the lady outside, he spun out before the rear door was closed. He swerved around the corner, hitting a lamp post with the rear door. With the door latched in place, he rolled into traffic and claimed the outer lane with one thought on his mind. *Where did they go?*

As he searched, thoughts of Danielle drifted in and out of his mind. For the next twenty minutes, he drove with near reckless abandon, weaving the cab in and out of lanes until he caught sight of them. He dropped back and began a cat and mouse game. The Caddy seemed to wander aimlessly until it took a side road. There, Alex cut the lights and came to a stop. By the dim light from a lamp post, Alex made out Matalino, who exited the car, followed by Candecki. They were headed to a walkway close to the Potomac.

About to jump out of the car, Alex heard the unmistakable popping sound coming from what seemed only steps away. Seconds later, Candecki reappeared.

Alex realized his chance to free Danielle, if she was alive, was about to evaporate. Once Candecki opened the driver's door, he started the car, backed up, and then began a slow U turn. Alex drew a bead on the driver's door, driving toward it like a raging bull. The impact sliced into it.

With the airbag in the cab deflated, Alex jumped out and headed toward Candecki, who lay unconscious across the console. Alex reached in and released the trunk lid. Somewhat dazed, he rolled to the back of the car to find Danielle. As he released her bindings and the duct tape over her mouth, she let out a shriek. He turned to see Candecki with both hands on a gun pointed directly at them.

Before he could say anything, a shot rang out. Candecki staggered and released a harmless shot overhead as he fell to the ground. The gun remained in his hand.

Their attention was drawn to Matalino, who had a smile on his face as he held his chest. He dropped to his knees and tried to speak, but a burst of blood oozed from his mouth.

# 47

Here it is," Kate said, handing Alex the two-page document.

Election night fever surged through the boisterous crowd located in the grand ballroom of the Hyatt Regency where red, white, and blue balloons were netted overhead. Meanwhile, a pianist tickled the keys with patriotic songs prior to a rock group scheduled for the next hour. Drinks flowed freely at the bar where the five hundred guests, more or less, meandered in and out of the room. Somewhat oblivious to the gala affair, Alex looked up with an approving smile. He handed it to Danielle.

Kate broke in as Alex, who had spent more than half the day searching for Danielle, gathered his thoughts. "The exit polls project Clarke as the winner. A number of precincts have already posted results. There's only a small margin of difference between them, with McClay slightly behind." She brushed aside her curly red hair. "But despite the seesaw battle, I've heard Clarke intends to declare the win. It's his style to take the upper hand."

Danielle replied, not surprised, "Cervasi intends to steal the election." Reading the news article, an expression of surprise crossed her face. "How do you think Clarke will react?"

Alex smirked, shrugging his shoulders. "I suspect he'll deny it. Win or lose this senatorial election, he'll point the finger at a conspiracy leveled against him by special interest groups who have other agendas. Then he'll ask for a special investigation that will go nowhere."

Disillusioned by the assessment, Danielle said, "If that's the case, we should hold off so we don't tip our hand too soon without the demonstrative evidence." She, like Alex, wasn't sure whether Clarke would categorically dismiss the article as political rubbish or acknowledge it as correct. Then what?

Alex eyes continued to survey the room. "Mind you, it's a hunch, but I like to strike when the iron is hot. With Candecki out of the picture, what we found in his possession is very damaging. That's why I had Kate make a photocopy of the Swiss bank receipt and Candecki's handwritten note to our esteemed congressman. And when this hits the news that Clarke was dealing with a hired gun that had FBI credentials that were forged ..." He raised his eyebrows for emphasis. "How would he explain it?"

Kate interrupted the conversation between them. "Cervasi and Denon are upstairs in the Presidential Suite with Clarke. Word has it they're about to return to the ballroom, undoubtedly with his acceptance speech. But I'm sure they'll be shocked when they see you, Danielle."

As she continued to stand on her tiptoes trying to locate Baker, Danielle, exasperated, said, "Baker has to be here somewhere. He wouldn't miss this."

Alex nodded his head agreeably. "With all the people crowded into this room, he has eluded us. But this place is actually crawling with police. Baker, Cervasi, and Pierce will never leave the premises."

"You know," Alex continued, "through all this, I remain a little unsettled by what Greyson had believed. That there's no guarantee that subliminal impressions have an effect. We don't have any evidence that it had an impact—it's pure conjecture."

Danielle offered, "I'm convinced that it had an impact. Answer me this: how do you measure a person's subconscious? You can't. Nor can you measure determination, grit, insight, or for that matter, talent. It's what we do as a response that can be measured. And here we have Clarke winning due to an encrypted cell phone message! But what I don't understand is why Candecki was at Greyson's office?"

Alex answered, "Apparently, Bateman said Greyson knew everything. So Candecki scheduled an appointment to meet Greyson, and I unexpectedly happened on the scene. Lucky for Greyson, otherwise he'd be dead."

With that, Clarke walked out onto the stage to the thunderous applause of the crowd. Leaning over slightly near the edge of the stage, he was glad-handing and waving to those in the gallery with an occasional two thumbs up. The crowd rocked with signs for Clarke and broke into a chant for the senator.

In the spotlight, he nodded thankfully to those around him. A few balloons were released prematurely into the crowd, which appeared right on cue as he withdrew what undoubtedly was a prepared speech. He beamed heartfelt gratitude to the reaction of the crowd. As he began speaking, Cervasi and Denon stealthily stepped into the background of the stage, smiling boastfully as though they had pulled off the big one.

Alex nudged Danielle. "Some entrance."

She had to admit the fanfare was astonishing similar to greeting a lost soul who had been missing for years. She bit her lip and took a short breath.

Alex grabbed her arm and said, "Let's go." He excused their cutting through the crowd until they reached the front row.

Danielle meticulously parsed through the individuals, surrounding the senator, at the podium. *Where was Baker?*

Alex nodded to Kate, who on cue handed the sealed envelope to a campaign aide. Clarke had already begun his canned speech. "I would like to thank each and every one of you for the support, the time, and the faith you've had in me during this campaign." He waved to a few people in the crowd and recognized those people who had a direct influence on his success.

Clarke continued with his off the cuff comments. "I haven't heard from my esteemed opponent, Thomas McClay, who ran a fierce campaign. And I thank him for being a worthy opponent. But as you know, we have closed the gap these last several weeks."

Danielle whispered to Alex, "I think he's got it all wrong. It was Owen's program that made the difference."

The aide strode across the stage and handed Clarke the envelope. He didn't appear startled, perhaps thinking it was a written statement of concession by McClay. He continued, "If this is what I think, it will clearly—" After he scanned the contents, he raised his eyebrows and cast a gaze at Cervasi.

He cleared his throat and said, "Excuse me, I ..." Again he paused for what seemed like minutes. Murmurs grew into a din within the crowd. He coughed and then raised his head as though looking for divine intervention. He cleared his throat before he folded Alex's article.

Clarke started again. "My years as congressman have been prosperous for me and my constituents. But," he coughed into a balled fist, "sometimes it's necessary to step aside and let a new breed take over. And with that, I ... ah ... I concede the election to my opponent, Thomas McClay. I wish him the best of luck and fully support him." He abruptly strode off the stage and retreated into a gaggle of news reporters.

Danielle, stunned by the announcement, had not expected this reaction. And from all indications, Clarke's supporters were equally speechless. She exchanged glances with Alex and Kate in the numbed crowd.

Alex's phone rang. He looked at the screen for the caller's name, but it appeared from the shrug of his shoulders and the blank expression on his face that the caller was not identified. "Hello." He squinted and handed the cell to Danielle. "It's for you."

Somewhat surprised, she answered with questioning eyes.

"Danielle," said the voice, which she recognized as Baker as she spun around in a circle looking for him, "*you won. We'll have to get together sometime.*"

# Epilogue

*New York, New York*
*Six Months Later*
*4:45 p.m.*

Karen swung around in her seat and arched her eyebrows at the sight of Danielle. "Well, let's see it." Her eyes beamed with anticipation.

Danielle stepped into the office and approached the desk with an outstretched hand, laying it on a stack of papers.

Karen leaned slightly forward for an examining look. And, for a moment, she appeared deeply absorbed as though she had never seen a ring up close. "Now that's so beautiful ... treasure it." Wiping a tear from her eye, she couldn't finish her words, as though she regretted her past. As Danielle pulled her hand away, Karen's demeanor and her mood changed, not allowing her past control the moment. "Sit down, sit down. Tell me what you've been doing."

"Alex and I are excited. We haven't set the date yet."

"Make sure I'm first on your list." She muted the music playing in the background. "That's better, now tell me about your new job."

Danielle settled back into the chair. "Challenging. I've got deadlines but not the same pressures as in private practice. As an adjunct professor, I've remained in the realm of politics teaching Election Law at Georgetown. And you? What have you been doing?"

"Me? I work with the new associates, keep the same hours. And now with Greg about to make senior partner, I'll be giving him a hand. I'm never going to change. HBR hired several forensic accountants to examine the books and records of Denon's financial activities. Apparently he was engaged in money laundering. It really makes you wonder where greed and good judgment intersect."

Danielle nodded in agreement. Those words rang crystal clear. For Denon, it was a psychotic desire for power and money. And now it was all gone. "I can't fathom how he could sleep at night. What made him cross that line?"

"I've seen a number of lawyers come and go over the years. Maybe they become desensitized from clients' wrongdoings or their moral fabric never existed in the first place. What makes great lawyers?" Karen stared fixedly in silent reflection. "Simply, I presume, the recognition of right from wrong, and then choosing the right course of action in the practice of law."

"To think, Cervasi, the pawn, and Denon, a conspirator, will both undoubtedly pay the ultimate price for Baker, the mastermind. And Baker, with all the police posted at the exits, leaves an empty wheelchair as evidence he was in that ballroom. He merely walked away." Danielle shook her head. "And then there's Owen." She dropped her head. "You know, I still think about him."

Karen returned, "You've turned the corner. Neither you nor I will ever know what made him get involved in the first place. Whatever the reason, we know he made the right decision in the end. And that was bringing the program to your attention and keeping it out of their hands for as long as possible."

"You're right." Danielle took a deep breath and exhaled forcefully. "I never thanked you for what you did on that fateful night when I sent you that text message."

"You needn't thank me, what are friends for? But I do have one request—I think I'd like to have a drink to celebrate your engagement."

"And a lifelong friendship. Do you have the time?"

"Why not?" Karen rose from her chair. "Mind you," she said with a wagging finger, "you're going to have to order me one of those fancy drinks."

Minutes later, they exited the building. Danielle hailed a cab in the dreary rain. As Karen got in, Danielle looked over her shoulder and spotted a black and white umbrella headed in the opposite direction.

# Acknowledgments

In the course of writing of this novel, a number of individuals unselfishly contributed their time, effort, and input toward its completion. At this time, I offer my express gratitude.

The collective wisdom and writing critiques of Marge Burke, Ed Kelemen, Judith Gallagher, Barbara Miller, and Mary Ann Mogus, a group of dedicated fiction writers made me a better writer.

Ann Burkholder, an avid reader of many great novelists, offered useful suggestions and valuable guidance.

Laurie Massafero, a creative writer and teacher, provided me a path to character development and the pace within the book.

To my staff, Angela Davis and Linda Shinners, my sincere gratitude for their invaluable assistance both related to the writing of this novel and dealing with the many headaches they encounter with everyday legal and tax problems experienced by our clients.

Finally, and an extra-special thanks to Cathy Levandosky, my legal assistant, who believed in and supported the project, for her advice, encouragement, and criticism (there were ups and downs with her comments that make me smile even now, but she was vital to its completion).

Lastly, although I consulted several computer specialists, if I have made any errors or misstatements related to computers, computer programs, or cellular communication, I apologize, and I can only say that I took and offer my literary license. The ideas, concepts, and thoughts conveyed in this novel are mine, and those computer specialists should be considered innocent. Also, the names of characters, places, and events are solely the result of my imagination. Any relationship to past events, incidents, and persons, living or dead, are a mere coincidence. If I have offended or demeaned any political official, detective, or police force, I again apologize, as I never meant to insult their fine work, and the ideas were needed to move the plot forward.

This is a work of pure fiction.

Lightning Source UK Ltd.
Milton Keynes UK
UKOW06f1633300316

271188UK00001B/65/P